Witchfinder

By
Wendy Saunders

Also By Wendy Saunders

The Guardians Series 1
Mercy
The Ferryman
Crossroads
Witchfinder
Infernum

The Carter Series
Tangled Web
Twisted Lies
Blood Ties

This book is the intellectual property of the author and as such cannot be reproduced in whole, or in part, in any medium, without the express written permission of the author.

Please note, that this particular book is not to be taken as historically accurate. Although I have included some historical information on Salem and the 17th Century Witch trials, I have also taken a lot of creative liberties, and consequently many situations and people referred to in this book, are entirely fictitious.

Copyright © 2018 Wendy Saunders
First published in 2016
All rights reserved.

ISBN-13: 978-1534849143

For my sister Stephanie,

Who has been my constant companion, my best friend, my confidant and the best sister I could have wished for.

Library items can be renewed online 24/7, you will need your library card number and PIN.

Avoid library overdue charges by signing up to receive email preoverdue reminders at

http://www.opac.northlincs.gov.uk/

Follow us on Facebook
www.facebook.com/northlincolnshirelibraries

---

www.northlincs.gov.uk/libraries

CONTENTS

PART 1. 1685 .... **3**
1. 5
2. 11
3. 25
4. 39
5. 53
6. 67
7. 81
8. 96
9. 114
10. 130
11. 143
12. 158
PART 2. 1695 .... **169**
13. 171
14. 185
15. 199
16. 212
17. 226
18. 241
19. 255
20. 273
21. 288
22. 303
23. 318
PART 3. PRESENT **337**
24. 339
25. 353
26. 368
27. 381
INFERNUM **405**
1. 407
BOOTHE'S HOLLOW **415**
AUTHOR BIO. **417**

Part 1.
1685

1.

Olivia groaned and rolled over, pressing her face into the grass and inhaling deeply. Her fingers instinctively flexed, and dug into the earth. Lifting her head suddenly she inhaled again. She could actually smell the grass.

Looking up into the sky she could see endless blue, and fluffy white clouds. Gone was the strange bruised light of the Otherworld, or the oppressive darkness of the Underworld. This was pure sunlight. She lifted her hand slightly and her skin glowed, and she could feel warmth tingling on her skin.

Pushing herself up, she tilted her head and listened. She could hear the birds in the nearby trees. She closed her eyes and pulled in a deep breath; she was back in the real world.

Her eyes narrowed as a new sound began to intrude upon her awareness, something unfamiliar, a strange kind of pounding noise.

Hands suddenly grasped her and hauled her to her feet, dragging her across the grass. She kicked back and spun around, her brow creasing in confusion when she realized it was Theo.

'Theo,' she breathed.

'Shush,' he warned, his gaze anxiously darting between the forest of trees which surrounded them. He suddenly pulled her behind a thick tree trunk and pushed her down, so they were both out of sight.

The pounding sound got louder, and louder. The curiosity gnawed at her, but she resisted the urge to poke her head around the tree to see what was going on.

'Theo,' she whispered.

Suddenly, he clamped his hand over her mouth and pulled her in as close as he could. Her eyes widened as two horses thundered by. She caught a brief glimpse of their retreating forms as they passed by. Each horse bore a rider, dressed in some sort of dark clothing, although she couldn't quite make it out from this distance.

Theo finally let out a breath and some of the tension drained out of his body. He looked down at Olivia, cupping her face gently in his hands.

'Are you okay?' he asked softly in concern.

'I'm fine,' she placed her hand over his.

'I thought we'd lost you there for a moment,' he frowned. 'What the hell happened back at the Crossroad? What was that green fire?'

'I have no idea,' Olivia shook her head. 'It came out of nowhere, and wrapped around me. I could feel it pulling at me.'

'Did it harm you?'

She shook her head. 'Did it hurt you?'

'I felt it,' he replied, 'when I grabbed you. It felt like it was burning, but it left no mark.'

'Well, we're here now,' she stood slowly. 'Where's Sam?'

'I don't know,' Theo answered worriedly, 'but he can't be far. We have to find him before anyone does.'

'Who were those riders?'

'I have no idea.'

'Then why did we hide?'

'Olivia, this is the 17th Century and you're wearing jeans and a backpack.'

'Oh,' she looked around, but all she could see were trees and grasslands. 'Are you sure we're in the right place?

The right time even?'

Theo looked around quietly, his eyes shadowed.

'Theo?' she looked at him in concern, noting his strained expression.

'We're not far from Salem Village, my family's farm is a couple of miles west of here. We need to get someplace safe and out of sight, until I can steal us some clothes. Once we blend in we can look around, but we need to be careful until we can establish the date. People around here know me, the other me,' he shook his head in irritation. 'The past me, must be around here somewhere. I can't risk anyone seeing me in two places at once.'

Olivia nodded, 'we'd better find Sam.'

Theo took Olivia's hand and led her through the trees, all the while glancing around warily.

'I know where we are,' he replied suddenly. 'It's the apple orchard belonging to my neighbor, James Wilkins.'

'Is that water I can hear?' Olivia asked as she tilted her head and listened.

'There's a small stream that runs along the border of his land.'

It didn't take long to locate Sam. They seemed to have been thrown down roughly in the same area, although unfortunately for Sam he must have taken the brunt of whatever the strange green fire had been back at the Crossroad. He was barely conscious when they reached him.

Olivia dropped down to her knees beside to him and rolled him over. He was pale and his body wracked with violent tremors.

'What do you think is wrong with him?' Olivia looked up at Theo in worry.

'I don't know,' he frowned, 'but if it hadn't been for Sam, we'd never have gotten you through the portal. Whatever that strange green fire was, it must have undone whatever it was Hades did for him. He's probably suffering from the after effects of being in the Underworld for so long.'

Olivia stroked his face gently in concern. 'Do you think he'll be okay?'

'I don't know,' he shook his head, 'we don't even know what he is.'

'I wish Louisa was here.'

'Me too,' Theo glanced around, 'but for now, we're on our own. Not too far from here, James has a barn he uses to store the apples in. We should be able to hide in there for the moment.'

'Are you sure?'

He nodded, 'Logan and I used to hide in there when we were children.'

She climbed to her feet, watching as Theo heaved Sam off the ground and slung him easily over his shoulder.

Luck appeared to be favoring them for the time being, and they managed to cut back through the orchard toward the barn without anyone seeing them. The barn itself was pretty far from the farmhouse, so they snuck in, dropping Sam down on the hay strewn ground and tucking him into the corner near a huge barrel of apples.

'Now what?' Olivia asked.

'Now we wait for it to get dark. I'll slip out and see if I can sneak up to the main house and steal some clothes for us. Once we can roam around a little more freely we can make a plan.'

'God,' she frowned, 'this is a nightmare. Sam's pretty much out for the count, we've got to try and avoid not only the past you, but anyone who knows you, and as if that weren't bad enough, there are now two Nathaniels.'

'I know,' he replied in frustration. 'If the one with your mother wasn't bad enough, the Nathaniel from my time is in his true form, and much more powerful. He'll know we're not from this time the second he sees us.'

'We'll just have to make sure he doesn't see us then.'

'That's easier said than done,' he shook his head.

'He's looking for Hester too remember?'

Olivia sighed and closed her eyes, rubbing her temples tiredly.

'Are you alright?'

'It's just a lot to take in,' she breathed, 'and I'm tired.' Her stomach growled loudly, 'and hungry apparently.'

'Here,' he reached into one of the barrels, and grabbed a couple of apples, 'eat these. I'll see if I can find some clean water.'

There was a sudden scuffling noise, and the sound of the barn door opening.

Olivia pulled her legs in and slid behind one of the large barrels of apples, holding onto Sam carefully, while Theo hid behind another.

'Hello?' a small timid voice called out. 'Hello?'

Olivia frowned, it sounded like a child's voice.

'Theo?' the child's voice called out.

Olivia glanced across at Theo and saw his eyes widen, as he instinctively turned in the direction of the voice.

'Theo, I know you're here, so you might as well come out.'

Unable to help it, Theo unfolded himself from his hiding place, stepping out into the light that streaked in from an opening higher up in the building. His heart stopped, as his gaze landed on the small dark haired child.

'I've been waiting for you,' she smiled.

'Tempy?' he whispered.

She smiled widely, and held her arms out for him.

He dropped down slowly in front of her and she wrapped her arms tightly around his neck. He folded his arms around her tiny body and crushed her to him, not wanting to let go, afraid that it wasn't real. His eyes burned with tears, and he found he couldn't swallow past the hard knot of emotion burning at the back of his throat.

Temperance pulled back and grinned.

'I brought you some clothes.' She looked down at him, in his jeans and boots. 'Your clothes are very strange. Where are your friends? I brought some for them too.'

'What?' he replied in confusion.

'The lady with the gold eyes, she's here too isn't she? And the boy with black hair?' she turned and retrieved the sack she'd dropped by the door. 'You'd better hurry up and change. Mr Wilkins is at market today but he'll be back soon.'

'Tempy,' he whispered, 'how do you know about the others? How did you know to find me here?'

'I saw you silly,' she shook her head.

'You saw me?'

'In a dream,' she smiled. 'There was another lady there that time. She wore a green dress, and had a bow and arrow. She told me you needed me to help you.'

She pulled out some clothes, and handed them to him as he sat staring at her in disbelief.

'I got one of Mary's dresses for your lady friend,' Temperance frowned. 'I hope Mary doesn't notice, she gets awful mad lately.'

'Mary?' his eyes widened as the pieces began to fall into place. 'Tempy, is Mary back at the house?'

'Of course she is,' she replied as if it was the most obvious answer in the world. 'She's back at the farm with the other you.'

'Tempy, is Mary sick?' he asked carefully.

'You know she is,' she answered seriously, 'the sickness is in her mind, and she's getting real bad.'

Theo closed his eyes and drew in a shaky breath.

If Temperance was still alive, and Mary was at the height of her madness, it could only mean one thing. The year was 1685. He wasn't sure what that strange green fire was, which had interfered back at the Crossroad, but something had obviously gone terribly wrong. They'd been thrown back ten years too early.

2.

Olivia struggled with the unfamiliar clothing, her fingertips fumbling with the ties of the petticoats she'd pulled on over her plain shift. Sitting down on a low cask, she pulled on a pair of long woolen stockings, and slipped her feet into a pair of plain leather shoes that pinched at her toes uncomfortably.

She gazed longingly at her favorite boots, which were laying amidst her growing pile of discarded clothes. Sighing in resignation, she stood and pulled on a simple woolen gown, taking care to carefully tuck the small golden compass, which still hung from the delicate chain around her neck, under her clothes so it could not be seen.

She'd spent a long time studying Salem, and this time period in particular. She knew the women of this era did not wear such trinkets. They were not even allowed to wear gold, or silver lace, or buttons, a practice enforced by strict laws. Reaching up, Olivia removed the small silver hoops from her ears, hoping no one would notice the tiny pin prick piercings in her ears.

She pulled on a jacket, made of the same coarse material as the dress, and fastened it. It was a deep russet color she knew would have been dyed from the Madder root, which produced red-based colors. She remembered this particular color had been popular, as it was supposed to represent humility. It was also scratchy and uncomfortable, and was no doubt made of wincey, a strong coarse fabric which was a combination of linen and wool and very popular for colonial clothing. However, reading about it in an historical reference book, was a hell of a lot different from having to actually wear the unforgiving fabric, she thought grimly.

She tugged at the stiff, starched white collar and eyed the matching white apron distastefully. Her gaze once again drifted to her beloved jeans, as she blew out a resigned breath and picked up the white apron, pulling the damn thing on.

Finally, she pulled her hair free of the ponytail, refastening it in a neat bun at the nape of her neck and securing a close fitting coif over her head. It was lucky she hadn't painted her nails before they'd left Mercy she thought idly, as she looked down at her hands. She'd just have to make sure no one saw her barefooted, as her toenails were still a bright bubblegum pink. Shaking her head in amusement at the thought, she glanced up and caught Theo looking at her with a strange expression.

'What?'

'Nothing,' he answered after a moment, 'it's just…it's strange seeing you looking like that.'

'You can talk,' she smiled, her eyes tracking down his body.

He was now dressed much as he had been that night in Mercy, when he'd appeared in the middle of the road and she'd nearly hit him with her car, a night which seemed like a lifetime ago.

Her head tilted as she studied him absently, he now wore a loose fitting linen shirt under a sleeveless cloth jerkin, which was fastened at the waist with a simple leather belt. His thighs were covered with a pair of breeches which fastened at the knee, his lower legs and calves were covered with long woolen socks much the same as she wore, and plain leather shoes covered his feet.

'You look like you've just stepped off the set of The Crucible,' she laughed quietly.

'The what?'

'Never mind,' she shook her head in amusement.

He watched her thoughtfully, as she bent down to scoop up her discarded clothes.

'We should probably burn our clothes.'

'Burn them?' she glanced up at him with a pained expression, 'but these are my favorite boots.'

'We can't risk anyone finding them,' he frowned. 'The backpack will have to go too. What have you got in there?'

'Not much,' she unzipped it and rummaged through the contents. 'A flashlight, a small first aid kit, an empty water bottle and Hester's Grimoire.'

'Most of that won't burn,' he mused. 'Maybe we could bury them.'

'That won't work,' Olivia shook her head. 'You can't bury it deep enough without the risk of discovery, and we can't have anyone finding a flashlight nearly two centuries before it's invented. Same goes with the water bottle; plastic won't be around for another couple of hundred years.'

'We'll have to hide it then,' he scratched the stubble at his chin thoughtfully. 'If we hide our clothes and the backpack, we'll just have to make sure we take them with us when we leave.'

'If we leave,' Olivia murmured, glancing down at Sam. 'In case it's escaped your notice, our ticket out of here is out cold, and we have no way of knowing if he'll have the juice to jump us through time when he wakes up.'

'We'll deal with that problem when we come to it,' Theo shook his head. 'Gather up the clothes and put them in the backpack. We'll find somewhere to hide it for the time being.'

'Not Hester's Grimoire.'

'Olivia,' he replied carefully, as she stuffed their

clothes into the bag, 'we're in Salem now. You can't go wandering around with a magic book. If you're caught with it in your possession, you may as well flat-out ask the magistrate to hang you for witchcraft.'

'I'll be careful,' she dropped the bag and stood, approaching him slowly. 'I can't leave it Theo, it's my responsibility. Wherever I go, the book goes.'

'I understand that,' he ran his hands up her sleeves, unconsciously pulling her in closer, 'but you haven't lived this life. You may have studied it in your books, but you don't know…you can't know how dangerous it really is. So much was omitted from the official record.'

'What do you mean?' she frowned.

'You remember I told you there were discrepancies in the historical books you showed me?'

'I remember,' she nodded, 'there was no mention of Nathaniel.'

'That wasn't the only thing wrong with them.'

'What?'

He shook his head as if trying to clear his thoughts.

'Olivia,' he told her seriously, 'everything you think you know about Salem and the trials is wrong. They recorded the absolute minimum they could, but the persecution of the witches started much earlier than the ravings of a couple of spiteful pre-pubescent girls. Nathaniel is here now, in his true form. Accusations of witchcraft are already being whispered in every corner of not only the village, but Salem Town itself. Why do you think I went to such lengths to hide the gift of foresight that both Temperance and I have? People have already begun to disappear.'

'They are taking people?' Olivia's eyes widened. 'Why?'

'I'm guessing Nathaniel is already searching for the Wests. He knows they have the book. He's using the excuse of witchcraft to take these people and torture them, trying to gain information.'

'How do you know?'

'There were whispers,' Theo replied. 'I heard a great many things in the village, and I had dreams. I dismissed them as nothing but nightmares at the time, but knowing what I do now...'

'Why didn't you say something before?' Olivia whispered.

'There was no point, it was in the past. It didn't impact what we were doing at the time, but now...'

'Your past is our present,' she breathed heavily. 'Well, shit.'

'Olivia,' he pulled her close, 'it is so dangerous for you to be here. These people are so paranoid they are accusing friends, neighbors, even family members, but the truth is none of them have ever seen a real witch in their lives. If they find out what you can do, what you really are...'

'They'll kill me,' she finished for him.

'Only if Nathaniel, the Nathaniel from this time, doesn't get to you first. You have to remember, he is in his true form not that rotting mess your mother forced him into. I barely harmed him back in Mercy, and that was when he was already weakened. If it comes down to a fight here and now, we have no weapon that would be effective against him.'

'Well then, we'll just have to make sure he doesn't find us,' she soothed him, 'but regardless, the book stays with me. I'll just have to take my chances. I can't risk it falling into the wrong hands.'

'Olivia,' he breathed, as his hand snaked around the back of her neck gently and he pressed his forehead to hers.

'I know,' she whispered, as she looked up into his dark eyes. 'We'll be okay.'

'I'm not worried about myself,' he murmured, 'but I can't lose you.'

'You won't,' she grasped his wrist firmly and

stepped back. 'We can do this, we just need to lay low until Sam regains consciousness.'

'That may be a while,' Theo glanced over at their friend who was still out cold on the ground. Temperance sat next to him, smoothing back his hair and pressing a damp cloth to his forehead.

'I think your friend has a fever,' she looked up at Theo.

'Damn it,' Olivia moved closer and dropped down next to him, checking his pulse and peeling back his eyelids.

'What do you think?' Theo crouched next to her. 'Can you do anything?'

'That's Louisa's gift not mine,' she shook her head. 'I wouldn't even know where to start.'

'You need to get him someplace safe,' Temperance looked up at her brother. 'I could go back to the farm and fetch the cart. We could hide him in the stables, or the barn.'

'No,' Theo shook his head as his gaze once again fell on his little sister.

His heart gave a helpless thud, as he watched her trying to make sense of the situation she found herself in. She had come to this place to find him, because she had seen it in a dream. A waking dream she called them, but he knew it was a vision she'd had. Even though she knew she would find him and his companions in their neighbor's barn, he could see she was still struggling with the concept that there were two versions of him.

'The younger version of me is still at our farm, remember Tempy?' he told her gently. 'He doesn't know anything about this.'

'Oh that's right,' she frowned, coughing slightly.

Her skin was pale and drawn, her eyes held dark circles, and a persistent cough was beginning to wrack her body. His heart clenched again painfully, she was already starting to show the symptoms of the fever which would claim her life.

It wasn't fair, he had finally been given a second chance with the sister he loved more than anything, and he was as powerless to save her as he had been the first time. It was cruel, the worst kind of irony, to be allowed to see her again only to be fated to watch her die once more.

Swallowing back the sudden rush of emotion threatening to choke him, Theo opened his mouth to speak, but stopped abruptly, his head turning in the direction of the barn doors. His eyes widened at the unmistakable sound of nearby voices.

'Quick hide,' Theo hissed as he yanked Sam off the floor and threw him over his shoulder.

Temperance scrambled deeper into the barn ducking down into the shadows between several large casks of cider, and open barrels of apples. Olivia scooped their belongings off the dusty floor and followed.

Theo dropped Sam down behind a large barrel, and dived into the shadows himself, just as the doors were flung open and the sound of three distinctive voices broke the silence.

'Didn't manage to make it to market,' a deep booming voice echoed from the rafters. 'You have quince you say?'

'I do,' a smoother, deeper voice replied. 'I also have a few plums left.'

'You don't say Wilkins,' the booming voice mused, 'bit late in the season for plums isn't it?'

'Not that late Reverend Alcott,' James Wilkins shrugged, 'but you are right, most of them were harvested shortly after midsummer. These were late ripening.'

'Hmmm,' George Alcott scratched his chin thoughtfully, 'are they inferior quality?'

'Not at all,' James answered easily, 'but if you prefer you can just take the quince.'

'Margaret is partial to plums, and I must say she makes a fine plum cobbler,' he decided. 'Very well, you win, Wilkins. I'll take the plums, the quince, and a couple of casks of your apple cider. I hear you're now using one of those fancy machines.'

'I do have a cider press now,' James nodded. 'It presses more apples in a fraction of the time.'

'Incredible,' George mused. 'I have to say Wilkins, yours is the finest cider for miles.'

'Well thank you very much Reverend Alcott,' James acknowledged the compliment with a slight inclination of his head.

'Have you tried Wilkins' cider yet Nathaniel?'

'I'm afraid Reverend Alcott, I have not yet had that pleasure,' a smooth oily voice replied.

Olivia's breath caught in her throat and she sank further into the shadows, as a tall slim man stepped forward. Her eyes narrowed in contempt, as her gaze locked on the true form of the demon Nathaniel.

He looked deceptively like a regular human, which is probably what he wanted everyone to see. Beneath his wide brimmed hat, his hair was as black as pitch. The crisp white of his stiff collar was a stark contrast to the austere unadorned black of his coat, and a medallion hung from his neck, pure silver and disc like.

Although she couldn't make out the details from this distance, Olivia knew it was the serpent seal, the symbol, which had been seared into the flesh of her mother's murder victims back in Mercy. The symbol, which was depicted as two intertwined serpents in the shape of an infinity symbol, represented Nathaniel and his brother, the demon Seth, who was trapped deep in the Underworld, at the mercy or pleasure, depending on your point of view, of the God Hades. Olivia's gaze narrowed, as she took in the medallion. It surprised her that he wore it so brazenly over his clothes, and that no one seemed to question it.

'Then please,' James stepped toward a small cask, 'allow me.' He broached the top and retrieved two tin cups from the shelf nearby.

'I've been working on something new, perhaps

you'd like to sample it?'

George lumbered forward in interest, his thumbs tucked into the wide leather belt, which was cinched in under his ample paunch. Nathaniel followed politely behind, his dark eyes glittering with an unreadable expression, as he watched James dip each cup in turn into the swirling amber liquid. George took a cup giving a loud sniff, before taking a mouthful. He swished it around his mouth and swallowed.

'Well James,' George stared at the liquid in the cup, 'I think you've outdone yourself this time. What is that flavor?'

'A blend of peach and apple cider.'

'Peach and apple you say?' his eyebrows rose as he drained the rest of his cup. 'That certainly is good, very good. I'll take two casks.'

'As you wish,' James smiled inclining his head.

'Margaret will enjoy it,' George turned to his companion, 'what about you Nathaniel? How do you like it?'

'Very good,' he muttered quietly handing back the cup, which looked as if it hadn't been touched. 'You certainly have a talent Mr Wilkins.'

'It's good of you to say so,' James answered.

'So you live here alone?' Nathaniel asked, studying James' face with more curiosity than he'd shown for the cider.

'I do.'

'Forgive me,' Nathaniel apologized smoothly, a cool smile curving the corner of his mouth. 'I am still quite new to Salem and have not yet had a chance to become acquainted with all of Reverend Alcott's congregation.'

James nodded in understanding, watching Nathaniel carefully.

'The orchard passed to me from my father,' he answered after a moment.

'You need a wife,' George snorted gruffly. 'Perhaps

I should have a word with Wilmott Howe, he has two daughters of marriageable age.'

'A generous offer,' James resisted the urge to grimace. He was well acquainted with Wilmott and his daughters, who in his opinion were barely old enough to marry. If he was ever inclined to take a wife, which he wasn't, it certainly wouldn't be one of the Howe girls. 'I appreciate the thought Reverend, but I am not looking to take a wife just now.'

'Suit yourself,' he replied, 'but I wouldn't leave it too long. You're not getting any younger you know, and you'll need a son, sooner or later. It would be a shame to allow the secret of your cider to die with you.'

'You're too kind,' James smiled.

'You have no other siblings?' Nathaniel asked, his beetle like eyes narrowing in interest.

'A sister,' James replied uncomfortably. He didn't know what it was about the young looking cleric, but he seemed to have some sort of interest in him and his family, that he was certain had nothing to do with his orchard, nor his cider.

'Does she live close by?'

'No,' he answered cagily, 'she married and moved away.'

'I see,' Nathaniel murmured, his penetrating gaze scrutinizing James' face slowly.

'Well,' George interrupted, 'as pleasant as this has been, I must be getting home. You'll see to it that the casks are delivered?'

'Of course Reverend Alcott,' James inclined his head. 'The Burroughs boy has been helping out, I'll see to it he has them delivered to your house by supper time.'

'Excellent,' he extended his hand. 'Shall we Nathaniel?'

'As you wish Reverend,' he bowed slowly, his eyes lingering on James' face a fraction longer.

James watched warily as the two men headed

toward the barn door. After a moment he moved to follow, but a sudden glint in the dim light drew his gaze to the dusty ground. His brow furrowed in confusion at the tiny silver ring, but before he could stoop to pick it up a sudden small cough came from behind him down between two large casks.

Nathaniel stopped suddenly and swung around, his eyes narrowed suspiciously.

James covered his mouth and coughed loudly as he stepped forward, covering the small silver ring with his foot.

'Forgive me,' James gave another small cough, 'the dust, you understand?'

Nathaniel's gaze darkened, narrowing on James' face once again.

'Of course,' he replied after a moment.

'Come along Nathaniel,' George called, 'let's not keep Margaret waiting. She has a rabbit stew ready for us.'

Nathaniel forced a cool smile for James, before turning and following the Reverend Alcott from the barn. After a moment, James bent down, and scooped the small silver ring off the ground and turned it over in his palm, studying it carefully. It was tiny and delicately crafted, with a tiny hinge on one side. He'd never seen anything like it. He frowned, wrapping it tightly in his fist, before he walked over to the door, watching through the crack as the two men hauled themselves into their saddles, and headed out, with their horses picking up the pace to a brisk trot.

He waited patiently until he was sure they were gone, before closing the door and stepping back into the dimly lit barn.

'You might as well come out,' he called into the shadows. 'I know you're there.'

Temperance finally stepped out.

'Temperance,' James greeted her, although she couldn't tell whether his tone conveyed surprise, or censure.

'Mr Wilkins,' she replied hastily, 'I wasn't stealing nothing. I swear.'

'I didn't think you were,' he smiled in amusement. 'You might as well tell your brother and his friends to come out, I know they're here too.'

Temperance said nothing, simply stood staring at him.

'Alright Mr Wilkins,' Theo crawled out of his hiding place followed by Olivia, who he kept tucked protectively behind him. 'How did you know we were there?'

'I heard your sister's cough.'

'No, I mean how did you know she wasn't alone?' Theo asked suspiciously.

James ignored the question and stepped closer, his eyes narrowing, as he studied Theo's face carefully.

'You're older,' he murmured as his gaze drifted over Theo's shoulder to Olivia, 'and you...don't belong here,' he spoke to her softly.

Theo stiffened and pulled her further behind him, his expression hard and guarded.

'I mean her no harm,' James held up his hand gently, as he stepped closer to them, as if approaching a skittish animal. 'I believe this is yours?'

He held out the small silver hoop, and as Olivia reached for it he dropped it gently into her outstretched palm.

'Thank you,' Olivia replied softly. She clutched her earring in her hand, mentally admonishing herself for being so careless.

She could feel the waves of anxiety pouring off Theo. His spine was as rigid as steel, his jaw clenched, and when she reached out to touch his arm she could feel his muscles corded tightly.

'It's okay Theo,' she murmured, as she stepped out from behind him, and got her first good look at James Wilkins.

He was as tall as Theo, and of a similar build. His hair was dark and wavy, hanging almost to his collar, with streaks of grey. If she had to guess she'd peg his age at late forties perhaps. His suntanned face was slightly lined, he had dark chocolate brown eyes and his mouth curved into a smile, as she continued to appraise him.

For an older guy, he was seriously good looking, but more than that, there was just something about him, something she couldn't quite put her finger on. One thing was for certain, he was not as he seemed, but even then she didn't feel threatened by him. If anything she felt completely the opposite.

'Temperance,' James looked down to the young girl, 'run along home now, before you're missed.'

He sensed her hesitation, as she turned to look at her brother.

'It's alright, I mean them no harm. They will be safe here with me.'

Temperance looked up at Theo, unconsciously seeking his approval. At the barest, almost imperceptible nod of his head, she glanced once more at James before disappearing out of the door, closing it quietly behind her.

'What are your intentions?' Theo asked warily.

'I am not going to tell anyone you're here, if that's what's bothering you,' James replied, 'but we should continue this conversation back at the house. I can't guarantee Nathaniel won't return.'

'What makes you say that?' Theo replied.

'I don't know,' James suddenly frowned, 'there was just something about the way he was looking at me. I don't trust him.'

'But you expect us to trust you?'

'That's your choice. I am simply offering you a roof over your head, a hot meal, and a bed for your friend. He is sick, is he not?' he glanced to where Sam was hidden in the shadows behind a large barrel. From the light in the barn, and their vantage point, there was no way he could've seen, or known about Sam.

'How do you know about that?' Theo whispered suspiciously.

'Theodore,' James sighed, 'I know a lot more than you might think.'

Theo stared at him, trying to gauge the man's sincerity. He'd always believed James Wilkins to be a fair and good man, but there was something about him that just didn't add up.

'Why should we trust you?'

'Well, you don't have a lot of options right now, do you?'

'He's right Theo,' Olivia stroked his arm reassuringly, 'we can't do this on our own, not while Sam is still out of it. We need help.'

'Look,' James turned and glanced uneasily at the door, 'I would feel a lot more comfortable back at the house. You have my word I mean you no ill will, but we have much to discuss, which we cannot do out here. Nathaniel and his cronies have ears everywhere.'

'You know what he is, don't you?' Olivia realized suddenly.

'I have my suspicions,' James replied.

'Just how much more do you know?' Theo asked.

'I know that you are not supposed to be here,' James raked his hand through his hair in frustration, in a gesture so familiar, Olivia's stomach clenched, and her mouth went dry. But if the gesture had tied her stomach in knots, the next words out of his mouth nearly stopped her heart.

'I wasn't expecting you both, for at least another ten years.'

3.

The light was dying as Olivia got her first look at James Wilkins' house. It was larger than she'd expected for a rural farmhouse; a south facing, timber framed, single storey building, with a shingle roof. She could see where the house had been expanded beyond its original design. A further two rooms had been built onto the ground floor, which would have originally just been one room, and a small kitchen garden was tucked neatly in front of the house to protect it from the north winds.

James led the way, glancing around to make sure they had not been seen, before opening the door and stepping aside to allow Theo to enter carrying Sam, who hung limply over his shoulder. Olivia followed, curiously glancing around the darkened room.

As she'd suspected, the ground floor was mostly given over to one large room which was dominated by a fireplace. A table stretched across the room, but upon closer inspection was actually little more than a long rectangular board resting on trestles. A single high backed wooden chair sat at the head of the table, with two benches either side. Candles were spaced at intervals around the room, some made from tallow and some from what looked like beeswax. The latter she knew would probably be reserved for special occasions being more expensive than the smelly tallow ones. A small bake-oven sat beside the fireplace, next to a stack of firewood.

She jolted slightly, as James shut the door abruptly behind her and bustled into the room, crouching down to light the fire. She watched him quietly in amusement, knowing she could have lit the fire, and all of the candles around the room, without even moving. Even with that errant thought she felt the power pool in her fingertips, heat and light tingling beneath her skin.

James stopped suddenly and glanced up at her, his eyes narrowing as she ruthlessly reined her magic in. James may not have been what he seemed, but she was still far from trusting him, and there was no way she was about to reveal her magic.

After a moment, James turned back to the fire, which had caught and begun to crackle merrily. He took a long taper and lit it from the dancing flames, moving steadily around the room, lighting candles and flooding the space with warm golden light. He then moved purposefully to the corner of the room where a small chest stood. Sliding it out of the way with a shrill grating noise he lifted a loose floorboard, revealing a small cavity beneath.

'You can hide your belongings in here,' he glanced up at Olivia.

She nodded and dropped in her backpack, which contained both hers and Theo's clothes. Their boots also followed the backpack. The only thing she retained was Hester's Grimoire, which was tightly wrapped up in a dull grey, utilitarian cloak.

'A little help here,' Theo sucked in a breath and rolled his shoulder, shifting Sam's weight. 'He's not getting any lighter you know.'

'Come,' James replaced the floorboard and shoved the chest back into place, before indicating toward a ladder which led upward to an open loft.

'We'll put your friend up in the loft; I have a bedroll up there he can use. He'll be safer tucked out of eyesight, his condition would be too hard to explain to anyone who might come calling.'

Theo nodded and followed James up the ladder, leaving Olivia to wander the large room. Two smaller rooms led off from the main one. These must have been the building additions she'd seen from the outside. She was intensely curious as to what they actually were used for, but thought it best not to go snooping. After all, she didn't want to offend James when he was risking a great deal to help them.

'It's just the keeping room,' a deep smooth voice spoke behind her, so close she jumped.

She turned to see James standing watching her. She'd heard of a keeping room, a kind of precursor to a kitchen, a food preparation area.

'I'm too curious for my own good,' she answered carefully.

'Theo is just settling your friend, he will join us shortly,' he replied after a moment. 'We haven't had a chance to be properly introduced,' he held out his hand. 'James Wilkins.'

'Olivia,' she murmured, purposefully omitting her last name. After all she wasn't sure she completely trusted James, and she certainly didn't want anyone to know she was a West, in case that information found its way back to Nathaniel.

'It's a pleasure,' he replied softly as his hand closed around hers.

She felt a sudden rush of power shoot up her arm, her eyes widened, and her mouth opened with a small gasp as she pulled away, abruptly snatching back her hand.

'Please,' James continued as if nothing had happened, indicating for her to take a seat. 'You must both be hungry.'

She quietly took a seat on one of the benches next to the table, and watched as James disappeared into the keeping room. If he'd felt the sudden jolt of energy when their hands had touched, he gave no outward indication of it, and seemed completely at ease when he reappeared a couple of moments later carrying a large pot, which he slid into the bake oven.

'That shouldn't take too long to warm,' he told her as he reached for a small cask and three cups.

'What is it?'

'Stew,' he smiled, 'mutton I believe. Rebecca Foster brought it for me earlier today.'

'Does that happen often?'

'Too often,' he laughed. 'All the single ladies of the village seem to feel an incessant need to feed me.'

'I guess you're considered a catch,' Olivia chuckled.

'A catch?'

'A desirable prospect for marriage,' she clarified.

'Aye,' he laughed lightly in return, 'something of that nature.'

'And no one has yet tempted you into matrimony?' her mouth curved in amusement.

He glanced at her, raising one eyebrow good naturedly.

'Sorry,' she shook her head smiling, 'it's that curiosity again.'

'Well,' he answered after a moment, placing a cup down in front of her, 'there is a long and complicated answer to that question, but for now let us say that I have no desire for a wife.'

Knowing not to push the subject further, she took a sip from her cup, allowing the light fruity liquid to dance across her tongue, releasing the unmistakable flavor of sweet peaches and tart apples to burst in her mouth.

'That's delicious,' she stared into the cup in surprise.

'Thank you,' he replied, with a pleased smile, before glancing up at the sound of Theo climbing back down the ladder. 'How is your friend?' he asked as he handed Theo a cup of his own.

'Still sleeping,' he took a seat next to Olivia. 'He definitely has a fever though.'

James nodded.

'So, are you going to explain what you meant when you said that you weren't expecting us for another ten years?' Theo asked bluntly.

'Theo,' James sighed as he shook his head, 'there is so much for me to tell you. I'm not even sure where I should start.'

'At the beginning would probably be a good idea.'

Olivia hid a smile behind her cup as she took another sip. Theo had obviously spent too much time with Jake. He was beginning to sound like him, right down to the sarcastic undertone.

The sudden thought gave her heart a sharp tug. It had been so long since they'd seen their friends, and she missed them terribly. Knowing there was nothing she could do about it, she pushed the thought aside and tried to focus on the conversation in front of her.

'Let me prepare supper first and then we will talk,' James told Theo, who nodded begrudgingly. After all, they were guests in the man's house and he had been nothing if not courteous and considerate.

They sat in silence, watching as James laid out three wooden bowls and spoons. In the center of the table he laid a thick dark loaf of bread, which he cut into chunky uneven slices. He filled a small jug with his delicious cider and set it beside the bread. When he deemed the stew ready he spooned it out into the bowls, setting one each in front of Olivia and Theo, with a thick slice of bread laid over the top. For the most part, they ate in companionable silence, unless they counted the suspicious glare Theo kept casting in James' direction.

Olivia took a spoonful of stew and froze, her cheeks puffed out like a squirrel. She sat for an uncomfortable moment, debating on whether or not to spit it discreetly back into her bowl, or swallow. She didn't want to give any offense and unfortunately for her she was unaware of the etiquette of spitting into one's dinner bowl in the 17th Century, something that hadn't been covered in her beloved history books. She decided to err on the side of caution.

Steeling herself, she forced herself to swallow down the greasy meat, ruthlessly fighting back the urge to gag. It was absolutely disgusting. She'd never had mutton before, if that even was what it was and to be honest she wasn't entirely sure, then there was no way in hell she was ever eating it again. She'd become a god-damn vegetarian if she had to.

As if the stringy greasy meat wasn't bad enough, the gravy was thin and watery, and a rather distressing grey color. She wasn't entirely sure what vegetables had been used, but they were a strange mixture of soggy overcooked mush, and hardened uncooked lumps. If this was what the ladies of the village were serving up to James, she wasn't surprised the guy was still single.

She glanced across to James, who was contentedly scooping it into his mouth with all the enthusiasm of a guy who'd obviously never tasted fillet steak in his life. Theo was also spooning the evil mixture into his mouth without any outward sign of distaste, his gaze locked on James, as if he was a puzzle he couldn't quite figure out. She shook her head and picked up the bread, which hopefully was a little more palatable.

She wasn't really surprised at Theo, she thought dryly. He grew up on this type of food, he probably had a cast iron stomach. No wonder he liked her cooking so much. She bit into the thick bread which wasn't too bad, just dry, making it a little hard to swallow. What she wouldn't give for some butter, and a jar of Liddy Mayberry's strawberry jam. She picked up her cup of cider and took a deep gulp to wash her bread down. At this rate she was going to spend her entire time in Salem hungry and, quite possibly, drunk.

Theo finished his meal and pushed his bowl away, before sitting back and taking a swig of his cider, waiting patiently for James to finish. He took his time, seemingly unaware of Theo glowering in his direction. He mopped up the last of the stew with his bread and swallowed it down slowly, before pushing his own bowl back and reaching for his cup. Their eyes met over the rim of his cup, as James took a casual sip.

'Thank you for the meal,' Theo broke the silence.

'You're welcome,' James replied. 'Unfortunately Rebecca Foster has limited skills when it comes to cooking, but she does try.'

His gaze fell to Olivia's almost full bowl in amusement, before rising to meet her apologetic eyes.

'Perhaps now you will tell us what you meant earlier and why you are helping us?' Theo interrupted.

'So impatient,' James shook his head, 'so like your mother.'

'My mother?' he frowned in confusion. 'What has my mother got to do with this?'

'First,' James glanced at both of them seriously, 'we must make an agreement, that nothing discussed here is repeated outside of these walls. All of our lives depend on it.'

Olivia nodded, glancing at Theo, who also inclined his head in silent agreement.

'I knew your mother very well,' James began quietly, his eyes distant and lost in memory. 'I remember the very first time I saw her. We were barely more than children, but I remember thinking she was the sweetest, most beautiful thing I'd ever seen in my life. She knew...' he smiled to himself, 'she knew the very first time she saw me.'

'Knew what?'

'That we were the same, not like the others.'

'I don't understand,' Theo frowned.

'Theo, haven't you ever wondered where you and Temperance got your gifts from?'

'I don't know what you mean,' Theo replied carefully.

'Yes you do,' James' voice was soft and sympathetic, 'but it's alright. I know that feeling, the feeling of denying your true nature, of hiding for fear of discovery. You don't have to admit anything, I know the truth and so did your mother.'

'And that truth is?'

'That you can see things before they happen, a kind of foreseeing.'

'Are you saying my mother could see things too?'

'Yes, your mother was gifted too.'

'And you?'

'I have my own gifts,' he replied vaguely, 'but we both knew we were the same. It's quite easy to identify others with power. We certainly weren't the only ones.'

'I really don't understand. Everything I thought I knew,' Theo shook his head his voice dropping to a whisper, 'you're telling me it was all a lie?'

'A lie that kept you safe,' James told him, 'that kept your sister safe.'

James watched carefully as Theo struggled to reconcile the dead mother he thought he'd known, with the woman James had obviously known very well.

'Theo,' James' hand twitched involuntarily as if he was fighting the instinct to reach out and comfort him. 'All of us with gifts of power are second, or third generation. Our parents and grandparents fled England and Europe, thinking they were fleeing persecution toward a new life, a better life. They saw the Americas as their New World, a chance to flourish, but what they found was a new society even more rigid and unforgiving than the one they'd fled from. In order to survive we learned to hide in plain sight. Most of us do not discuss our gifts with anyone, not even amongst each other. If you recognize one of your own kind, it is never spoken of. Emmy and I were the exception.'

There was something in his voice when he spoke of Theo's mother, something so wistful, and filled with years' old hurt.

'You loved her?' Theo whispered.

'For my sins,' James admitted. 'Yes, I loved her, for all the good it did me. Her father must have known about me. He didn't want her married to someone magically descended, because it would increase the chances of her children being gifted too.'

'Why wouldn't he want that?'

'Your grandfather was a fearful man Theo, he remembered the Old World. He'd watched his own grandmother accused of witchcraft when he was but a boy himself. He watched what they did to her. He wanted nothing to do with the legacy which ran through his veins. If his gift had been a limb he would have severed it without a second thought, but he couldn't, and as he couldn't cut it out, he thought to breed it out.'

'So, she married my father?'

'She had no choice,' James replied bitterly. 'Her father had her married to Matthias Beckett, before she was barely old enough to be a bride.'

'I'm sorry,' Olivia spoke up, her voice soft and sympathetic.

'Old miseries,' James shook his head, 'that cannot be changed.'

He blew out a deep breath filled with pain.

'Your grandfather got his wish,' he continued softly, 'for a while at least. Your brother Logan was born without any abilities and she knew he would be safe, but then you were born. We knew from early on you had the gift of sight. We tried to keep it hidden as much as we could, but you were always jabbering on...' James smiled as he looked up at Theo, 'about a girl with golden eyes, who had a bow made of fire...'

His eyes cut across to Olivia, his gaze warm and amused.

'You finally found her I see.'

Theo's eyes narrowed warily and his lips tightened, choosing not to confirm or deny anything about Olivia.

'We finally managed to convince you to stop talking about it, and for a while everything was alright. Then your mother gave birth to Temperance and she...' his voice broke, as he drew in a deep breath.

'After Emmy was gone I had to sit by and could do nothing. Although you didn't realize it, I watched over you both as much as I could, but you belonged to Matthias, there was nothing else I could do.'

Theo nodded silently.

'What did you mean about us being ten years too early?' he asked.

'Your mother and I knew that as one century gave birth to a new one, a great madness would descend upon Salem. Darkness would walk among us, and with him he would bring a wave of death. Brother would turn upon brother, and the blood of the innocent would be spilled in search of an ancient power.' James' voice had dropped to a whisper, and his dark eyes deepened.

'You would stand at the center of the madness, with a woman by your side, a woman with hair of midnight and eyes of gold. In her hands she would hold flames of deep lavender. To your other side stood a young man, who seemed to carry on his shoulders the weight of endless years, and in his hands he held time itself.'

'A vision?' Theo asked.

'Then there must be a way,' Olivia muttered to Theo. 'If they've seen us there must be a way for us to jump forward.'

'Are you certain?' Theo turned back to James.

'Nothing is certain,' he shook his head. 'I can only tell you what we knew, and you my friend, are not supposed to be here, not yet anyway.

I saw you today at market, the younger you. I don't understand everything, but I know that you have been jumping through time, and now you have reached a place where you have caught up with yourself.

We have to be very careful now. Until we can sort this mess out, and get you both back to the time you are supposed to be in, we have to make sure no one sees you, especially you Theo. Not so much Olivia, no one here knows her. I may be able to pass her off as a relative.

My older sister married over twenty-five years ago, and moved away to another town with her husband. No one has seen her since they left, so I should have no trouble convincing people Olivia is my niece, which may give her a little more freedom.'

'I see,' Theo frowned. 'What we need is a way to help our friend Sam. We can't leave here until he is recovered, but we don't know for certain what is wrong with him, or how to revive him.'

'I take it his illness is magical in origin?' James questioned.

Theo's jaw once again tightened.

'Theo,' James sighed in frustration, 'I understand you're reluctant to admit to anything, but we are not going to resolve anything if you cannot bring yourself to trust me. I swear, I mean you and Olivia no harm.'

'That's easy for you to say.'

'Yes, it is,' James conceded, 'so I will prove it to you.'

James impulsively reached across the table and grasped Theo's hands. It was like a door had opened in his mind. Layers and layers of memories crashed in on him, memories of his mother, memories that he knew weren't his.

It was like being thrown into a pool of ice cold water. The shock and intensity of it made his breath catch in his throat, and for a second he found himself unable to release his breath.

Suddenly the memories were wrapped up in intense emotions; pain, loss, regret, pride and above all a deep abiding love, so intense, Theo roared in pain.

Ripping his hands free he stood abruptly, stumbling back over the bench he'd been sitting on. His vision cleared and fixed on James, who was sitting pale and shaking as he looked up at Theo, seemingly just as shocked at the intensity of their link as he was.

'I'm sorry,' James breathed heavily, as he closed his eyes, 'I only meant to show you. Speaking of your mother out loud, after all these years, has obviously affected me more than I thought. It was not my intention to cause you pain, only to prove to you...'

'Prove what? That you knew my mother? Well you've certainly done that,' he hissed from between gritted teeth, as he tried to get the trembling in his body to subside.

'No, to prove you could trust me,' James replied. 'You know what I am now, you hold my life in your hands.'

'He's right Theo,' Olivia spoke quietly, her eyes soft and understanding, 'I know this is hard for you, but we have to find a way to trust each other.'

He regarded Olivia silently, turning over her words in his mind before finally turning back to James.

'Don't ever do that to me again,' he warned.

James nodded contritely in agreement. 'I am truly sorry.'

Theo resumed his seat at the table.

'I think there may be a way to help your friend,' James said quietly.

'How?' Olivia asked curiously.

'My neighbor, Samuel Parris, he has a West Indian slave in his household, a girl he brought back from his family's plantation in Barbados. Her name is Tituba.'

'Tituba?' Olivia's gaze snapped to his; she'd heard the name before. Anyone who thought they knew anything about Salem and the witch trials, knew the name Tituba. She was the slave Betty Parris, and her cousin Abigail

Williams, had accused of witchcraft.

'She has a great deal of power. Sometimes Samuel would bring her to market, and I could sense it whenever she was near. I've heard whispers of her curing illness. She may be able to help. I have a delivery to make to the Parris place tomorrow, Olivia could come with me. I'll introduce her as my niece, and try to distract the family long enough for her to speak with Tituba.'

Theo sat frowning. It was clear he didn't like the idea of Olivia going anywhere without him, but equally he knew he couldn't risk anyone seeing him.

'Theo, we need to help Sam,' Olivia told him. 'We have to try.'

'I know,' he reached out unconsciously to touch her face. 'I just don't like letting you out of my sight.'

'Believe me I know that,' she smiled covering his hand with her own, 'but we are going to have to take some risks.'

He sighed in resignation, 'I know.' He turned to James, 'If anything happens to her...' he warned dangerously.

'I will protect her with my life, I swear to you.'

Theo glared silently at him, as if gauging his sincerity. Finally he nodded.

'You should both get some rest,' James told them as they stood and stepped away from the table. 'You two should take my bed, it's through the doorway in the next room.'

'We can't take your bed,' Olivia frowned.

'I assure you it's no trouble,' James shook his head. 'I have a spare bedroll, I'm quite happy in front of the fire.'

'You should know we're not married,' Theo told James.

'I didn't hear that,' James smiled, as he cleared the bowls from the table, 'now take your woman to bed. She looks like she needs some sleep.'

Theo turned to Olivia and saw her yawn. Her skin

was pale and there were dark circles under her eyes.

'Come on love,' he took her hand and bent to scoop Hester's Grimoire from the floor, before leading her from the room.

Olivia smiled gratefully at James, as Theo led her through the keeping room and into another room, where a sturdy wooden bedstead dominated the room and a large chest was pushed against the wall. As soon as they were in the room the candle burst into flame.

'Sorry,' Olivia yawned.

He'd noticed she had less control over her power when she was tired, and right now she looked dead on her feet. It was as if everything that had happened, since the moment he was dragged from Mercy through the gateway to the Otherworld, had finally come crashing in on her.

He tucked the book safely under the pillow and turned back to Olivia. She stood still and let him undress her, like a doll. He stripped her down to her linen shift, before scooping her up and settling her in the bed, pulling the bedclothes up to her shoulders. She was already dozing when he stripped down and slid into bed next to her, pulling her safely into his arms. He blew out the candle, but as he closed his eyes an endless reel of memories that didn't belong to him played around and around in his head. He sighed deeply, a frown creasing his brow. Sleep would be a long time coming.

4.

Olivia's eyes flew open and she shot out of bed, heading for the keeping room. She grabbed the small wooden bucket she'd seen the night before, and dropped to her knees as she started heaving unmercifully, violently expelling the contents of her stomach.

'Olivia?'

She was vaguely aware of Theo's voice, as she continued to throw up for what felt like an eternity. When the heaving of her stomach finally subsided, she looked up weakly to see Theo standing in the doorway, looking at her in concern.

'Are you okay?'

'Do I look okay?' she whispered miserably, as she turned her head back to the bucket, and began to heave once again.

She felt him kneel down beside her, and after a moment his hand was on her back, rubbing soothing circles. She murmured something, but the words were lost in a muffled echo.

'Sorry, I didn't quite catch that?'

She lifted her head out of the bucket, and drew in a shaky breath, as she looked up at Theo's amused expression.

'I said I'm never eating mutton ever again,' she rested her aching head against the rim of the bucket. 'Tell James to stay away from Rebecca Foster, she's obviously trying to kill him.'

'The food is very different here,' Theo chuckled lightly as he smoothed back her hair, which was plastered to her clammy forehead, 'and the living standards are too. It will probably take your body a while to adjust; you've been through a lot lately.'

'Why aren't you sick?' she frowned.

'I grew up without a mother, in a house where none of us knew how to cook. Trust me, I've eaten some pretty questionable meals in my time.'

'I hate you right now,' she whispered, 'and your lead lined stomach.'

'I'm sure you do,' he smiled as he stroked her hair. 'Are you finished?'

'I think so.'

He tucked his arms gently around her back and under her knees. Lifting her easily, she curved into his body exhaustedly as he headed back towards the bedroom.

'Wait Theo, I can't leave that mess. I have to clean up.'

'I'll take care of it love.'

'You shouldn't have to clean up after me,' she frowned.

'Olivia, I spent most of my life on a farm swilling out pigs, and mucking out cows. I think my constitution is strong enough to handle a little vomit.'

'Still,' she grumbled, as he laid her back on the bed.

He tucked the bedclothes back over her and laid his hand on her forehead.

'You don't seem to have a fever.'

'That's because it's not a virus,' she propped herself up on her elbows. 'I told you, it's probably food poisoning.'

She squeezed her eyes closed and forced herself to

take deep even breaths, fighting the wave of intense nausea at the mere thought of the oily, stringy meat sliding down her throat. Her mouth flooded with moisture, and she clamped her lips shut, swallowing convulsively. Probably best not to think about it. She fell back against the pillow and blew out a shaky breath.

'God, I would sell my soul for a toothbrush right now.'

'I'm sure you would,' Theo smiled. 'Wait a moment.'

She watched patiently as he slipped from the room, reappearing moments later with a cup.

'Here,' he lifted her head, wrapping her fingers around the cup. 'Sip slowly, it should take away some of the taste without making you sick again.'

She took a small hesitant sip and experienced the smooth, light, fruity flavor of James' peach and apple cider. It wasn't exactly ginger ale, but it soothed her ragged throat.

'Better?' Theo asked.

She nodded, resting her throbbing head once again on the pillow, as Theo placed the cup on the edge of the chest nearest the bed.

'Where were you?' she asked, suddenly realizing that not only had he not been in bed with her when she'd woken so abruptly, but that he was fully dressed.

'I was checking on Sam.'

'Oh,' she replied, 'how is he?'

'Much the same,' Theo shook his head. 'I don't know what else to do, his fever isn't breaking.'

'There's not much we can do at the moment except wait it out. What time is it anyway?'

'Still early,' he answered easily as he pushed her hair gently back from her face.

'And James?'

'Up with the dawn. He's down in the orchard and won't be back for some time. You should rest.'

'But we were supposed to visit Samuel Parris,' she

struggled to get up. 'I should get dressed.'

'Sleep first,' he pushed her gently back against the pillow. 'You can't go anywhere while you're sick. Sleep and we'll see how you are when you wake. James isn't expected at the Parris house until late this afternoon, there's plenty of time.'

'I don't know,' she frowned.

'For God's sake Olivia,' he rolled his eyes. 'For once in your life, can't you just do as you're told?'

'You're very bossy all of a sudden,' she smiled.

'Then it'll make a nice change from you being the bossy one,' he replied. 'I don't like it when you're sick, it worries me.'

'And it'll worry you less if I take a nap?' her eyebrow rose in amusement.

'Yes.'

'Fine then. I'll take a damn nap, if it makes you happy.'

'It does.'

'Well then.'

He chuckled as he shook his head. 'I'll check in on you later,' he stood and dropped a kiss on her forehead.

'Kay,' she murmured, as she snuggled back down into the bed, already drifting off.

James ran his hands down the thick trunk, as he glanced down the row of trees either side. The others seemed to be flourishing, all except the one in front of him. The leaves were beginning to curl at the edges, and the fruit was small and underdeveloped. Frowning slightly, he ran his fingertips down the rough bark, closing his eyes as he felt the tree pulsing beneath his gentle touch.

It was sick, he could sense it. He dropped to his knees and pressed his fingers into the soil at its roots. His breathing slowed, and his heartbeat faded into the background. He could feel everything.

Pressing his awareness further down into the earth,

he could feel layers upon layers of rock and sediment. The top layer of soil was not as rich in minerals as he'd have liked, but then again, the lands surrounding his property were not known for being lush and fertile.

In fact, from the moment the colonists had settled, it had been a battle to grow certain crops. It was almost as if the land itself was fighting man's possession, all except his land. He felt the earth, was a part of it. He sensed its moods and needs, he tended it like a lover, made sure it flourished. There was a reason his orchard was known for miles for its quality and abundance.

The earth felt a little dry, the roots a little brittle. It had been a good while since they'd last had a good soaking, as the passing summer had been hotter than usual.

Concentrating, he reached further into the ground, searching for moisture, until he finally sensed a small stream of water deep down in the earth. He pressed a little harder, nudging it with his mind and forcing it open a little wider, until a small trickle of water started seeping upward into the surrounding earth.

Satisfied, he turned his attention back to the tree. Some sort of pestilence, he mused, chewing his lip thoughtfully. He could sense dark patches deep in its core. If he didn't deal with it quickly, it could spread to the surrounding trees.

He pressed his palms against the trunk and reached into the tree with his mind. Starting at the roots, he checked the sick young tree inch by slow inch, burning away any sign of rot. Finally satisfied he'd got it all, he stood and opened his eyes. Reaching for a strip of linen, he tied it around the branch, to mark the tree, so that his laborers would know not to pick from this tree during harvest. It would need time to recover, perhaps by next season it would produce the quality of fruit to suit his standards.

He stepped back and looked up at the tree smiling softly, anyone else would not be able to detect the difference, but he could.

A small breeze rippled through its branches, rustling the leaves, which already seemed to be relaxing like an unclenched fist. The tree itself almost seemed taller, as if previously it had been hunched over in pain. He patted the bark fondly and stepped away, stopping abruptly when his eyes fell on Theo, who was watching him with a mixture of curiosity and suspicion.

'What were you doing?' Theo asked.

'The tree was sick,' James answered easily. 'I was just treating it, before the rot spread to any of the other trees.'

'How?'

'Do you really want the answer to that?' he replied with a slow smile.

Theo didn't reply, his eyes narrowing as he studied James speculatively. He didn't give his trust easily, especially not now, not when one mistake could potentially expose Olivia. But there was something about James, something he couldn't quite figure out.

He'd known this man from afar, for most of his life, and he'd never once suspected he was different. It was almost as if he'd stepped back in time, and he was actually seeing the life he'd lived before with completely different eyes.

How could he have been so blind? Had the signs always been there? Had he been so consumed with keeping himself and his sister hidden, he'd not noticed, that they were not the only ones with a secret.

'You look as if you are having an argument with yourself,' James told him softly.

'I haven't been gone that long, but I'm finding nothing is as I remember it,' he finally admitted.

'Nothing ever is,' James patted his shoulder companionably. 'Come walk with me, we have much to talk about.'

'Such as?'

'You were not wrong, when you said nothing is as

you thought it was,' James began, as they walked slowly along the rows of apple trees. 'You were too young to know the truth before. You were so caught up in protecting yourself, and your sister, and quite rightly so, but now you can't ignore it any longer.'

'Ignore what exactly?'

'The truth about Salem, about the people in it,' he blew out a deep breath as he tried to organize his thoughts. 'What I told you last night was true. Many of us with unusual gifts are descended from magical families. We aren't in anyway what they say we should be. We don't worship the devil, and we don't summon evil spirits. We are as god fearing, as the ones who would wish us harm.

Our families fled the Old World, believing, foolishly perhaps, that this would be a sanctuary for us, a place free from persecution. But it was not to be so.

If the others find out about us, it will cost us our lives. There is no reasoning with fear, and many believe any form of magic is inherently evil. Once we realized it was not going to be the haven we had wished for, we had to make the best of our new home. We knew we could not survive by ignoring who we are, denying our true natures.'

'I don't understand,' Theo shook his head.

'You denied your gift for years, and now you have no control over it. I suspect it is the same for Temperance, but a gift like that with no control or instruction, is a great risk. The less control you have, the more likely it is to manifest in front of the wrong people.'

'I see,' he frowned.

'I can help you,' James offered. 'I can teach you how to use your visions, instead of letting them use you.'

Theo stopped abruptly, staring hard at James.

'Why?'

'Why what?'

'Why would you help me? Why risk the exposure?'

'Because,' James sighed, 'because you are your mother's son, because I care what happens to you and

Temperance, because I would give my life to protect you both.'

'She was that important to you?' Theo asked.

'Your mother was everything to me,' he whispered painfully.

'Do you have visions too?' Theo asked after a moment.

James shook his head and they both began walking slowly once again.

'No, that was your mother's gift. I don't see things like she did. I have more of…a knowing I suppose you'd call it. I don't see things before they happen, but sometimes I just know something is about to happen.'

'I'm not trying to be rude or ungrateful, but if you don't have visions how do you expect to help me?'

'Emmy and I grew up together, we were inseparable. We explored and refined our abilities together. I was there when she learned to control her visions, I can tell you what she told me. The knowledge would have passed to you from her eventually if she hadn't died. I suppose in a way it still will, just through me instead.'

Theo continued to walk in silence for a few moments before finally nodding.

'Thank you,' he murmured.

James let out the breath he hadn't realized he was holding, and relaxed the tight set of his shoulders.

'Well then,' he grinned, 'we may as well begin.'

'Now?'

'Are you planning on staying in Salem for long?' he asked pointedly.

'Not if I can help it,' Theo replied.

'Then we have to make the most of the time we have,' James told him. 'We'll use the barn, no one should see us in there.'

Olivia rolled over and lifted her head. She had absolutely no idea what the time was, or how long she'd slept, but she was forced to admit her stomach felt better. She sat up gingerly, as if daring her stomach to begin revolting against her once again, but it remained still and calm, apart from a loud growl which informed her that she was hungry.

Swinging her legs over the side of the bed, she reached for her petticoats. It didn't take her as long to dress this time, now that she was starting to get the hang of the fiddly layers of clothing. She stepped into her uncomfortable leather shoes, after making sure the compass and chain around her neck was concealed carefully beneath her clothes.

Pulling her hair back, she once again fastened it in a low bun at the nape of her neck, before pulling the close fitting cap over her head. Satisfied she was presentable enough to not raise any questions she left the room, making her way through the keeping room into the main room, which was also empty and silent.

Climbing the ladder to the loft, she quickly checked on Sam. He looked dreadful. Despite the fever, his skin had taken on a grayish hue, instead of the usual flushed pink of someone with a high temperature. They would have to do something and quickly. They had no way of getting any fluids into him, and with his temperature burning like an inferno he would soon dehydrate, which would only complicate matters further.

She was worried, very worried. He seemed to be getting worse, and she wasn't even sure what was causing it. She carefully removed the cloth from his forehead and dipped it into the almost empty bowl of water, before wringing it out and placing it back on his forehead. Satisfied he was in no immediate danger, she climbed back down the ladder, and left the farmhouse in search of Theo.

'We're going to start small,' James told Theo, as he sat on the edge of a cask of cider.

'Small?'

'Eventually you will be able to look forward and see big events before they happen, but for now we are going to try for just a few moments into the future.'

'What good will that do?' Theo frowned.

'It will do a great deal of good,' James told him patiently. 'Being able to see something just before it happens will give you a distinct and definite advantage. Imagine being able to see your enemy's intentions, before he even knows it himself. Will he step to the right and throw a punch? Will he step to the left and grasp a weapon? Imagine being able to see an accident before it happens? If you can see it, you can change the outcome.'

'Okay then,' Theo breathed out, 'so what do I do?'

'Focus,' James' voice was low and smooth. 'Close your eyes and find your center, the place where you are at peace. Block out all distractions.'

Theo felt a sudden sharp thud against his shoulder, which knocked him back, making him lose his balance on the barrel.

'What the hell?' he growled and opened his eyes as he steadied himself.

James was standing a few feet from him, grinning and tossing an apple back and forth between his hands. Theo looked down to the ground and noticed chunks of apple at his feet, and flecks of pulp stuck to his jerkin.

'Did you just throw an apple at me?' he asked incredulously.

'Maybe next time you'll duck,' he chuckled. 'Close your eyes and try again.'

Scowling, he did as he was told, taking a calming breath and trying to focus. If he could see the apple before it impacted his body, he could deflect it, or avoid it. Now he understood, this was the test. He had to see what James was going to do, before he did it. If he could see it, he could change the outcome, just like James said.

'Ouch,' Theo's eyes flew open, as another apple smashed against his other shoulder.

'I can hear you thinking all the way over here,' he grinned. 'Stop thinking, and focus...again.'

Again, and again, he tried. He took a shot to the arm, to his shoulders, his knee, and his stomach, which almost knocked the wind from him. The final straw was when it hit him in the forehead, leaving a reddened mark, and showering him with chunks of apple.

'Enough,' he roared, glaring dangerously at James as he raked his hand through his dark hair, sending a scattering of pulp and pips to the ground.

'Sorry,' James winced, 'I wasn't actually aiming for your head.'

'Then you're a lousy shot,' Theo growled, looking down at the apple piled around his ankles, 'and you're wasting your apples.'

'I have more,' he shrugged.

Theo looked up suddenly. Olivia was close by, he could feel her.

The door of the barn rattled slightly, before creaking open enough for her to slip through. She stepped further into the space, catching sight of Theo, who looked slightly damp, and disheveled, and James who was standing close by, biting nonchalantly into an apple. Her gaze dropped to the floor, which was liberally littered with what looked like chunks of apple.

'Have you two finished playing?' she asked dryly.

James chuckled as Theo made his way over to her.

'Are you okay?' he asked, ignoring her question. 'Are you feeling better?'

'I am actually,' she nodded, 'just hungry now.'

'Here,' James tossed her an apple, which she bit into gratefully.

'Thanks,' she mumbled, as she chewed and swallowed, turning back to Theo. 'I've just checked on Sam. I'm worried Theo, he seems so much worse.'

'We'd better go take a look then,' Theo turned to James.

'You head back to the house,' he told them, 'I still have work to do. Come and find me, if you need me.'

Theo nodded and took Olivia's hand, pulling her out of the barn and heading back towards the house.

'What exactly were you two doing?' she asked curiously.

'Don't ask,' Theo flushed lightly, shaking his head.

She tossed her apple core as they reached the house, and opened the door.

'You go and sit with Sam,' Theo told her. 'I'll fetch some fresh water and cloths.'

Nodding, she headed into the house alone, taking a moment to retrieve the Grimoire from the bedroom, before she climbed back up the ladder and settled herself beside Sam.

She pulled the cloth from his forehead, noting that in the twenty minutes she'd been gone, the wet cloth was now bone dry. Wishing she had a thermometer, she unwrapped Hester's book and flicked open the pages. Maybe there was something in it she could use.

She covered the book quickly, and looked up as she heard steps up the ladder, relaxing when she saw Theo's head of dark hair appear. He settled the bowl of water down beside him, and dunked the cloth a couple of times before wringing it out and laying it on Sam's forehead.

'His temperature seems to be getting higher,' Olivia frowned. 'If it gets any worse, he could end up having a seizure.'

'Have you found anything in the book?' he nodded at the familiar shape she'd hastily concealed beneath her dress.

'No, not yet.'

She pulled the book clear, and opened it once again. The now familiar black ink appeared on the page, undulating like lapping water. The letters formed, and then reformed, and then changed again.

'Show me a way to help Sam,' she whispered, running her fingers across the dry parchment.

Before, when she'd asked the book for guidance it had rather helpfully obliged, but it seemed not this time. The words just kept shifting on the page, as if it couldn't decide what to settle on. She stared at it a little longer, before sighing and closing the book.

'I guess we're on our own this time,' she looked up at Theo.

'I guess so,' he frowned. Taking another cloth and dunking it in the water, he loosened the linen shirt he'd changed Sam into the night before, and squeezed the cloth directly onto his chest, allowing the cool water to fall on his sweat slicked skin.

'We need to try and get some fluids into him,' Olivia told him. 'If we don't, he's going to dehydrate, before his fever has a chance to break.'

'Cider?' Theo asked.

'He needs water,' she shook her head. 'Where did this water come from?'

'The stream at the edge of James' land I would imagine,' Theo replied.

'Is it clean?'

'I don't know,' Theo shrugged. 'I seem to remember the stream being quite clean, but I don't know that I'd drink from it.'

'I think we're going to have to risk it,' she murmured, staring at Sam. 'Go and get some more, and grab a cup.'

She watched as he nodded and climbed back down the ladder. She tucked the book back into the cloak and wrapped it up tightly, knotting the material and placing it next to her.

She pulled the bowl of water Theo had just refilled closer, and held her hand over the liquid. Looking around, carefully checking she was alone, she allowed her magic to flow to the palm of her hand, the heat making her skin tingle. The water beneath her hand began to bubble and jump around the bowl, as she heated it way past boiling point, hoping that the intense temperature would burn away any bacteria.

When Theo returned, they waited patiently for the water to cool down to drinking temperature, taking turns over the next several hours to feed him sips of water and bathe his burning body. Olivia was next to him stroking back his wet hair, when they heard the sound of someone climbing the ladder. Both she and Theo looked up as James' face appeared.

'How is he?' he glanced over at Sam's prone body, which now shook and shuddered uncontrollably.

'He's getting worse,' Theo replied.

'It's time for me to head to the Parris place,' James looked directly to Olivia. 'I think at this point, Tituba might be your only hope.'

Olivia gathered her skirts in her hand, and tried to stand, but Theo's hand shot out and grasped her wrist. She knew he was worried about letting her out of his sight.

'Look at him Theo,' she whispered, 'he needs this. We don't have a choice.'

He looked back down at Sam, before finally blowing out a breath.

'Just be careful.'

'I will,' she nodded, and squeezed his hand reassuringly, before turning to follow James back down the ladder.

5.

Olivia reached out and took James' hand as he helped her up into the wagon. Settling her skirts around her she sat down on the hard wooden bench, watching as he climbed up beside her and reached for the reins. Clucking lightly at the horses he nudged them into a slow walk. The casks in the back jostled against the ropes which held them in place and the wheels creaked.

'It's a pleasant afternoon for a journey to the village,' James remarked conversationally as they rolled ponderously down the dirt road.

'Uh huh,' Olivia replied non-committedly.

They rode in companionable silence for a short while, the farmhouse behind them disappearing as did the forest of apples trees, giving way to open farmland and a hard packed dirt road which meandered in no particular line. Rather than intentionally being cut into the ground it seemed to have been worn down over time by the continuous passing of horses' hooves and wagon wheels.

Olivia watched curiously as James took a deep breath, inhaling the fresh air, a small smile playing at his lips.

'You seem happy.'

'And why shouldn't I be?' he turned to her, the smile still on his lips. 'It's a beautiful day, my business is doing well, I have the company of a beautiful woman and I finally have the chance to…'

He broke off suddenly, almost as if unsure of his next words.

'A chance to?' she prompted.

He blew out a deep breath.

'I finally have a chance to know Theo.' His gaze fixed on the horses in front of him thoughtfully. 'It has been difficult.'

'How so?'

'I have had very little dealings with Matthias Beckett.' His sunny expression suddenly darkened, 'he is a difficult man.'

'And when you say difficult?' Olivia asked curiously.

'Has Theo spoken to you of his father?'

Olivia stared at him for a moment, her lips thinning as she scrutinized him thoughtfully.

'Forgive me,' he shook his head, 'you don't need to answer that question.'

They carried on down the road, the wagon bumping sharply at every slight dip and rock.

'He has told me a little,' Olivia finally broke the silence. 'I know there was no love lost between them and that Matthias drank quite heavily, and although Theo has never said as much I get the impression he was heavy handed with all of his children.'

James' head whipped around sharply as he studied Olivia, his eyes dark and his jaw clenched tightly.

'I was afraid he might be,' he sighed after a moment. 'There was nothing I could do. After Emmy died I had no access to the children. In the eyes of the law and God they belonged to him. I could not take them away, not even to protect them.'

'That must have been very frustrating for you,' she murmured thoughtfully.

'You have no idea how much it has pained me over

the years to watch them from afar, to catch glimpses of them, but not be allowed to know them, to speak to them, to be of any comfort to them.'

'Then you should treasure this time you have with Theo,' Olivia smiled impulsively, covering his hand with hers. All of a sudden she felt a deep sympathy and connection with this sweet man.

It was clear to her, even if he did not speak the words aloud, that he loved Theo very much. She relaxed into the uncomfortable bench finding that, with a greater understanding of this man the more she felt comfortable in his company. She knew Theo was still suspicious of James' motives and she didn't blame him. The problem with Theo was that he was under a great deal of stress, seeing his sister again, and re-living the pain and loss of his mother. He was incapable at this moment of judging anything impartially.

'I intend to,' he smiled. 'So tell me Olivia, where do you come from?'

'A place a few hours ride from Salem town,' she told him carefully, substituting the word 'drive' for the word 'ride.' After all, there was no way she was going to explain modern day transportation to him.

'I see,' James nodded, 'and how did you and Theo meet?'

'Well,' she frowned, trying to edit the version of how they met. It was really hard not giving away specifics and she found she had a new understanding of how hard it must have been for Sam to have withheld certain things from her. Damn it, she really hated time travel. 'Theo was sent to help me.'

'Are you in trouble then?' he frowned.

When am I not in trouble? Olivia thought dryly. 'It's complicated,' she answered with a sigh.

'I wish you could both trust me,' he sighed.

'It's not so much a question of trust,' Olivia told him softly, feeling bad for the guy who was obviously trying real hard to understand the situation they had all landed in the middle of. Deciding to take a little leap of faith she pulled in a deep breath. Her gut was telling her she could trust this man, and so far her gut had not steered her wrong.

'James,' she spoke quietly, 'I come from a different time, from a time far into your future.'

'I know,' he nodded.

'You do?' she replied with some surprise.

He nodded again, seemingly organizing his thoughts before speaking once more.

'Emmy saw a great many things. At the time not all of it made sense, but I have not forgotten a single word she breathed to me, especially when it concerned Theo. Not only that, but I have my own limited gifts when it comes to foretelling.'

'How much exactly do you know about me?' she asked curiously.

'I know you come from a time and place many, many years from now. I know that you have been betrayed by your own blood and that a great evil overshadows you. It is hunting you, because you have a great destiny. There is something important you have to do and it can only be you. Theo is deeply entwined in that destiny.'

'I see,' she murmured as she watched him.

'I also know that you hold fire of deep lavender in your hands and yet it does not burn you. The fire is more an extension of you than an outside force.'

That was interesting, Olivia thought. Twice now he had referred to her wielding a lavender colored fire, but that was not one of her abilities. She could call Earth fire, the easiest fire there was, as it was part of the mortal world. It was gold and red and filled with warmth. She could also call Spirit fire, which was a cool silver flame and which carried with it, the sense of thousands of souls. She was also able to summon Hell fire of deep sapphire blue flames edged in jet black. Vast and all-encompassing, it was as seductive as it was powerful and carried with it the weight of thousands upon thousands of years. Perhaps in time the strange purple fire would be another skill she would add to her abilities.

'You seem to know much about me James.'

'You can trust me,' his mouth curved with an amused smile.

His expression was suddenly so familiar a sneaking suspicion began to grow in her mind.

'Can I?'

'An exchange of secrets then,' he offered, 'so you will feel less vulnerable. You may ask me anything at all and I will answer truthfully.'

'Alright then,' she tilted her head slightly as she watched him, 'what exactly is your ability? Your magical ability I mean?'

'It's hard to put into words,' he frowned thoughtfully. 'I feel the Earth, I am at one with it.'

He seemed to struggle explaining to her what he was able to do and she wasn't surprised. Other than Theo's mother, he'd probably never discussed it with another living soul.

'I can sense its change of mood,' he continued. 'I can nurture it or change it, or even move it.'

'I see,' she nodded in understanding, 'your element is Earth.'

'Element?'

'There are five elements that make up all of creation,' she told him. 'Earth, Air, Fire, Water and Spirit. In magic it is possible to call upon all five elements, but certain people have a very strong affinity for one element in particular. My element is Fire, I understand it, I can control it and it is a part of me, a part of who I am. You have a very strong affinity for Earth, it is a part of you.'

'Yes that is it exactly,' he answered, relived that she seemed to understand.

He looked back at the road, scanning his surroundings.

'We'll come upon the village soon,' he told her. 'I will introduce you as my niece, the daughter of my sister Ann and her husband Thomas Wardwell. They left Salem after they married and moved to Plymouth, where his people are from. It was so long ago I doubt anyone will question us, although it's probably best if we tell them you are married and that your husband is away. It would not be seemly to have a young unmarried woman in my household, even if she is my niece. We need a name for your fictional husband.'

Olivia frowned thoughtfully as she searched back through her memory turning over the historical facts and lists, trying to come up with a name that would not sound out of place.

'How about Oldham?'

'Very well then, I'll introduce you as Olivia Oldham.'

'You'd better introduce me as Livy Oldham' she frowned. 'It's probably best that no one here knows me by the name Olivia.'

'Is there someone in particular you wish to avoid hearing that name?'

'You are too astute,' she replied as if musing to herself. 'How much do you know about the cleric known as Nathaniel.'

'I know enough to avoid him whenever possible,' he scoffed as he noted the serious expression on Olivia's face. 'I have sensed great darkness in him, in truth I have tried not to place myself in his path if I can help it. He is not what he seems.'

'No he is not,' she agreed.

'You know what he is don't you?' his eyes narrowed.

'I know enough to know you should continue to avoid him,' her jaw tightened.

'Is he a danger to you?' James frowned.

'Let's just say I would prefer not to announce my

presence to him.'

'Very well,' he nodded.

Before long buildings started to come into view, tall and rectangular, some of reddened wood, others with dark wood clapboards and pitched roofs. A few were lower, more squat and probably only one level. The noise level began to build and now the peaceful afternoon air was filled with the chatter of villagers, the laughter of children and the insistent squawk of a battery of hens wandering aimlessly.

'I see Corey's hens have gotten loose again,' James chuckled. 'I told him to shore up his fence.'

Olivia glanced around and saw most of the houses had simple wattle fences, which came up to maybe waist height, bordering off their plot of land. Children ran the dusty worn paths under the stern eye of the other residents. James navigated the narrow paths skillfully, slowing his pace to a safer crawl as the children laughed and chased the wagon.

They finally came to a stop beside a low fence, beyond which was a pretty little wild flower garden and a taller rectangular house. Clearly a two storey house which spoke of wealth, it had a steeply pitched roof and dark wood clapboards. The windows were glass, reinforced with thick black metal strips in a recurring diamond shape pattern. To the side stood a small wooden shed with a broad overhang, beneath which were stacks of neatly chopped firewood.

James climbed down from the wagon and tethered the reins to the fencepost before reaching up to help Olivia down. He turned in the direction of the house and she followed him hands folded neatly at her waist, her eyes demurely cast downward. She had a part to play now, as she had to make sure no one suspected that she didn't belong there.

James knocked firmly at the door and waited patiently as it creaked open slowly. A young house servant, a girl of perhaps fourteen, answered the door, staring silently at them both with wide eyes.

'Good afternoon,' James smiled easily. 'I am here to see your master girl. Be so good as to fetch him.'

She curtsied and disappeared. A few moments later a tall man in his late thirties appeared. He was dressed soberly in a dark colored coat, his lank brown hair hanging to his shoulders.

'Ah James, there you are,' he nodded. 'Come in.'

He stepped back allowing them to pass, his gaze landing with interest on Olivia.

'I apologize for the absence of my wife, but Elizabeth is at present unwell and not receiving visitors.'

'I am sorry to hear that,' James nodded. 'I shall pray for her swift recovery.'

'You are too kind,' Samuel responded. 'I don't believe you met the children last time.'

'No, I have not yet had that pleasure.'

'My children Thomas and Betty,' he indicated toward three young children playing in front of the fireplace. 'The other girl is my niece Abigail Williams.'

Olivia glanced over at the three children playing happily on the ground in front of the huge open fireplace, where a fire burned cheerily. They seemed to be playing some kind of game which involved a wooden board with pegs in it. Small clay marbles were scattered on the floor next to them and in amongst them were small wooden objects, which looked a lot like jacks. It was incredible really Olivia thought, three hundred years separating her generation and theirs and yet they still grew up playing the same games.

She turned her attention to the children themselves. The boy was a sweet little thing with chubby cheeks and dark wavy hair and couldn't have been more than four years old, but it was the girls who had really piqued her curiosity. Abigail Williams and Betty Parris were two of the names most synonymous with the infamous witch trials. It was their accusations which led to the arrest of Tituba, Sarah Good and Sarah Osbourne in February of 1692.

Her gaze narrowed as she studied them both. The older one, Samuel's niece Abigail, was about five years old and the younger, his daughter Betty, was maybe three years old. They looked so sweet, so innocent. It was hard to believe that in a mere seven years' time their accusations and spiteful theatrics would set in motion a chain of events, which would lead to so many innocents being condemned to death.

'Perhaps you'd like to introduce your companion?' Samuel suggested pointedly.

'Beg your pardon,' James inclined his head lightly. 'This is my niece Livy Oldham, the daughter of my sister Ann. She hails from Boston. Her husband has recently sailed aboard 'The Deliverance' bound for the West Indies and in his absence Livy has come to visit, to satisfy her curiosity about the Orchard.'

'Well, you are gaining a reputation for quality I'll admit,' he conceded grudgingly before glancing at Olivia. 'You have no children of your own yet Goody Oldham?'

'No Sir,' she replied quietly. 'My husband is often away for long periods of time. We have not yet been blessed with the joy of a child.'

'It is not just a joy, but a sacred duty,' he replied solemnly.

'As you say,' she agreed contritely. 'I pray that I will be judged worthy of such a duty.'

He nodded, somewhat mollified by her answer and her deference.

'James you have brought the cider I requested?'

'I have,' he answered easily. 'I brought your usual cider and two casks of applejack, but I have also brought a gift. A new flavor of cider I have been working on.'

'New you say?' he huffed.

'Aye, apple and peach. It has been well received by

the folks who've already tried it. Perhaps your wife may care to sample it; it has a sweet and pleasing flavor.'

'Maybe,' he shrugged. 'You'll be wanting some help to unload then?'

'I can manage.'

'Nonsense,' he turned toward the back of the room to the open doorway. 'JOHN!' he bellowed, loud enough that the small boy Thomas flinched.

A few moments later a tall dark skinned man stepped into the room, so tall and broad he almost filled the entire doorway.

'Sir?' his voice was a deep and pleasing rumble.

'Where are Tituba and Rebecca?'

'You wish I fetch them?' his voice was a rich baritone filled with a thick island accent.

Olivia cast her mind back to her history books. This must be John Indian, Tituba's companion and the only other slave Samuel Parris had brought back from his failed plantation in Barbados. She could not seem to recall the name Rebecca though, perhaps she was a house servant borrowed from a neighbor, while Elizabeth Parris was abed ill.

'Yes, yes,' Samuel snapped irritably, 'and be quick about it.'

John nodded and disappeared from the room. They stood in silence for a moment and then the young girl of fourteen scurried in followed by a taller, slim, dark skinned woman. Her wild raven hair was tamed beneath a demure coif. Although she wore the clothes of a proper puritan woman, it did nothing to mask her exotic beauty. As she entered the room her eyes flickered to Olivia, pausing for the barest of moments before she lowered them again. Olivia almost sucked in an audible breath with the punch of power that hit her. James hadn't been wrong when he said he'd felt the edges of her power when he'd been in close proximity to her.

'Rebecca take the children upstairs, Tituba clean up

their mess. John you come with us,' Samuel barked orders before turning back to James. 'You can tell John here which casks to take, then we can retire to the study and settle up with coin.'

'Of course,' James inclined his head.

Olivia stepped to the side allowing the three men to pass. Samuel swept imperiously from the room. A man used to power and privilege, he did not give Olivia a second glance.

The man was an absolute prick, Olivia thought to herself as she bit her tongue. She knew that his personality and conduct were very typical of his time, but it still didn't change the fact that she instantly disliked the man.

The girl named Rebecca scooped the children from the floor and ushered them nervously from the room. Olivia turned her attention to the fireplace where Tituba was kneeling and picking up the children's discarded playthings, avoiding Olivia's gaze. Checking that they were indeed alone Olivia hurried across the room and dropped down in front of the beautiful slave woman.

'Tituba?' Olivia whispered, 'I need your help.'

Tituba ignored her and continued to pick up the clay marbles, dropping them into a small cloth sack.

'Tituba please,' Olivia tried again.

'You not supposed to speak with I,' she glanced up at Olivia. Her eyes were a startling ocean blue and the longer Olivia stared into them, the more she could have sworn she heard the hiss and roar of the waves breaking upon the shore. 'Go and wait for Mister Wilkins otherwise risk discovery and bring punishment.'

'Tituba, I am not trying to get you into trouble with your master,' Olivia whispered, 'but I need your help. Please...my friend is dying.'

'Then that is a matter for your God,' her voice held the same musical lilt of the islands as her companion John.

'It is not as simple as that, he has a fever that won't break. There is nothing else we can do and he is too important to leave his survival in the hands of fate.' Olivia reached out and grabbed her hand and felt a jolt of power sear up her arm. 'I swear I mean you no harm, but I cannot save him alone. I need your help…please.'

A sudden intrusion of voices had them both pulling apart and standing abruptly. Olivia moved back a distance, watching warily as James re-entered the room followed by Samuel.

'Come Livy,' James indicated for her to follow, 'we have taken enough of Goodman Parris' time.'

Olivia moved to stand obediently at James' side, but she risked a brief glance at Tituba, who was watching her with troubled eyes. There was no way she hadn't felt the jolt of power when she'd grasped her arm.

'Samuel,' James nodded as he stepped out of the main door back into the garden. Olivia bobbed in a small curtsy and followed, feeling Samuel Parris' eyes boring into her back.

James kept his silence until they reached the wagon and glanced around warily to make sure they would not be overheard.

'Did you speak with her?' he asked in a hushed whisper.

Olivia nodded, her brow curved into a frown. 'I don't know that it did any good, she's afraid of exposing herself.'

'Do you think she will help?'

'I just don't know,' she shook her head.

'Well then I suppose all we can do is wait and hope,' he told her softly. 'Come, I have a few more casks to deliver and then we shall return, and pray that your friend's fever has broken.'

It took another few hours before they were once again on the worn path traveling back toward James' home. For the most part they journeyed in silence, each lost in troubled thoughts.

The sky burned in wild slashes of pink and purple

as the sun descended slowly toward the horizon. By the time the wagon came to a stop in front of the house, the brightly blazing sky had given way to the dark curtain of night, filled with tiny pinpricks of starlight.

James jumped down from the wagon and reached up, grasping Olivia around the waist to lower her gently to the dusty ground.

As they walked to the door it swung open abruptly and Theo stepped out, pulling Olivia roughly into his arms. She smiled as her arms snaked around his waist, holding him in return and breathing in the warm comforting scent of him.

'Are you alright?' he pulled back suddenly, holding her face gently in his hands, his gaze running over her body as if checking for injury.

'I'm fine Theo,' she smiled softly as she cupped his hand against her face. 'James took good care of me.'

Theo looked up at James, his gaze losing a little of the mistrust as he nodded at him.

'What about Sam? Olivia asked, 'has his fever broken yet?'

Theo stared down at Olivia, the tension in his jaw tight and visible.

'What?' she asked worriedly sensing his change of mood. 'What is it?'

His eyes, when they locked back on hers, were dark and filled with concern. 'There's something you should see.'

She took his hand and hurried into the house. Hoisting her skirts as she climbed up the ladder to the loft, she settled down beside Sam. His body was wracked with deep shudders, his shirt clung to his skin and was soaked through with sweat. Olivia cupped his face gently and turned his head toward her. A startled gasp escaped her lips as she took in his appearance. Deep winding veins of a sickly green color spread from his throat, past his jaw and crawled like vines across his cheek. His eyes were now open but unseeing, the whites of his eyes riddled with the same sickly green veins.

'What the hell is that?' Olivia breathed heavily. 'I have never seen anything like it.'

'Nor I,' Theo shook his head.

Suddenly Sam began to thrash violently, his eyes rolling back in his head and a fine filmy froth appearing at the corner of his lips.

'What is this?' Theo's eyes widened.

'Damn it,' Olivia swore, 'he's having a seizure. Help me with him.'

'What should we do?'

'Roll him onto his side so he doesn't choke on his tongue,' she told him as she grasped his flailing arms, 'and hold him, so he doesn't hurt himself.'

Theo held him as gently as possible, while Olivia stroked his hair and soothed him.

'Did you find the girl?'

'I did,' she nodded.

'And will she help?'

'I don't know.'

'Olivia,' he reached for her hand, 'if she won't help us, Sam will die.'

She glanced up at him her eyes filled with pain. 'I know…' she whispered brokenly.

6.

Olivia rubbed her brow with the back of her hand, then continued to wipe the sweat from Sam's body with a damp cloth. Tears burned the back of her eyes as she noted the toxic green plant-like vines, which were spreading like poison across his skin. Suddenly he started shaking violently once again.

'THEO!' she yelled as she pinned him down.

Theo clambered up the ladder and dropped down beside Sam as the tremors began to fade.

'That's the fifth one he's had,' Theo frowned. 'They are increasing in frequency.'

'I know,' Olivia whispered, 'but without modern medicine I don't know how to help him,' she looked down. 'Even if we had access to a hospital, I don't know that it would do any good.'

Theo looked up at her as she rubbed her forehead slowly in frustration.

'You should get some rest Olivia,' he told her gently, 'you have not left his side since you returned. The hour is late; there is nothing more you can do for him tonight.'

'Maybe,' she murmured, 'but I can at least make sure he is not alone.'

'I can do that,' he reached for her.

'I can't leave him,' she shook her head.

'Together then,' Theo replied.

'Together,' she whispered, linking her fingers with his over Sam's body.

There was a sudden loud knocking at the door. Who would be calling at this hour? Theo looked across to the ladder as they heard James stride across the room, his boots echoing on the wooden floor. A moment later the door opened and the sound of hushed voices drifted up to the loft. At the sound of steps upon the ladder Olivia looked up hopefully.

James appeared at the top of the ladder and Olivia's heart jolted hard in disappointment.

'We have a guest,' he told them softly as he moved away from the ladder.

Olivia held her breath as a head appeared revealing jet black hair which fell in long tight curls, followed by skin of dark cocoa and the startling blue eyes of a Caribbean ocean, framed with thick sooty lashes.

'Tituba,' Olivia breathed heavily in relief.

The woman climbed the rest of the way up the ladder and stepped out into the loft, moving to sit beside Sam directly opposite Olivia. Theo moved out of the way of the beautiful slave woman and stood beside James, watching curiously.

Tituba had discarded her tight fitting coif which tamed her unruly hair, in favor of allowing it to tumble down her back in wild spirals. Her dress was plain blue without the apron and restrictive collar. The neck of her dress was open at the collar, revealing the long slender column of her throat, at the base of which was a strange looking pendant. It was about the size of a marble, made of dark blue glass, and suspended on a leather thong. It seemed like just a plain blue ball of glass, but as her gaze narrowed and she looked closer, for a second she could have sworn she'd witnessed a micro burst of lightening within its crystalline depths.

Tituba removed the plain woolen shawl at her shoulders and leaned forward to cradle Sam's face, gazing into his unfocused eyes.

'Thank you for coming,' Olivia whispered. 'I know you risk a great deal by being here.'

'You know nothing,' Tituba looked up, her tone much more sure and commanding than that of a slave. 'If I am discovered it will mean more than a whippin.'

Olivia nodded in understanding.

'Your friend is dying,' she ran her fingertips lightly across his burning skin, tracing the rope-like vines of poison.

'Is there anything that we can do?' Olivia whispered desperately.

'The poison must be purged from him body,' the musical lilt of her accent was a balm, giving Olivia hope.

'Can you do that?'

'Not I,' Tituba told her, her clear blue eyes holding Olivia's gaze, 'but you can.'

'Me?' she frowned, 'how?'

'Tell me how he come to be sick,' she demanded, 'the truth or I cannot help you.'

'He was trying to save me,' Olivia told her. 'I'm not entirely sure what happened. There was a green fire.'

Tituba nodded.

'It is the fire which burn through him body beneath the surface, spreading like a disease. It must be purged or he die.'

She stroked his skin lightly as if sensing the toxic fire burning his body from the inside out.

'What is it?' Olivia frowned.

'Demon fire,' Tituba looked up. 'I 'ave seen it's like before, an ocean away when I was a girl. A demon come to the island bringing with him disease, and in his bare hands he held fire as green as the leaf of the Baobab tree. The fire burns wild, it destroys, it hungers, it cannot be controlled, it cannot be contained. It feeds and it destroys, that is it only purpose.'

'Demon fire,' Olivia breathed, her eyes widening.

'That is why it must be you, Daughter of Fire. Only you can draw it out and you must.' Tituba reached out and grabbed Olivia's arm, awakening the bolt of power, which shot up her arm, jarring bones and making her veins throb uncomfortably. 'You must draw it out as poison from a wound, it is him only chance.'

'I don't know how.'

'Yes you do,' Tituba took Olivia's hands and pressed them to Sam's chest. 'Feel the fire.'

Olivia closed her eyes and reached out. Tituba was right, she could feel the fire burning through Sam's veins, wild and out of control.

The room faded away, as did Tituba's voice. The feeling of Theo's watchful presence hovering protectively over her shoulder, and James' curious gaze, it all faded away. She could feel the pounding of her own heart throbbing in her ears, her hands and arms trembling with anticipation as she reached out.

The fire burned before her, she could see it. Flames of emerald green, vast and powerful. Her breath caught in her throat and everything froze, a moment in time when the whole world almost seemed to cease turning on its axis and the universe to hold its breath, waiting to see what she would do. Her fingertips inched slowly forward and her fists clenched.

The roar was deafening. Her head fell back, her mouth open in a soundless scream, as her hands closed around the fire. It engulfed her, the heat and lick of the flames scorched her body. This was like nothing she'd ever experienced before.

Her Earth fire was a joy and a deep love. It completed her and was as easy as breathing. Her Spirit fire was cool and ageless. When she held it in her palms it was like cradling the beating heart of a thousand souls. Her Hell fire was vast and powerful, the kind of power that held wisdom and centuries of secrets.

But this... this Demon fire was wild and untamable. It destroyed and devoured. There was no containing it; it fought and scratched at her. It was like trying to ride the whip of a dragon's tale. All she could do was hold on for dear life and pray it did not consume her.

Underneath the fire she felt Sam's heartbeat falter. The fire did not want to let him go. She steeled herself and tightened her grip. It writhed and tried to escape her, but she gritted her teeth and pulled harder. The veins of green flame slowly and inexorably retreated from Sam's body and wound itself around her arms like vices, sinking viciously into her skin. She pulled back, breathing heavily through the pain until the last of the flame-like tentacles snapped from Sam and dug into her flesh.

She stood up shakily, backing away from Sam's exhausted body. Her vision was washed with green as if she were looking through colored glass. Her body shook and trembled violently as she fought to keep a tight rein on the fire.

'YOU MUST RELEASE THE FIRE!' Tituba shouted urgently.

'I c...can't,' she gasped through the intense agony.

'RELEASE IT OR IT WILL DESTROY YOU!'

Olivia threw her head back, her arms outstretched as a scream tore from her lips. She let go and felt the fire rip from her body, exploding out of her in a shock wave of pure emerald flames. The circle of fire stretched outward in a ring of energy, knocking the others to the ground as it flashed through the walls of the house like the ripple of a still pond after a pebble had been thrown in. The circle widened, gradually fading as it began to tatter and dissipate.

Olivia's eyes rolled back in her head and the whole world went dark. She didn't even feel Theo rush to his feet and his arms encircle her as she crumbled lifelessly to the ground.

Olivia rolled over, her aching body seizing up in protest, every muscle screaming like an abscessed tooth. She blinked and opened her eyes as the room swam back groggily into focus. Her head was pounding inside her skull and as she attempted to sit up a powerful wave of nausea rose, bright and urgent.

She crawled out of bed as quickly as she could, but it felt like her body was crawling through syrup. The room swayed and faltered around her as she clutched the wooden timber of the door frame. Stumbling forward into the keeping room she dropped to her knees and crawled across the floor.

Once again, she grabbed the bucket and heaved unmercifully. She hadn't eaten the night before and there was pretty much nothing to come out, but the relentless dry heaves were almost worse than if she'd had a full stomach. Once she'd finished she lay down on the floor, too exhausted to move. There wasn't a single inch of her body that didn't hurt.

Feeling a soft soothing stroke across her forehead she slowly opened her eyes and looked up into Theo's concerned face.

'Sick again?'

'I think someone should just shoot me,' she murmured miserably.

He scooped her limp body gently off the floor and carried her back to bed. Tucking her in, he climbed in beside her and sat with his back against the head of the bed.

'What happened?' she inched over painfully and laid her head in his lap.

'You collapsed.'

'Yeah I figured,' she murmured. 'What about Sam?'

'He's doing better,' Theo sighed, 'his fever's broken and the strange green veins across his skin have disappeared. He hasn't woken yet, but he seems to be resting peacefully so we're letting him sleep.'

'How long was I out?'

'About two days,' Theo frowned.

'Two days, seriously?' Olivia looked up at him. 'No wonder my stomach's empty.'

'I'll fetch you something to eat if you're feeling up to it.'

'As long as it's not stew,' she grimaced. 'I may never eat it again.'

'No,' he smiled softly, 'not stew, but you need to eat something. That green fire took a lot out of you. I have to admit Livy, you scared me half to death when you collapsed.'

'Sorry,' she mumbled.

'I'm worried about you,' he replied, as he ran his fingers through her hair soothingly.

'I'll be okay,' she yawned sleepily. 'We never did get that vacation did we?' she murmured.

'Vacation?'

'If we ever make it home, I swear we are going to spend an entire month on a beach somewhere in Tahiti, doing nothing but swinging in a hammock, sipping cocktails and making love to the sound of the ocean.'

'Will you be wearing a bikini?'

She laughed tiredly.

'Get some sleep love,' he settled her down.

By the time he'd climbed off the bed and headed toward the door she'd already drifted off again.

'How is she?' James asked softly as Theo stepped out of the room, closing the door behind him gently.

'I don't know,' he frowned in concern. 'I've never seen her this exhausted. Something's not right.'

'I'm not surprised she's exhausted,' James said as they stepped further into the main room. 'I've never seen anything like what she did the other night.'

'That? Oh that's nothing,' Theo shook his head, a small smile tugging the corner of his mouth. 'You should see what she can do with Hell fire.'

'Hell fire?' James' eyes widened.

'It's not as bad as it sounds,' Theo hastily amended.

James was so easy to talk to and so comfortable to be around that several times over the past couple of days Theo had almost forgotten himself. No matter how enlightened James was when it came to witchcraft and supernatural powers, he still had to remind himself that James was raised a puritan as he had been. James had not had the benefit of spending the last several months three hundred years into the future, which had given him a somewhat broader perspective.

'Hell fire is the name of a very ancient and vast power. It doesn't mean that it's evil,' Theo shook his head as he tried to explain. 'The world is so much more complicated than you realize.'

'I'm beginning to see that,' James breathed thoughtfully. 'Do you want me to fix her something to eat?'

Theo shook his head. 'We'll let her sleep for a while longer.'

'Do you want to practice again?' James asked.

'It depends,' Theo smiled slowly. 'Are you going to throw more apples at me?'

'Maybe,' he laughed, his smile matching Theo's.

It wasn't long before Theo was once again standing in the barn, scowling and covered in pieces of apple pulp.

'You're not concentrating,' James frowned.

'I'm trying,' Theo growled, 'but it's a bit hard to focus when you're being attacked by fruit.'

James chuckled. 'Are you ready to go again?'

'What are you doing?' a small voice interrupted.

'Tempy?' Theo turned, an unconscious and genuine smile gracing his face.

The small skinny dark haired girl sat on a large cask, swinging her legs as she watched them with curious eyes.

'Hello Temperance,' James turned to watch her.

'Hello Mr Wilkins,' she replied.

He winked and tossed her an apple, which she caught easily.

'What are you doing?' she bit into her apple.

Theo sucked in a breath as he briefly considered making something up, but the truth was he'd never lied to Tempy before. For so long it had only been the two of them with this huge secret between them, but now they had James.

He glanced over to her, his heart clenching painfully. She had no clue how little time she had left. He wondered idly if they'd known about James before, if they'd known about their mother, if it could have somehow made a difference. He shook his head frowning slightly. Probably not, it's not like James could have cured her of the illness that would take her life. But just for once it was nice to not feel so alone. He walked over to his little sister and dropped down to his knees, so he was more her height.

'James is helping me to learn how to control the things we see,' he told her softly.

'The waking dreams?'

'Yes,' he nodded, 'they're called visions.'

'But how does he know?' she frowned. 'You said to never tell anyone.'

'I know I did,' he told her, his voice low and serious, 'but James, well you see he is special like we are.'

'Does he have the dreams too?' her little brow wrinkled.

'Not exactly, he has his own special gift, but he knew our mother really well.'

'Was she special too?' she whispered.

'Yes,' he smiled, 'she was like us. She could see things before they happened.'

'But what can he do?' she turned to stare at him.

James walked over to her and gently took the half eaten apple from her hand. He pulled a pip from its core and turned it over in his palm.

'Watch,' he told her softly.

The tiny little seed in his hand twitched and rolled over. A minute seam began to open up, splitting the side of the small pod and a thin white vine snaked out. Slowing elongating and coiling slightly as it grew, the end began to darken into a green color. The seed casing finally split and fell away, an empty husk, as the end began to bud and split into two. The two edges unfurled and spread out into delicate little leaves.

'I feel the earth Temperance,' he told her. 'I can feel it grow and change beneath my feet. I can sense its moods. I can make things flourish.'

'Like your apple trees?'

'Yes,' he smiled nodding.

He placed the small fledging plant carefully on top of one of the barrels, making a mental note to go and plant it out in the orchard once they were done. He turned back to Theo and Temperance, unaware that the tiny seedling had slid from its perch and tumbled to the floor. Being so tiny and delicate, it slipped between the cracks in the floorboards and toppled to the damp moist earth below. Neither did James notice when its roots continued to grow, spearing down into the soil and throbbing with new life as it spread out and took root.

'What was he trying to show you?' Temperance asked.

'To focus on seeing into the future by only a few moments. To control the vision so it does not come unbidden.'

'Can't you do that already?' she replied in confusion.

'No,' he frowned, 'why? Can you?'

'Of course I can silly, I thought you could too.'

Theo's brow creased thoughtfully as he studied her.

'Let me have a turn,' she jumped down off the cask and walked over to where Theo had been standing.

James hesitated as he looked down at the small dark haired child who looked so much like her mother.

'It's alright Mr Wilkins, you won't hurt me,' she assured him.

He picked up another apple and drew in a deep breath.

'Well alright then,' he replied quietly.

Temperance closed her eyes.

James threw the apple and Theo held his breath. He'd thrown it softer than he had with Theo, but his eyes still widened slightly in surprise as Temperance's hand shot out and caught the apple with ease.

'What?' Theo breathed, 'how did you do that?'

Temperance opened her eyes, focusing slowly on the apple clutched in her tiny fist.

'How did you do that?' Theo asked again.

She looked up at her brother and blinked slowly. 'It's hard to explain,' she frowned. 'It's like reaching out, but not with your hands.'

'With your mind,' James supplied helpfully.

'Yes,' she nodded.

'But I was doing that,' Theo frowned.

'Were you thinking about the apple, or about Mr Wilkins?' she asked after a moment.

'The apple.'

She shook her head. 'But the apple doesn't decide where it is going to end up,' she tilted her head slightly.

A small smile curved the corner of his mouth, could it really be that simple? Instead of focusing on the apple he should have been focusing on the intent before it was thrown. He should have been focusing on James.

'Again,' he told James as Temperance skipped toward the cask and Theo moved back to his previous position.

James nodded and picked up another apple. Theo closed his eyes and took a deep calming breath. He let go of the frustration and annoyance and for the first time relaxed enough to really open his mind.

It was incredible, it was like walking through an open door into a completely different reality. He could feel everything around him as he breathed in the sharp scent of apples, the slightly damp smell of the hay and the earthy wood tones of the barn itself. Outside the air above them felt heavy, laden with the promise of an oncoming storm. He could feel his sister watching him with curious eyes and a few feet away was James.

Theo pushed out further with his mind, this time it was slightly easier. Although his eyes were firmly closed and he could physically see nothing, in his mind the picture of James stood out in sharp relief and exacting detail. He could feel the strength of his muscles moving and contracting as he tossed the apple thoughtfully back and forth between his hands.

Theo reached out further and his lips parted on a silent gasp, he could feel James' thoughts weighing his indecision, felt the muscles in James' arm contract seconds before he subconsciously made a decision. Just for a split second Theo saw the apple fly through the air toward his left shoulder and his hand close around it. A few seconds later his body seemed to react instinctively and as his fist clenched he felt the small hard orb in his palm. Opening his eyes he looked down, his fingers slowly unfurling. His breath caught in his throat as he stared at the apple in the palm of his hand.

'You did it!' Temperance clapped happily.

Theo glanced up at James who was looking at him with a strange kind of expression. Was it pride?

'Again?' James smiled.

'Again,' Theo grinned as he tossed the apple back to him.

Each time it got a little easier to focus and Theo got a little faster. After a dozen or so times he found he could predict easily when, where and how James would throw.

'Let's try something a little harder,' James bit into one of the apples watching Theo and Temperance.

'A game?' Temperance asked.

'Of sorts,' James replied. He dug into his pocket and came up with a metal coin flicking it toward Temperance. 'Take it and hide it.'

She grinned as her tiny hand closed around the coin and with a small delighted laugh she disappeared into the shadows of the huge barn.

'Hide and seek?' Theo raised a brow questioningly.

'Just wait a moment.'

They stood in an easy companionable silence until Temperance suddenly reappeared.

'Right,' James turned to Theo, 'find the coin, but there will be no physical searching. You have one chance, you have to go to the exact place it's hidden. You have to know where it is, not just look. Do you understand?'

Theo nodded and turned toward the vast barn. It really was big, filled with stacks of cider filled casks and barrels of apples. Stacks of hay were neatly piled throughout the barn and two ladders led up to a loft above. If he had to search the regular way, there was a chance he would never find the small coin. No, he had to see it, but how? He closed his eyes and relaxed.

At first he tried to reach out toward Temperance, focusing on his little sister as he tried to see where she would go to hide it, but it wasn't working. Then he understood, it was because it had already happened, he wasn't looking ahead to the future because Temperance had already hidden it.

Instead he tried a different approach, he needed to see himself finding the coin. Drawing in a deep breath he focused inward. The images flashed through his mind as clear as day, he saw himself standing in the farthest corner leaning down behind a cask of applejack. Sweeping the straw aside he saw the coin jammed down between the wooden planks of the floor.

Opening his eyes, he threw an amused smile at his sister and disappeared toward the back of the barn reappearing a few seconds later with the coin in his hand. Temperance laughed in sheer delight, clapping her hands once again.

'Me now, I want a turn.'

James jumped up onto a large cask taking another bite of his apple.

'Go ahead,' he smiled at Theo, 'you hide it and give Temperance a chance to find it.'

Hours passed, darkening clouds swept across the sky as the sun reached its peak in the midday sky and began its slow descent toward the horizon, giving way to late afternoon.

Theo and Temperance smiled and laughed as they took turns in hiding a plain old coin and trying to see if they could find it. For a few precious hours they were free, able to be who they truly were, with no fear of consequence except to delight in the strange gift of foresight which burned through their veins. Taking such simple pleasure in each other's company neither Theo nor Temperance noticed how James watched them with intense eyes and an unfathomable expression.

7.

Olivia opened her eyes slowly. The massive pounding in her head seemed to have subsided into a dull ache and her eyes felt like they were full of grit. Rolling over onto her back, she glanced around the room. Light was pouring in through the window, which had been opened slightly to let in the crisp fresh air. The sharp tang of ozone wafted in on the breeze indicating that a storm was brewing.

Taking a deep breath, she pushed herself up and swung her legs over the side of the bed. Her stomach growled loudly causing a shaky laugh to escape from her lips. Her body was so out of sync after her trip to the Otherworld and the Underworld, and then being thrown back three centuries into the past, that half the time she didn't know if she wanted to eat, sleep or just plain throw up.

Standing slowly, she smoothed down her plain linen shift and reached for her petticoats. There was no way she could stay in bed all day, she definitely needed something to eat and she wanted to check on Sam. The longer they stayed in the past, the greater the chance that they would irrevocably damage the timeline and as far as she knew Sam was the only one who could leapfrog them through time. After all, they still needed to track down her mother and the Nathaniel from her time, before they could cause any damage of their own.

She sighed in annoyance as her fingers once again fumbled with the ties on her petticoats. Her hands shook slightly and her body still felt weak. Reaching for her dress she yanked it over her head and buttoned up the bodice. Making sure the compass was safely nestled between her breasts and hidden from view she left her dress unbuttoned at the throat, foregoing the severe collar and apron. She also ignored the tight fitting cap, instead opting to leave her hair loose so it fell in deep dark midnight waves down her back. Although her headache was nowhere near as bad as it had been, her scalp still felt tender and she simply didn't feel like scraping her hair back into a tight uncomfortable knot.

She just hoped she didn't run into anyone other than Theo or James. Then again she had no real need to leave the house. Her first priority was helping Sam recover otherwise they would be trapped, going the long way around to 1695 by waiting ten years, instead of having Sam jump them forward instantaneously.

She closed her eyes and sighed, she really didn't think she had it in her to do ten years of mutton stews, pigeon pies, no indoor plumbing and most importantly no toothbrush. She was forced to reluctantly conclude that history was much more fascinating when looking through the eyes of a historian. The reality of it was fascinating, but really uncomfortable for someone who'd grown up in a world of modern comforts.

Smoothing down the deep blue material of the new dress James had provided for her, she tucked her hair behind her ear. Her hands felt strange, prickling like she had pins and needles. She splayed her fingers and held up her trembling hands in front of her.

A gasp of shock escaped as a strange green glow wrapped itself around her fingers and palms like an eerie phosphorescent mist. Then as quickly as it had come it was gone again. She blinked and stared hard at her hands, wondering if she'd imagined it.

A low sound suddenly caught her attention, a harsh guttural whisper. She tilted her head, her brow frowning as she strained to make out the words. Turning slowly, she tried to pinpoint the strange voice. It seemed to be coming from somewhere near the bed. She took an unconscious step closer. The voice seemed to fade in and out like a badly tuned radio station. She strained harder but the voice faded away until she was once again alone in the silent room.

What the hell was going on?

Her gaze dropped down to her hands once again, but as she turned them over and studied them carefully she could detect nothing out of the ordinary. Perhaps the stress was finally getting to her, maybe she was going crazy.

She laughed self-deprecatingly. Poor Theo, he'd just got rid of one mad wife and now he was going to be saddled with her wild hallucinations. Shaking her head lightly, she cast the thought aside. It was probably nothing and just the strain of everything that had happened recently. She wasn't kidding when she'd told Theo she wanted a break. If they ever got back home in one piece she was going to drag him to the nearest tropical island and not move for a month…possibly two.

She slipped her stockinged feet into her leather shoes and turned toward the door. She stepped out into the main room, it too was silent apart from the odd crackle of the fire, which had begun to bank low. She shivered slightly and wandered over to the fire, longing for the warmth and familiarity of the gold and red flames.

'Wake up,' she whispered, 'it's getting cold in here.'

The fire burst merrily into flame, bathing her in its warmth and light. She sighed in pleasure, feeling it seep into every pore in her body. For the most part it wasn't that cold out yet, but the summer was dying. Although they may snag a bit of Indian summer yet, fall was snapping at its heels and there was a slight bite to the early evening air, which seemed to echo down into her bones. If she were honest though, it seemed to have little to do with the weather, it was something else. Something dark was out there casting a shadow over everything, she could feel it.

Shaking off the morose feeling crawling slyly up the back of her neck, she headed up the ladder into the loft. She stopped suddenly and glanced down at the figure huddled up in a blanket on a bed roll. A small smile tugged at her lips as she dropped down next to him and smoothed his jet black hair from his forehead. His skin had lost some of its sickly grey pallor and was once again a healthy color. She wished he'd open his blue eyes and smile at her again so she could see those dimples of his.

She sighed and tucked the blanket tighter around him, he looked so young. He was not the same Sam she'd known from her time, the Sam who'd brought Theo to her. That Sam had been around her age, well he'd looked about her age she amended her thoughts, although she suspected he was far older than she could imagine.

He'd exuded strength and power and seemed to have this unshakable faith about him. He was a man who knew his purpose, his destiny and was confident in his abilities. But this Sam, curled up in front of her, sleeping peacefully for the first time in days, was so much younger. They'd spent a great deal of time together in the Otherworld and she'd become extremely fond of him, in fact she cared a great deal for him. She was glad he would recover; for a while there she'd been so afraid he wasn't going to make it. Now she just hoped to high hell that when he woke up he had enough Mojo to jump them ten years into the future. That was, of course, if he could figure out how to do it, as the ability to jump through time was something this younger version of him had yet to attempt. God, she rubbed her eyes tiredly, it was never simple. Why did it always feel as if the odds were stacked against them?

She looked up suddenly and frowned. Something

didn't feel right. She turned and looked toward the window. All of a sudden the light seemed dimmer somehow. She could feel something dark, something cold lurking nearby. She stood, slowly reaching out with her mind, past the house, beyond the boundaries and the orchard. There was a blackness, that was the only way to describe it. It was like a small void of nothingness. Not like the Void between worlds she'd experienced in the Otherworld. No, this blackness wasn't empty, it was filled with a cold evil. She shivered, her eyes narrowing. Whatever it was, was moving toward the house.

Theo swung open the door and stepped into the main room followed closely by Temperance who was glancing around in curiosity.

'I've never been inside Mr Wilkins' house,' she frowned, 'are you sure?' The small girl covered her mouth and began coughing once again.

'It will be fine, James said he would join us back at the house,' Theo assured her as he listened to the persistent racking cough with a concerned frown.

'Well if you're sure,' she replied softly.

'Why don't you sit by the fire,' he picked a chunk of apple from his hair and laughed lightly, shaking his head. 'I'm going to wash up and check on Olivia.'

Temperance nodded, watching him disappear into one of the back rooms. Instead of moving to the small wooden stool by the cheery fireplace, she moved further into the room curiously drinking in her surroundings. She'd never left the farm except for exploring the land surrounding their property, in fact the furthest she'd ever gone was Mr Wilkins' orchards. So being invited into his home was something of a novelty. It was scrupulously clean she noticed, but welcoming. She was so busy staring around the room she wasn't aware of the sudden movement behind her until it was too late.

The muffled scream died in her throat as a slender

hand clamped tightly over her mouth, roughly pulling her backward. She struggled as an arm wrapped around her middle, effectively pinning her arms to her sides. She felt herself pulled back against a body and struggled as she looked up at the person holding her.

Olivia looked down at the writhing child in her arms, watching as the recognition slowly dawned in her eyes. Temperance stopped moving and Olivia removed her hand from her mouth slowly pressing her finger to her own lips, warning her not to make a sound. Olivia's gaze shot across to the window.

Her arms tightened around Temperance as she dragged her quickly across the floor and pressed them both back against the rough wooden front door, holding her breath tightly as a face suddenly appeared at the window. She didn't move an inch, she didn't dare even breathe, her fingers trembling slightly as she held the small girl.

A wave of nausea swamped her as the darkness she'd felt before pressed up against the window, she could sense him. Her brow furrowed as her vision narrowed and everything was suddenly brought into sharp relief. She could feel Temperance's heart thunder beneath her hand like the wing beat of a small bird. Her breath caught in her throat, aware she could feel the wind ripple ponderously through the trees outside the house; the ominous dull squeak of long spindly fingers trailing down the glass of the window.

Edging away from the door as slowly as she could, she tried to keep them away from the piercing beetle-like eyes peering through the glass.

The face disappeared and Olivia almost breathed out a sigh of relief until suddenly the door handle at her back began to turn slowly. Her eyes widened and her heart jolted in her chest. Grabbing Temperance, she pushed her forward to the back of the room as the sound of the latch lifting echoed through the room, followed by the slow creak of the hinges as the door inched open.

Olivia pushed Temperance through the door into the bedroom. Theo looked up as they entered the room, his hands still in the small basin of water perched atop a heavy wooden chest. His hair clung damply to his head and small rivulets of water slid down his naked chest as he grabbed a clean linen shirt and pulled it roughly over his head. Glancing at Olivia in confusion he opened his mouth to speak but paused, holding his breath, as Olivia held her finger to her lips and shook her head vehemently. Registering the slight panic in her widened eyes, he stepped forward.

'Nathaniel,' she mouthed silently.

Theo scowled, cursing under his breath as he pulled them both behind him protectively and peered carefully around the doorway.

The door swung open slowly and Nathaniel's black eyes narrowed. He lifted his face slightly, a barely perceptible tilt of his head as if he was sampling something in the air. His black hair hung to his shoulders beneath the wide brimmed felt hat, which cast his unmarred face partially into shadow, giving him an even more menacing appearance, if such a thing was possible.

His long, thin tapered fingers flexed and curled into fists against his coat and the muscle in his jaw tightened. Stepping forward into the still room the heel of his leather shoes echoed hollowly against the wooden floor. He paused, his head turning in the direction of the roaring fire as it hiccupped and danced drunkenly in the large fireplace. His gaze narrowed and once again he drew in a deep breath, as if tasting the air. He took an ominous step into the room and then another, scanning his surroundings with intense scrutiny.

Theo drew in a breath, his heart pounding so loudly he feared it would be heard half a continent away. This was not the Nathaniel from Mercy, the pathetic mismatched Frankenstein of a creature Isabel West had ripped from a devil's trap and forced into a prison of rotting flesh.

No, this was the Nathaniel he remembered from his Salem, the Nathaniel with no such limitation. This was the demon in his true form, unfettered, unhindered and Theo feared, undefeatable. If it came to a fight they had no way to defend themselves against an ancient and powerful demon lord.

Not only that, they couldn't afford to expose themselves to him. Not only would it put them all in danger, including Temperance and James, but it could conceivably change the time line. He pulled in a deep resigned breath, at this point there was only one logical course of action… run.

'The window,' he mouthed to Olivia.

Nodding in agreement, she moved as quietly as she could toward the window and pushed the handle up swinging it open carefully. Grabbing Hester's Grimoire from under the bed, ensuring it was once again bundled up in an old cloak, she dropped it out of the window, watching as it landed in a small pile of early autumn leaves.

Gathering up her skirt she hitched up her petticoats and stepped up onto the small chest and climbed out of the window. She paused for a moment, legs dangling, before dropping to the ground. Turning quickly, she reached up and held out her arms for Theo to lower Temperance carefully out the window after her.

Theo scooped his tiny little sister into his arms and lifted her to the window and then Temperance let loose a sudden cough. Theo froze, his gaze darting toward the open doorway. Sucking in a breath he practically threw her out of the window into Olivia's arms and climbed up onto the chest grasping the window frame. Olivia pulled her into her body and pressed them both against the wall beneath the window.

Nathaniel looked up sharply, his ears pricking up at the sudden sound. He stalked through the main room his gaze fixed intently on the back room. The door swung open to reveal a sleeping room. A large timber framed bed dominated the room and a small chest sat underneath the window which was open, letting in a cool breeze. His footfalls echoed ominously across the floor, slow and deliberate as he approached the window.

Theo pressed his hand carefully over Temperance's mouth praying to God she did not begin to cough again. They pressed themselves against the wall beneath the window, there was no way to make a run for it. They'd heard the steps across the floor and if they moved now they would be clearly visible. All they could do was pray he didn't lean out of the window and look down.

Nathaniel scanned the room his gaze narrowing suspiciously. The whole house hummed with power, an ancient power he'd not felt in centuries. He inhaled again trying to pinpoint its source, but it seemed to be everywhere. His long pale fingers wrapped slowly around the window frame and stepping nearer he slowly began to lean forward.

'Nathaniel?' a stern disapproving voice snapped behind him.

Nathaniel paused, a small amused smile tugged briefly at his lips, but disappeared swiftly as he turned, schooling his features into a mask of contrite concern.

'Goodman Wilkins,' he spread his hands in a gesture of supplication. 'I am so glad to find you in good health.'

'I am afraid I do not grasp your meaning,' James replied coolly. 'Perhaps you will explain, as soon as you have offered a reason as to why you are in my home uninvited.'

'Forgive my unpardonable manners,' Nathaniel answered smoothly. 'I should never be so presumptuous as to enter a house without invitation, but I do assure you my actions were motivated purely by concern for your well-being.'

One of James' eyebrows rose questioningly.

'I was invited to dinner by Reverend Alcott and sampled some of your highly lauded applejack. I came by to purchase some for myself and I knocked several times, to no avail. Assuming you were not at home I resigned myself to seek you out in the orchard when I heard a terrible coughing from the house. Fearing you had succumbed to illness I ventured inside to offer aid.'

'You are too kind,' James replied carefully, 'but I'm afraid you must have been mistaken. I am not unwell, nor was I in the house.'

'Perhaps you have a guest?' he enquired with a deceptive casualness.

'No, it is just me,' James' back stiffened.

'Well then,' Nathaniel turned to leave, his gaze falling on the apron and coif Olivia had left laying across the chest and which now had a dirty boot print pressed into the material. His eyes flitted to the open window before turning back to James, a cool smile gracing his thin lips. 'As you say I must have been mistaken.'

'Thank you for your concern,' James stood aside so he could leave the room.

Nathaniel barely inclined his head before walking from the room. James followed him to the front door, watching as he mounted his grey mare and nudged her forward into a slow walk.

'Good day to you Goodman Wilkins,' he nodded once again.

As soon as his back was turned James closed the door and bolted it. Turning sharply on his heel he ran back through the house to the bedroom and leaned out of the window as Theo, Olivia and Temperance looked up.

'Quickly,' he told Theo, 'before he doubles back.'

Nodding in agreement he lifted Temperance and passed her through the window to James. Olivia was next, with the book tucked safely under her arm. Once she was safely through, he hoisted himself back up and through the window.

'Hide,' James hissed.

Theo grabbed both Olivia and Temperance and dragged them to the floor below the window, while James watched passively as a dark figure seated on a grey mare appeared at the edge of the orchard.

Nathaniel resisted the urge to peel back his lips and snarl at the offensively arrogant human. He sat astride his stupid slow horse watching James through the window of his stinking little hovel. He was hiding something, he was sure of it. The whole place reeked of magic. His fingers tightened on the reins as he jerked the horse away from the house and back toward the road to the village. Whatever James Wilkins was hiding, he was going to find out what it was.

'I think he's gone now,' James looked down to the three of them huddled on the floor.

Theo nodded as he climbed to his feet, helping the other two to stand.

'I think you had better tell me exactly who Nathaniel is and what he wants with you both.'

Theo's eyes darted to Temperance. It was obviously something not to be discussed in front of the child. James nodded, recognizing the silent agreement that they would tell him once she had returned home.

'Why don't we go and sit in the other room and have a drink. I brought in another cask of the peach and apple cider you favor Olivia.'

'That would be lovely James, thank you,' Olivia replied brightly, not wanting to alarm Temperance any more than necessary. Taking her tiny hand in hers she smiled down at the girl with a lot more confidence than she felt. 'Have you tried Mr Wilkins' peach and apple cider Temperance?'

'No,' she shook her head. 'Father brings us apple cider from market, but it has a bad taste,' she wrinkled her nose in distaste.

Olivia chuckled lightly, 'well I can guarantee Mr

Wilkins' is a lot better.'

Theo watched gratefully as Olivia led his sister into the other room ahead of them.

'Do you think he'll return?' Theo turned to James.

'I don't know,' he frowned as his gaze fell on the soiled apron and coif. 'He knew I was lying about having anyone else in the house. I just hope he doesn't speak with Goodman Parris, after all I introduced Olivia to him as my niece. If Nathaniel finds out he may take it upon himself to return.'

'Well there is not much we can do about it at the moment,' Theo raked his hand through his hair in frustration, the sleeve of his shirt falling further down his arm from his wrist to his elbow.

James' eyes widened suddenly as his gaze locked on Theo's arm.

'What is that?' he reached out and grabbed Theo's wrist.

He looked down and silently cursed. He'd forgotten about the tattoo, which curved and twisted up his arm from his wrist to his shoulder in vines of blue, black and silver. How the hell was he going to explain that to James. He didn't even know what a tattoo was, let alone the fact it magically transformed into a weapon, which could kill supernatural creatures.

'It's nothing,' he jerked his arm back, fastening the cuff more securely and grabbed his leather jerkin, pulling it over his head roughly.

James frowned in confusion.

'James,' Theo sighed, 'I'm sorry, but there are just some things I cannot explain. I hope you can understand and accept that.'

James continued to watch him silently and Theo prayed that he wasn't pushing him too far. James had been so kind and understanding up to this point, but he knew everyone had their limit. He just hoped they weren't approaching James' limit, because the more they told him the more they risked the timeline. Finally James nodded, seeming to accept that for now.

'We should wait until we're sure Nathaniel is gone and then I'll see Temperance home.'

'That's not a good idea Theo,' James shook his head. 'You can't risk running into your brother or anyone else who might know you.'

They walked back into the other room. Olivia and Temperance were sat at the long rectangular table sipping from a small tankard. Temperance took a large gulp as she lowered the cup and grinned directly at James.

'This is so good Mr Wilkins.'

His gaze softened and he smiled at her softly.

'I'm very happy you think so Temperance.'

She drained the cup and wiped her mouth on her sleeve. 'Thank you for the cider Mr Wilkins, but I have to go home now or father will get mad.'

James' mouth thinned at the mention of Mathias Beckett and his eyes followed her to the door, his expression unreadable.

'I still don't like the thought of her going alone,' Theo scowled.

'She'll be fine' James murmured, his eyes still locked on the small girl as she crossed the room, 'besides I can track her movements all the way back to the Beckett farm. Even if I'm not with her, I'll know if anything is wrong.'

'You can do that?' Theo asked in surprise.

'Not with everyone,' he replied after a moment.

Olivia watched James carefully at his admission, her fingers tapping her cup thoughtfully.

'Even so,' Theo replied, 'I think I'll just see her as far as the tree line and make sure she's not followed.'

James didn't argue, he just watched in silence as Theo followed her out of the door.

Olivia's soft voice suddenly broke the silence. 'Are you going to tell him?' she asked bluntly.

'Tell him what?' James asked as he turned to face her.

Olivia pursed her lips speculatively, 'that he's your son.'

'What?' his eyes widened suddenly, 'that's not...he's...' he shook his head.

'James,' Olivia's eyes held his sympathetically.

He sighed after a moment, the automatic denial dying on his lips.

'How did you know?'

'Little things,' she murmured thoughtfully, 'little expressions, mannerisms. You share a lot of traits you know, he also has your smile and your eyes.'

'You are too perceptive,' he replied stiffly.

'James,' she blew out a deep breath, 'I've seen the way you look at him.'

'How do I look at him?' he frowned in confusion.

'With such love and longing,' she replied easily, 'and pride.'

'Pride?'

'Familial pride,' she shook her head, 'but it's not just him, you do it with Temperance too.'

James' back stiffened uncomfortably and his lips clamped together, as if he didn't trust the words from his mouth.

'Theo's brother Logan was born within a year of Emmaline's marriage to Matthias Beckett wasn't he?' Olivia continued quietly. 'Then there was a gap between his birth and Theo's, which is unusual in this day and age. Add into that the fact that Logan has no magical abilities, but both Theo and Temperance do. If I had to guess, I'd say that Logan is Matthias Beckett's child, but Theo and Temperance are both your children.'

'Is that true?' a harsh voice rasped from the open doorway.

James and Olivia both turned to look and found Theo standing frozen in the doorway, his eyes blazing with anger and confusion.

'IS IT TRUE?' he shouted.

'Theo you have to understand...' James stepped toward him.

'IS IT TRUE?' he growled again.

James stopped as he sucked in a sharp breath.

'Yes, it is true,' his dark eyes locked on Theo's, pleading for his understanding. 'You are my son.'

James' heart sank as Theo coldly turned his back on him and stalked back out of the house, slamming the door with a violent and resounding crack.

8.

As the door slammed with an uncomfortable finality, James turned back to Olivia, who was watching him carefully.

'Perhaps you should speak with him,' James spoke quietly.

'No.'

Olivia continued to stare up at James. It wasn't that she didn't want to go after Theo, but she knew there would be time enough for her to comfort him later. Right now he needed the truth and that was something she couldn't give him.

'I'm sorry James, I like you I genuinely do, but this is your mess to clean up,' she shook her head lightly. 'You need to go and talk with him.'

'How can I?' he asked quietly, 'how can I possibly explain this to him?'

'Men,' she sighed in exasperation, 'just open your mouth and talk. It doesn't matter if it doesn't come out exactly right, what matters is you tell him the truth and let him come to terms with it in his own time.'

'But what if he won't forgive me?'

'That's a chance you're going to have to take,' she told him sympathetically. 'Do you want a chance to truly get to know your son?'

'More than anything,' he whispered.

'Then this is your chance, don't waste it.'

Slowly James inclined his head before turning and walking out of the door, leaving Olivia sitting alone at the table. He checked around the house and then the barn, but there was no sign of Theo. Knowing he wouldn't have gone far and risk someone seeing him, James began the slow and painstaking process of searching the orchard. Frustrated and worried, he wandered the rows of apple trees, wondering how he was going to explain to Theo what his mother had meant to him and him to her.

He knew it wouldn't be easy for Theo to accept, their upbringing strictly forbade adultery and fornication. It was a brutal way to describe what had been between him and Emmaline. How could he begin to explain that they were the other half of each other's souls? That ever since she'd been gone it was as if a piece of himself was missing?

He shook his head at his thoughts, frowning as he searched the tree line with his eyes. He was about to give up and return to the house to see if Theo had gone back to Olivia, when his gaze fell on a figure sitting propped up against the trunk of one of the trees.

Theo's angry gaze was fixed on a small twig as he turned it over and over in his hands, twisting it and causing it to splinter slowly. He didn't look up as James' shadow fell over him nor did he acknowledge his presence.

James sighed and sat down on the cool hard ground, the early autumn leaves crinkling under his legs as glanced sideways to Theo.

'I know you are angry with me Theo, but I have much to tell you. If after hearing what I have to say you wish to never speak with me again, I will accept your decision.' He studied Theo's profile looking for some kind of response. 'Will you hear me out?'

Theo's jaw tightened, but he offered no answer. James waited a moment longer. Theo hadn't given an instant refusal, so James could only take his silence as a tacit agreement, giving him an opportunity to tell Theo his story.

'I remember the very first time I saw your mother,' he began quietly. 'I was in church with my parents when I looked across and saw her. Long dark curly hair and big brown eyes. I was only eight years old at the time and she, a full year younger. I remember thinking she was the prettiest thing I'd ever seen. Emmaline and her parents had newly arrived from the New Hampshire Colony, her father Lucas was a cooper. A few days later he came to visit my father bringing with him casks he'd made, but that was not all he'd brought. Emmaline rode with him in the wagon and while he and my father discussed business we played together in the orchard.'

James' voice softened as he lost himself in memory.

'I think I lost my heart to her that very first day, the moment she smiled at me. We were inseparable. I think it was always an unspoken agreement between our parents that when we were of age I would ask for her hand.'

'Why didn't you?' Theo asked finally.

'I never got the chance,' James scowled at the painful memory. 'I came into my gift late. I was almost a man when I realized I had certain abilities. Unfortunately, Emmy's father realized too. Do you recall I what I told you about him?'

Theo nodded slowly, 'that he didn't want her marrying anyone with magical blood because he was afraid her children would be born different too.'

'Exactly,' James' jaw clenched involuntarily with anger, 'he was a coward for many reasons. Once Emmy and I realized I had the gift too, we knew her father would never allow us to marry. We planned to run away as far as we could and start a new life together.'

'What went wrong?'

'I travelled into Salem Town to the port with my father. He had some seedlings being brought from England for the orchard and we were to collect them, but when we arrived we learned there had been a storm off the coast and the ship was delayed. Our trip ended up taking longer than expected. Emmy's father saw an opportunity, and while I was gone he married her to Matthias Beckett.'

'So when you returned...'

'The woman I loved belonged to another man,' James shut his eyes as if to shut out the pain. 'I felt so betrayed, I'm ashamed to admit I blamed her. When your brother Logan was born nine months later I crawled to the end of a bottle of hard spirits and stayed there for the next three years. There was a chance I may have never sobered up, I certainly didn't want to.'

'Why did you then?'

'Illness swept through the village and surrounding areas, apparently some kind of pestilence brought in on one of the ships. By the time it had run its course half the colony were dead. Neither my parents nor hers survived. I didn't have a choice, I had to sober up and take over the orchard otherwise I wouldn't be able to afford to drink myself into oblivion.

Slowly I began to re-join the living, resigning myself to a life without Emmy. But this place isn't that large and our paths were constantly crossing as we tried to help the village rebuild itself and recover the loss of so many of our neighbors. I avoided her as much as I could. It was torture every time I saw her and her little boy, but I could see how much she was hurting and her pain was more than I could bear. It was only then I realized how much she'd suffered and the lengths her own father had gone to, to see her married to Beckett.'

'What do you mean?' Theo asked suspiciously.

'I should have known Emmy would never have betrayed me, she would never have agreed to marry him.'

'Then how did she end up married to him?'

'From what I understand Emmy and her father fought terribly when she refused to marry Matthias, but he overrode all her objections,' his voice betrayed his anger.

'And then he tricked her into drinking a calming draught he had bought from Goody Giles. It is a draught used to calm those afflicted with an illness of the mind. It is supposed to inflict a kind of dreamy lassitude. She was barely aware of what was going on around her when he married her to Matthias without her consent. By the time she came to her senses it was already done and that bastard had already…'

He broke off unable to finish his sentence, but it didn't take a genius to figure out what Matthias Beckett had done to his new bride, while she was still practically unconscious and unable to fight him off.

Theo dropped his head into his hands, gripping his hair so tightly a sharp pain speared across his scalp. He'd thought his opinion of his so called father, Matthias Beckett, could get no lower, but it seems he was wrong. It killed him to think of the suffering his mother had endured at the hands of that monster.

'It was done,' James breathed out painfully, 'they were man and wife before God. There was nothing either of us could do. We tried to ignore our feelings and slowly we began to rebuild our friendship.'

'But you became lovers,' Theo frowned, 'you committed adultery. She broke her sacred vows.'

'I know,' James shook his head slowly, 'we never meant for it to happen. We tried to fight it, but in the end we couldn't.'

'Is that it?' Theo replied coldly. 'You left her there with that monster and used her for your own gratification?'

'It wasn't like that,' James replied angrily. 'I begged her to leave with me, to run away, even before you and your sister were born. I wanted to take both her and your brother away. I even booked passage on a ship back to England, where we could disappear. I would have given up everything I had ever known for her, but she wouldn't leave.'

'Why not?'

'She never gave me an answer,' he shook his head

in frustration. 'She just said she had to stay in Salem, no matter what happened.'

'She had visions, powerful ones?' Theo asked.

James nodded his head.

'Do you think she saw something? Something that stopped her from leaving?'

'If she did, she would never tell me what it was,' James sighed. 'It killed me Theo, you have to understand. Knowing that she was married to Matthias was bad enough, but when you were born it absolutely destroyed me. Knowing that you were mine and that I had no claim on you, knowing that you would be raised by that bastard and it only got worse when your sister was born. Then Emmy died, I had no access to you, no claim. I even considered stealing you away in the night but…'

His voice once again trailed off.

'So you really are my father,' Theo asked after a moment.

'Yes,' James replied quietly. 'I know in the eyes of God and society what we did was considered a sin, my soul may be damned for all I know, but I don't regret a single moment I spent loving your mother. She was everything to me, every single beat of my heart, every breath I took. The only thing keeping me from following her to the grave was my love for you and your sister.'

Theo looked up at the man beside him, studying him intently.

'You love me?'

'Yes I do,' he replied, his eyes dark. 'You are my son. I have loved you from the moment you were born, even before that. I placed my palms on your mother's swollen belly and felt you move beneath my hands, so restless, so impatient to be born, and I loved you so much. I wish with all my heart things could have been different, that I could have been the father you deserved, but I'm here now and if you'll let me I can be your father now.'

Theo turned away, his hands trembling as he pulled

in a shaky breath.

'I need…' he shook his head, 'I need to be alone right now.'

'Theo I…' James broke off abruptly at the sound of a horse approaching. Not wanting anyone to see Theo he climbed to his feet. Dusting the leaves from his clothes, and reluctantly giving Theo the space he required, he headed across the rows of trees toward the noise.

'Morning James,' a familiar voice called out.

James relaxed as he recognized the rider approaching. The man sat comfortably relaxed in his saddle, a confident smile playing on his lips.

'Justin,' he smiled in greeting. 'What brings you out this way?'

'A visit to an old friend,' he laughed, as he swung down out of the saddle.

'It's a long way for a visit,' he inquired curiously.

Justin laughed again good naturedly. 'Sarah is with child again.'

'A cause for celebration,' James shook his hand. 'Such a blessing.'

'That it is,' he nodded. 'Perhaps this time it will be a boy.'

'God willing,' James nodded.

'Anyway Sarah insists she must have some of your apple and peach cider.'

James laughed. 'You rode all the way from Salem Town to fetch some of my cider for your wife?'

'Aye,' he replied somewhat sheepishly, 'and perhaps some of your applejack for the girls.'

'Ah,' James smiled wistfully. He knew his friend doted on his wife and two young daughters and the part of him that was still raw from talking about his past, lamented on the fact that he'd never had the chance to do that with his beloved Emmy and their children.

'How are Mercy and Hope?'

'Growing like weeds,' Justin laughed.

'Come up to the house and have a drink,' James invited.

'Thank you,' James pulled on the bit, encouraging his horse to trot obediently beside him as they walked companionably past the rows of trees. 'I must admit it has been a long ride.'

'How are things in town?'

'The same,' Justin shook his head. 'Rowdy.'

'Something should be done,' James frowned.

'Aye it should,' he agreed. 'I have a cousin who has sent word from Boston where he settled with his wife and sons. The watch they established there to keep order appears to be extremely successful by all accounts.'

'Do you think something like that would work in Salem?'

'I think it would,' Justin nodded. 'One constable, six watchmen and a few volunteers should maintain some sort of order.'

'Perhaps you should bring it to the attention of the magistrate.'

'Me?' Justin laughed shaking his head. 'I am just a humble merchant and I fear not up to the task.'

'I think you would be perfect,' James shrugged. 'You are an honorable man, you are well liked and well respected. I think you'd be the perfect choice for the post of constable. I know there's no one I'd trust more.'

As they walked in a comfortable silence toward the house Justin frowned in concentration, wondering if James' ridiculous idea actually had merit.

Olivia sat thoughtfully staring into her empty cup, hoping that Theo and James were coming to terms. She knew it was a lot to expect Theo to accept, after all it was not the way he was raised. To learn, after all this time, his mother was not the woman he thought she was and that he was in actual fact another man's bastard, it was hurting him and she couldn't bear to see him hurt.

She wished desperately she could help, but knew that this was something he had to work through in his own time, just as she had when she'd learned her mother was not only alive but a psychotic killer and that her father had lied to her for most of her life. It left her feeling helpless and she didn't like it one bit.

Her fingers tapped out a restless beat on the table top and she wondered idly if she should go looking for them. She stood abruptly, intending to grab her shawl and search the orchard for them, but as she turned she jolted in surprise. She was not alone.

'Tituba?' Olivia gasped, her hand on her thundering heart. 'You startled me.'

The beautiful slave woman stood calmly in front of her, her blue eyes sharply fixed on Olivia, who could have sworn for a moment she could smell the briny scent of tropical seas and hear the crash of the waves upon the sand.

'Olivia,' she spoke slowly, her lilting musical accent putting emphasis on the 'O' in her name.

'How did you get in here?' Olivia's eyes narrowed suspiciously.

'You are not the only one with gifts,' she replied in amusement. 'I wanted to speak with you alone.'

She seemed different Olivia realized. She didn't have the submissive posture and tone of a slave, as she'd had the day they had met at Samuel Parris' house. Then again, Tituba had witnessed her pulling demon fire from her unconscious friend, so she supposed that was bound to change her perspective of her.

'Can I offer you a drink?'

Tituba's mouth curved in amusement. 'A white woman offerin' a black woman a drink? A black slave?'

'I'm not like the others,' Olivia shrugged.

'I see dat,' she shook her head. 'I can't let anyone find me here.'

'Tituba why did you come?'

'I come to warn you,' her blue eyes burned. 'The demon fire you release the other night lingers still, its scent upon the air. Others have noticed.'

'Others?' Olivia frowned. 'Who?'

'The one with dark eyes, the one they call Nathaniel. He feels its power caught in the air, like a fly in a spider's web. He is drawn to its power.'

Olivia's eyes narrowed as she studied the young woman. Something in her voice, in the way she referred to Nathaniel, made her slightly suspicious.

'You know what he is, don't you?'

Tituba stared at Olivia, her lips thinning. 'I know what he is and I know what he want. You do not belong here Olivia and the longer you stay the more dangerous it become for you and for your friends.'

'I can't leave,' Olivia shook her head, 'not yet. It's complicated.'

'Not so complicated I think,' she stepped forward slowly, her voice soft and lulling. She reached out her slender finger, trailing it lightly down Olivia's throat to her clavicle and then reached beneath her open collar. Her finger hooked around the delicate gold chain and drew it out slowly, revealing the compass Olivia had concealed beneath her clothes.

'This…' Tituba balanced the intricate compass on her fingertips.

Olivia snatched it from her and grasped it protectively in her fist, her eyes widening.

'How do you know about that?'

'I feel its power,' she replied easily. 'It is old, ancient, one of a kind and yet…part of a whole.'

'That makes no sense,' Olivia frowned, 'besides it doesn't work.'

She nearly added 'outside the Underworld,' to that statement, but caught herself just in time. Tituba might be a woman with power of her own but she was still, at the heart of it, a 17th century slave and Olivia seriously doubted she'd be able to accept half the things Olivia had seen or experienced.

'It will work for you,' Tituba insisted, 'if you take the time to learn its secrets.'

Olivia tucked the compass back into her clothes, effectively ending the conversation.

'I must go now before I am missed.'

Olivia nodded, watching silently as she slipped back through the doorway.

'Be very careful with her Olivia.'

At the sound of the familiar voice her face broke into a wide smile. She spun around to find Sam standing behind her. Stooped slightly in exhaustion and wrapped in a blanket, he offered her a small smile, his dimples winking to life.

'SAM!' she rushed to him, wrapping her arms around him and pulling him in for a hug. 'I was so worried about you,' her brow folded into a frown, 'and what do you mean be careful of her?'

'She's not what she seems,' he told her seriously.

'What do you mean?'

'What did I miss?' he suddenly changed the subject.

Deciding not to push him for an answer, she led him to the table and nodded for him to take a seat. Maybe if he understood how Tituba had helped her to heal him he might be less distrustful of her. So she poured him a cup of James' delicious peach and apple cider and filled him in on everything that had happened since the moment they'd crash landed in James' orchard. From meeting Temperance and James, to visiting Samuel Parris, drawing the demon fire from Sam's body with the guidance of Tituba and finally figuring out James was Theo's biological father.

'Wow,' Sam's brows rose in surprise, 'it seems I slept through quite a bit.'

'Understatement,' Olivia muttered.

Sam sat for a moment, silently staring into his

empty cup.

'Demon fire?' he asked after a moment

'Yeah,' Olivia replied.

'What was it like?' he leaned forward, his eyes lighting with interest.

'Terrifying,' she replied quietly. 'It was like being poised on the highest peak of the universe's scariest roller coaster, feeling that moment when you plunge, almost as if you're suspended in a single moment of time. Your breath is trapped in your lungs so you can't even scream, so you hang on tightly, white knuckling it, and praying to whatever God you believe in that you're not going to die. I have never felt so out of control in my entire life.'

'Olivia,' he blew out a breath, 'you're damn lucky it didn't kill you. It is the most violent and unstable of all the elemental fires. It can't be controlled and anyone who has ever been foolish enough to try and master it has been torn apart.'

'Shit,' Olivia swore under her breath.

'Yeah, not a good area for experimentation.'

'Just do me a favor okay and don't mention it to Theo. It'll just freak him out and he's got enough to deal with right now.'

Sam nodded.

They both looked up as the latch rattled and the door opened. Olivia's eyes widened in surprise and for a second she had to do a double take of the achingly familiar, tall blonde man, who walked into the house beside James.

'Justin, this is my niece Livy and um...' his gaze slid across to Sam, not expecting him to be up and about so soon after his illness, 'her brother Samuel,' he improvised as he introduced them. 'Livy, Sam, this is my good friend Justin Gilbert.'

'A pleasure,' he smiled at them and Olivia's heart did a somersault.

He was the spitting image of her best friend Jake, right down to his mischievous blue eyes and infectious smile. She watched him in fascination as he turned and spoke with James. He even had the same laugh, it was really incredible. She was actually meeting someone she could only assume was one of her dearest friends' ancestors.

It really was a small world after all.

The grey storm laden sky had given way to night as Olivia paced the sleeping room, which was bathed in candlelight. Theo had still not returned and she was beginning to worry. James' guest Justin had stayed for supper upon conclusion of his purchase of James' cider. The company had been pleasant and the conversation lively. Sam had eaten like he hadn't eaten in weeks and really that wasn't too far from the truth. While he'd been out of it, the fire which raged within his body had taken a lot out of him. Although he was up, awake and eating, he still looked too pale and far too gaunt.

After Justin had departed Olivia had excused herself to her room, but she was unable to relax. She'd intended to settle in with Hester's Grimoire and search for anything they could use to jump through time. After seeing Sam she wasn't sure at all if he'd have the strength to do it, and they still needed to find a way to get to 1695. She'd climbed on the bed...she'd climbed off it again. She tried sitting under the window on the chest, still she couldn't settle, which is how she'd ended up pacing the room. Despite having stripped down to only her thin linen shift, in preparation for bed, she was close to tossing a cloak around her shoulders and heading out into the dark silent orchard to look for Theo.

She stopped pacing and turned as she heard the door open behind her.

'Theo,' she breathed in relief, 'where have you been?'

He shrugged silently.

'In the Orchard,' he replied after a moment, 'then in the barn. I needed some space.'

She stepped back watching him quietly as he kicked off his shoes and woolen socks and discarded his jerkin. Yanking his shirt over his head he climbed onto the bed in only his breeches and sat with his back propped up against the head of the bed.

'You haven't eaten,' Olivia sat down on the edge of the bed next to him. 'You missed supper.'

'I'm not hungry,' he murmured reaching for her. His hand snaked underneath her hair, cupping the back of her neck, the pad of his thumb grazing her jaw gently as his dark eyes fixed on her.

'Talk to me,' she whispered.

'What is there to say?' he sighed, dropping his hand.

She sat patiently waiting for him to organize his thoughts.

'I'm having a hard time reconciling what they did,' he frowned. 'I was raised to believe adultery was wrong, a sin against God, but then I think about you, and I understand. I understand what it is to love someone so much you would risk everything for them, break every single rule for them. But understanding why, doesn't change the fact I was born of a mockery of a marriage, and lies.'

'No,' Olivia told him firmly, 'you and your sister were both born from love, and I think that is better than being born from duty.'

This time her hand cupped his face, drawing his gaze back to hers.

'Theo, I know the kind of religious upbringing you were subjected to. I know this is hard for you to accept, but you can't have it both ways.'

'What do you mean?'

'You can't judge them so harshly, when by Puritan standards and laws, what we've been doing is considered just as bad,' she reminded him. 'You are technically widowed and I've never married, so we're not committing adultery, but we're lovers outside of marriage. Life's not black and white Theo. Your poor mother was denied the man she truly loved and forced into a violent and unhappy marriage, in which she stayed to protect her children from your harsh society. You can't fault her or James for trying to grasp onto any single moment of happiness they could.'

'Maybe not,' he shook his head, 'and part of me is so damn grateful she did have James. My mother was a kind and loving woman, she didn't deserve a man like Matthias Beckett.'

'But?' she prompted, sensing there was a 'but' in there somewhere.

'But' he continued, 'it's like I woke up and everything I ever believed was a lie. I was raised to believe witches and magic were evil, only to discover the people peddling that crap were descended from witches themselves. The whole thing just reeks of hypocrisy.'

'It makes you question everything, doesn't it?' she replied sympathetically.

'I always thought I knew my mother, knew exactly who she was and I mourned her. God, I mourned her every damn day, only to find out she wasn't the woman I thought she was and that I never really knew her at all.'

'You did know her Theo, in all the ways that counted. Okay, so she couldn't tell you James was your father and she couldn't tell you about her magical gifts, but she loved you, she protected you and that's all that matters. That's what you have to hold onto. Hold onto her love for you, everything else will come in time.'

'Is this how you felt, when you found out the truth about your parents?'

'What, you mean when I found out my dead mother wasn't actually dead, but a psychopathic serial killer and that my father wasn't a killer, but had lied to me most of my life?' her lip curved in amusement. 'Yeah, you know how messed up I was, but you know what?'

'What?'

She climbed up on the bed next to him, lifting her shift out of the way as she swung a leg over him, settling in his lap astride his thighs. She leaned forward and took his face gently in her hands.

'I got through it because I had you. Even when I felt like I was shattering into a thousand pieces you were the one who held me together, and now it's my turn to do that for you.'

'Livy' he breathed, pressing his forehead to hers, 'do you have any idea of how in love with you I am?'

'Probably about the same as I am with you.'

His mouth lost some of the grim lines and curved with a small self-deprecating smile.

'I don't know why you put up with me.'

'Guess I'm just crazy,' she smiled back.

He pulled back, his dark eyes holding hers.

'Crazy enough to marry me?'

Olivia's smile faded slightly as she searched his face.

'Depends,' she replied softly. 'Are you asking me as a knee jerk reaction to your parents not being married and you and I living in sin?'

'I'm asking you because I can't stand to live a single moment of my life without you and I belonging to each other in every way possible. I'm asking you, because I want to promise you forever. I'm asking you, because it's what I want, not because its expected.'

A small smile played on her lips.

'Then yeah,' she murmured, 'crazy enough to marry you.'

'Is that a yes?' his face broke into a wide smile.

'Yes,' she laughed, as his hands slid into her hair, gripping the nape of her neck, and his lips crashed down on hers.

The second his tongue traced the seam of her lips her mouth fell open with a hum of pleasure. He tasted her slowly and thoroughly. Her fingers released the firm muscles of his shoulders and plunged into his thick dark hair and gripped tightly.

His hands slid down her neck to her shoulders grasping her shift and dragging it down her arms letting the soft material pool at her waist. She couldn't help the groan of helpless pleasure that escaped the moment he filled his hands with her swollen breasts, moaning as he dragged his thumbs across her nipples, grazing the sensitive peaks.

She rolled her hips, rocking forward in his lap and feeling him hard and ready between her thighs. They hadn't made love since the night she'd found him in the abandoned psychiatric hospital in the Otherworld and she'd missed him, missed the intimacy and desperate pleasure of feeling him inside her.

It burned through her blood now like a drug; passion, as bright and intense as her fire. Her need for him was beyond words. She suspected from the way he devoured her mouth, digging his fingers into her hips as his hardness pressed against her core, that he felt it too, the intense need they had for each other.

'Theo,' she gasped against his mouth, 'please…'

He shifted her slightly in his lap, his lips never breaking contact with her as he loosened his breeches and pushed them down past his hips. His hands skimmed up her thighs pushing her shift up until he was grasping her naked buttocks. She slid down on him achingly slow, until he filled her completely, moaning into his mouth at the sudden feeling of fullness. He couldn't help himself as he thrust up inside her, helplessly lost to her. Her back arched, changing the angle and increasing the friction, her posture unconsciously offering her breasts to him. He closed his mouth over one of those pretty little peaks, increasing the suction until he felt her muscles tighten around him, causing him to lose his hold on her nipple and drag in a sharp gasp of intense pleasure.

His hands gripped her hips desperately as she rode him, her hips undulating against him. She drove him to the point of madness, until all he could see was her whiskey colored eyes deepening to molten gold, her midnight hair spilling down her back like an inky waterfall grazing his thighs, all of which added another layer of sensation.

His gaze held hers and despite the sheer intensity of being inside her, he could see her smile playing on her lips as their eyes locked. She rocked her hips forward again, taking him even deeper and he was unable to stop the groan which tore from his throat.

'Shush,' she clamped her hand over his mouth, her breath hot and teasing in his ear. 'Your dad will hear us.'

He growled and tossed her on her back, making her laugh breathlessly as he followed her and plunged back inside her. Her laugher died in her throat to be replaced with a deep moan as she arched up into him.

'God!' the breath rushed from her lungs as he skillfully rolled his hips, angling himself so he hit that place inside her which made her see stars.

'Such blasphemy,' he breathed into her ear this time, his mouth curving as he nipped her earlobe playfully.

'Theo please,' she gasped as he set a torturous pace.

His hands skimmed the length of her arms until he reached her hands and linked their fingers. He lifted her arms pinning them above her head by their entangled fingers. She wrapped her legs around his hips as he drove her up, higher and higher until she couldn't think, couldn't do anything but breath him in. His lips took hers once again, drinking in every moan, every gasp, absorbing every single part of her she gave to him so freely, until finally they both shattered.

This…he thought to himself breathing heavily, his heart pounding so loudly he could hear it in his ears. What he felt right now, his intense love for the woman pinned beneath his body, this was worth breaking every rule for and in that moment he understood…she was the other half of his soul.

9.

Olivia lay awake staring at the rough wooden beams of the ceiling that were, for the most part, concealed by the deep shadows of the room. Theo was sprawled naked over the bed beside her, lying on his stomach with one arm wrapped around her waist, his breathing deep and even. Drawing in a frustrated breath she carefully slipped out from underneath his grip so as not to wake him. She couldn't say exactly what had woken her. She'd been dreaming, but already the dream was fading, slipping from her grasp as fine and insubstantial as mist. It was important somehow, she was sure of it. She swung her legs over the side of the bed and sat there for a moment, trying to grasp the loose threads of the dream. It was not a dream she realized with a slight jolt, she'd been remembering something, something Theo had said to her back in Mercy.

    She rubbed her forehead in frustration as if the action could nudge loose the elusive thought she'd been chasing. She felt unsettled, as if she were forgetting something important, but she just couldn't put her finger on what it was. She stood and stretched, feeling the pull of her overused muscles. She stepped over her shift, which had been discarded along with Theo's breeches at some point during the night when he'd made love to her again.

Not bothering to pull her garment back on she stood in front of the window. She could barely see anything outside. The pale moonlight was mostly obscured by huge swirling storm clouds, as the rain hammered down against the roof of the house. Perhaps the rain had woken her or the distant rumbles of thunder.

No, she frowned, that wasn't it. She couldn't explain it, there was something she was missing, some detail that was right under her nose. What the hell was it?

Suddenly a new sound intruded over Theo's soft snores and the pounding of the rain against the window, a strange sibilant whispering. It wasn't the first time she'd heard it. She canted her head to the side, straining to make out the words, or even the language that was being spoken, but it was too soft and there were too many distractions. She continued to listen for a moment longer, but it began to fade and was soon replaced by the howl and shriek of the storm. Shaking her head she wondered if she'd imagined it.

Tired and frustrated, but not able to sleep she turned back to the window, watching as the rivulets of water streamed down the surface. The driving rain had let up slightly and was now a soft constant drumming against the panes of glass. Without realizing it she picked up the compass, which still hung from the chain around her neck. She stroked it absently with her fingertips as she gazed out of the window, lost in thought. She didn't even notice that Theo was no longer snoring, nor did she hear him pull the blanket from the bed, wrapping it around himself as he climbed out of bed and moved to stand behind her. She jolted slightly as his warm sleepy arms snaked around her waist, drawing her naked body in against his own as he wrapped the blanket around both of them.

'What is it love?' His voice was roughened by sleep as he murmured against her ear.

'Couldn't sleep,' she turned in his arms reaching up on her tiptoes to press a soft kiss against his mouth.

'Come back to bed.' He wrapped his arms around her tightly and lifted her, carrying her back to the bed.

Whatever random thought Olivia had been trying to hold on to tattered and drifted away and as they sunk back down into the warm bedding, all she thought of was Theo.

With the dawn came no respite from the storm. The skies wept openly with a continuous downpour, thunder rolled ominously across the sky, punctuated every now and then by a jagged slash of lightning. The storm seemed to perfectly mirror Theo's mood. James had disappeared early in the morning with an excuse of work he needed to do in the barn, and although that may have been true, to a certain extent, Olivia was sure the decision was made in part with the desire to give his son some space. However, as the day wore on Theo's mood darkened and he became more and more restless.

Olivia, thinking it best to give him some space, had withdrawn to the fireplace where she sat pouring over Hester's Grimoire, looking for some clues as to how they were going to manage jumping ten years into the future. Finally, in frustration, she slammed the book shut and wrapped it in the old tattered cloak she'd been using to conceal it. She couldn't seem to concentrate.

Although she couldn't recall the details of her dream from the night before, she still had the unsettling feeling she was missing something important. It was something Theo had told her in passing, she was sure of it, but try as she may she couldn't bring it to mind.

Giving up on that particular trail of thought, she pulled the compass from the collar of her dress and eased the chain over her head so she could inspect it more closely. Everyone seemed to be so concerned with the small golden compass which, quite frankly, didn't even work that well. Still, Hades himself had gone out of his way to give it to her, insisting it would work if she simply took the time to 'figure it out' as he'd told her in his usual dry tone. It had been the same with Tituba. She'd said the compass would work specifically for her, if she took the time to learn its secrets.

Why her? she frowned silently. What was so special about her? And why was everyone being purposefully vague? Why didn't the damn thing come with an instruction manual? She turned it over in her hands again, flipping open the lid. It was a compass, for all its delicate craftsmanship, it was still just a compass. What more could it possibly do? Okay, so it had taken them to the Crossroad Epsilon while they'd been in the Underworld. But then again, they were in the Underworld at the time, a place which had ancient magic woven through the very fabric of its existence. Would it even work in the real world?

Closing the lid, she turned it over to study the underneath. There was nothing there, it was just plain smooth metal, but as she turned it on its edge she could feel another fine groove, which ran around the circumference of the compass. Curiously she grasped it gently in her fingertips and twisted slightly, as if twisting the cap off a bottle. Much to her surprise it rotated smoothly and with a quiet click it flipped open on a small spring.

Her mouth fell open in a silent surprised, 'Oh.' The top opened to reveal a compass face, but underneath was a small concealed compartment. She lifted it closer and studied it carefully. When the lid had sprung open, the internal mechanism had also triggered something else. A tiny golden triangle had flicked out in the center and now stood on its narrow edge. Underneath it were markings and engravings.

It was…a sundial she realized after a moment, a miniature sundial and it was incredible, so tiny and yet so detailed. Strangely enough a glint of color caught her attention and in the center of the sundial was a flash of blue stone. It wasn't smooth and round, but more a jagged scar, which split the face of the golden metal to reveal a shard of deep blue crystal. Now that the stone was exposed, she could feel the strong thrum of power pulsing through the metal into her palm. It was like the exposed shard of crystal was a vein, throbbing and pulsing with life. Maybe they were right, maybe it was more powerful than she thought.

What was it Hades had said to her?

'It's a compass Olivia, so ask yourself what does a compass do?'

A compass? she frowned. Well, it was an instrument for determining a direction. It shows the way to your destination, but it was more than that.

Her frown deepened and her lips pursed as she tried to follow the thought through to its conclusion. The compass hadn't just shown her the way to the Crossroad, it had taken her there. In fact, it had taken her there because she had specifically asked it to. Tituba was right, the compass would work for her.

So what was the sundial for? If she broke down the thought process the same way she had with the compass, the sundial was a way of telling the hour of the day using the shadow cast by the sun's position. Essentially it recorded the passage of time…

Holy shit!

Olivia's hand trembled slightly. What if this was the answer? If the Compass could transport them across distance, what if the sundial could transport them across time? If she could just figure out how to make it work. She tried to think back to the Underworld, to the moment it had transported them to the Crossroad. What exactly had she done? Holding the small sundial close to her face she took a deep breath.

'Wake up' she whispered, her warm breath fanning across the deep blue stone.

The tiny golden triangle trembled slightly, then twitched. Her heart gave a sharp thud of excitement and her breath caught in her throat. This was it, this was somehow the answer if she could just figure it out. She looked up as the door banged open abruptly, letting in the driving rain as James stomped into the house, dripping water across the floor.

Reluctantly, she closed the sundial and pulled the chain back over her head, tucking the compass safely back under her clothes. She needed to think about this some more before she started experimenting with jumping through time, and even then there was no guarantee that it would work. All she had right now was a theory and a vague one at that.

James removed his wide brimmed hat and cloak, stepping closer to the fire where Olivia sat.

'Storm's getting worse, I'd say we're going to have a few days of this. Doesn't look as if it's going to blow over anytime soon.' He held his hands out to the flames, shivering as the warmth began to slowly seep into his fingers.

Olivia happened to glance over at Theo as James mentioned the storm. She saw his face pale and his jaw tighten.

'I think I'll heat up some of the apple cider. I can feel the damp all the way down to my bones,' James murmured as he disappeared into the keeping room to retrieve one of the broached casks.

Olivia moved from her seat by the fire, wandering over to where Theo sat.

'What is it?' she asked quietly.

'It's nothing,' he scowled.

'Theo.'

'The storm,' he sighed.

'What about it? Storms have never bothered you before,' she frowned in confusion.

'It's this storm in particular,' he told her pointedly. 'I remember it...I remember exactly where I was and what I was doing the first time I experienced it.'

She watched him, patiently waiting for him to explain.

'I was at the market with my brother, but we were delayed returning home because of the storm. I left Temperance home with Mary.'

Olivia closed her eyes and her chest tightened wretchedly. She remembered Theo telling her about this. While he was gone Temperance died from a fever. She'd known the child was sick when she'd seen her the day before, but she had no idea that they'd run out of time.'

'I don't know if I can do it Livy,' he breathed painfully. 'I know we're not supposed to interfere, but I don't know if I can lose my sister all over again.'

Olivia opened her mouth to speak, but abruptly shut it again as James entered the room. They could not discuss this in front of him, after all Temperance was his child too. The last thing the man needed to know was that his daughter was about to die and that they had no choice but to stand by painfully and let it happen, because they could not afford to compromise the timeline.

Olivia looked up as James swept back into the room, pouring some of his apple cider into a pot and setting it to warm over the fire. She didn't know what to do, how to help Theo. It must be killing him knowing that only a few miles from where they were now, his sister's condition was deteriorating and that it would ultimately lead to her death.

There was nothing they could do. Even if they could interfere with the timeline and somehow not cause catastrophic consequences, they had no way to help the girl. Olivia was not a healer, not the way her great aunt had been. She had rudimentary skills at best. If only they had access to modern medicine they may have stood a chance, but it was impossible.

It was Temperance Beckett's fate to die of fever in Salem in 1685 and as much as she would give anything for it not to be so, there was nothing they could do. She felt so helpless and absolutely sick to her stomach when she thought about that sweet, beautiful little dark haired child.

If only her Sam, the older version who knew how to jump through time was there, maybe he could've helped her.

Theo couldn't sit still. He paced the floor, stopping in front of the window, watching as the water pounded against the glass. He knew what Olivia was thinking, he could read it as plain as day on her face. He could easily see the play of emotions upon her features; helplessness, hurt, and desperation. He knew she was trying to come up with some solution. She didn't want Tempy to die any more than he did, but she was right, some things cannot be changed no matter how much he might wish differently. He knew he shouldn't interfere, he knew he should stay hidden away safely in James' house, but the thought of Tempy dying alone and in pain, with no one to watch over her but his mad wife, was tearing him apart.

A thought had occurred to him, and try as he might he could not dissuade himself from it. Tempy was sick, there was no denying that, there was no way to cure her, but that didn't mean she had to die alone. If he couldn't save her, then he was going to make damn sure she died in his arms, knowing she was loved and safe. He swallowed past the knot of grief burning at the back of his throat and took a deep breath, forcing back the wave of pain and focusing on the details.

He knew that the past version of himself was not at the Beckett farm, nor was his brother Logan. They were both miles away, holed up at a cheap inn waiting out the storm. Mary was at the house, but by now she would be at the height of her madness. There was little chance she would notice that he looked ten years older than the Theo who'd just left for market with his brother. There was only one problem.

Matthias Beckett.

The man Theo had thought was his father, the man who made their lives a living hell. He had hoped he would never have to see him again, but if he was very careful he might not have to. By the time Temperance had died and

Mary had been hung, his father, or so called father, he shook his head to remind himself, was already coming to the end of his life.

By this point he was a fat bloated mess, never sober and barely able to function. His eyes were yellowed, his nose a nasty bright red protuberance upon a face that was covered in thin spidery looking, broken veins. The chances were, he would barely be conscious and even if he was, like Mary, he probably wouldn't be cognitive enough to realize Theo was different. He could do it, he mused. He would do it. His fists clenched involuntarily and his jaw set in determination; Tempy was not going to die alone.

'Come sit,' James called to Theo.

Olivia was already sitting at the table as James poured the warm, spicy scented drink into a cup and handed it to her. 'It will ward off the chill in the air.'

Theo slid onto the bench next to her and James poured him a cup too.

'I have something for you Theo,' James told him quietly. 'I think it may help you to come to terms with everything, at least I hope it will.'

Theo looked up, silently watching as James placed a cloth covered bundle on the table in front of him.

'It belonged to your mother, she gave it to me shortly before Temperance was born,' James' eyes darkened with grief. 'I think she knew what was coming. She gave me this and told me to keep it safe and to give it to you when you were old enough.'

Theo looked down at the tattered rough cloth, which was tied in a loose knot. The bundle itself looked vaguely rectangular and quite flat. Reaching out with shaking hands he fumbled with the knot twice, before he was finally able to separate the fraying strands. Pressing his lips together thinly, he unfolded the edges of the material and breathed out slowly. In front of him was a thin tattered looking journal.

James smiled sadly as he cast his gaze upon it.

'I gave that to her when we were younger,' he looked up and met Theo's gaze.

He could feel the depth of James' love for his mother and the deep endless anguish her death had caused him. For a moment, he could see how raw the other man's pain was and he had to turn away from it, unable to look into the face of such loss and not bleed for him.

'When I was a boy my father, your grandfather, would take me travelling with him all over the colonies. He was always looking for rare or new seedlings to plant in our orchard. He was bound to the earth the same as I am and he wanted nothing more than to create and grow the best fruit in New England. One time we went to Boston and I brought back that journal for Emmaline. It was one of her most treasured possessions.'

Theo reached out with trembling fingers and opened the worn cover. His chest clenched painfully as he read the first few lines.

Dearest Theo, if you are reading this then I am long since gone and you have now learned the truth from your father James...

Theo slammed the book shut, his hand resting on the cover, his eyes squeezed tightly shut. His breath caught and his heart knocked painfully against his ribs.

'She knew,' he whispered, opening his eyes and staring up at James.

'Yes,' he replied sympathetically, 'she knew everything. She knew she was going to die. She knew you would meet Olivia. She knew you would find your way to me. It is all there in that book.'

'You read it?' the words came out on a rush of grief that made them sound harsher than he'd meant to.

'Not all of it,' James shook his head. 'Once I realized what it was I hid it, until the day I knew you would need it.'

'What do you mean, once you realized what it

was?' Theo frowned.

'Theo,' James sank tiredly into the seat opposite him, 'when your mother realized what was going to happen to her, she sat down and began to write that journal…for you. She knew she wouldn't be here to guide you, to teach you how to use your gift, so she wrote it all down in there. All her memories, her love, her guidance, her most private thoughts, all laid bare…for you.'

Theo felt the tears burning at the back of his eyes and a hot ball of misery sat like lead at the back of his throat, threatening to choke him. She hadn't abandoned him after all. She'd left him everything he needed. She'd left him the most precious parts of herself.

'In this journal,' Theo began shakily as he looked back to James, 'she wrote everything? She wrote that you are my father not Matthias?'

James nodded.

'She wrote about the magic, the visions, all of it?'

James nodded again.

'And you kept it, all of these years, for me?'

James stared at Theo not trusting his voice.

'You kept it for me,' Theo continued, finally realizing the depth of James' love for him. 'You kept it, knowing that if it was discovered in your possession, if it fell into the wrong hands, you would be tried for witchcraft?'

'Yes,' James croaked finally. 'I knew you would need it, not just so that you could learn to control your gift, but because you deserved the chance to know your mother, even if it was only through her words on a page.'

'You risked too much,' Theo shook his head. 'Do you have any idea what would have happened if this book had fallen into the wrong hands?'

'I don't care,' James replied, 'you are my son Theo. I would risk everything for you.'

Theo couldn't breathe, couldn't swallow past the knot of pure emotion choking him. A tear spilled over and meandered slowly down his cheek as he beheld the man in front of him.

All his life he had felt displaced, unimportant, unloved. Abandoned, first by the death of his mother, then the emotional abandonment and abuse he had endured at the hands of the man he had thought was his father. He'd feared Matthias Beckett, he'd hated him and all his life he had lived in fear that the anger and pain that consumed him would manifest itself as the very worst qualities of Matthias Beckett.

For the first time in his life, Theo acknowledged the stark fear he'd always carried deep within his heart. That somehow, someday, he would turn out just like his father, that he would hurt Olivia, whether by design or otherwise.

But now he knew he bore no part of that man. He was James Wilkins' son by blood and all of the best parts of himself, he now knew came from the man in front of him. James was loving and honest and loyal. He was truly the best man Theo had ever known and for the first time in his life Theo experienced what it was like to feel truly loved by his father.

'Thank you,' Theo mouthed the words rather than spoke as no sound would come out.

James nodded in response, his own eyes glassy and not trusting his voice either. In that moment a kind of understanding and acceptance passed between them.

'What did I miss this time?' Sam startled them as he dropped down onto the bench next to Olivia.

'Your timing is impeccable as always Sam,' Olivia replied dryly as she poured him a cup of warm cider, distracting Sam, and giving James and Theo time to collect themselves.

'That's a hell of a storm blowing out there,' Sam drained the cup in one go. 'It woke me up.'

'I'd thought nothing short of an apocalypse would wake you up,' Olivia smiled.

Sam chuckled. 'I think I've slept enough to last me

a couple of lifetimes. Now I'm so hungry I could devour an entire herd of cattle. What's for supper?'

'There is some stew left,' James chuckled, as he climbed to his feet. 'I'll settle it to warming for you.'

'Thank you James,' Sam grinned.

'You're looking so much better,' Olivia's eyes narrowed as she scrutinized him carefully. 'How are you feeling?'

'Not quite my old self,' he replied 'but definitely better.'

'Glad to hear it,' James interjected. 'Olivia love, why don't you cut Sam a couple of slices of bread to be getting on with while the stew warms.'

Nodding in agreement she rose gracefully from the bench. She retrieved the loaf of thick dark brown bread from the sideboard and brought it back to the table. Fetching a plate and knife and some thick milky looking butter she set it down in front of him.

'Theo,' she stroked his face gently as he sat staring numbly at his mother's journal. 'Why don't you take a few moments in the other room with the book?'

She knew he was churned up inside, with a dozen turbulent emotions he didn't want to let loose in front of James and Sam.

Nodding slowly he stood, but as he swept the journal from the table several loose pieces of parchment scattered to the floor.

'What are these?' he frowned as both he and James stooped to pick them up.

Theo began to stack the ones he'd picked up, glancing at them in interest. They were sketches.

James smiled softly in remembrance as his fingers trailed the pages lightly.

'My drawings,' he replied. 'I would draw these for Emmy. She kept them all.'

'You drew these?' Theo's brows lifted in surprise. They were so similar to his own that he now realized where he had got his gift for art from.

'Yes I did,' he handed them back to Theo as they both stood. 'They're yours now.'

'Hang on, you missed one.' Olivia bent and scooped up the last piece of paper, but as she held it out she glanced down at what was drawn on it and her mouth fell open on a startled gasp.

Theo leaned over to see what Olivia was looking at and his heart clenched. It was a portrait of his mother. Even though he hadn't gazed upon her face in years her features were still burned upon his heart.

'That's my mother,' Theo whispered.

'This?' Olivia held up the paper. 'This is your mother?'

Theo nodded, frowning slightly at the shock registered on her face.

'What is it Livy?'

'I've seen this woman before.'

'What?' Theo shook his head in confusion. 'Where?'

'This is Tammy Burnett,' she told him pointedly, 'the mayor of Mercy.'

'That's not possible,' Theo shook his head. 'My mother is dead.'

'But Temperance isn't,' she whispered to herself as the pieces slowly started to slide into place, like moves on a giant chessboard.

'What did you say?'

'She always looked so familiar and I couldn't put my finger on why,' Olivia shook her head. 'I can't believe I didn't see it.'

'See what?'

'She looked familiar because she looked like you.'

'I don't understand, what are you saying exactly?' Theo frowned.

Suddenly it all snapped into place. That strange elusive memory of Theo she'd been trying to recall for days, now blazed into life in her mind and she could hear Theo's voice so clearly.

'Mary was completely mad by then, ranting about a man appearing and disappearing before her eyes.'

'He did it,' she muttered as her gaze fell on Sam, 'he figured out how to jump through time.'

'Olivia, you're not making any sense.'

'Theo,' she grasped his arms, a smile breaking out on her face, 'don't you see? Temperance is alive and she's living in present day Mercy as Tammy Burnett.'

'How is that possible?'

'Sam,' she glanced across at him. 'Theo, don't you remember, when you were telling me what happened to Mary, you said she was completely mad, that when you found her she was raving about a man who…'

'Appeared and disappeared in front of her eyes,' he finished for her, his own gaze tracking across to Sam.

'You said Mary burned the body, but you never recovered Temperance's remains did you?'

Theo shook his head.

'That's because we covered it up, it was us all along don't you see,' she shook her head, her words falling out in a tumble as she tried to explain herself. 'That's probably where Sam got the idea to pull you from the burning barn later on. Fire covers all our tracks and closes the timeline. History recorded that Temperance Beckett died on the 28th September 1685 of Juvenile Fever, but no body was ever discovered.'

'What do you mean Temperance is going to die?' James interrupted hotly.

'She won't if I can help it,' Olivia told him then she turned back to Theo. 'Don't you get it? We were here the first time around, we were always here. Sam pulls Temperance out before she dies and we cover it up by making everyone think that Mary burned her body.'

Theo stared at Olivia his mind working furiously

now, trying to find some flaw in her logic as desperate hope burst to life in his chest.

'Theo,' her voice was breathy as her face broke into a wide smile, 'we can save your sister.'

10.

'What in God's name is going on?' James demanded impatiently. 'What do you mean you can save his sister? What is going to happen to Temperance?'

Theo glanced down to Olivia who'd moved closer to him. A look passed between them, a look which was filled with questions.

'It's your choice how much you want to tell him,' Olivia whispered to Theo.

'The timeline?' Theo shook his head.

'Doesn't matter much at this point when it comes to James,' Olivia replied softly. 'He knows enough about us to realize that we have come from another time and he probably suspects more. I don't know how much your mother saw or how much she shared with him, but I think he's proved he can be trusted to keep whatever we tell him to himself.'

Theo's gaze cut across to his father and he sighed.

'Theo, she's his daughter. He deserves to know the truth.' Olivia reached out and grasped his arm gently.

He stared down into her eyes, trying to decide whether or not telling James was the right thing to do. Either way the man was going to lose his daughter, but maybe knowing she was alive and well, but living in a different time, would bring him a small measure of comfort.

'You'd better sit down,' he replied after a moment.

James glanced at Olivia, his expression a mix of curiosity laced with worry. She nodded once in reassurance and watched as he took a seat at the table.

'Before we tell you anything,' Theo warned, 'we must have your word you will not tell another living soul.'

'You have my word,' he agreed.

Another silent look passed between Olivia and Theo as they tried to decide how much to reveal.

'You may as well tell him all of it,' Sam reached for a piece of thick dark bread, slathering it in butter.

'But you said…'

'That was the other me,' Sam took a bite and chewed thoughtfully. 'Regardless, I think we're going to have to start taking a few risks. We'll try and keep the timeline as intact as possible, but I think Olivia is right. It doesn't necessarily apply to James as he already had foreknowledge of the future thanks to your mother Theo. I think we'll be safe enough as long as he doesn't act on any information we give him or share it with anyone else.'

'Who am I going to tell?' James interrupted angrily. 'I just want to know what is happening with my daughter.'

'Go ahead Theo,' Olivia breathed, 'tell him all of it.'

Theo dropped back down onto the bench opposite James, trying to organize his thoughts.

'About ten years from now I die,' Theo began, 'or at least that's what everyone will believe. There was a fight between my brother Logan and myself in the barn back home. In the struggle a lamp was knocked over and the barn caught fire. Logan made it out, but I didn't. To everyone who witnessed the fire, I died that night. As my body was never recovered they just assumed there was nothing left. In reality, Sam here, or rather an older version of Sam, pulled me out of the barn at the last moment and took me forward in time. Three hundred years forward.'

'Three hundred years?' James' mouth fell open in shock.

'Yes,' Theo nodded, 'that's where I met Olivia.'

James turned, his wide dark eyes on Olivia. 'You...you were born...'

'I was born in the year 1986,' she told him gently, 'in a town not far from Salem, that doesn't exist yet and won't do for at least another twenty years.'

'Anyway,' Theo continued. 'I settled into Olivia's time believing I would never again return to Salem, to my time.'

'What changed?' James asked with a frown of confusion as he tried to process the fantastical tale.

'A lot of things I won't explain to you and you will have to accept that,' Theo replied. As much as James was willing to at least accept the possibility of time travel, Theo didn't think he was ready to hear about the Underworld, lost Crossroads and Greek Gods.

'So what does this have to do with Temperance?' James asked.

'She died,' Theo breathed out painfully, 'or so I always believed. I was away at market with Logan when we were delayed by a storm. This storm. We took shelter at an inn and waited it out, but it lasted for days. When we finally returned home, it was to be informed by my father,' Theo stopped suddenly shaking his head, 'told by Matthias Beckett,' he corrected himself, 'that Temperance had succumbed to a fever and died. My wife Mary, in her madness, had apparently burned Temperance's body, so there was no way to confirm their story and no reason to believe they'd lied.'

'But they did lie?' James asked in confusion.

'No,' Olivia disagreed. 'They honestly would have believed what they were saying was the truth, but now I know differently.'

'I'm not sure I understand,' James frowned.

'Temperance is alive, and living in the town where I was born, during my time. Which means she was pulled through time the same way Theo was. Again the fire would have covered up the lack of a body.'

'If what you are saying is true,' James answered in confusion, 'that would mean that…'

'We're running out of time' Olivia confirmed. 'We must save her before this storm blows itself out and the younger version of Theo and his brother Logan return.'

'But how; how will you save her?' James asked looking across to Sam. 'Forgive me Sam, but you don't look as if you have the strength to stand for a long period of time right now, let alone jump through time.'

'You're not entirely wrong,' Sam frowned, washing down the bread with a mouthful of cider, 'besides I've never even tried it before.'

'Perhaps you are wrong Olivia,' James replied, 'and it is not Temperance living in this town of yours, but a distant ancestor who merely looks similar.'

'I'm not wrong,' Olivia shook her head, 'not about this.'

'But Sam said it himself,' he argued. 'He has no idea how to travel through time.'

'Actually I didn't say I had no idea,' Sam intervened, 'I just said I'd never tried it.'

'What?' Theo turned to Sam. 'You think you know how to do it?'

'I have a theory,' Sam mused thoughtfully. 'You remember the conversation we had Olivia, about time in your world being like a river?'

She nodded, trying to cast her mind back. 'You said it only flows in one direction because it's linear.'

'That's right,' he replied, pleased that she'd remembered. 'I also theorized that there were fixed points in time, events of such importance they cannot be changed and that time might butt up against those points. As they can't be moved or changed those events would redirect the flow.'

'Rippling out and causing thousands of alternate timelines,' Olivia finished for him. 'Yes I do remember, you wondered if you could ride those timelines like a wave.'

'It's a little more complicated than that,' Sam tapped his fingers against the table, 'but I did spend a great deal of time thinking about it. In fact, I've been thinking about it ever since you told me the older version of me is able to navigate through time, and I think I know how I did it. However, I haven't had time to test my theory.'

'Can't you test it now?' Theo asked.

'No,' Sam shook his head. 'James is right about one thing, I'm weakened right now and I still haven't fully regained my strength. If I'm even going to try to attempt what you're suggesting and pull your sister through time into the future, I need to conserve every ounce of strength I have.'

'So you're just going to what; grab Tempy and hope for the best?' Theo growled.

'It's the best I can do right now Theo, I'm sorry,' Sam replied. 'I'll try, that's all I can promise. Like I said, it's a theory. I've got no way of knowing if it'll work until it does.'

'Or doesn't,' James frowned. 'Look I understand all of you are trying to help, but if Temperance really is sick we should call the doctor and see if he can help her.'

'He won't be able to James,' Olivia replied softly. 'I know it's a lot for you to take in all at once and a lot to ask you to take on faith, but this really is her only shot. If Sam fails, she will die.'

'No pressure then,' Sam murmured sarcastically.

'Sam I know you can do it,' Olivia turned to him, 'I have faith in you. Now you have to have faith in me and I'm telling you Temperance is alive and living in Mercy.'

'Very well,' he shook his head. 'You know I'll do

what I can, but there is something else you're missing.'

'What's that?' Theo asked.

'Just say you're right and this works. Say I manage to jump Temperance three hundred years into the future, the chances are it's going to use up whatever strength I have left. I won't be able to come back for you. You will be stuck here in 1685, while your mother and the other Nathaniel are causing God knows what kind of trouble ten years ahead of you in 1695.'

Olivia turned to look at Theo and a silent agreement passed between them.

'Then we'll take the long way around,' Olivia told him.

'You'll stay in Salem for the next ten years? Just waiting for your mother and Nathaniel to show up?'

'If we have to,' Theo agreed. 'It's a small price to pay to save my sister.'

'It's too risky,' Sam told them. 'If you change even the slightest thing, the consequences…'

'We know,' Olivia replied, 'trust me you've told me often enough. But if I am right and Temperance Beckett is Tammy Burnett, then by not saving her you'll be changing the future.'

'Time travel gives me a headache,' Sam growled. 'I don't do well under the weight of this kind of responsibility, that's why I left my…'

'Your what?' Olivia asked curiously as his voice trailed off.

'Nothing,' he stiffened in his seat, 'never mind.'

'Look Sam,' Olivia replied, 'we've all got to grow up some time. You need to make a decision. Will you save Temperance or attempt to jump us ten years into the future to stop my mother and Nathaniel?'

'Sometimes I wish I'd never met you,' he grumbled.

'I'm sure you do,' she replied, a small smile tugging at the corner of her mouth. 'Now put on your big boy pants and make a choice.'

'Fine,' he breathed. 'I'll do what I can for Temperance, but try and stay out of trouble for the next decade. I don't need to remind you that there is another younger version of Theo walking around. Theo is essentially going to have to hide from everyone for ten years and you Olivia, I don't think I need to remind you what is going to happen in the next few years. If they find out what you are, you'll be the one hanging from the tree on Gallows Hill.'

'They won't find out,' Olivia assured him.

Staying in the past at the height of the Salem witch trials wasn't her first choice, but at this point it couldn't be helped. If they had to stay, maybe they could relocate to Boston or New Hampshire, anywhere that Theo wouldn't be recognized.

Then they could return after the trials, but before her mother and Nathaniel arrived from the Underworld. It wasn't a flawless plan, but it was the best she could come up with, unless of course she figured out a way to make the compass work. There was always the possibility that she could use the strange compass Hades had given her to jump herself and Theo through time. Of course she didn't want to bring that up just yet, in case it didn't work. Right now they needed to deal with the situation regarding Temperance and time was running out.

'So are we all agreed?' Olivia asked, 'we try to save Temperance?'

She looked at each of them in turn as they nodded in agreement.

'Okay then,' she replied. 'Theo, tell me exactly what you remember Mary and Matthias saying about the night Temperance was supposed to have died.'

'There's not much,' Theo shook his head trying to cast his mind back. 'He was drunk and she was mad, neither of them were making much sense. All I know is that at some point during the storm, Mary saw a man appear and disappear. Matthias didn't see anything, so my guess is that he was passed out drunk.'

'What about the fire?' Olivia asked. 'Mary said Temperance's body burned, but where? In the house? The barn? Outside?'

'In the house,' Theo frowned thinking back. 'Actually I remember thinking how strange that was. The fire was inside the house, it burned the whole of the section where Tempy's room was. There was literally nothing left of the room or the hallway leading to it, but the fire didn't spread beyond that. It burned hot enough to destroy everything in that room, but it didn't move beyond the confines of the hallway. Most of the house was left intact and we later rebuilt that section. Logan at the time thought that it hadn't spread because of the heavy rain.'

'That's not right,' James interjected. 'Matthias' house is timber. Surely if it had caught alight the fire would have spread too quickly. Even if the rain did douse the flames it would have destroyed more than just one room.'

'Not if it was my fire,' Olivia mused.

'What?'

'What if I was the one who started the fire to cover up Temperance's disappearance? I could have controlled the flames, kept it to a small area and stopped it from burning out of control, knowing that the heavy downpour could have explained away the small amount of damage incurred.'

Theo glanced at her his eyes widening. An impossible hope began to bloom in his chest and he allowed himself to truly hope that Olivia was right. If she was, it meant his sister was alive and well and if they ever managed to return to Mercy, she would be there waiting for him.

A sudden rumble of thunder roared across the sky, so close the windows rattled.

'If we're going to do this,' Theo glanced up at the roof as the rain continued to pound down upon the house, 'we do it tonight.'

Olivia nodded in agreement. 'I think you're right. There's no way to tell if we've timed it exactly right, but we already know Temperance is sick. If her condition has worsened, we can't afford to wait any longer. Sam do you think you can handle it tonight?'

'I can't see how putting it off another night would make much of a difference. It's either going to work or it's not. I say we take our chances.'

'Okay then,' Theo stood glancing out of the window, 'we wait until it's fully dark. It will lessen the chances of anyone seeing us or recognizing me, although the chances of anyone being out in this storm are slim.'

They all nodded in agreement. They knew they didn't have long before darkness would descend and so they made the most of the time they had.

Theo made Sam something to eat, while Olivia gathered up Emmaline's journal and Hester's Grimoire, not wanting to leave them out in the house where anyone could find them. As they had already caught Nathaniel snooping around the house, she debated on taking them with her to the Beckett farm, but the rain was hammering down in a torrential downpour and she didn't want to risk either of the precious manuscripts being damaged. So she reluctantly relinquished them to James, who hid them in the small space under the floor, where they'd hidden their original clothes and the backpack containing the flashlight.

Ducking back into the bedroom, she quickly braided her loose hair back from her face and pulled on a dark grey cloak, before wandering back out into the main room to find Theo and Sam both wearing cloaks and wide brimmed hats.

'Where's James?' Olivia asked.

'Saddling the horses,' Theo replied.

'Theo,' Olivia frowned, 'I didn't want to say anything earlier, but I don't think it's a good idea James comes with us.'

'What? Why?' Theo replied. 'If we didn't want him involved why did we tell him everything?'

'Because he needed to understand what we were doing and why,' Olivia answered. 'At the end of the day that's his daughter and he deserved to know the truth. Besides he'd overheard too much, he was going to demand answers no matter what we did.'

'So why don't you want him to come with us?' Theo shook his head. 'Like you said, it's his daughter. You can't think he's just going to sit by and do nothing.'

'Olivia's right,' Sam joined in, 'that's exactly what he has to do.'

'Why?'

'For his own protection,' Olivia told Theo. 'He has to remain above suspicion, no matter what happens. We don't know what we're walking into tonight, but I do know one thing. If Mary or Matthias accidentally see me it won't matter because neither of them know who I am, likewise with Sam. Neither of them are lucid enough to realize that you are not their Theo, but they do know James. All it takes is for one of them to mention him being there and it will make people see him differently and we can't afford to have anyone looking at him with any kind of suspicion, especially not this close to the outbreak of the witch trials.'

Theo sighed, he could see the sense in what they were saying, but he knew James was not likely to accept their opinion. Especially if it meant he would not be able to help Temperance and Theo couldn't blame him. If he had a child and he knew they were in danger, nothing would stop him from rushing in to protect them. He knew James would feel the same way.

'He's not going to like it,' Theo told them seriously.

'I know,' Olivia replied quietly, 'but it's for his own good. We can't risk exposing him, especially not with Nathaniel on the loose. We don't want him tying James to your family in any way.'

Their heads turned as the door rattled and swung open, banging in the violent draught James brought in with him.

'I have the horses tethered to the tree out front,' he stepped into the room and closed the door behind him. 'Are you ready?'

'Not quite James,' Olivia straightened as she faced him calmly. 'I'm really very sorry, but you can't come with us.'

'You can't mean that?' he scowled.

'I'm sorry James,' she repeated, her voice softening in sympathy. 'I wish there was another way, but we can't risk you being exposed. It's for your own safety.'

'Damn my safety,' he stepped closer to Olivia angrily, 'that's my child. I'm not going to just sit by.'

'James that's exactly what you are going to do, we really don't have time to argue about this.'

'I'm not arguing, I'm going and that's all there is to it.'

'No you're not,' Olivia replied firmly.

'And just how are you going to stop me?'

She sighed, reaching out and pressing her two forefingers to his forehead.

'Sleep,' she whispered.

James' eyes rolled back in his head and he crumpled to the floor.

'Damn it Livy,' Theo dropped to the ground and rolled him over to check he was alright.

'He'll be fine Theo,' she replied, 'but we need to hurry. I don't know how long he'll be out for.'

'Sam help me,' Theo hooked his hands under James' arms.

Sam grabbed his feet and between them they moved him closer to the fire so he'd be warm and comfortable.

'Okay let's go.' Theo stood up and strode past the

other two, pulling open the door and stepping into the driving rain. His gaze scanned the darkness and through the murky downpour, he finally saw James' horses tethered to the tree. He crossed the small expanse of sodden grass and leaves, with Olivia and Sam trailing in his wake.

'Do you know how to ride?' Theo asked Olivia, having to raise his voice over the howl and shriek of the wind.

'No,' she replied.

'Sam?'

'Don't worry about me,' Sam confidently swung himself up into the saddle. 'You take care of Olivia.'

Theo nodded as he too grasped the saddle and swung himself up. Reaching down he grabbed Olivia's arm and pulled her up behind him.

'Hold on to me,' he shouted back to her.

He felt her arms snake around his middle, grasping on firmly. Stretching his arm behind him he held her in place. With the reins firmly held in his other hand he dug his heels into the horse's flanks and nudged him in the right direction.

They set off at an easy canter, weaving their way through the trees of the orchard, with Sam close by. Once they hit the outer boundary of James' land with nothing but open fields ahead they urged their horses into a flat out run, praying that they didn't get caught out in the open and struck by lightning.

At the edge of the orchard, under the thick canopy of trees, a dark figure sat aside a horse. He watched the two mounted figures take off across the field, disappearing into the deluge. His large young stallion danced impatiently beneath him, his inky black coat glistening in the rain and a fine mist snorting from his nostrils, as his ears pinned back flat against his powerful head. Nathaniel leaned forward and stroked the jittery creature thoughtfully.

Now where were they disappearing to in the darkness and in the middle of a raging storm? His black beetle-like eyes narrowed in curiosity as he nudged his horse forward.

    Maybe he'd just see where they were off to in such a hurry.

11.

Theo reined his horse in under the wet and dripping canopy of trees. It pranced impatiently under the weight of the two riders, as if it could sense their unease. Olivia peered around Theo and got her first glance of the Beckett farm, the cold austere place where Theo had grown up. She couldn't make out a lot of the detail as the night was too dark and the moon was obscured by a swirling maelstrom of dark clouds. Every so often jagged shards of lightning would burst across the sky, while rain poured to the sodden muddy ground, like a giant pail emptying out high above them.

Theo slid down to the ground, before reaching up and lifting Olivia from the horse. Sam was already on his feet and Theo joined him as they tied the reins to a nearby tree. Satisfied that the horses were secure he turned to Olivia and grasped her hand. Together they crept as stealthily as they could, past the edge of the tree line, which opened up onto a field leading to the Beckett farmhouse.

It sat back in the distance, and set against the fury of the storm it appeared as a dark and ominous building. Bleak and uninviting, there was only one tiny pinprick of light coming from an upstairs window, glowing a sooty orange in the wake of the storm.

They came to a fence at the boundary of the

Beckett land and had to pause for Theo to help Olivia climb over the small squat fence. Normally nimble on her feet, the constant downpour had saturated her clothes until they were dripping wet and heavy. With every step she took the weight of her soaked petticoats, dress and cloak, slowed her down. They began their trek across the field towards the house, but her shoes kept getting stuck in the mud, making her feel as if she were trying to wade through molasses.

She pulled the hood of her cloak further over her head, but it did absolutely no good at all. The rain continued to pound against her unprotected head and face, she found herself almost wishing for one of the stupid looking hats Sam and Theo were wearing, although it didn't look as if they were faring much better than her.

When they finally reached the small yard in front of the house she almost sighed in relief, but it was short-lived. The tall foreboding structure blocked some of the wind, but the cold seemed to seep right down to her bones causing her to shiver violently.

The three of them pressed themselves up against the wet, black clapboards of the farmhouse. Theo peered carefully into the window, but could see only darkness. There didn't seem to be anyone downstairs. Not daring to raise his voice above the howl of the storm in case anyone heard him, Theo raised his hand and indicated that they should follow him.

He crept forward carefully, constantly on the alert and ready for trouble, until he reached the door. Lifting the latch, he swung the door open slowly and cautiously peered into the darkened room. He couldn't see anything. He paused for a moment listening for the drunken snores of the man he once called father, after all it was not unusual for the man to be passed out in the chair by the fireplace, but there was nothing. Stepping more fully into the room, he pulled Olivia in behind him, raising his finger to his lips in warning. Sam stepped in behind them and closed the door silently.

Cut off from the occasional flashes of faint light from the lightning streaked sky, the room was plunged into darkness. The fire was dead in the cold empty grate and without any kind of light, they would not be able to navigate the house without alerting either Mary or Matthias.

Wishing fervently for her flashlight, Olivia had no choice but to use her magic. Opening her clenched fist she allowed one of her fiery dragonflies to burst into flame. Smaller than her usual ones it danced over her shoulder keeping low and discreet, casting a muted light for them to see a few feet ahead of them, but it was enough. It would have to be, she couldn't risk any more. Especially not here, not now...not in Salem.

Keeping Olivia's hand firmly in his, Theo crept quietly across the room toward the stairway leading up. Uncertain what they were walking into, his heart started pounding in his chest. It seemed so loud to him he was afraid the others could hear it. He felt the dryness of his mouth and the old familiar fear, a remnant of his childhood.

He climbed the stairs slowly, a slow curl of dread unfurling in his stomach. His father was up there, and for one brief moment he was that scared boy once again. The hairs on the back of his neck stood on end and he could feel the panic clawing its way through his chest.

Even as he clenched his hands to still the trembling, he felt Olivia's smaller hand in his, damp from the rain, yet warm and comforting. She squeezed back, a tangible reminder that he was not that little boy anymore and that Matthias was no more than a sick old man.

The first room he came to was one he knew very well; the one both he and his brother and sister knew to avoid at all costs. His father's room. Even now, he could hear the loud even snores coming from the door, which stood slightly ajar. Forcing down the sudden jolt of panic he swallowed convulsively and grasped Olivia's hand tighter as if to remind himself that she was real, that he wasn't the boy or even the young man that he had been. His heart pounded as he reached out toward the door with shaky hands.

Matthias Beckett was snoring, the distinct symphony of the seriously inebriated. It was obvious that he was out for the count and that they could have quite easily crept past his room, bypassing him completely, but something stopped Theo. It was almost as if he had something to prove to himself. He had to know that this man, the one who had terrified him for most of his life, no longer held any power over him. It was a personal demon, one he knew deep in his heart he had to face or he would always wonder if the monster from his memory really matched up to the man of flesh and blood.

As if understanding that a part of him needed this, Olivia let go of Theo's hand and stepped back. He glanced down at her, her beautiful face bathed in the firelight of her magic dragonfly, her deep whiskey colored eyes regarding him seriously. She nodded slowly, encouraging him to take that final step and lay a ghost of his past to rest once and for all.

Steeling himself, Theo turned and quietly pushed the door open. The golden light behind him spilled softly into the room, which reeked of stale sweat, cheap spirits and urine. Theo stepped further into the room, his gaze fixed on the prone figure slumped across the bed, one muddied boot resting on the floor and the other smearing more filth on the already grotesquely soiled bedding. A loud gurgling snore reverberated through the small room, masking Theo's steady footsteps, until finally he stopped, forcing himself to look down upon the man who had once terrified him beyond all reason.

He didn't know what he had expected to feel in that moment, perhaps hate or uncontrollable rage? Resentment or maybe even a small lingering curl of fear?

But instead he felt nothing. He looked down on the man he'd built up in his mind, the man he'd remembered as being so tall and powerful and evil. But that was not the man lying on the bed before him, thin, emaciated and stinking, passed out drunk and clinging onto an empty bottle like a lost lover, a thin trickle of vomit drooling down from his slack rubbery lips.

His eyes were sunken and dark, and his skin waxy and unpleasant looking. He looked so small and pathetic. Theo found that he couldn't dredge up even the slightest bit of fear, nor pity. Mathias Beckett's face and body now reflected back the ugliness he'd concealed on the inside for so long. He would not live long now.

Theo glanced down at him, he was not part of this man. He was not fated to walk the same path, a secret fear he'd always had deep inside him. A fear he'd never even admitted to himself. But now he knew the truth, James was his father. This pathetic creature sprawled out in front of him was nothing, less than nothing, and it was oddly liberating.

He felt a soft tender squeeze at his arm and he glanced down to find Olivia standing next to him, her eyes filled with understanding. Her grip slid down his forearm entwining her fingers with his own. Theo smiled down at her and nodded. There was nothing left in this room for him now, he was done. They both crept out and pulled the door behind them. Sam's eyes locked on Theo's, as if he too understood the inner demon Theo needed to lay to rest.

They started off again, down the narrow passageway. A dim light spilled out from an open doorway further along and as they neared it they could hear the sound of someone pacing the room. Closer still and an agitated muttering joined the shuffling footsteps. Olivia pulled her dragonfly back in, watching as it disappeared back into her outstretched palm, a soft muted glow beneath her skin. She couldn't risk anyone seeing it and the room they were heading for seemed to be lit anyway. There was only one problem.

Mary.

As they neared the room, they could hear her muttering to herself, random phrases, which made no sense and were punctuated every so often by a harsh wracking cough. Olivia glanced up at Theo and he inclined his head as if to confirm her suspicions. Mary was in Temperance's room. Her heart sank. If they wanted to get to the little girl they were going to have to go through Theo's mentally unstable wife. This was not going well. If Mary created a scene, it might wake Matthias and then they'd have to deal with them both.

'We need a distraction,' Olivia mouthed to both Theo and Sam.

Sam nodded and disappeared back down the dark passageway. A few moments later they heard a crash downstairs. Theo grabbed Olivia, pulling her past the door to the room and pressing them both into the shadows. Mary suddenly appeared at the door and Olivia had to bite back a startled scream. The woman looked like something from a horror movie. Her hair was matted and dirty, and she wore a long, severe looking, high necked white nightgown, which revealed dirty feet and overgrown gnarled toenails. Her skin was so white it was like chalk and her blue eyes were wide and wild.

Her gaze darted back and forth, as she tried to accustom her eyes to the darkness after the lamp light of the room. A loud snore from down the passageway caught her attention and she hurried from the room, her hands flicking absently at her nightgown, as if she were trying to brush away something that only she could see.

She disappeared into the darkness and seeing their opportunity Olivia and Theo slipped into the room. Temperance was lying on the bed, heaped with dozens of blankets which were almost smothering her. Olivia rushed to her side and could just about make out the tiny pale face beneath the mountain of bedding.

Reaching out to touch her forehead she swore inwardly, the child was burning up. She began to strip off the blankets covering her. It was almost as if, despite her madness, Mary was trying to help Temperance by keeping her warm, but she was only making it worse.

'Tempy,' Theo whispered shaking her urgently.

Temperance let loose another hacking cough, followed by a distressing wheeze.

Suddenly Olivia felt herself being yanked violently back by the hood of her cloak and dragged across the floor. She looked up, struggling to release the clasp of her cloak, which was biting unmercifully into her neck and cutting off her oxygen. Mary hovered above her shrieking wildly, her mouth snarling, revealing brown dirty teeth.

'MARY NO!' Theo reached for her, roughly pulling her off Olivia, who rolled over and coughed, dragging air back into her lungs.

Mary shrieked like a harpy, twisting in Theo's arms as she viciously clawed down the side of his face, drawing blood. He lost his grip on her for a moment and she started back toward Olivia. He rushed forward and grabbed her from behind, hauling her back against his body and pinning her arms to her sides, as she hissed and snapped, trying to bite him.

Olivia glanced across to the bed, which had suddenly begun to shake and bang against the floor. Temperance was convulsing on the bed, her eyes rolling back in her head and her body stiffening with a seizure. Olivia climbed to her feet, rushing to the bed.

There was no time left. Temperance's fever was too high and causing her to have a fit. It was now or never. No longer caring about waking Matthias or what Mary would witness, she opened her mouth and screamed.

'SAM!'

He materialized out of thin air next to the bed and looked down at the seizing child. Reaching down he scooped her into his arms. Mary let loose a scream and threw her head back, connecting with Theo's nose and causing his eyes to tear, forcing him to momentarily loosen his grip. She shoved him back and he lost his balance, stumbling to the floor.

Her wild, mad eyes locked on Sam cradling Temperance's now limp body. She grabbed the lamp perched on a chest next to the bed and launched it at them both. By the time it reached the other side of the room it was too late, Sam and the sick girl had both disappeared. The lamp hit the wall and exploded, spraying burning oil across the floor and bed. The flames quickly took hold and began to spread.

Mary saw the flames and screamed in murderous rage, fleeing the room. Smoke began to fill the room as Olivia crawled across the floor toward Theo.

'Theo,' she croaked.

'I'm here,' she heard his voice and felt herself being hauled to her feet. 'Come on, we have to get out of here.'

They stumbled out into the passageway, the flames licking at their backs and consuming the doorway. Theo grabbed Olivia's hand and together they ran back down the darkened corridor. As they passed by Matthias' room Theo suddenly paused and looked back toward the flames. After a brief internal struggle, he swore then turned, kicking open the door to the room. He darted inside as smoke began to fill the passageway.

'Theo!' Olivia called to him, trying to see what was going on, her eyes burning from the smoke as she coughed and tried to cover her mouth.

'Keep going Olivia,' he appeared with an unconscious figure draped over his shoulder.

He descended the narrow stairs with Olivia following closely behind him. They hit the bottom step and made their way back across the dark main room toward the door, which had crashed open in the violent wind.

Theo disappeared out into the storm, but as Olivia moved to follow him, she felt a body crash into her, dragging her to the ground. Disorientated, she tried to stand, but someone grasped the back of her head and slammed it against the hard wooden floor. Stars burst behind her eyelids and pain erupted across her forehead.

She was vaguely aware of a trickle of warmth spilling down her face. Groggy and confused, she struggled to rise and merely succeeded in rolling onto her back, but she was not alone. Mary climbed on top of her, pinning her to the ground and wrapping her claw like hands around her throat, squeezing viciously. Olivia clutched at Mary's hands as her air supply was once again cut off, but the woman's grip was too damn strong.

Letting go of Mary's hands, knowing that she wouldn't be able to prize her loose, Olivia reached out pressing her fingers to Mary's forehead.

'Sleep,' she croaked.

The effect was instantaneous, much as it had been with James. Mary's eyes rolled back in her head, her fingers loosened around Olivia's neck and she collapsed on top of her, crushing her chest. Using the little strength she had left, Olivia dragged in a deep lungful of much needed air and pushed the dead weight off her body. Mary rolled unconscious to the floor as Theo rushed back in.

'Olivia!' he rushed to her side. 'I'm so sorry, I thought you were right behind me.'

'I was,' she coughed, 'until your wife tackled me like a god damn linebacker.'

'Are you okay?' he lifted her to her feet.

'I'm alright,' Olivia nodded at the unconscious woman. 'Grab her, we can't leave her in here until I've dealt with the fire.'

Theo nodded, scooping Mary up and slinging her over his shoulder as he had with Matthias. This time, he waited for Olivia to leave the house first and then he followed her out into the rain.

    James groaned and rolled over. His head throbbed painfully and for a moment he was back at that moment in time after Emmy's death, when he'd crawled to the bottom of a bottle and stayed there for three years. His body felt heavy and slightly shaky as he gingerly pushed himself upright. His head spun and his vision swam in and out of focus. Pulling in a deep breath, he stood and grasped onto the fireplace, closing his eyes and waiting for the spinning to stop. When he finally regained his equilibrium he opened his eyes and glanced around the room. The fire had banked low and barely cast any light into the now darkened room. The storm still howled outside and he realized he was alone. He wasn't entirely sure what had happened. One moment he was arguing with Olivia about Temperance…

    Suddenly it all came rushing back to him. He started toward the door, yanking it open so violently he heard the hinges groan and splinter slightly. He glanced out, squinting into the driving rain, and realized the horses were gone. Swearing softly to himself, he ran out into the rain, knowing it would take him twice as long to reach the Beckett place without his horse. Undeterred he set off. No matter what happened or how long it took him, he was going to help his children, whatever it took.

    Olivia turned and watched, as Theo placed Mary down next to Matthias under the small lean-to where the firewood was kept neatly stacked. She backed up across the open space in front of the house and looked up until she could see the flames licking up the side of the building.

    Stretching her arms out she opened her mind, searching out the heat and flames of the fire. She closed her eyes so she could focus easier. In the driving rain she could hardly see anything, so she would have to rely on her other senses. Feeling the cold rain stinging the tender skin of her face and washing away the sickly smoke she tried to clear her mind, once again reaching out toward the fire, which was beginning to burn out of control. She could see the gold and red strands of the flames wild and untamable, as beautiful as they were deadly, but she did not fear it. The fire was hers, it would never harm her.

A quiet, dreamy kind of lassitude fell over her as she grasped onto the flames, soothing them as she would a fractious child until they slowly began to bank down. With the rain and her own control of the flames, the fire finally smothered itself and petered out. Part of the roof had gone and there was nothing left of Temperance's room but a charred out blackened hollow. The rest of the house remained intact though.

Breathing heavily, Olivia glanced up at the house in satisfaction. They'd done it. Mary and Matthias were alive, the house largely remained standing and Sam had taken Temperance. She just hoped that they had made it to present day Mercy safely.

'Well, well, well,' a cold voice spoke from behind her. 'Now there is something you don't see every day.'

Olivia spun around in the direction of that chillingly familiar voice.

'Nathaniel,' she hissed and without thinking she drew her hands apart and her bow burst into blue black flames of pure Hell fire.

'Interesting,' his eyes widened as he beheld the fiery bow she wielded. 'Now you really have my attention.'

Olivia swore under her breath. She should have stopped and thought, not just reacted, but now she had Nathaniel in all his demon glory standing in front of her, and he knew she had power.

She felt Theo step in beside her and watched him from the corner of her eye. His jaw was set in a grim determined line and as he raised his hand, the molten metal set deep into his skin melted, running down his arm to coalesce in his palm. It didn't form the knife Olivia had originally transformed for him, but instead became the sword Hades had adapted, and this time, as it met the sure grip of his fist, the blue black blade burst into flames, rippling in the rain with a fusion of sapphire Hellfire and cool silver Spirit fire.

'Nathaniel,' Theo ground from between his teeth, 'walk away. This does not concern you.'

Theo would have loved nothing more than to split the smirking demon in half like a corn husk, but he had to remind himself this was not the rotting misshapen creature Isabel West had trailing after her, but Nathaniel in his true form. Theo was not entirely confident that their weapons would actually make a difference. At this point the best they could possibly hope for was to distract him long enough to escape.

'Theodore Beckett isn't it?' His black oily eyes narrowed as he tried to place Theo's face. He glanced briefly at the Beckett house behind him. 'I don't know the woman though…yet…her I'm very interested in.'

Theo growled, stepping partially in front of Olivia, as if to shield her from him.

'I mean it Nathaniel,' he warned ominously. 'You don't want to fight us.'

Nathaniel eyes suddenly widened and he looked at them both in surprise, as if only just realizing something.

'You don't belong here,' he spoke slowly. 'You don't belong in this time frame.'

His mouth curved into a cold gleeful smile.

'I am going to enjoy learning your secrets,' his fingers flexed unpleasantly as he took a step closer.

Olivia's eyes narrowed as she took aim, releasing her grip and letting loose a bolt of pure black fire from her flaming bow. It streaked through the streaming rain and hit its target with a sickening thud, knocking Nathaniel back several paces as he skidded through the slimy mud. Regaining his balance he looked down at the smoking burn dead center of his chest, then raised his head again, his face splitting into a feral grin.

'Itches a bit,' he replied coldly.

As he charged toward Olivia, Theo spun her around behind him and lunged forward, running Nathaniel through with his sword. The blade appeared protruding from his back and he let out an animalistic cry of rage and pain. The flames of the sword licked through his wound, filling the stormy air with the sickening stench of burning flesh. Nathaniel gripped Theo's arms and threw him back. Losing his footing on the slippery waterlogged mud Theo rolled to the ground, sliding a few feet away.

James hurried through the trees toward the outskirts of the Beckett property. He could see figures close to the house and he quickened his pace, praying that he was not too late. He bypassed his horses tethered nearby to a tree and headed toward the boundary.

Nathaniel grasped Olivia by the throat hauling her so close to his body she could smell his fetid breath.

'What are you?' he growled. Flecks of bloodied spittle appeared at the corners of his mouth. 'How is it you can call the ancient fire?'

Olivia struggled against his death like grip, clawing at his hands to try and get loose. He wasn't holding her tight enough to cut off her oxygen, just enough to cause her pain and prevent her from escaping.

'How is it you came to be here in this time?'

Lightning lit up the sky and he caught a glimpse of something shiny at her throat, partially concealed beneath the open collar of her dress. He hooked his cold finger beneath the chain and withdrew the compass, his eyes widening in pure shock. His fist closed around the compass and he held it up to her face.

'Where did you get this?' he demanded.

Olivia tried to speak, but all she could manage was a croak as his fist tightened on her throat in fury.

'THIS BELONGS TO MY BROTHER! WHERE DID YOU GET IT?' he roared.

Olivia's scrambled at him weakly, trying to get him to release her throat. In his incandescent rage, he didn't seem to realize he wouldn't be able to get an answer out of her if he choked the life from her. A glint of light reflecting off the dark shiny metal of a blade cut across her vision and the pressure on her throat was suddenly released.

She fell to the ground sliding through the mud and gasping for air. A shrill scream split the air and as she looked up she saw Nathaniel throw Theo to the ground before stumbling backward himself, clutching the stump of his arm, which had been severed at the elbow and was now gushing thick black blood.

Olivia glanced across at the discarded limb lying beside her in the mud. Resisting a shudder of revulsion, she peeled back the limp fingers and pulled the compass free. She could feel it pulsing in her hand, the lid flipped open and as she saw the hand spinning wildly she knew what she had to do. Her heart pounded wildly in her chest and her breath came in short adrenalin filled gasps.

Nathaniel's furious pain filled eyes locked on hers and he peeled back his lips in a hate filled snarl. He started toward her, lurching unsteadily. Olivia dug into the mud hauling herself across the soaked ground toward Theo.

She reached him and grabbed on tightly, squeezing her eyes shut. Her grip tightened around the compass, so hard it bit into the soft flesh of her palm. She felt it burn white hot against her skin, heard Nathaniel's wrenching cry of denial and suddenly everything around them shifted and blurred.

They lay on the ground, not moving, watching as the space around them went light, then dark, and then repeated itself over and over again. It was almost as if they remained constant, in the same space but time had sped up, passing through endless rotations of day and night around them and all they could do was hold onto each other and hope they ended up in the right time.

Nathaniel raised his face to the sky and howled in outrage as Olivia and Theo disappeared before his eyes. He looked down at the stump of his arm, raising it in front of him. The bleeding had slowed to an unpleasant ooze and before his eyes the limb started to elongate and stretch. The bud appearing at the end split into five and continued to grow until he had a completely new arm. He flexed the fingers experimentally a few times and bent it at the elbow.

Satisfied it was as good as the original, he glanced down to the ground where his discarded limb bubbled and decomposed, disappearing into the mud. Steeling himself and reining in his fury, he glanced back at the Beckett house. His black eyes were cold and his mouth thinned into a bitter line. He would be keeping an extremely close eye on the Beckett family from this moment on.

James pressed himself back against the tree out of sight, his heart beating wildly and his eyes wide in disbelief. Had he really just seen the young cleric Nathaniel grow back a severed limb? He couldn't believe it, he'd known there was something not right about him, but he had no idea…

There was no way to get into the house now, not with Nathaniel so close. He now understood what Olivia had been trying to tell him about being exposed. Olivia and Theo were gone, so he swallowed hard and ruthlessly smothered his pain. He looked up at the Beckett house and saw the fire damage to the structure just as they'd described. He could only hope and pray that they had gotten Temperance out in time.

Sneaking back through the trees, he untied the horses and set off back toward his house. He couldn't let Nathaniel suspect him of complicity. Olivia and Theo may be gone, hopefully having jumped successfully through time, so now he was going to have to wait and protect their secret at all costs.

12.

Mercy Medical Center
December 1983

Harriet leaned over the nurses station, her gaze running over the doctors' notes she'd been handed and sighed. There was no way she was getting out on time. She glanced up at the clock and frowned. Her shift ended five minutes ago, but she still needed to dress a wound, check another patient's stats, restock the exam rooms and all while trying to cover the front desk, as the temporary desk clerk seemed to have disappeared with her boyfriend again.

'Harry,' another nurse shot past her, 'we need a bedpan for the patient in 2.'

'Why can't you get it?' she called after her retreating form.'

Damn it, she swore under her breath. It was always crazy around the holidays, but despite the fact that everyone seemed to be trying to poison themselves with bad eggnog, falling off ladders or trying to electrocute themselves with fairy lights, it was usually fun. However right now, she was having a lot of trouble finding her Christmas spirit. Half the staff were out sick with the flu and they were desperately understaffed. She glanced back at the clock, sighing again, there was no way she was going to make her date in time.

She glanced across at the huge gaudy tree Dougie, the maintenance guy, had dumped unceremoniously down in the middle of the ER. It was slightly wonky, a bit bald on one side and covered with so many decorations and angel hair, it was like Santa had just vomited up Christmas all over it. Still, a small amused smile crept across her face, the damn thing was so ugly it was kinda cute.

She shook her head and turned toward the small radio sitting on the nurses' station. Kim Carnes voice was once again filling the air. It wasn't that she minded her singing about Bette Davis' eyes, but to tell the truth she was getting slightly sick of hearing it on repeat. Reaching for the dial, she turned it to a different station picking up the upbeat sound of Olivia Newton John getting physical, which to be honest wasn't much better. Twisting it again she finally settled on John Lennon and Yoko Ono's Merry Christmas (War is over) a song which may have been over ten years old, but she still loved it. It was a song which never failed to make her feel Christmassy and yet humble at the same time. Lost in the song and humming happily to herself she jolted at the sudden voice behind her. Turning her head she saw her friend Joelynn and offered her a tired frustrated smile.

'I see Hazel has done a disappearing act again.'

'Her boyfriend turned up with a limp sprig of mistletoe and a bad apology and I haven't seen them for the last hour,' she rolled her eyes.

'Eeew, the girl has no class. It'd take a lot more than that to win me back if I'd caught my man gambling my rent money on a poker game.'

Harriet's eyes narrowed as she studied her friend carefully. 'What have you done to your hair?'

'Do you like it?' Joelynn fluffed her hair, the ends had been dyed a bright almost white blonde leaving the roots still her dark natural colour. She'd also scrunched it into wild curls and tied it back from her face with a length of thin lace.

Harriet's gaze continued on, taking in the rather large crucifix's dangling from her ears to the dozens of black rubber bracelets at her wrists.

'You do know you're not Madonna, don't you?'

'You can talk,' Joelynn smirked. 'What's with the Brooke Shields?'

Harriet's hand automatically went to the large barrel curls and flicks of her soft shoulder length brown hair.

'I had a date,' she frowned.

'Had?' she raised once dark eyebrow.

'I'm not going to be able to make it now.'

'With who?'

'Johnny finally asked me out,' she smiled shyly.

'Johnny? As in John Gilbert?' Joelynn's eyebrows shot up. 'He's cute.'

'I know,' Harriet sighed.

'Harry,' Joelynn spoke softly, 'go on your date. I'll cover for you.'

'But your shift doesn't start for another hour.'

'And yours ended ten minutes ago. Just because they're short staffed and you're here, doesn't mean you have to pick up everyone else's slack. Besides, I'm here now so I may as well start,' she shrugged out of her coat and hooked it over one arm, smoothing down her white nurses' uniform.

'Are you sure?'

'Please,' she rolled her eyes, 'you've been making eyes at John Gilbert for the last six months. If the guy finally plucked up the courage to ask you out, you can't stand him up.'

'You're the best,' Harriet threw her arms around her friend and squeezed hard.

'Yeah, yeah, I know,' she grinned. 'Just make sure you name your first child after me.'

'But you hate your name.'

'Fine,' she conceded, 'you can use my middle name instead.'

'Which is what?'

'Louisa,' she replied.

'Actually that's a really pretty name.'

Joelynn started laughing.

'God,' Harriet rolled her eyes. 'I can't believe we're talking about baby names, we haven't even gone on a first date yet.'

'And you won't if you don't hurry,' Joelynn shooed her along, 'you still need to change out of your uniform yet.'

'Okay, okay,' she laughed as she skirted around the nurses' station and headed for the locker room.

But as she crossed the waiting area, a strange flicker caught the corner of her eye. As she turned to look more fully, a very young looking, dark haired man suddenly appeared, cradling a small child. Harriet frowned in confusion, she could've sworn he hadn't been standing there a moment ago.

'Sir?' she saw him stumble, 'Sir, are you alright?'

'Help her,' he croaked, stumbling forward into Harriet. 'Help her.'

He pushed the young girl into her arms. The action, combined with the sudden weight of the child, had her dropping to her knees and when she looked up the man was gone.

Ignoring him, she turned her attention back to the small girl. She looked to be not much more than eight or nine years old. She was dressed only in a thin, long white nightgown, which was clammy and damp with sweat. She was burning up. Harriet could feel the heat of the girl's body through her nightgown and her breathing was labored.

'HELP!' she called out, 'SOMEBODY HELP!'

Joelynn rushed to her side as she grasped the tiny

child carefully and lifted her, heading for one of the empty exam rooms, with her friend hurrying along behind her.

'Find Doctor Hughes now!' Harriet told her. 'She can't breathe.'

She laid the child down on the crisp white bed as Joelynn darted from the room.

Temperance opened her eyes slowly, blinking against the muted light. Everything looked fuzzy and out of focus. She tried to swallow, but her throat was so painful, it was like she had swallowed a pincushion full of needles. She shut her eyes against the throb and sway in her head, taking a deep breath. It was only then she realized she could breathe easily. It no longer felt as if a large slab of stone was pressing down upon her chest. She sucked in a deep lungful of air, which no longer triggered a painful bout of coughing.

She opened her eyes again and slowly the room began to swim into focus. Her brow folded in confusion and her eyes widened. This time when she sucked in a breath it was in panic and fear. She pulled herself up the firm bed and glanced around.

The room was very strange, it was so bright. The walls were painted a crisp cold winter white and a large window dominated one wall. She looked down at her body noticing she was dressed in a clean nightgown, which was pale yellow and scattered with pictures of tiny daises. The bedding covering her was also the same bright white as the walls and folded neatly over a pale pink blanket. There was a table by the end of the bed and on it stood a pretty pot with flowers in it.

She managed to keep her fear and panic under control somewhat, that was until she tried to sit herself up but as she moved her arm it felt strange and uncomfortable.

Looking down, she noticed something long and thin sticking out of the flesh of her arm. Her mouth fell open, but before she could let loose a horrified scream a larger hand clamped over her mouth. She began to struggle, her wide terrified eyes turning to the intruder, but realizing that she knew him she stopped struggling.

'Shush Temperance it's alright. I know you are very frightened right now and that all this seems very strange, but I have things that I must tell you and I don't have much time before we are discovered. Now I am going to remove my hand and I need you to promise you won't scream, okay?'

Silently the small girl nodded, and he slowly pulled his hand back from her mouth.

'Sam?' she croaked, frowning suddenly. Her voice sounded very strange to her own ears, almost as if it didn't belong to her.

'It's alright,' he replied, 'don't try to talk, rest your voice. You've been very sick and they had to keep you asleep for a while and put a tube into your throat to help you breathe.'

'How long?' she mouthed.

'You've been here nearly two weeks now.'

'Where am I?' she whispered hoarsely. 'Where's my brother and Olivia?'

'They are still in Salem,' he frowned shaking his head. 'You need to listen to me very carefully now Temperance. Everything you have ever known is about to change. You are no longer in Salem and the year is not 1685. You are in a town called Mercy and I have brought you over three hundred years' forward into the future. It's going to take a while for you to adapt to your new home, so the less you say the better. You can't tell anyone where or when you are from.'

'I want to go home,' she whispered as her dark eyes filled with tears.

'I know,' he took her tiny hand gently, 'but trust me, there is nothing left there for you. Olivia and Theo are going to join you; they don't belong in the past any more than you do, but they have something they have to do before they can come back, something very important.'

'When will I see them?'

'Not for a long while,' he shook his head sadly. 'I'm so sorry Temperance, I tried to get you as close to their time as possible, but this is the first time I've jumped time and I'm still weakened from my illness. I was aiming for the 21st century but we've ended up in 1983, well '84 now, judging by the New Year's hangovers out there at the nurses' station.'

Temperance looked at him blankly.

'Look, you won't understand everything that is going on right now, but these are good people and they will take care of you while you wait for Theo and Olivia. I don't have the strength to jump you through time so you're going to have to stay here for the moment.'

'You,' she mouthed as her voice began to fail again.

'I can't stay,' he breathed heavily, 'I'm very sick Temperance, I have to go home.'

Her eyes narrowed as she studied him thoughtfully. He was right he did look sick. His skin was a pale clammy grey, his eyes betrayed pain and fatigue he was desperately trying to mask and his hands, even as he gripped hers trying to offer her some measure of comfort, were damp and trembling.

'Will you come back for me?'

'One day I hope,' he replied tightly. 'Listen, there are only a couple of things you need to know. Keep your mouth shut, watch and learn. Soon you will learn how to blend in. Secondly, don't tell anyone your real name, we need to keep you safe, keep you hidden. Do you understand?'

She nodded slowly.

'I have to go now,' he whispered urgently when they both heard hushed voices outside her room.

He dropped a kiss on her forehead as the door

opened and a man in a white coat walked in, holding some sort of rectangular object. Temperance looked back, but Sam had already disappeared.

'Ah good, you're awake,' Doctor Hughes glanced down at the chart in his hands. Pushing his spectacles back up his nose he perused her notes, 'well everything is looking good here.'

He took a seat, perching on the edge of her bed as he placed a cool professional hand on her forehead.

'You gave us quite a scare there young lady,' he smiled down at her kindly. 'You've been suffering from acute Pneumonia with a secondary bronchial infection, a nasty one at that. It was touch and go there for a while. How are you feeling?'

She opened her mouth to try and speak, but as she swallowed past the sharp pain, she closed it again and simply nodded instead.

'Throat hurting a bit I should imagine?'

She nodded again.

'Don't worry sweetheart that will pass,' he reached over to the small locker next to the bed and poured a glass of water from a small plastic pitcher. 'Here take a small sip, not too much yet.'

Temperance lifted her head as he brought the cup to her lips. Taking a small sip as he suggested, the cool liquid soothing her ragged throat slightly.

'Now young lady,' he picked up his clipboard once again, his expression slightly more serious. 'We have been unable to locate the young man who brought you in, nor have we been able to ascertain your identity and contact your family. Can you tell me your name?'

'Tempy,' she tried to reply, but her voice croaked and failed her again, leaving her to partially mouth the word.

'Tammy?' he repeated, scribbling it down on her chart.

She opened her mouth to correct him but shut it

again abruptly, as Sam's warning came flooding back to her. She couldn't tell him who she was, even if he did seem like a kind man.

'Your last name?' he prompted.

She stared at him silently.

'How about your family, can you tell me who they are?' he continued gently. 'Your mother? Father?'

Temperance shook her head mutely.

'It's okay,' he patted her hand sympathetically.

'Knock knock,' a cheerful voice called from the other side of the door accompanied by an actual knock.

The door swung open cautiously and a friendly face surrounded by a mop of permed hair, appeared.

'Is it alright to come in?'

'Yes, yes, by all means,' Doctor Hughes smiled.

The door opened wider and the smiling lady walked in, followed by a taller man with salt and pepper hair and a bushy greying mustache.

'Tammy,' Doctor Hughes turned toward Temperance with a reassuring smile on his face, 'this is Susan and Ed Burnett, they are foster parents. If it's alright with you, once we're satisfied you are fit enough, they're going to take you home with them until we can trace your family or make other arrangements.'

'Hello Tammy,' Susan took a small hesitant step toward the bed, 'Ed and I are very much looking forward to getting to know you, we're very happy to take you home with us. Is that okay with you?'

Tempy shrugged, sliding further down into bed and turning on her side away from them. It didn't really matter what she wanted. She was stuck in this strange place, with all these strange people and she couldn't even tell them her real name. She squeezed her eyes shut as she felt Doctor Hughes weight lift off the bed and begin to speak in a hushed tone with the Burnetts.

The tears burned behind her closed eyelids as she swallowed past the hot ball of misery and grief in her throat. Was it alright, they'd asked her. Well the answer was no…nothing would ever be alright again.

Part 2.
1695

13.

Isabel West's gaze narrowed shrewdly as she focused on the thin curl of smoke snaking up from the chimney of the small wooden cabin, nestled among the trees. The light was dying, the sky already bleeding into a vibrant pink bruised with violent purple slashes. There was a slight bite to the air, which was filled with the promise of autumn, and a light scent of musky damp moss that carried on the breeze. A mad rush of orange, russet and gold leaves tumbled across the floor of the forest, rustling in the wind and washing over Isabel's heeled boots.

The cabin itself was small and squat, probably only one room. It was solidly constructed of rough-hewn logs, the pitched roof was punctuated with a small ramshackle chimney, which leaned alarmingly in the wind and looked as if either magic or blind luck were holding it together. A wide overhang was pitched over the front of the cabin and could be loosely described as a porch, a rather poorly constructed one at that.

Isabel turned her attention back to her companion, who was glowering at her back, so fiercely she could feel the waves of hatred prickling her skin like needles.

Turning around more fully, she faced him. Her eyes were no longer the deep aged whiskey color of all the West women, but now burned a bright unusual lavender hue, thanks to the deal she'd made at the Crossroads. She ran them over his misshapen form as Nathaniel glared up at her with venom burning through his expression. His decaying fleshy body was stitched up so tightly with magic, to stop him from escaping, that he could now no longer stand up straight and instead had the shortened, crooked posture of a hunchback. A heavy black cloak covered the worst of his damaged body, but could not in any way disguise his awful face.

When Isabel had originally raised him from the devils' trap back in Mercy, she'd forced him into a body of human flesh, which she'd pieced together with body parts from several young men that she'd murdered with the express purpose of creating his custom built prison.

What she hadn't accounted for was the body degrading so quickly, and she'd been forced to stitch him back together with some pretty strong magic, to keep him under control and to prevent him from escaping. Unfortunately she could do nothing about the decomposing flesh, nor the God awful stench of death and decay which followed in his wake.

She looked down at him in distaste. His face had always resembled Frankenstein's monster, with his mishmash of features awkwardly stitched together. Now however, his eyes had turned a gruesome milky white and his mouth was sewn shut with large black clumsy stitches, the kind a child would produce when first learning to sew.

'Something you wanted to say to me Nathaniel?' she taunted, raising one slender sculpted brow.

His hand curled into enraged claws. She was sure he would have peeled back his lips in an animal like snarl, if she hadn't sewn them together to prevent him from speaking. However a deep gurgling growl did bubble in his throat and he launched himself toward her, hands outstretched, as if he was not sure whether he wanted to scratch her eyes out or wrap his fingers around her pale slender throat and choke the life from her.

She laughed derisively when he collided with an invisible barrier and was pushed back a good few paces.

'You still can't harm me Nathaniel,' she smiled coolly, 'no matter how many times you try.'

His eyes burned with malice.

'You are beginning to try my patience,' she warned him dangerously. 'I'll only keep you with me for as long as you are useful and it suits my purpose. If you continue to be counterproductive, I won't just leave your foul mouth shut, I will sew up your eyes and your ears, and drop you back into that pit of a devil's trap. There you will remain for eternity, deaf, blind, mute and sealed in a coffin of rotting human flesh.'

Nathaniel's fists clenched furiously and for a second his damaged hate-filled eyes held her cool gaze, before he finally looked away.

'That's better.'

She glanced down at her clothes. She was still wearing her fitted black slacks and a soft silky sapphire colored shirt, along with her heeled polished leather boots. That just wouldn't do, she needed to blend in to gain her ancestors' trust and right now she stuck out like a sore thumb.

Pursing her lips thoughtfully for a moment, she raised her hands covering her face. Her palms swept over her face and hair and trailed down her body, her form blurred in their wake, and when she was done she was no longer wearing her 21st century clothes.

She now wore a dark grey cloak and a long deep blue dress over her petticoats, woolen stockings and leather shoes. Her dark hair was tucked under a neat, close fitting coif. She briefly ran her fingertips over her cheekbone and up to her temple. The vicious looking burn scar she'd had since that long ago night in Mercy, when she'd faked her death and disappeared, was no longer there, another gift from the Crossroad.

'So much better,' she murmured, glancing down at

her body to check everything was in order. Then she looked down at her new attire once again, pressing her finger to her lips. It still didn't look right. It was a little too new, too respectable.

In order to gain the sympathy and trust of Hester, her twin sister Bridget and their mother, she needed to look a little more vulnerable, a little more desperate. Stroking her hands down the roughened fabric of her dress, she watched as it aged beneath her touch, appearing more tattered and worn. Smoothing her fingers along the line of her jaw a deep, dark, angry bruise appeared.

'Perfect,' she thought to herself.

She shrugged into her disguise a couple of times, satisfied the glamour spell was firmly in place. She silently marveled at how effortless it was to conjure and maintain. A glamour spell was one of the easiest charms in a witches' arsenal. As a teenager she'd struggled with it, she hadn't even been able to call forth enough power to add blonde highlights to her dark hair. She felt it now though, the low thrum of power burning through her veins, and it was heady and intoxicating.

She was so close now, so close to claiming the book that was her birthright. Infernum, the Hell book…the book that should have been hers all along. Just as Hester's Grimoire should've passed to her, would have been passed to her if her mother and aunt had not betrayed her, casting her aside in favor of her own daughter Olivia.

Isabel's lip curled in resentment, they should not have been so quick to brush her aside. She may not have had the power of the other West women, but they should not have turned on her.

Once she had the Hell book in her possession, she would take the power her ancestors had been too afraid to use. Then, she thought self-righteously, no one would ever underestimate her again.

She looked up, shaken loose from her thoughts by

the low murmur of voices nearby.

'Nathaniel,' she called him abruptly, 'leave now. I can't have them see you or even sense your presence. I want you to venture into Salem, but carefully. You cannot be seen. Once there you are to locate my daughter. I have no doubt she followed us here from the Crossroad and if you find Olivia, I can guarantee she'll have the Beckett boy with her. I've come too far for them to interfere now.'

He looked at her and she could've sworn she could see a smirk pulling taut the thick blackened stitches at his mouth.

'You are not to harm either of them,' she told him bluntly. 'All you need to do is make sure you keep them well away from this cabin and the West girls. I will deal with my daughter when the time comes.'

Nathaniel continued to stare at her.

'I suggest you don't test my resolve,' she told him coolly. 'Harm a single hair on my daughter's head and you will find yourself back in the devil's trap, while your brother rots in the Underworld.'

His pale eyes flashed and his fists clenched once again.

'Do I make myself clear?'

He nodded tightly.

'Go then, before you are discovered,' she dismissed him callously.

She watched as he disappeared into the forest in the opposite direction to the low chatter of female voices, then she deliberately placed herself in their path and unceremoniously dropped to the ground. Laying still and quiet as a mouse, she waited to be discovered.

Nathaniel stalked furiously through the forest. He wanted to throw his head back and howl out his pain and frustration to the uncaring skies, but he couldn't. That bitch Isabel had seen to that. As if the painful clumpy stitches weren't bad enough, they were sealed with strong magic, making it feel as if his jaws were actually welded together. Even if he could find a knife capable of cutting the stitches, he was certain he still wouldn't be able to speak.

That fucking whore, he hissed to himself in the deep recesses of his mind where she couldn't hear him. He'd underestimated her, she'd played him and he'd paid dearly for that mistake.

Ripped from the Underworld and his allies, only to be thrown back to the stinking, filthy 17th century. It was like being thrown into a giant cesspool of human filth and depravity, all masked with the righteous propaganda of the clergy. He'd not exactly enjoyed it the first time around, but it had amused him. The blatant hypocrisy and sadistic cruelty of the so called men of faith, using their God and his stupid commandments to justify their own perversions. And it had been a perversion. He could smell their arousal, almost taste their excitement, while they had pinched, mutilated, tortured and violated the females they had accused of witchcraft. It would have been pathetic if it hadn't been so amusing.

Still, it didn't mean he had wanted to return to that time. He had a somewhat more refined palette now and an agenda of his own. Isabel may have the upper hand for the moment, but she was delusional if she thought he was just going to roll over and allow her to scratch his belly and toss him a couple of stringy scraps.

He knew she had no intention of using the power of Infernum to break his brother Seth free from his prison in the Underworld. No, he was going to have to re-adjust his plan. Although she didn't realize it yet, Isabel had actually done him a favor. She'd dropped him down in the exact place and time he could find an ally, one whose loyalty he would never question, and that ally was…himself.

His past self was walking the streets of Salem freely and in his true unfettered form. It wouldn't take long for them both to figure out a way to break this disgusting prison of pig flesh Isabel had forced him into. The other version of himself would also be able to help him to summon Zachary, although it would be difficult. After the disaster at the Crossroad, he would imagine his faithful second in command had gone into hiding. He had no doubt that not only would Hades be tearing the Underworld apart brick by ancient brick searching for him, but that if he returned to Hell then he would be trying to stay off Lucifer's radar too.

There was still a chance to salvage this situation though, he just needed to get his hands on that book. Once he had the Hell book in his hands and unlocked its secrets, he would be unstoppable. He would rip that witch whore Isabel to pieces and then he'd do the same to her daughter. Theo he'd take his time with, for all the inconvenience he'd caused him, maybe even make him watch what he did to Olivia.

He repressed a shiver of pleasure at the thought of the pain he would bring to the humans, and that was before he'd even started on the others. He'd raise his brother Seth from his cage and together they would deal with Hades and Lucifer and anyone else foolish enough to stand in their way. They'd tear down the walls of the Hell dimensions, all of them. Hell, Sheol, Tartarus, they would all fall, the carnage spilling out onto the human infested Earth and once the plague of humanity was wiped clean they would climb the mountain of mortal corpses to the gates of Heaven itself and paradise would belong to them.

Now all he had to do was find the past version of himself.

'Hester come on, mama's waiting,' Bridget sighed, as she juggled the pile of twigs and sticks in her arms.

'I'm coming,' Hester hurried to keep up with her twin sister's brisk pace.

'Hurry up, it's going to be dark soon and you

know mama doesn't like us being out after dark.'

'The dark doesn't bother me,' Hester grinned, clutching her own armful of firewood tighter.

'Me neither, but I'd just as soon not make mama cross,' Bridget rolled her eyes. 'Besides, I'm hungry.'

'You're always hungry.'

'Am not,' Bridget frowned.

'You are too, you always have a second helping.'

'It's because I'm growing, mama says so. That's why I'm taller than you.'

It was true, despite the fact the girls were identical in every other way, Bridget was indeed a little taller than her sister.

'Fine,' Hester conceded with a small grin. Bridget was just too easy to tease.

'What's that?' Bridget stopped, her expression wary as her gaze fell on a rumpled heap of material lying amongst the rainbow leaves.

'Come on,' Hester darted forward.

'Hess be careful,' Bridget called out, but it was no good, Hester had already approached the pile of cloth giving Bridget no choice but to follow her impulsive sister.

'It's a lady,' Hester let the sticks she was holding drop to the ground and fell to her knees beside her. 'I think she's hurt.'

'Come away Hess,' she frowned. 'Mama said not to go near strangers.'

'She's not,' Hester murmured.

'Not what?'

'A stranger.'

'What do you mean? Have you seen this woman before?'

'No,' Hester shook her head thoughtfully.

'I don't understand,' Bridget replied.

'I don't either,' Hester turned to her sister. 'Run to the cabin and fetch mama, she'll know what to do.'

'I don't want to leave you.'

'I'll be fine,' Hester replied. 'Hurry though, we're losing the light.'

Torn between leaving her sister on her own with an unconscious stranger, or going to fetch her mother Bridget wavered, her face wrought with indecision.

'Bridey go!' Hester told her firmly.

Unable to resist her sister's command, she darted back into the trees toward their cabin, running as fast as she could. Fortunately it wasn't too far and she could already see it from where they had been standing, but she still had an inexplicable feeling of unease.

Hester watched her sister run back to fetch their mother, but as she disappeared amongst the trees Hester turned her attention back to the woman lying unconscious on the ground. There was something familiar about her, something she couldn't quite put her finger on. She wasn't sure what to think, as so many conflicted emotions crashed in on her.

The woman wasn't a stranger, of that she was certain. However, there was something about her that made the tiny hairs on the back of her neck stand on end. The mysterious lady had power, she could feel it thrumming through the air surrounding them both, and when she leaned forward and tentatively touched the cool pale skin of her cheek, a jolt of energy surged through her fingertips and up her arm.

There was something else that was strange about her, something only she would be able to see. Her gift, as her grandmother had called, was that she was able to see people's 'threads'. The threads of life, her grandma had explained, the long colorful strings that bind all life together. Very few witches could actually see them, but she was one of them. It was like looking at the world through a spider's web of brightly colored yarn. Every person was connected to each other in one way or another, by different colored threads. Except for this woman. Her threads were dull muted colors, not at all the vibrant rainbow colors she was used to. No, this woman's threads were a pale washed out version and they weren't attached to anything. It was like they'd been severed with a huge pair of scissors and lay scattered on the cold hard ground around her.

She didn't trust her, she didn't trust anyone who was adrift, with no ties to anyone or anything, but she couldn't ignore the fact the woman was most likely injured and needed help. Her heart wouldn't allow her to turn away anyone who was in need. She looked up and was glad to see Bridget hurrying back through the trees with their mother in tow.

'Hester love are you alright?' she asked breathlessly as she approached, pulling her shawl tighter around her shoulders against the wind which had now picked up.

'I'm fine mama,' she looked down at the unconscious woman, 'but she's not.'

'Let's see,' she dropped down next to them and laid her hand gently on the woman's forehead. 'There's no fever thankfully.'

The woman stirred with a groan.

'There, there, take it easy,' she soothed in a gentle voice.

She looked down at the woman and felt the same strange jolt of recognition of power, but couldn't quite place it. Maybe it was just like recognizing like, for there was no doubt in her mind the woman lying on the dirty ground was a woman of power, and given everything that had happened in Salem over the past several years, she had a good idea what she had been running from.

'Alright, take it easy love,' she soothed. The woman's eyelids fluttered and opened slowly, and she found herself staring into the deepest pair of lavender colored eyes she'd ever seen. No wonder the woman had been running. With eyes such a beautiful and unusual color she would have been a target for every Witchfinder within a ten-mile radius.

The woman blinked groggily and flinched, as if afraid of the woman and two children leaning over her.

'Shush it's alright, we mean you no harm,' she smiled warmly. 'My name's Abigail, Abigail West and these are my two daughters Hester and Bridget.'

'Is…Isabel,' she swallowed lifting her head weakly, 'my name is Isabel Connell.'

'Well Isabel, can you sit up?'

'I think so,' she replied, shakily pushing herself up into a sitting position. 'I'm sorry, where am I?'

'In the forest, just east of Salem Town,' Abigail replied softly.

'Salem?' her eyes widened fearfully. 'I'm sorry I have to keep moving, I can't let them find me.'

In a panic she started to rise, but was held back by Abigail's firm grip.

'It's alright,' she assured her, 'we're far enough away from the main town. You're safe here.'

'No, I've heard about Salem,' she shook her head. 'I can't stay.'

'You're in no condition to be going anywhere,' she told her firmly. 'When was the last time you ate?'

'I don't…' she shook her head, 'I don't remember. I had to keep moving so they didn't find me.'

'Who?' Hester asked suddenly, 'so who doesn't find you?'

'Hester,' her mother admonished, 'you bite your tongue. Can't you see the poor woman is afraid and we know what that feels like, don't we?'

Hester nodded slowly. Her head may have dropped contritely, but her piercing whiskey eyes continued to watch the strange woman intently.

'Come to the house, won't you?' Abigail offered.

'I don't want to be a bother,' Isabel shook her head.

'Nonsense,' Abigail took her hand and helped her

to her feet. 'It's no bother at all.'

Isabel effected a convincing stumble, causing Abigail to wrap Isabel's arm around her shoulders to steady her.

'Poor thing, you must be exhausted,' she started back toward the house taking most of Isabel's weight as they stumbled across the forest floor toward the cheery little cabin. 'Don't forget the firewood Hester, there's a chill in the air tonight.'

'Yes mama,' Hester replied dutifully, as she stooped to retrieve the sticks she'd dropped earlier.

Once back inside the house Abigail settled Isabel into a chair by the cheerful fire and retrieved a blanket to place over her legs.

'You just sit there for a bit and get some warmth back into your bones.'

'You're too kind,' Isabel's eyes glazed with tears as she blinked to keep them from spilling over.

'It's been a while since anyone has shown you a kindness, isn't it?' Abigail spoke softly, her eyes brimming with sympathy and flickering over the bruise along Isabel's jaw.

'You have no idea,' Isabel breathed heavily.

'Oh I think I have a fairly good idea,' Abigail replied seriously. 'Having to hide what you are.'

'I don't know what you're talking about,' Isabel stiffened.

'Yes you do,' Abigail nodded, 'but it's alright, you don't have to admit anything. Just know that you are with kin and that you are safe.'

Isabel looked up at her, her expression unreadable.

'Well then, time for some supper I think,' Abigail smiled genuinely. 'The girls will be starving by now, they're growing like weeds. Do you have any children Isabel?'

'A daughter, once,' she murmured.

'Once?'

'I lost her,' she replied quietly.

'I'm sorry,' Abigail replied sympathetically. 'There is nothing in this world worse than the loss of a child.'

'I don't know,' Isabel muttered, 'there are some things worse.'

'Life's been hard for you, I can tell,' she answered after a moment, 'but you mustn't let it take you to a dark place.'

Isabel sat watching quietly as Abigail handed her a steaming cup.

'It's tea,' she told her gently, 'made from herbs. It will help you regain your strength and soothe you.'

'Thank you,' she murmured, taking the cup and cradling it in her hands.

Abigail did not speak further for a while, seeming to allow her some time to herself. Isabel sipped her tea, quietly watching as the other woman busied herself preparing a simple meal of vegetable stew and warm fragrant bread.

Taking a moment to glance around the room, she noticed it was indeed one large room. A huge stone fireplace dominated one side of the cabin and alongside it was a small preparation area, where she kept her plates and utensils.

There was a small rough table and benches and in the corner, warming by the fire, were thickly folded wads of material, which she assumed were bedrolls. There were no beds anywhere, which implied the three of them simply slept on the floor in front of the fire at night. Primitive, but cozy.

'Where is the girls' father?' Isabel asked after a moment.

Abigail paused as she lifted a pot of stew from the warming oven, a momentary shadow of pain crossing her features.

'He died two winters past now.'

'I'm sorry,' Isabel murmured.

'It's just me and the girls now,' Abigail carried the

stew to the table and set out the bowls. 'Bridget, Hester you go and wash up now,' she called to them.

'What about you?' Abigail turned her attention back to Isabel.

'What about me?'

'You have a man? A husband?'

'I did once,' she replied quietly, her expression hardening as she unconsciously rubbed her chest. For a moment she was transported back to the house, the fire, the heat. The sensation of the knife sliding into her chest, gripped in both his hands and hers as they struggled. His eyes, she'd never forget his eyes for as long as she lived, the way his gaze locked with hers as the knife tore through her flesh.

'He betrayed me,' she answered finally, 'and stole my daughter.'

'So you are all alone now?' Abigail sighed.

'Something like that.'

'Well not any longer,' Abigail decided. 'You'll stay with us for a while.'

'No,' Isabel shook her head, 'you've been so kind and welcoming, but I couldn't impose on you like that.'

'I insist,' Abigail replied firmly, one hand propped on her hip.

Turning to ladle the stew into the bowls Abigail didn't see the cool calculating look in Isabel's eyes, nor did she see the satisfied smile curving the corner of her mouth.

14.

Light, dark. Light, dark. The strange flickering lights which surrounded them finally began to slow and Olivia could almost see the turning of day to night and back to day again. It was so weird, watching the passing of time, the turn of the seasons, the people who passed by them, so close they could almost reach out and touch them and yet unaware of their existence, because it was like someone had hit the fast forward button.

It was almost dizzying as they lay on the hard ground of the Beckett farm clinging onto each other, filthy, exhausted and covered in mud. The spinning sundial on the compass finally slowed and came to a stop, and so did time. They both looked up to find they were lying on the ground in the middle of the farm and it looked to be about mid-day, judging from the sun's position in the sky.

'Are you okay?' Theo pulled Olivia close checking her for injuries.

'My throat's a bit sore as both your wife and Nathaniel tried to choke the life out of me.'

Theo's expression hardened.

'One of these days I am going to kill him,' he bit out coldly.

'We can only hope,' she murmured.

Theo hauled his protesting muscles off the ground

and pulled Olivia up, gently wrapping his arms around her and burying his face in her hair as if to reassure himself that she was indeed okay.

'Do you think we hit the right time period this time?' Olivia asked looking around. 'You know, for a farm it's awfully quiet around here.'

'You're right,' Theo frowned, glancing around the place he'd once called home. 'Something isn't right.'

'We need to figure out when the hell we are,' Olivia stepped back and glanced up at the house.

The section of the house which had been destroyed by fire that night, had now been demolished and rebuilt. The clapboards covering the exterior of the house were somewhat worn and weather beaten, indicting they'd been gone a fair while since the night of the storm.

'We should go and find James,' Theo told her.

'I hope he's alright,' Olivia replied worriedly. 'If Nathaniel had followed us from the orchard that night, it might lead him to suspect James was involved somehow.'

Theo's heart thudded in his chest. Damn it, she was right. They needed to find out what had happened after they left that night.

'Okay, we head to James' house,' he nodded in agreement.

The unexpected slamming of a door and heavy footsteps suddenly startled them. Theo grabbed Olivia and pulled her in close to the side of the house. In the distance they could see a tall dark haired man in a black coat and breeches striding towards the barn, with some sort of book tucked under his arm.

They both backed up slowly, hoping he didn't see them, but for some reason he suddenly stopped and turned around, glancing in their direction. Theo pulled Olivia down behind the woodpile where they both crouched, almost holding their breath. Unable to control her curiosity Olivia peeked carefully around the neatly cut logs stacked in front of her and her breath caught in her throat. The man standing in front of the barn scanning the property behind him was Theo. She turned back to look at her Theo, crouched protectively beside her, almost to reassure herself that it was indeed him and he'd not somehow slipped around in front of her.

This really was the weirdest thing she'd ever experienced, seeing Theo in two places at once. Her eyes narrowed as she studied the man in front of her. He didn't seem younger. In fact, he looked identical to her Theo, which meant they must be pretty damn close to the time Sam pulled Theo from the burning barn and jumped him through time, dropping him in Mercy right in front of her car on Halloween.

'Damn it,' she swore under her breath, 'he's coming this way.'

'Who?' Theo whispered, unable to see around her.

'You are,' she mouthed, her eyes wide in panic.

Theo had intended to head straight to the barn. It was the only place he felt comfortable these days; the only place not filled with painful memories. There wasn't much to do on the farm now. It had fallen into a shocking state of disrepair since his brother Logan had taken a vow as a Witchfinder and left to work for Nathaniel.

Theo sighed.

He'd tried to keep the farm going for as long as he could, but it was no use, his heart just wasn't in it. Temperance was gone, his mother was gone. He'd failed Mary and now she too was gone. His father Matthias was gone also, although his was the only passing he did not lament. Logan was all he had left and so he'd made a decision. He'd left the farm behind and joined him in Salem. It had been a mistake, thinking he could save his brother. He thought he could pull him back from the edge of whatever dark abyss he was perched so precariously on, but he had been wrong. Logan didn't want to be saved and all that had happened was that Theo had nearly lost himself in the process.

In the end he'd given up, he'd come back to the only home he'd ever known, a place he loathed from the bottom of his wretched broken heart. He'd tried to revive the farm, but by then it had been too late, too neglected. He couldn't do it on his own and no one had wanted to help him.

He was tarnished now, not only by Logan's reputation, but by his own. Everyone knew what they had done, the Beckett brothers, the blood they had spilled. He was alone now.

He'd managed to coax the land to grow just enough to get by and trade enough of the surplus for meat since all the livestock were long gone. None of the traders at market dealt with him fairly, they knew he had limited options and would be forced to take the ridiculous prices they offered.

Still, he probably deserved their scorn and their derision. In fact, he probably deserved a hell of a lot worse. He sometimes wondered if it was worth it, if maybe he should leave Salem, start afresh somewhere else. Somewhere no one knew him or the Beckett name. Maybe he should change his name and sever the last link to the cold cruel man who'd sired him and then ruined him.

But something kept him there, he wasn't sure what exactly. Perhaps it was the dreams he had, or more specifically the woman in his dreams, so beautiful it almost hurt to look at her. She had long dark midnight colored hair, which spilled down her back in deep waves. Her eyes were the color of a fine aged whiskey, which could darken to a passion-filled amber or burn a molten gold. He dreamed of her almost every night now. Her soft voice, breathing his name, burned through his veins like a wild untamable fire, leaving a devastating trail of lust and need in its wake. He could feel her fingertips grazing across his skin every time he closed his eyes. He knew her scent, it was dark and smoky, coiling around him, binding him to her.

He let out a sigh; if only she was real. If only he could find her. But she wasn't real, she was most likely a figment of his imagination, a pale specter he had conjured to keep himself from going mad. Only the problem was she wasn't pale, nor was she a specter.

She was warm, her skin touched with a golden hue, her body pulsing with life and when she touched him she brought him back to life too. When he was with her, he was no longer the broken empty husk of a man who'd lost too much, but a living breathing man whose heart beat in time to her siren's call.

He didn't want to admit it, even to himself. But she was who he was waiting for. He dreamed of her, standing with him in this very house. So no matter how much he despised it, he would never leave it because he was waiting for her and he would continue to wait, even if it took him the rest of his life.

He was almost at the barn door, his journal tucked carefully under one arm, when he suddenly froze. He felt a shiver of recognition skitter up his spine causing him to shudder, even as he turned and looked behind him.

For a second he'd felt her. Was she real? Or were his dreams finally giving way to delusions. He had to know, he had to know if he was losing his mind. He walked slowly towards the lean-to, which covered the stack of firewood he'd chopped only the day before. His heart was racing and his palms were clammy. The closer he got the more he could feel her. His heart was pounding wildly now as he approached the wood pile, another few steps and he would know. He held his breath, his pulse pounded in his ears as he rounded the corner and looked down.

Nothing, there was no one there.

He almost laughed out loud as he scrubbed his hand over his face. He really must be losing his mind. Did he really expect her to be hiding behind a wood pile in his yard? Disappointment warred with the absolute lunacy of his expectations. Shaking his head, he turned away and headed back towards the barn.

'That was close,' Olivia breathed from around the corner of the house, as they both stepped out of the shadows and watched the other Theo disappear into the barn and close the door behind him.

Theo stood quietly staring, his brow creased into a frown.

'What?' Olivia asked in concern, 'what is it?'

'I don't remember doing that,' he replied. 'He's me and yet I don't remember doing that, nor this farm.'

He cast his eyes across the empty paddocks and overgrown fields.

'I don't remember it being so run down,' he shook his head before turning his gaze back to Olivia. 'Something has changed, something is different.'

'Are you sure?'

'I'm positive,' he replied. 'I never lived on the farm alone, even after I returned from Salem. I employed three hands and got the farm back up and running again.'

'We need to find James,' Olivia took Theo's hand.

Nodding in agreement they started back across the overgrown fields, cutting through the tall grass the same way they had come before and hoping that James was home.

The farmhouse looked much as it did when they'd left, the orchard was quiet and still. The breeze rippled through the trees, rustling the leaves as it went, and silently they crept up toward the house. There didn't seem to be any of James' workers about, despite the fact that it was midday. It was the same as the Beckett farm, nothing felt the same. The atmosphere felt heavy and oppressive, almost as if the town itself had borne witness to the worst of humanity and was still reeling from the experience. Everything seemed to be sad and muted.

As they approached the door Theo let go of Olivia's hand and crept to the window, peeking through carefully. After all they had no idea how much time had passed or even if James was still there, and not knowing what they were walking into just made them both that much warier.

Cupping his hand against the glass as he looked in, Theo could see a man seated at the table with his back to him. The figure's posture may have been hunched over, but Theo would know that man anywhere.

'James…'

Glancing around the room to check he was indeed alone, Theo headed back toward the front door. Not bothering to knock he simply lifted the latch and walked into the room, with Olivia following behind.

James spun around in his seat at the sound of someone entering his house uninvited. His eyes widened and his mouth fell open in shock.

'Theo?' he whispered, as if he could not quite believe his eyes.

He rose slowly from his seat, his gaze fixed on Theo. They stood for a moment, staring, locked in a silent communication and neither not quite knowing what to do. Then suddenly Theo strode across the room in a few quick strides and wrapped his arms around his father.

'Theo,' James' voice broke as he fisted his hands against Theo's back and held him tightly.

Olivia's eyes filled with tears as she watched the two men embrace. So much was left unsaid between them, but they seemed to have reached some kind of mutual understanding and in that moment she knew Theo had finally accepted James as his father.

James released Theo and turned his gaze on her.

'Olivia,' he croaked as she rushed forward and wrapped her arms around him tightly.

He pulled back and cradled her face gently in his hands.

'Are you alright?' he frowned, glancing down at her filthy muddy clothes.

'I'm fine,' she smiled, grasping the hand that held her cheek so tenderly.

'Temperance?' he turned to look at Theo, 'did Sam get her out in time?'

'We think so,' Theo nodded, 'but we can't know for certain, until we return home.'

James let out a deep shuddering breath as he squeezed his eyes shut. 'I've waited ten years to find out what happened to you all.'

'The year is 1695?' Olivia gripped his hand tightly.

He nodded slowly and she let out a relieved breath.

'What happened?' James asked quietly, 'I saw…'

He shook his head, dropping his hands from Olivia's face.

Theo watched as he struggled to find the words. He could see the turbulent emotions playing across James' face. Obviously restless and trying to organize his thoughts, James moved toward the fire and stared into the dancing flames.

Theo frowned as he watched him move. He walked slowly and with a very pronounced limp that he'd not had the last time he'd seen him. That was not the only thing that was different. He was thinner and his dark hair was much more liberally shot with grey, but as he raked his hand through his hair, in the signature gesture Theo had so often used himself, he saw a deep scar which ran from his temple, down the side of his face and along his jaw, to disappear into his collar.

'What happened to you James?' he asked softly.

'So much,' he shook his head, dark thoughts clouding his still handsome face. 'So much I've seen, so much has happened.'

Looking up from the soothing flames he looked his son directly in the eye.

'Tell me what happened the night you went after Temperance.'

'We made it to the farm,' Theo began. 'Matthias was passed out drunk, he never even knew we were there. However, Mary was another matter. We found her with Temperance, there was no other way around it. Tempy was in a bad way and we had so little time. We tried to distract Mary, but she walked in on us as Sam disappeared with Temperance. In her madness and panic she threw a lamp, which lit up the whole room. We managed to knock Mary out and get everyone out of the house, while Olivia stopped the fire from spreading. We thought we were safe, but as we made it outside…'

'Nathaniel was waiting for you,' James replied.

'How do you know?' Theo frowned.

'Because I was there,' James whispered. 'I saw…I woke up on the floor and you were all gone.'

He turned his piercing gaze on Olivia who had the grace to look guilty.

'I am sorry about that,' she told him softly. 'I was trying to protect you. I didn't want Nathaniel or anyone else to have any reason to become overly interested in you.'

'It didn't make a difference in the end,' James muttered.

'What do you mean?' Theo asked.

'I mean, Nathaniel followed you to the Beckett farm from here. He knew you were both connected to me somehow, so even if I hadn't followed you the moment I came around, he would have still come here looking for me.'

'Is that what happened?'

'Not at first,' James blew out a tired breath. 'I followed you to the Beckett farm when I woke. By the time I got there you were both out in front of the house with Nathaniel, but before I could come to your aid Theo cut Nathaniel's arm off. I saw the severed limb fall to the ground and you both disappear in the blink of an eye. But what I saw next...' he shook his head as if even after all these years he still couldn't reconcile what he'd witnessed.

'What did you see James?' Olivia asked curiously.

'His arm, it...' he frowned, 'it grew back, right before my eyes.'

'Did he see you?' Theo asked.

James shook his head again. 'No, I retrieved the horses and returned home.'

'But he came looking for you?'

'As I said, not right away.' James returned to the table and took a seat.

'For so long I looked over my shoulder, waiting for him to confront me. I watched as he gained more and more influence in town, until finally the first open accusations came. Samuel Parris' daughter Betty and his niece Abigail; such foolishness. I don't think they ever meant it to go as far as it did. But Nathaniel seized upon their accusations, whispering in the right ears until a full blown witch fever seized the town. It was madness, so many innocents hung, but far more died in the jail. At one point Salem jail was filled to bursting, everyone seemed to seize upon the opportunity to settle every disagreement and petty squabble with an accusation of witchcraft. I kept to myself as much as I could, hoping it would pass and sanity would return but...'

'But?'

'I realized Nathaniel had not forgotten about me at all, he'd simply been biding his time, waiting for the right moment. He came to my door late one night with Stephen and your brother, and a warrant for my arrest.'

'Logan?' Theo's gaze snapped up to meet his serious eyes, 'came to arrest you?'

James nodded.

'What happened next?' Theo asked, his eyes deeply troubled.

'At first I was taken to Salem Jail, but it was

overrun and afforded little chance for the privacy he required to question me. He sent Logan and Stephen to search the house.'

'Your house?' Olivia's eyes widened in panic, 'Hester's Grimoire? Emmaline's journal?'

'Both gone,' he told her softly, his voice filled with remorse. 'I'm so sorry Olivia, I tried to hide it from them but…'

'Nathaniel has them both?' she asked fearfully.

He nodded slowly, 'the Grimoire for certain. He admitted it to me.'

'No!' Olivia's head dropped into her hands as she shook it in denial.

'Livy,' Theo dropped down on his haunches in front of her, gently grasping her wrists and pulling them away from her face.

'I should never have left it here,' she swallowed hard. 'It was my responsibility and I allowed it to fall into Nathaniel's hands.'

His heart clenched painfully at the expression of hopelessness and guilt on her face. He knew she'd never let the book out of her sight, but at that moment she'd only thought of him and his sister. A testament to her love for him, it was also a debt he'd never be able to repay. Because of her his sister was still alive, he hoped.

'What if Nathaniel figures out how to use Hester's book?'

'Livy love,' he comforted her, 'you know as well as I do, that Grimoire is protected by blood magic and some pretty potent other magic. No one but you has been able to read it, not even your mother. I'm willing to bet that he hasn't been able to do much more than stare at the cover.'

'God, I hope you're right. It has been passed down my family for centuries, protected and treasured by generations of Wests. Hester's Grimoire is part of my legacy and I just tossed it aside and forgot about it.'

'No you didn't,' he told her firmly. 'None of us

could have predicted what would happen.'

'He's right Olivia,' James interrupted, 'none of this is your fault.'

'We'll get it back I swear,' Theo promised her.

She stroked his face gently, smiling gratefully as he turned back to James, waiting for him to continue with his story.

'So what happened after that?' she asked James.

'When Nathaniel realized he wouldn't be able to force any answers from me in the jail with so many witnesses, he had me moved to his private residence,' he continued. 'He'd had a house built in town, specially commissioned, and I was unfortunate enough to experience why.'

James glanced up noting their worried expressions.

'The house has a room concealed below ground, a cellar of sorts where he likes to…question his guests.'

'He tortured you?' Olivia whispered in horror.

James looked away, unable to stand the sympathy and concern in her honey colored eyes. Turning his haunted gaze toward the fireplace he reached down deep inside, forcing himself to finish telling them the truth, even if it meant disturbing memories he wanted to shut away forever.

'I don't know how long exactly I spent in Nathaniel's cellar but I do know I didn't break,' he turned his gaze back to Theo. 'I never said a word about you.'

'James,' Theo whispered painfully, 'I never wanted you to get hurt because of us…because of me.'

'Theo, I would suffer through the pain a thousand times gladly if it meant protecting you,' he squeezed his eyes shut momentarily. 'I failed you before, leaving you with Matthias. I was not going to fail you again.'

'Is that why you walk with a limp now?' Theo's jaw tightened furiously. 'Did Nathaniel do that to you?'

'He left me with many reminders of our time together,' James replied grimly, 'but I have learned to live with them.'

'How did you escape him?' Olivia asked suddenly. 'I know Nathaniel. I can't imagine he would've let you walk away, especially without giving him the answers he wanted.'

'That's the strange thing,' James frowned. 'There were only three people who knew I was at Nathaniel's house. Nathaniel himself, Stephen and Logan. I thought for sure I was going to die in that house. When Nathaniel couldn't get what he wanted from me I honestly believed he'd kill me. I lost track of days, I have no idea how long I was there, and just when I thought the worst, my friend Justin came for me with the watchmen.'

'Justin?' Olivia repeated.

'You met him briefly before, Justin Gilbert. He was originally a merchant, but well-liked and respected in the community, with a reputation for being fair and just. As the trials began to wind down, a watch was established in Salem to restore order and Justin was appointed as constable. He picked several good men he trusted and made them watchmen. It was they who restored sanity to Salem, as much as the magistrates would have you believe differently.'

'How did Justin know where to find you?'

'That's just it, I don't know and we have never spoken of it again,' James replied quietly. 'I owe him my life.'

'So he showed up and Nathaniel just handed you over?' Theo asked in confusion.

'Exactly and that's the odd thing, Logan found the Grimoire and the journal in my house, in my possession, and I know he handed them over to Nathaniel. He had more than enough evidence to go before the court and have me sentenced to hang for witchcraft.'

'So why didn't he?' Theo wondered.

'He wouldn't have wanted to hand over the book,' Olivia replied. 'Hester's Grimoire is extremely powerful, it contains some pretty hefty magic. There's no way he'd want to hand it over to the court as evidence and risk it being destroyed. He's searching for the Wests and now he has a direct link to them. If he can figure out how to use the Grimoire, it will lead him back to Hester herself. Likewise, it served no purpose to kill James. He still had answers Nathaniel wanted and so he was worth more to him alive than dead. My guess is he's waiting for everything to die down and people to forget then, he'll try to get to James again.'

'He's been very patient then,' James frowned, 'because it's been years and he hasn't so much as nodded in my direction.'

'Trust me,' Olivia answered solemnly, 'he hasn't lost interest in you in the slightest. He's waiting.'

'There's too many things about this whole situation that just aren't right,' Theo scratched the stubble along his jaw and frowned.

'What do you mean?'

'I don't remember any of this,' he replied.

'I don't understand,' James answered in confusion, 'of course you wouldn't remember, you weren't here.'

'Yes I was,' he reminded him. 'The younger, past version of me was, and I spent a great deal of time in Salem Town with Stephen and Logan the first time around. I was with my brother most of the time and I can tell you with a hundred percent certainty that you were never arrested. In fact, I do remember you helping out the watch, as one of the volunteers.'

'What does this mean then?'

'It means,' Olivia's heart sank, her eyes squeezing shut miserably, 'that somewhere along the line we've managed to change history.'

15.

Nathaniel watched as the crimson liquid tumbled smoothly into the glass. Picking it up he swirled it once, and then again, before he took a small sip, allowing the full bodied flavor to dance across his tongue. Turning around slowly his gaze fell upon the tall slightly paunchy man standing in front of him, sweating nervously.

'Reverend Parris,' Nathaniel replied coolly. 'Just what exactly is it you think I can do for you?'

Samuel Parris shifted uncomfortably, his fingers tightening on the wide brimmed hat he held pressed against his chest.

'I thought you might speak with Stoughton on my behalf,' he answered nervously.

'And why would I do that?' Nathaniel smiled slowly.

'Nathaniel please, be reasonable,' a bead of sweat rolled ponderously from his temple. 'You were the only one who walked away with his reputation intact.'

'I fail to see your point,' he sipped his wine slowly, savoring the taste, a delicious vintage made all the more sweeter by his guest's obvious desperation.

'Nathaniel,' he drew in a shaky breath spreading his hands in supplication, 'what more can I do? I've already made a public apology yet they've refused to pay me several times. If this continues, my family will be ruined. I've heard that the governor himself has issued an invitation to Reverend Joseph Green, which can only mean that they are going to have me replaced. It is only a matter of time.'

'And you expect me to intervene with the new governor on your behalf?'

'If you could,' Samuel breath heavily in relief. 'I would very much appreciate it.'

'Again,' Nathaniel swirled the liquid in his glass, 'why would I do that?'

Samuel's face dropped.

'You and Governor Phipps had only one job,' Nathaniel replied slowly, 'and you couldn't even do that properly. So now you will suffer the consequences. Phipps has already returned to England and I have it on very good authority that he is already dead.'

'Dead?' Samuel swallowed hard, as the color drained from his face.

'That's right,' Nathaniel smiled unpleasantly. 'There are whispers that it is God's retribution for the part he played in the death of so many innocents.'

'But if that is true we are all damned,' Samuel whispered.

'Not all, not I'

'But you…you…'

'I did nothing,' he answered innocently. 'My name and signature appeared on no arrest warrants. I did not sit as one of the judges in the court of Oyer and Terminer, nor did I accuse any of the prisoners.'

Samuel's face fell further as he realized Nathaniel was right.

'Nathaniel please,' he begged, 'my family…'

'Will suffer, not only for your sins, but those of your daughter and niece also,' he replied dismissively, placing his glass down on the table. 'Now if that is all, the hour is late.'

Samuel swallowed hard, having no choice but to follow Nathaniel, who was already moving toward the door. Stepping out into the cool night air, he turned and opened his mouth in a last attempt to reason with him.

'Good evening Reverend Parris,' Nathaniel cut him off before he could utter another word.

Mustering what little pride he had left Samuel's spine stiffened, his lips tightening into a thin angry line as he replaced his hat on his head and gave a curt nod.

'Good evening Nathaniel,' he murmured tightly, before stepping down from the doorway and disappearing into the night.

Nathaniel stood for a moment in the darkness, shrouded by the light spilling from his open doorway. He breathed deeply, a small smile playing at the corner of his lips. He'd enjoyed that. The sheer desperation of the man, he'd reeked of it. He had no illusion that the man had not thought of his family at all. Samuel Parris was such an easy man to read, he'd been motivated to come to Nathaniel's door for one reason and one alone, self-preservation. He'd been quick enough to shift the blame after the trials, as had the former Governor, William Phipps.

It was amusing the way the humans schemed and plotted against one another. So quick to cause death and pain to their fellow man, or woman in this case. The witch trials had been an interesting diversion he had to admit. He'd hoped it would last a little longer as they had not quite produced the result he'd desired. He still had not managed to locate the Wests. He knew they were somewhere close, but so far they'd managed to remain hidden from him. He had hoped, when he'd first set the wheels in motion, that the witch hunt would drive them out into the open, but unfortunately it had simply produced the opposite effect. It had driven them deeper into hiding.

Still, he mused, stroking his chin thoughtfully, he was close; he could feel it. Perhaps it was time to pay another visit to Mr Wilkins. The man knew something. Whether or not it pertained to the West women he had no idea, but he was involved somehow.

He needed to figure it out. How had the man become involved with time travelers and who was the woman who was able to conjure Hell fire? That was something no human had ever been able to do and more than that, how had a human woman ended up with his brothers' compass, when his brother Seth was still Hades' prisoner deep in the belly of the Underworld.

Stepping back into the house and closing the door behind him with a firm click, he headed back into the study. Reaching up to the heavy wooden bookcase he retrieved a thick rectangular object. He walked slowly to the heavy antique desk which he'd had brought over from England, and laid the item out, unwrapping the dark velvet covering.

The dark leather-bound volume stared back at him, taunting him. He ran his hand over the face of it, his fingers dancing a breath above the binding itself. Even now he could feel the magic pushing him away. He'd learned the hard way when the book had first come into his possession, that it did not want him to learn its secrets. The witches' book was guarded by heavy and potent magic, sealed with blood. He'd tried everything he could think of and still it would not submit to him.

Nathaniel sat down in a tall backed leather chair, winding his fingers together as he gazed at the Grimoire pensively. The book may have been in James Wilkins' possession, but it did not belong to him, of that he was absolutely certain. Wilkins may have some lingering magical talent, third generation if he had to guess, but he was certainly not a powerful witch. No, the book belonged to someone else. The woman he'd seen that night at the Beckett place? It was entirely plausible. He'd sensed an incredible amount of untapped power within her, not to mention her ability with the ancient fire.

But how was James Wilkins and Theodore Beckett connected to her? After some digging he'd been able to find out that Wilkins had introduced her to Samuel Parris as his niece, Livy Oldham. However, a quick trip to Boston, where James' sister was living with her husband, had proven her identity to be a lie. James' sister had no daughter, only a son who had been only fourteen years old at the time. Now ten years later, he was no closer to discovering her true identity.

He'd kept an extremely close eye on Theodore Beckett after that night, but it quickly became obvious the man knew nothing of magic, nor the girl. No, the Theodore Beckett he'd seen the night of the storm was an older version of him, which meant he had yet to meet her. He thought that by gaining control of his brother and by extension Theodore himself, by involving them in the witch trials, he might've gained some measure of control over them.

But controlling Theodore Beckett had been a lot harder than he'd thought. He did not seem to be as weak minded, nor as easily manipulated as the others had been. He'd only had a tenuous hold on him, which at best had proved to be as elusive as trying to hold smoke in his bare hands. He'd broken away, distanced himself even from his brother and Nathaniel had lost his only leverage. He'd stepped back and allowed him to return to his farm, but he'd still kept a close eye on him.

His brother however had been an entirely different matter. He'd been so angry, so bitter. Manipulating Logan Beckett had been like plucking ripe fruit from a tree and so far the man had proved to be extremely loyal, not to mention resourceful.

It was he who had brought him the book. Although he still wasn't sure how Justin Gilbert had found out James was being held at his house. He'd had no choice after that but to release the man and keep his distance, he was far too valuable to risk. Wilkins had answers, answers he needed. He'd kept his distance, but the time was coming when he would have to make his move. If he could not make the book submit to him he had to find out why.

A sudden knocking at the door had him rising and wrapping the book once again. Carefully placing it back onto the highest shelf away from prying eyes, he headed out of the study and back to the door. This time when he opened it he was greeted by the bright eager gaze of Stephen Holborne. A lowly man, born the son of a peddler, Stephen was a greedy and ambitious man with no conscience and even less scruples. He didn't care what Nathaniel asked him to do as long as he was well paid for it.

'Stephen,' he greeted him quietly.

'Nathaniel,' he nodded, 'I have some information for you.'

Nathaniel gazed out into the darkness behind him, as if to make sure he was alone, before stepping back and indicating for the stocky man to enter his home. Shutting the door with a soft click, Nathaniel led the way back into the main sitting room. Moving toward the fireplace he stoked the dying embers to reignite them and added another log to the muted flames.

'Well?' he turned to the other man, 'you said you had information.'

He ran his eyes over the man before him. Stephen was not very tall, stocky in build, but with powerful looking arms, which gave his body an odd sort of mismatched appearance. His hair was a dull, golden orange and his eyes were a weak watery color as they locked on Nathaniel.

'I thought you might like to know, Theodore Beckett visited James Wilkins this afternoon and he had with him a woman, a pretty thing with dark hair.'

Nathaniel's eyes widened in interest. 'Did you manage to find out who she is?'

'I got close enough to hear him call her Olivia.'

'Is that all?' he pursed his lips, his eyes narrowing in displeasure.

'Not quite,' Stephen continued, 'you see I'd also been keeping an eye on the Beckett place, which is where I first saw them. I followed them both to the Wilkins place.'

'So,' Nathaniel shrugged.

'Here's the thing,' Stephen warmed to his tale. 'I saw Beckett walk into his barn and not a moment later I saw him on the opposite side of the farm with the woman.'

Nathaniel watched Stephen carefully.

'There is no way he could be in two places at once. I couldn't figure it out, until I saw them both at the same time. There's two of them.'

Still Nathaniel remained silent.

'That's devil magic,' he concluded. 'Then I ask myself why you would set me the task of watching both properties and it occurs to me that you might've known something about this.'

His pale calculating gaze locked on Nathaniel's dark beetle like eyes.

'Information like that would be worth a lot…to the right people.'

'I see,' Nathaniel replied calmly as he moved toward an ornate cabinet, which held a bottle of wine and glasses.

'Figured you would want to be the first to make me an offer.'

'You thought right,' Nathaniel pulled the stopper and poured the dark liquid into the glass. Picking it up and slowly walking across the room he handed the glass to Stephen, who took it with some surprise as he'd never been offered a drink in Nathaniel's house before, certainly not as an equal. A smirk appeared on his face and he gripped the glass as Nathaniel circled him slowly.

'Tell me something,' Nathaniel asked softly, 'does anyone else know you're here?'

'No,' Stephen raised the glass to his lips, 'I came straight from the Wilkins place.'

'That's what I thought,' he smiled, reaching out.

Stephen's head snapped to the side with a sickening crunch and his body dropped to the floor in a heap. The glass shattered across the hard wooden floor and the crimson colored wine pooled around his lifeless hand.

Nathaniel stepped callously over the corpse littering his floor and poured himself a drink. Taking a thoughtful sip he stared into the fire. Until he figured out what was going on he would need an ally. He glanced back at the dead man in disgust. Someone he could trust. Someone like Zachary.

The younger demon had proved his worth and his loyalty dozens of times over the centuries. He didn't like to pull him from his assignment in Hades' domain, but then again there was no one he trusted more, other than his brother, and as he was currently Hades' permanent guest Zachary was the next best choice. Of course he'd need a disguise, something which would allow him to circulate amongst the people. After all they were still a little skittish around strangers. Stupid humans, he scoffed. However, he took another sip of his wine… his run-in with Stephen had provided a solution.

Grabbing the dead man's boot he pulled him unceremoniously through the house, dragging him effortlessly by one limp lifeless foot as if the stocky dead weight was nothing. He entered his study and dropped the body to the ground at the side of the room. Draining his glass in one, he set it down on his desk and leaned down to the floor. Grasping the corner of the carpet, he pulled it back revealing a huge blackened pentagram burned into the bare floor. Scrawled across it, in and around the pentagram itself, were intricate spidery looking sigils.

He moved toward a small chest in the corner of the room and pulled a small bronze key from his pocket.

The lock turned with a well-oiled click, and lifting the lid he began to pull out various items, bundles of dried herbs and a bag of foul smelling soil which carried with it the unpleasant stench of decomposition. He pulled out several thick stumpy black candles inscribed with more sigils, followed by what appeared to be a feline skull and a cruel curved birdlike claw.

The ticking of the clock echoed behind him as he took his time arranging the items on or around the pentagram, muttering in a strange guttural language as he moved. Once he'd arranged everything to his satisfaction, he lit the black candles which were spaced at intervals between the points of the star. They began to give off an oily grey smoke, which soon filled the air with an unpleasant smog punctuated only by the sooty orange glow of the candle flames.

He began to chant again, an ancient, complex language which rose and fell in cadence. The ground began to throb and bubble, as if the wood itself had become liquid. It stretched and heaved as a shape resembling an arm pressed upwards.

Suddenly the strange fluid floor split, like a membrane. One arm clawed its way out, followed by another, then a head and torso. Nathaniel stepped back, watching in satisfaction as the figure clawed its way out. When its body was finally free the ground once again hardened. The creature unfolded itself, standing slowly. Completely naked, its flesh appeared raw and painful, as if his entire body had been flayed and burned. His black beetle like eyes scanned the room until they fell upon Nathaniel.

'Zachary.'

'Nathaniel,' his voice was a growl, which sounded wet somehow. 'Why have you summoned me?'

'I need you to do something for me.'

'I was already doing something for you, unless you no longer consider the release of your brother a priority.'

'You are well aware that nothing is more important than Seth.'

'Then why am I here?' he growled again.

'Because I require your assistance, and other than my brother there is no one I trust more than you.'

Zachary stared at him before closing his eyes and inhaling deeply, pulling in the surrounding air and tasting it.

'The human world,' he sneered, 'never changes. I can still taste the fear and corruption.'

'You should fit right in then,' Nathaniel gave a sardonic smile.

'I haven't been topside since…'

'Constantinople,' Nathaniel finished for him.

'Yes, the fall of Constantinople,' he smiled in remembrance, a truly frightening expression on his damaged face. 'I did so enjoy the Ottomans, they were so…creative.'

'I seem to recall you getting quite creative yourself, when you were chasing down the fleeing Greeks.'

'Good times.'

'Indeed.'

'So what exactly is it you need from me?' he asked.

He followed Nathaniel's gaze to the rumpled form at the side of the room. 'You don't expect me to wear that?' he asked in disgust.

'An unfortunate necessity my friend,' Nathaniel replied.

'A pig suit?' he scoffed. 'I'd rather go back to hell.'

'As I said it's a necessity. I need you to blend in.'

'But they stink,' he looked at Nathaniel who remained silent, his expression unmoved. 'Very well,' he hissed, stalking towards the corpse.

His body began to undulate, his skin rippling and softening and as he reached the body his form began to melt. He leaned over and poured himself into Stephen's chest, leaving no wound. The corpse jerked once and then settled. Suddenly his eyes opened, no longer pale blue, but now black like Nathaniel's. He sat up abruptly then climbed to his feet. Stretching out his arms and staring at his hands, he walked across the room. His movements were stiff and jerky at first, but as he moved they smoothed out into a fluid gait.

'Urgh,' he said in disgust, his voice now sounding just like Stephen's. 'Human flesh is disgusting, it makes my skin crawl to be wearing this.'

'It will not be for long my friend,' Nathaniel reassured him, picking up a bottle of wine and holding it up in front of him questioningly.

Zachary didn't bother to answer, nor did he wait for Nathaniel to pour him a glass. He simply plucked the wine from his hand and drank straight from the bottle, not stopping until it was empty.

'Better?' Nathaniel asked in amusement.

'Not even slightly,' he grumbled. 'I still have a disgusting taste in my mouth…now tell me what is going on.'

'We have time travelers.'

'Really?' his eyes widened in surprise, 'that's rare. How are they managing it?'

'They have Seth's compass,' his darkened expression was suddenly murderous.

'Are they human?'

Nathaniel nodded.

'There's only one way they could be in possession of the compass,' Zachary mused thoughtfully.

'Hades has to have given it to them.'

'But why?' Zachary shook his head. 'He doesn't get involved in the human world. He doesn't like them very much. In fact, from what I hear, he hasn't been topside in over two thousand years.'

'The only reason he would involve himself is if we are getting close to finding a way to free my brother,' Nathaniel surmised.

'Maybe,' Zachary replied thoughtfully, 'so who is it? Who has the compass now?'

'A woman, I'm not sure who she is yet. I think her name is Olivia. I first encountered her ten years ago.'

'And you allowed her to slip through your fingers?' Zachary shook his head. 'You're losing your touch.'

'Hardly,' Nathaniel retorted acerbically. 'She disappeared that night but she's finally resurfaced.'

'So grab her and question her,' he shrugged.

'It's not quite that simple.'

'Why?'

Nathaniel started at the beginning. He told Zachary of the Wests and his search for them, how he believed he was getting close. He went on to explain about Salem and the witch trials, James Wilkins and the Becketts, particularly Theodore and his connection to the girl. How there were two of him, a past version and a time traveling version. He told him about the Grimoire and the fact that it was found in James' house, but he was certain it belonged to the woman and finally he told him that she could conjure Hell fire.

'That's not possible,' Zachary frowned. 'No human has ever been able to conjure the ancient fires.'

'And yet she did, and not by some fluke or accident. I saw her with my own eyes. She drew a bow of Hell fire from thin air, loaded with a bolt of pure black flame.'

'And you're sure she is human?'

'Yes,' he shook his head frowning, 'I touched her skin. I felt her heartbeat pound beneath my grip, she is human. But there is something else there, something I don't understand. A vast well of power as yet untapped.'

'Wait a minute,' Zachary held up his hand, squeezing his eyes shut as he rifled through Stephen's memories. He turned over every memory of Logan and Theodore Beckett, before going back to study the face of the woman Stephen had seen just hours earlier heading for the Wilkins house.

'Hades obviously has some interest in this girl if he gave her the compass, but it's not only that. She is able to use it, not just to cross distances, but to jump through time. Even your brother wasn't able to make it do that.'

'I know,' Nathaniel scowled.

'We need to get our hands on that girl,' Zachary's eyes narrowed.

'That's why I summoned you,' he answered. 'I don't want to involve Beckett and Wilkins yet, their involvement is peripheral at best. It's the girl; she's the center of everything. If we can break her, I get the feeling she'll be a goldmine of information and not only that, I think she might be able to help me find the Wests.'

'What makes you think that?'

'Because of the Grimoire, it belongs to one of the West women. I felt it when I touched it the very first time.' He looked down to the healed burn scars, which marred the palm of his hand. 'If she had this book in her possession, it means she has some sort of tie to that family. It's all connected somehow.'

'So we need the girl.'

'Yes,' he answered, 'but I don't want Beckett interfering. Right now I don't have any interest in him. That may change, but I don't want the trail to lead him here, to lead him to me. I need time with her…uninterrupted time.'

'Consider it done' Zachary smiled coldly. 'By this time tomorrow she'll be yours to do with as you please'.

16.

Olivia peeled the muddy gown from her body, pushing it awkwardly past her petticoats. Glancing down at her hands, she cringed at the dirt embedded under her nails. Trying to ignore them as best she could, she started to pluck and pull at the strings of her petticoat. She looked up as Theo entered the room, carrying another bucketful of cold water.

'Where's James gone? I heard him leave.'

'He said he had some chores to do out in the orchard.' Theo closed the door and dumped the contents of the bucket into the cramped bath tub he'd dragged into James' room, so that Olivia could bathe in privacy. 'But I think it was an excuse to give us some time alone and him some time to think.'

Olivia sighed heavily as she dropped down onto the side of the bed.

'We're doing it to him again aren't we?' she frowned.

'What?'

'Dragging him into our mess, putting him in danger,' she breathed out slowly. 'When I think about what Nathaniel put him through and what these last ten years have been like for him, I feel so…'

'Guilty?' he finished for her as she nodded. 'I

know, I do to.'

'We keep bringing this to his door,' she frowned. 'I just wonder...'

'Wonder?'

'Where it's all going to end?' she replied as Theo pulled her to her feet and unlaced her petticoat for her, letting it pool on the floor. 'Last time he was arrested and tortured, what if this time it costs him his life?'

'I know,' Theo replied quietly as he gazed down into her troubled eyes. 'I've asked myself the same question a dozen times since we got here.'

'And?'

'I don't see how we can do this without him,' he sighed reluctantly. 'I want the best for him, I want him to be safe and happy, but also selfishly I want to spend as much time as I can with him. I mean, if by some miracle we manage to stop your mother and the two Nathaniels and return to Mercy, I'll never see him again.'

'I know,' she stroked his arms comfortingly, 'but this is getting too dangerous for him. We need to retrieve the books from Nathaniel, we can't leave Hester's Grimoire in his possession. Which means, as crazy as it sounds, we're going to have to break into his house. I don't think we can risk James with that kind of exposure. We may have no choice but to distance ourselves from him, for his own good.'

'Olivia,' Theo shook his head, 'we can't go after the book, at least not right now.'

He saw her frown and open her mouth to object as he rushed ahead. 'I know the book is important, but so is Hester or have you forgotten the deal we made at the Crossroad? We came back here to stop your mother and the present day Nathaniel from tracking down Hester and her family. Now as important and powerful as her Grimoire is, it's nothing compared to what will happen if either your mother or Nathaniel get their hands on Infernum. You know what's at stake. We can't lose sight of that, especially not now we're so close. The Grimoire will have to wait. Hester has to be protected at all costs because...' his voice softened as he cupped her face in his hands, 'if anything happens to her, you'll never be born, and you and I will never meet. I can't let that happen. Hester has to be our priority, we have to find her and stop your mother.'

'You're right,' Olivia sighed, 'I know you are. It's just, I was trusted with the Grimoire and I failed. I allowed it to fall into the hands of a demon. The whole family destiny thing they've been shoving down my throat since the moment I set foot back in Mercy, was about how my family were the guardians of the Hell book, Infernum and how it's our responsibility to keep it protected and hidden. Well how can I do that, when I can't even keep a book of spells from falling into the wrong hands?'

'Livy,' he stroked her tangled hair back from her muddy face, 'that wasn't your fault.'

'Don't sugar coat it Theo,' she scowled. 'You can't call extenuating circumstances on this one. I was supposed to keep it safe and I didn't, end of story... I failed.'

'You're too hard on yourself,' he shook his head.

'I can't do this,' she whispered, 'it's too much, all this expectation and destiny crap. I can't help feeling Hades, Diana, Bridget, Aunt Evie, all of them have backed the wrong horse. I'm not the person they're making me out to be.'

'I know it all feels a little overwhelming. You've had a lot thrown at you in a very short space of time.'

'I just can't do it,' she shook her head, her eyes filling as she tried to breathe through the oppressive weight which settled firmly on her chest. 'It's too much pressure, I feel like I'm going to break. Any moment I'll just shatter, dragging everyone down with me.'

'You won't shatter,' he wrapped his arms firmly around her, pressing her against his warm body. 'Do you remember what you said to me the other night?'

She looked up at him, her brow furrowing thoughtfully as she shook her head.

'You said when you found out the truth about your parents, the only thing that kept you from falling to pieces was me.' He tilted her head back, his thumb tracing the line of her jaw tenderly. 'That hasn't changed and it never will. I'm right here holding onto you and I won't let go, not ever.'

'You'll stay with me?' she whispered.

'Always,' he murmured, brushing his lips softly against hers.

'I just want to go home Theo,' she spoke quietly.

'I know,' he released his hold and stepped back slightly. 'Look, you're tired and dirty. Why don't you have your bath, you'll feel better for it. Then we can decide where we go from here.'

'I suppose,' she sighed.

'You might want to heat the water up though, it's a bit cold.'

Olivia let go of him and knelt down next to the tub, dipping her hand into the freezing water and shivering. Allowing her magic to pool in her fingers she watched in satisfaction as, after a moment, small tendrils of steam began to rise from the water. She let her hand glide through the water, which was now somewhere between warm and pleasantly hot. She looked up and caught Theo's amused expression.

'What?'

'You would have saved me so much time,' he shook his head. 'You have no idea how long and painstaking a task it was to warm the water to bathe Tempy when she was younger. That's why she was dirty more often than not.'

"Well I can't stay dirty,' Olivia grimaced, 'it's making my skin crawl. When we get back to Mercy the first thing I'm doing is getting in the shower and I may not leave it for several days.'

She lifted her arms as Theo grabbed the bottom of her shift and lifted it over her head. Taking hold of his hand to steady herself she lifted one foot and stepped into the tub. It was small and cramped, but the water felt so good against her skin. Wrapping her arms around her knees she let out a sigh of contentment.

'James said he left your spare clothes from last time in the chest, so at least you'll have something clean to put on afterwards.'

She nodded as she watched him retrieve a small jug and a linen cloth, which he handed to her along with bar of soap. Dunking the cloth into the water and wringing it out she scrubbed her face until her skin was flushed and pink.

'You really don't like being dirty do you?' he chuckled, kneeling down next to the washtub and dipping the jug into the water to fill it.

'And I suppose you do?' she tilted her head back so he could rinse her hair.

'You forget that I grew up here and without a mother. The only time Logan and I bathed was when we got rained on,' he smiled fondly. 'With Tempy we did try to make more of an effort to keep her clean, being a girl and all, but the truth is she had as much of an aversion to washing as we did. Then again if we'd had indoor plumbing with hot and cold running water, not to mention showers, we probably could have been persuaded to clean ourselves every so often.'

Olivia smiled as he took the cloth and soap from her and began to wash her back.

'Tell me about Logan?' she asked quietly.

Theo's fist clenched involuntarily against her back. She could feel the tension in the corded muscles of his forearm, but as his dark gaze settled on hers she reached out with damp fingers, smoothing the wrinkle which had appeared between his brows.

'Not the way it ended,' she whispered softly. 'Go

back to a happier time when you were children.'

She watched as Theo visibly relaxed and resumed washing her back. A small smile played at the corner of his lips as he remembered.

'He was so funny.'

'Funny?'

'You wouldn't have thought it if you'd met him later, but as a child he had such an incredible sense of humor. He was always laughing and playing jokes on me. I used to say that he could never take anything seriously,' Theo sighed. 'He proved me wrong, very wrong.'

'What was it, do you think, that changed him?'

'I used to think it was the death of our mother.'

'And now?'

'I'm not so sure,' he shook his head. 'Maybe it was lots of little things that built up over time. I think it started with the death of our mother and the way our father treated us, the general atmosphere of fear and intolerance of anything different.'

'Did he know?'

'About?'

'You and Temperance? Your magical gifts?'

Theo shook his head frowning.

'No, I thought I was protecting him, but I've often wondered if I made a mistake. Maybe if I'd let him in he would've been more sympathetic to those who were accused. If he could've seen them as being just like me and Temperance and not servants of the devil.'

'He sounds like a fanatic.'

'Maybe if things had been different,' Theo murmured, 'but once Nathaniel got his hands on him, the Logan I knew was gone. It was always as if he were two separate people. I never could reconcile the loving, funny, loyal brother I knew, with the cold, cruel, angry and bitter man he became.'

'I'm sorry,' Olivia replied quietly, knowing the words were inadequate.

'Some things can't be changed,' he handed the cloth back to her.

'That's just it,' Olivia frowned thoughtfully, 'I'm not so sure about that. Theo, you do realize that sooner or later we may run into Logan?'

'I know,' he answered resignedly.

'You need to prepare yourself,' she warned.

'I'll be fine Livy,' he told her, 'I'm not the same man I was the last time I saw him.'

'Well he might not be either,' she murmured.

'What do you mean?'

'Theo, we've changed the timeline. You said it yourself things are different. There's no way we can predict how dangerous your brother is or what sort of man he is. He may not be the same man you remember.'

'Damn it,' he frowned.

'I know,' she replied, 'the problem is I don't even know what it was we changed. It could be a million different things, it could even be something really tiny, and we have no idea how far the damage has spread.'

'What do you mean?'

'When we get back to the future, it may not be the reality we left behind. We're working with a completely different reality now to the one we knew. This is why we're not supposed to mess with time, to prevent things like this from happening.'

'What if we go back and change it back?'

'We can't,' she shook her head, 'we don't know what we changed and even if we could pinpoint it, there's the potential for us to make things even worse by just trying to repair one thing. All we can do at this point is go with it and try to limit our exposure.'

'That's easier said than done. For all we know your mother and the other Nathaniel are out there causing all sorts of damage.'

'Exactly,' Olivia laid back against the tub and drew in a troubled breath. 'God, I hate time travel.'

Her gaze was drawn to the golden compass, which lay innocuously nestled between her breasts against her damp skin. The night they jumped through time Nathaniel had recognized it she realized with a start. Casting her mind back she tried to remember that moment. He'd said the compass had belonged to his brother.

Picking it up she turned it over in her fingers as the candlelight reflected from its shiny surface. It had belonged to the demon Seth and now Nathaniel knew she had it in her possession. Her brow furrowed thoughtfully, it wasn't safe for her to keep it. She'd already lost the Grimoire, there was no way she wanted to explain to Hades how she managed to let the compass pass into the hands of Nathaniel.

'What are you thinking about?'

'The compass,' she mused. 'Did you know it belonged to Nathaniel's brother Seth?'

'What?' Theo replied in surprise, 'are you sure?'

She nodded slowly, 'he recognized it and wanted to know how I came to have it.'

She pulled the chain over her head and sat up, displacing the water as she did. Quietly she slipped the chain over Theo's head, so it lay nestled in the open collar of his linen shirt.

'What are you doing Olivia?' he frowned. 'Hades gave the compass to you.'

'I know,' she replied, 'but Nathaniel knows I have it now. It's not safe for me to wear it and there is no one I trust more than you.'

'Olivia,' he whispered.

'I know it's a lot to ask…'

'I'll take care of it,' he told her softly as he stroked her face.

'You know,' she trailed her fingers along the stubble at his jaw, 'you're pretty dirty yourself. You should probably get in here with me.'

His mouth curved into an amused smile as he

looked down at the tub.

'We'd never both fit in there.'

'Never say never,' she smiled as she grabbed him and yanked him into the tub.

Caught off balance he toppled into the tub on top of her, splashing water all over the floor and soaking his clothes. Laughing in delight she hooked her legs over the side of the tub so he could kneel in the water without crushing her legs. Bracing his weight on his arms as he gripped the edge of the tub either side of her, he looked down into her amber eyes.

'We should get you out of these wet clothes,' she whispered against his mouth as she slid her hands under his shirt and grazed her fingers up his torso.

He pulled back and yanked his shirt over his head letting it drop to the floor with a wet splat. Taking his weight once again, with one hand gripping the edge of the tub, his other slid around her ribs and underneath her, pulling her body close to his as he took her mouth. Olivia felt his kiss right down to her toes. It was always like this with him, he consumed her until all she could do was breath him in.

'You know,' he pulled back slightly, 'this is not acceptable Christian behavior.'

'Good job I'm not a Christian then,' she smiled against his mouth.

'And... most husbands and wives don't share baths either.'

'Well you haven't married me yet,' she nipped his bottom lip.

He growled and took her mouth again. Her breath came in short ragged bursts as his hand left the small of her back and plunged between her legs stroking her maddeningly. Her back arched and she left out an involuntarily gasp as he quickly drove her up to the very edge and over.

Her breasts pressed against his damp chest, the

light dusting of hair scraping against her sensitive nipples. Her hands fumbled at the ties of his breeches, loosening them as he continued to taste her mouth. She shoved them down, barely managing to get them past his hips before he thrust deeply into her body and let loose a growl of satisfaction. She practically climbed up his body wrapping her legs tightly around his waist, while he set an urgent and punishing pace for both of them, proving that despite the small tub he was very creative when it came to small spaces.

Her fingers tangled in the dark curls of his hair, gripping tightly as he rode her hard. The pressure deep in her core began to mount, the tantalizing and desperately sharp edge of passion so close, almost within reach. Neither of them were going to last long, they were too desperate, too lost in each other. All the danger and stress and uncertainty of their situation drove their lovemaking to an urgent and frantic pace, desperate to experience the closeness and completion that they could only find in each other.

Olivia threw her head back as her body tightened, clamping down on him in her release as he pressed his face into her exposed throat and followed her down, breathing heavily. His heart was pounding in his chest as he lowered her and she slid bonelessly back into the water.

'Wow,' she panted, looking at him through heavily lidded eyes, 'and you said we couldn't both fit in the tub.'

He snorted lightly with laughter, dropping a kiss on her lips. He somehow managed to yank his breeches the rest of the way off and haul them over the side onto the floor to join his shirt.

Olivia once again hooked her legs over the side as he turned around putting his back to her. Unfolding his long legs from under him he hooked them over the end of the bath so his feet were almost touching the floor and leaned into her so his back was pressed against her breasts.

Sighing in contentment he smiled as Olivia

retrieved the cloth and wrapped her arms and legs around him, smoothing his hair back from his face and washing him gently.

'You know,' he said after a moment, 'as soon as we get back to Mercy I'm going to have you in front of a preacher quicker than you can say I do.'

'Are you now?' she smiled in amusement.

'I'm serious,' he twisted his head and glanced up at her. 'I'd marry you now, but we'd have to have the banns read and I can't really call any attention to us. After all Samuel Parris is still the Reverend in Salem and he knows you as James' married niece, not to mention the fact that he knows the other me.'

'It's fine Theo,' she chuckled, 'I can wait until we get home.'

'How exactly will it work?' he asked after a moment, his brow furrowing in thought.

'Well,' Olivia stroked the cloth soothingly across his chest, 'we get all our family and friends together, we get a ring and you say I do and I say…'

'Very funny,' he replied dryly, 'I meant you're not a Christian. We can't marry in a church can we? I mean, how does a witch get married exactly?'

'It depends,' she shrugged.

'What do you mean?' he asked curiously.

'Well I was thinking…' she stopped as he turned more fully toward her grinning. 'What?'

'You've been thinking about our wedding?'

'I may have given it a passing thought,' she replied innocently.

'Tell me what your thoughts are.'

'Well, I figured we could get married on the plot of land down by the lake and um…well your sister is the mayor of Mercy. I thought she'd probably have the authority to perform the ceremony. If not I'm sure we could get her ordained online or something, I mean there's probably a way around it. I just thought it would be nice if she officiated.'

He sat silently staring at her.

'What do you think? I mean, I guess if you really need a church or a preacher I could…'

'I think it's perfect,' he interrupted, his voice slightly rough. 'I would love for Temperance to be a part of it.'

She smiled softly and bent her head to kiss his lips.

'I love you,' she murmured.

'And I love you,' he smiled back.

They both looked up as they heard the door open in the other room, followed by the sound of footsteps across the floor.

'I think James is back,' Theo sighed and reluctantly pulled himself from Olivia's embrace. Climbing out of the tub he dried himself off and dressed in the clean breeches and shirt he'd borrowed from James earlier. Looking up and catching sight of Olivia, his mouth fell open and his mouth suddenly ran dry once more.

She stood, slowly rising out of the water like Botticelli's Venus, smoothing her long dark hair back and wringing it out. He watched her climb out of the bath and dry herself off.

'What I wouldn't give for some moisturizer,' she muttered reaching into the chest in the small room, looking for the spare shift she'd left last time. Finding the garment she was looking for she pulled it over her head and retrieved the comb from the chest. Glancing at the contents she smiled softly as she realized that James must have kept everything of hers, despite not knowing if they were ever going to return. That man, she shook her head, was such a sweetheart. It was easy to see where Theo got his temperament from.

Scooping the dirty muddy clothes from the floor she shoved them in the corner of the room, knowing that she'd have to wash them and hang them out to dry in the morning.

Climbing up onto the bed, she began to comb the snarls out of her hair, watching as Theo opened the window and picked up the bucket. He began to scoop the dirty water from the bath tub and dump it outside. By the time Theo had emptied out the majority of the water, she'd not only combed her hair out, but used her magic to dry it.

She yawned tiredly and shivered, climbing under the covers.

'You should get some sleep love,' Theo closed the window and dropped the latch.

'I'm so damn tired all the time,' she yawned again. 'You know, by tomorrow I might have worked my way up to feeling bad we've kicked James out of his bed again.'

'I'm sure he doesn't mind,' Theo smiled as he pulled the bedding over her and dropped a kiss on her upturned lips. 'Rest, I'm going to go and speak with James.'

'Mmmm,' she mumbled settling down into the bed.

Her eyelids felt like they were lined with lead, so heavy she could barely keep them open. She was vaguely aware of Theo dragging the empty bath tub out of the room and shutting the door behind him, before she slid into a deep dreamless sleep.

She couldn't have said how long she'd slept when she was awakened by a deep shudder. Opening her eyes she sat up, squinting slightly as her gaze adjusted to the darkness in the room. The door was still closed and Theo's side of the bed still empty. Judging from the low murmur of voices in the other room she guessed he was still talking with his father.

Sitting up further she glanced around the room trying to identify what had woken her. She shivered again and realized with a frown that the window was wide open. A freezing cold draught whistled into the room.

Strange she thought to herself, she could've sworn Theo had closed and latched the window.

Swinging her legs over the edge of the bed, she winced as her bare feet landed on the freezing cold floor. Hurrying across the room to the window to close it she suddenly stopped. There was a strange, ugly, undulating fog obscuring the ground outside the window, a greasy unpleasant smog. With a sudden start she realized she'd seen something similar once before, in the woods outside her house when she'd been lured from her bed in her sleep.

A sense of dread filled her and her heart began to thud loudly in her chest as a sudden surge of adrenalin fueled fear flooded her veins.

She wasn't alone.

She turned abruptly toward the door, but before she could even move, everything suddenly went black. Before she could even let out a scream, she was falling into darkness.

17.

'Do you feel that?' Theo frowned, placing his cup of cider down on the table and turning around on the bench.

'What?' James queried.

'It's cold, like a draught.'

The cool gust of air once again washed over Theo, dancing gleefully down his neck with spindly fingers, making the hairs stand on end. Pushing back from the table he stood and headed toward the back room where Olivia was sleeping. His heart jumped in his chest and his eyes widened in alarm as a thin greasy roll of smog wafted through the crack beneath the doorway.

He threw open the door. The entire floor of the room was covered in the eerie undulating fog and a quick panicked glance at the empty rumpled bed confirmed his worst fears. Olivia was nowhere to be seen. His eyes shot across to the window which he'd closed earlier in the evening and which now stood wide open to the chilly night air. Rushing across the room, ignoring the smog which seemed to snap at his ankles, he grasped the window frame looking out into the darkness. The dirty fog was even thicker outside, carpeting the ground and stretching all the way back into the orchard itself. The sharp tang of ozone ominously scented the air and the fog seemed to glow with an eerie phosphorescence.

'OLIVIA!' he shouted desperately out into the dark night.

He vaguely registered James rushing into the room behind him, but Theo had already climbed out of the window and disappeared into the orchard, swallowed by the fog as he screamed her name.

Olivia blinked slowly, her head bobbing limply on her neck. She blinked again and the room spun, making her feel nauseous. Her whole body throbbed and ached as if she were recovering from some sort of virulent strain of flu. She shivered violently and once again tried to lift her head. Whatever she'd been knocked out with sure as hell packed a punch. She swallowed painfully past the dryness in her throat, forcing her eyes open. Slowly the room stopped spinning and the splashes of muted color began to sharpen back into focus.

She could feel the hard wooden chair beneath her. Still clothed in only her shift her body trembled, not because the room lacked warmth, but more from the trauma her body had sustained from being knocked unconscious, although how she was knocked out was a mystery. She tried to shift her legs to a more comfortable position only to discover she couldn't move them, not even an inch, due to the tight bindings restraining her ankles and knees and fixing them to the legs of the chair. She tugged at her arms only to find they were similarly restrained.

'I see you're finally awake,' a cold familiar voice spoke from the doorway.

Olivia turned toward the voice, ruthlessly steeling herself against the wild pounding in her chest. She twisted her arms trying to get free, but the bindings were too tight.

Glancing down she could see that her wrists were bound to the arms of the chair with strange thin reeds that had been braided together to form a thicker rope. Tightly interwoven in the rope was a sweet smelling vine of small white flowers. Her wrists burned and chafed, already red raw and oozing small trickles of blood, even though she had not struggled against her bonds. In fact, the rope itself seemed to be reacting to her skin.

She reached for her magic intending to burn not only the rope, but the whole damn house if she had to, but realized with a start that she couldn't. She could feel her magic bubbling just below the surface of her skin, writhing like a trapped animal howling to be free, but she couldn't access it.

'I wouldn't bother trying to use your power,' he smirked. 'That rope is something a little special I prepared just for you. It is designed specifically to bind not just a witch's body, but her magic too.'

Her gaze hardened and unwilling to show any fear she raised her chin. She'd defied the God of the Underworld, she faced the Titans, pissed off the Judges of the Underworld and dunked a drunk Goddess. There was no way she was going to cower before a demon.

'Nathaniel,' she replied coldly.

'So, you know who I am then?' his mouth curved in amusement.

He stepped smoothly into the room, a velvet covered item tucked under his arm. It didn't take a genius to figure out what it was. She watched him warily as he set it down on his desk, leaning against the heavy piece of furniture.

'I must admit,' he replied curiously, 'you have me at a disadvantage Olivia.'

Her eyes narrowed.

'Yes, I know your name,' he leaned closer and she cringed at the sharp unpleasant scent of him, 'but that's all I know for the moment. But don't worry, before we are done here, you will tell me everything.'

'I doubt it,' she replied.

'Oh I think you will,' he smiled. 'You'll find I can

be very persuasive.'

'I'm sure you are,' Olivia threw his smile back at him, 'but I don't plan on being here that long.'

'No one knows you're here Olivia. Just who do you think is coming to save you, Theodore Beckett?'

'Trust me, it won't take him long to figure out where I am,' she sneered. 'If you start running now, you might be able to find a slimy pit to crawl into and hide from him, but I seriously doubt it.'

He barked out a laugh, a cruel sound devoid of any warmth or humor.

'And what exactly is he going to do to me? Scratch me with his little knife again?' he held up the hand Theo had severed previously and wiggled his fingers. 'It didn't do him much good last time, as you can see.'

'Oh I wouldn't worry about that,' she replied coolly. 'This time I'll have him cut you into so many pieces there'll be nothing left to grow back.'

Nathaniel's eyes suddenly narrowed.

'Maybe we should deal with Mr Beckett,' he mused thoughtfully. He reached across the desk and retrieved a small silver bell before shaking it lightly, the merry tickling sound at odds with the tension filled air.

A few moments later a man Olivia did not recognize came stomping through the doorway. His hair was a dark strawberry blond, his eyes small obsidian orbs which glared balefully, first at her then at Nathaniel.

'A bell?' he growled. 'Do I look like a servant?'

'Zachary,' Nathaniel sighed.

'Zachary?' Olivia's gaze snapped to him in surprise. 'You're Zachary?'

Her mouth pursed thoughtfully as she studied the man with renewed interest. It had to be an earlier version of him she surmised, not the one who had been helping the later Nathaniel to destroy the Crossroads.

'So you know Zachary too?' Nathaniel raised one dark brow slowly. 'Now you are making me curious.'

'I know of him,' she shrugged, her gaze running up and down Zachary's form before allowing herself a slow smile. 'Last I heard he was about to take an extended vacation as Hades' guest…I can't imagine he would have enjoyed it as much as Hades did.'

'Hades?' Zachary queried sharply.

'You two,' she shook her head contemptuously. 'You really have no idea who you're dealing with, do you?'

Zachary lunged forward and roughly grabbed her throat. When he spoke he was so close his rank breath fanned across her face.

'Then why don't you enlighten us?' he hissed angrily.

'Zachary,' Nathaniel snapped, 'that's enough.'

'Let me have her Nathaniel,' he begged. 'I will wring the truth from her.'

'I am well aware of your skills,' he answered calmly, 'however, I wish to question her myself. I need you to deal with Theodore Beckett.'

'I thought you had no interest in him?' he glared at him accusingly.

'I don't, but if what the girl says is true he may become a problem for us.' He leaned back against the desk tapping his fingertips against the wood thoughtfully. 'Kill him, and the younger version of him just to be sure.'

'If you touch him I will destroy you,' Olivia growled as she struggled so forcefully against her bonds that the chair slid across the floor.

Zachary smiled cruelly, sensing that they'd touched a nerve. He leaned down over her until they were almost face to face.

'Would you like me to bring you back a little keepsake Olivia?' he whispered provocatively. 'Tell me, which body part would you like me to bring you as a gift? His head? His heart? Something else?'

'He's going to cut you to shreds,' she hissed, 'then we'll see who's missing body parts.'

'She's a spirited little thing isn't she?' Zachary turned and grinned at Nathaniel. 'Don't use the needles on her until I return, I wouldn't want to miss that.'

'Oh I'm sure we'll have plenty of time with this one,' Nathaniel's mouth twitched in amusement. 'Something tells me she won't break easily.'

Zachary turned to the door throwing her one last smirk before disappearing.

Once they were alone Nathaniel turned back to the desk and carefully unwrapped the dark velvet covering. Slowly and deliberately he peeled back the edges, revealing a book she was very familiar with.

Hester's Grimoire.

She glanced at the book impassively before looking up at him.

'Do you know what this book is?'

'A Good Housekeeping Guide?' she shrugged.

The slap cracked hard against her cheek, snapping her head to the side. Nathaniel smoothed his coat and readjusted his sleeve calmly before returning to his perch on the desk.

'Try again Olivia.'

'Is it a copy of Macbeth?'

Crack.

Her head whipped to the side again. Ignoring the sting of his palm across her reddened cheek she turned her defiant gaze back on him.

'No?' she queried. 'Is it… a copy of a Thousand and One Arabian Nights in the original Arabic?'

Crack.

This time she tasted the metallic tang of blood in her mouth. Spitting it out unceremoniously onto his expertly crafted rug, she looked back up at him.

'Wait…wait, I've got it,' she smiled through bloodied lips, 'it's a discourse on Meditations on First Philosophy by Descartes.'

'I knew you were going to prove troublesome,' he

breathed and with a mock sigh he turned and retrieved a roll of coarse material from a nearby cabinet. He unrolled it carefully on the desk making sure she could get a good look at it. Her stomach clenched when she saw it contained dozens of cruel looking implements.

'I can see we're going to have to do this the hard way.'

She straightened in her chair, stiffening her spine as she glared at him with hate filled eyes.

'But first,' he leaned over her and yanked open the neck of her shift. 'Where is it?' he growled seeing her bare throat.

'What?' she asked innocently.

'You know exactly what,' he hissed in her ear. 'Where is my brother's compass?'

'Ohhh,' she exhaled theatrically, 'you mean my compass?'

His jaw clenched tightly.

'I traded it,' she shrugged.

'You did what?' he replied slowly.

'Yeah,' she smiled smugly, 'to a peddler…for some magic beans…'

This time his hand balled tightly in anger as he smashed his fist into her jaw. She bit her lip to stop herself from crying out in pain, determined not to give him the satisfaction.

Fighting to get his anger under control he turned back to the table. 'Now,' he said, allowing himself a moment as he perused the selection thoughtfully, 'do you have any last requests before we begin?'

'Yeah,' she growled through her rapidly swelling jaw, 'untie the ropes.'

He stared at her for a moment almost as if trying to judge if she was serious or not. Clearly sarcasm was lost on him. Choosing to ignore her comment he turned back to the assortment and selected a wicked looking pair of metal pincers.

'Right then,' his smile was sharp as ice, 'shall we begin?'

The pale spectral light of dawn had begun to break over the tree line, trying to burn back the fog, which still filled the orchard and rolled over the ground surrounding the house.

'Any luck?' James called to Theo as he reappeared from the orchard.

'Nothing,' he growled.

'Come back into the house,' he told him, glancing at his clothes. He still wore only his breeches and thin shirt, long woolen stockings and leather shoes. 'You'll freeze to death out here.'

Scowling Theo stalked silently back into the house, with James limping along behind him, trying to keep up.

'Theo,' James began, but Theo slammed the door and headed straight for the bedroom returning moments later with his jerkin and cloak. 'What are you doing?'

'What does it look like?' he snapped. 'I'm going to look for Olivia.'

'It won't do any good until the fog burns off, you'll just end up wandering around in circles throughout the orchard.'

'She isn't in the orchard.'

'You don't know that,' he replied pointedly. 'From what you told me about the last time you saw this kind of mist, it lured her out into the woods while she slept. She didn't realize she'd left her bed. You can't be sure the same thing hasn't happened again, nor discount the possibility of her leaving of her own free will.'

'She wouldn't do that. There is no way she would have climbed out of the window in the middle of the night, half dressed, in the freezing cold, and not said anything to me.'

'She would if she'd been sleepwalking.'

'It wasn't sleepwalking last time,' he dragged his hands through his hair in frustration. 'Last time she was lured out into the woods, she didn't know what was happening.'

'How do you know the same thing hasn't happened this time?'

'Because Olivia is a lot more powerful and aware than she was last time. She knows how to protect herself, protect her mind from outside influence. The one thing you can say about Olivia is, she never makes the same mistake twice.'

'So where does that leave us?'

'Someone took her, and I'm going to get her back.'

He threw his jerkin on and tightened the belt before slinging his cloak around his shoulders and heading toward the door.

'Theo wait!' James limped after him, grabbing his own cloak, which was hung by the door. 'Theo will you just wait a minute and think this through.'

He followed him into the stables and watched as he began to saddle one of the horses.

'You have no idea where to start looking,' James pointed out.

'I have a pretty good idea,' Theo said darkly, 'and believe me, by the time I'm done with Nathaniel he's going to wish he'd never crawled out of Hell.'

'You don't know for certain it's Nathaniel. It could be her mother or the Nathaniel she brought with her.'

'No,' Theo shook his head, 'Isabel is too single minded. She wants the book, which means she wants Hester. All her focus right now is on finding the Wests, she's not interested in Olivia other than keeping her from interfering.'

'And the other Nathaniel?'

'Isabel has him bound up tightly with magic. He

can't do anything without her say so, besides when she raised Nathaniel from the devil's trap the body she bound him into was sealed with blood magic. Not only her blood, but she used Olivia's as well, which means as long as he's trapped in that body he can't harm her.'

'But that's not true of the other Nathaniel?' James replied slowly. 'He can still cause her harm?'

'He is in his true form, he has no restrictions. He can do whatever he wants,' Theo growled.

'But why go after Olivia?'

'There are so many reasons,' Theo shook his head, tightening the cinches on the saddle and adjusting the foot straps. 'He knows she has possession of the compass, which not only belonged to his brother Seth who is imprisoned in the Underworld by Hades, but Hades himself gave the compass to Olivia.'

''Hades?' James eyes widened.

'Look,' Theo's gaze locked on his father's, 'the night we left, he saw her conjure Hell fire, something apparently no other human has ever been able to do. Add into that her tie to Hades and to his brother, and he wouldn't be able to resist. He'd want answers, answers she has and you know he'll torture her to get them.'

James' face hardened as he reached for the other horse and began to saddle her quickly and efficiently.

'What are you doing?' Theo frowned.

'I'm coming with you,' he replied matter of factly.

'The hell you are,' Theo swore. 'You've been too exposed already because of us. You can't go up against Nathaniel again, this time he'll kill you.'

'Theo,' James' face softened at his son's obvious concern for him, 'Olivia is my daughter now. Do you really think I would risk any less for her than I would for you? Witch or no witch, she's my family and I love her. There is no way I am letting Nathaniel do to her what he did to me.'

After a brief moment's internal debate Theo

finally nodded in agreement.

'We have to hurry,' he waited as James finished up and they led their horses out into the chilly morning. 'He's already had her for hours. God only knows what he's done to her.'

'I'll take you to his house in Salem,' James replied, 'but we have to be careful Theo. You said yourself that time has already been changed. We can't risk damaging it any further.'

'I'm going to get Olivia back, even if I have to tear Salem apart brick by brick.' Theo swung up easily into the saddle his eyes flashing dangerously, 'and I don't give a damn about the timeline.'

It took longer than he would've liked and Theo bristled at the delay, but they were riding old working horses used to pulling a wagon at a slow laborious pace and delivering casks of cider. By the time they arrived in Salem they'd lost another couple of hours. They tethered the horses and continued on foot hoping to blend in with the crowd and draw less attention to themselves. Through the winding streets, past street vendors and beggars they ducked and weaved. Past the briny scent of the docks and the incessant screech of gulls they made their way into the wealthier section of town.

They ducked down an alley, stepping around piles of waste and passed by a faded green door with no markings as they headed toward the other end. When they reached it, the alley opened out into a wide street and on the opposite side were several houses.

'There,' James pointed at the large house directly opposite them. 'That's Nathaniel's house.'

'I see he's done well for himself. Last time I was here he was lodging with the Alcott's,' Theo murmured, his eyes narrowing as he took in the details of the two storey house.

'He is very highly regarded by the selectmen and

the clergy,' James glanced at the house darkly, trying not to remember the last time he had been within its walls. 'Although he makes a point to never expose himself too much to the public eye, never underestimate the level of his influence, nor the full extent of his reach.'

'None of that matters right now,' Theo frowned, 'all I care about is getting Olivia back in one piece.'

'It's too exposed,' James looked around noting the number of people on the street. We can't break into the house without someone seeing and we can't exactly walk up to the door and knock.'

'If I have to, that's exactly what I'll do,' he replied tightly, 'but for now let's get closer and see if there's another way in.'

Letting out a deep frustrated breath, James finally nodded his agreement.

'Okay then, let's go.'

Theo took a step forward out onto the street, but suddenly felt himself grabbed roughly and dragged back into the alley. Spinning around he was shoved against the wall and pinned by a large tall body.

Theo's eyes widened as his gaze fell on the one face he'd both missed and loathed, and not in equal measure.

'Logan?'

'Shush,' Logan hissed quietly, 'we can't stay here, it isn't safe. You need to come with me.'

'I'm not going anywhere,' Theo's eyes flashed back to Nathaniel's house, 'I have to…'

'I know about the girl,' Logan interrupted him. 'If you want to save her you have to come with me.'

'Where?'

'Somewhere we can talk,' his eyes flicked to James. 'It's not far.'

'Theo,' James spoke softly, 'we need a better plan if we are going to get to Olivia. He's one of the people closest to Nathaniel, he may be able to get us in. We should at least listen to what he has to say.'

Theo cast one last longing glance toward the house where he was certain Olivia was been held. So close and yet so far away. Knowing that he needed help if he was to have any chance of getting out of that house alive with her, he turned back to his brother and nodded reluctantly.

Logan released his grip on him and started back down the alley toward the same nondescript door they'd passed by earlier. They followed him curiously until he stopped and rapped hard on the door three times. The door slowly creaked open. A pair of beady blue eyes set in a ruddy face appeared, studying each of them in turn until returning to Logan. Nodding his head, the man opened the door fully and stepped back.

All three of them stepped into the small, cramped, low beamed room. Rough tables and benches filled the space, and a large fireplace was set deeply into the far wall a small fire burning weakly to ward of the chills and draughts of the poorly maintained building. A bar was tucked at one end of the room surrounded by kegs and casks and beside it was a set of stairs that led up.

'This is an inn?' Theo asked warily. There had been no signs or anything by the door.

'Of sorts,' Logan replied. 'Welcome to the Salted Bone.'

'The Salted Bone?' Theo's head snapped up in surprise as his mind was cast back to Jackson's pub in Mercy which bore the same name.

'Aye,' Logan nodded. 'This is Thomas, he runs the place.'

'You wouldn't be a Murphy by any chance would you?' Theo asked curiously.

'How did you know?' Thomas confirmed suspiciously.

'Lucky guess,' Theo replied, relaxing slightly. 'So this is an inn then?'

'I'll explain that later, for now come with me.' He led them past the bar and up the stairs, but paused and turned back to Thomas. 'Our friend will be here shortly, please send him up when he arrives.'

Thomas nodded and they continued up the stairs.

'Who is coming?' Theo asked. 'What is going on Logan?'

'In here,' he indicated an open door.

They stepped inside noting the small wooden chair and the dresser, upon which stood a wash basin and jug. A small bed was tucked against one of the walls and a fair sized window looked down onto the street below and gave a completely unhindered view of Nathaniel's house.

Theo turned away from the window to look back at his brother. This was the brother he'd loved so desperately and looked up to as a child, yet also a man who'd betrayed him and sent so many innocents to their deaths at the end of a rope. The man who, the last time he'd seen him, had tried to kill him and then left him to die in a burning barn.

So many conflicting emotions crashed in on him, he didn't even know where to start. This was a man he couldn't trust, a man that should be his enemy. He was Nathaniel's shadow. How was he supposed to believe anything Logan had to say? For all he knew he was using his relationship with Theo to delay him so Nathaniel could torture Olivia.

That thought alone should have had him walking out of the room, but there was something in Logan's expression, something in the way he looked at him. He was not the same bitter and angry man he'd left behind the night Sam had pulled him forward in time and dropped him in Mercy. No, he seemed different somehow, softer, more like the Logan from his childhood, the Logan he had loved.

'Theo,' Logan stepped toward him slowly, his voice low. 'We have much to discuss.'

He wasn't sure if he could trust this man. Everything in him told him he shouldn't, everything he knew, everything he remembered screamed that he was dangerous, that he would betray him, but Olivia's words kept coming back to him.

'Theo, we've changed the timeline, you said it yourself things are different. He may not be the same man you remember.'

'I think you'd better start talking,' Theo replied curtly.

Logan sighed, knowing this was not going to be easy.

'Theo,' he began, 'I know about Olivia. I know she is a witch and I'm here to help you get her back.'

'Why?' he frowned in confusion, 'I don't understand why would you help us?'

'Because…' Logan reached inside his coat and pulled out a tattered book that Theo instantly recognized. It was their mother's journal.

'I know everything…'

18.

Olivia's breath caught in her throat, the pain so intense she couldn't breathe, as she was thrown roughly to the hard ground of the cellar. She heard the door close as she lay motionless, unable to move. The room was dimly lit by candle light, but it didn't make a difference, she didn't want to move. Every tiny movement caused an excruciating pain to shoot up her arm, through her shoulder and across her upper back, and from the way her arm hung limply at her side, like a primate, she was pretty certain her shoulder was dislocated.

'Olivia?' a strangely familiar voice spoke softly. 'Olivia?'

She'd recognize that lilting musical island accent anywhere. Lifting her head slowly and sucking in a sharp breath at the pain shooting across her shoulder, she twisted her head in the direction of the voice and blinked as her eyes adjusted to the dim light.

'Tituba?' she croaked, her rough voice sounding foreign to her ears.

'Olivia,' Tituba repeated in concern. She tried to get closer, but there was a sudden chink of chains and her movements halted. 'Olivia, I can't get no closer, you 'ave to come to me.'

'No, I'm good' Olivia muttered, dropping her

head down on the ground. 'I think I'll just stay here for a while.'

'Olivia!' Tituba's voice snapped with authority, 'don't close your eyes, don't sleep. You 'ave to move, I can't help you unless you come close.'

She knew the beautiful slave woman was right, she shouldn't go to sleep. Somewhere in the back of her mind she knew that with the trauma her body had sustained there was a chance she could go into shock. But she was so tired, physically and mentally exhausted.

It wouldn't end, Nathaniel may not have gotten any answers from her yet, but it was only a matter of time before he came back and began again. In fact, the only reason he'd stopped was because her body had passed its point of tolerance and she kept passing out. So he'd dragged her broken body down to the cellar to rest, before he started on round two.

She could feel the numbness creeping in again and her eyes drifted closed.

'OLIVIA!' Tituba snapped again, 'open your eyes!'

She was right, she had to fight, she couldn't give in. If she stood any chance of getting out of this house of horrors she had to move. Raising her head again she forced herself to roll over. A pained cry tore from her lips as her shoulder pulled again, but at least it was no longer trapped under the weight of her body. Her left arm dangled uselessly at her side. Not only was her shoulder dislocated, but her hand was a mess.

When Nathaniel had first removed the pincers he'd amused himself by pulling off her nails, one by one and just when she'd thought it couldn't get any worse he'd proceeded to break every single bone in her left hand, starting with each of her fingers. She couldn't even feel it now, let alone move it. She'd tried not to look at it as it now resembled canned ham.

Fortunately, she thought, he hadn't had a chance to fuck up her other arm yet, so at least she could still use that and one of her legs. Her right leg was a different matter. There were several puncture marks which ran the length of her leg, where he'd slowly screwed vicious looking white hot metal pins into the bone along her shin.

Knowing she had to move, she gritted her teeth. Steeling herself against the jolting agony, she slowly and painstakingly dragged herself along the floor, inch by torturous inch. It seemed to take an eternity, the room silent but for her labored breaths. She could feel Tituba watching, feel the waves of sympathy and concern rolling off her.

When she was finally close enough Tituba reached out and pulled her the rest of the way. Collapsing exhaustedly into her arms, her breaths came in deep gasps. It was only by good fortune that Tituba was chained to the wall by her ankle, which left her hands free. She pressed and probed Olivia's shoulder, while she tried not to cry out in pain.

'Your shoulder is out of place,' she told her softly, 'I will have to put it back.'

Olivia nodded slowly, knowing it was going to hurt like hell.

'Brace yourself,' she told her, wrapping her arm around Olivia's torso and gripping her arm firmly.

Gritting her teeth, she couldn't quite silence the groan of pain and rush of nausea as Tituba cracked her shoulder back into place. She grabbed onto the slave woman with her good hand, squeezing her eyes shut and taking deep measured breaths until the pain slowly began to subside.

Although her shoulder still hurt like hell, she felt almost instant relief once it was back in place and no longer dangling uselessly. As the feeling suddenly rushed back into her damaged hand she sucked in an involuntary gasp.

Tituba stroked her hair back from her swollen face and crooned to her softly as if she were a child. Her jaw was badly swollen and bruised, her lip was split and one eye was almost swollen shut.

'I bet I look good, don't I?' Olivia murmured in a low scratchy voice.

'Trust me, being locked in this place I seen a lot worse.'

'How did you end up here?'

Tituba sighed, her head dropping back against the wall.

'After I was accused by Betty and Abby, I was beaten and arrested. I was put on trial along with the others.'

'But they didn't hang you?' Olivia replied in puzzlement. 'Don't get me wrong, I'm real glad they didn't, but it doesn't make sense. As a black slave, accused of witchcraft, I would've thought they would have been desperate to make an example of you.'

'Plenty of them were,' she replied.

'Then how?'

'Nathaniel,' she replied. 'He know I had magic in me, just as he know the others who hung did not.'

'He made sure you were protected from the death penalty,' Olivia whispered, 'because he wanted you alive?'

'Yes. I was left to rot in the prison. When sanity finally return and the court finished, all the accused were released but I. I was not free, I was still Master Parris' property. He did not wish me to return and so I was sold to a new master. When they took me from the prison I thought I would be taken to a new household, but instead I brought here. Nathaniel hired another man to buy me on his behalf so no one know I'm here.'

'How long have you been here?'

Olivia felt rather than saw her shrug.

'It doesn't matter, there no way out for me.'

She picked up the chain and rattled it. Olivia's eyes narrowed as her gaze landed on the metal band around the woman's ankle. The lettering inscribed deeply into the metal was familiar. She'd seen that design before on the demon collar her mother and Nathaniel had put on the Ferryman. No wonder she couldn't escape, the chains were probably blocking her powers the same way the rope had blocked her own.

The rope.

Olivia glanced down to her own wrists, the rope wasn't there. He'd untied her from the chair and left the rope attached to the chair instead of her. He probably figured she was too weak to cause any trouble.

Moron.

Reaching deep down she felt for her power. It was there and despite her exhaustion she could reach it. Turning to look at Tituba her good eye narrowed. If the shackles used on Tituba were indeed the same as the ones used to restrain Charon, then she should be able to break them the same way.

'Help me sit up,' she croaked.

'Olivia you should rest.'

'No,' she shook her head, 'help me.'

She reached out and grasped Olivia gently and after a few awkward moments she managed to help her into a sitting position. Cradling her damaged hand against her chest Olivia laid her other hand gently on the metal. It felt cool to the touch and vibrated like a plucked string as she traced her fingers along its surface. The writing suddenly glowed with sapphire blue fire and she knew it was the same as the demon collar, forged in Hell fire.

As it had before, in the Turkish baths of the abandoned Boatman hotel back in Mercy, the whole room seemed to fade away and her eyes drifted closed. She could hear a low murmur, a whisper in the furthest corner of her mind, a language so ancient it had not been spoken in millions of years. A language from the very beginning of time. It spoke to her soul and she realized with a start that she recognized it. It was the same voice which had been whispering to her since the moment she'd landed in Salem.

When she opened her eyes they were no longer a warm whiskey color, but deep blue, and held within their depths countless eons and such a vastness of power. The words rose unbidden to her lips as she murmured the language that came to her so easily. The shackles grew warm under her touch and as she wrapped her fingers around the side and tugged, it came apart in her hand with an inaudible click.

When she looked up, Tituba was watching her intently. She didn't appear at all surprised, but instead seemed to be appraising her in some way. Olivia's eyes had lost the bright blue flame and settled back into their warm natural whiskey color. But the whispering didn't stop, she could still hear it.

'Do you hear that?'

'Hear what?' she asked Olivia curiously. 'What exactly do you hear?'

'Whispering,' she murmured absently, her attention firmly fixed on the voices.

'What do they say, the whispers?'

'I'm not sure exactly, I don't think I can put it into words. The language is old and very complex.'

They both looked up suddenly as they heard footsteps on the stairs leading down to the door. Olivia grabbed the hem of Tituba's ragged dress and pulled it over her ankle, to hide the fact she was no longer shackled.

'When he comes for me,' Olivia spoke quickly, 'you have to let him take me.'

'Olivia no,' she shook her head.

'You have to,' she rushed on. 'While he's distracted with me, sneak out and find Theo.'

'I'm not leaving you.'

'Please,' Olivia breathed, 'you have to find Theo and warn him the demon Zachary is going to kill him.'

The door suddenly swung open and Nathaniel strode toward them. Wrapping the witch rope around her throat he pulled her backward, dragging her away from

Tituba.

'I realized I'd forgotten to restrain you. I thought you'd be in too much pain to cause any mischief,' he smiled as he looked down at her where she lay on the floor, breathing heavily. 'I see I underestimated your recovery time.'

'Go to hell,' she hissed.

'Already been,' he replied humorously as he hauled her up easily and slung her body over his shoulder. 'I hope you're looking forward to this as much as I am.'

She said nothing, watching Tituba's face as he carried her from the room and back up the stairs toward the study. Before she knew it she was tied back in the chair, and now the witch rope burned at her throat as well as her wrists.

'Now where were we?' he leaned over the instruments which he'd yet to use.

She watched as he pulled out what looked like three long, thin, wickedly sharp needles but as she looked closer she could see a spiral of metal winding the length of each of them, making them look like long thin corkscrews.

'I know Zachary wanted me to wait for this part,' his mouth curved, 'but I'm sure he'll forgive my impatience.'

She clamped her lips together as he lined up one of the needles against her shoulder and slowly pressed it into her skin, she bit her lip so hard she drew more blood. But as he slowly began to twist it, viciously screwing it deeper into her flesh and through her bone, she couldn't bite back the scream of white hot agony which ripped from her throat.

Theo looked up at his brother in confusion.

'What do you mean you know everything?' he asked cagily.

'After James was arrested Stephen and I were sent to search his house.' he turned to James contritely. 'Sorry about that.'

James' eyes narrowed and his jaw clenched tightly.

'While Stephen was in the other room, I found the first book, the book of magic,' he shook his head softly in remembrance. 'I knew what it was, it seemed to confirm everything they were saying about James. But then...I found this.'

He held up his mother's journal.

'I recognized her handwriting straight away,' he continued. 'At first I couldn't understand why it was there or what was going on. I was going to hide both books until I could look at them and decide what to do. But unfortunately Stephen walked in. I managed to hide mother's journal in my coat, but he'd already seen the witch's book. I had no choice but to hand it over to Nathaniel.'

He took a deep breath, his eyes locking on his brother.

'I took the journal home with me and spent every minute reading it. Then I went back and read it again and again. It was like walking out of the darkness into the sunlight and for the first time in years I could see everything so clearly. See every single mistake I'd ever made. I could see where my hate and anger had led me.'

'Reading that book was like finally being able to breathe again. I could hear mother's voice in my head with every page I turned.'

He shook his head, restlessly pacing the room, absently stopping in front of the window and looking down upon Nathaniel's house.

'I took a long hard look at the man I was, at the man I had become and I didn't like what I saw. She wouldn't have wanted that for me.' He turned to look at Theo, his eyes dark and filled with pain. 'She would've been ashamed of me.'

Theo kept his mouth shut, he didn't know what to say, didn't know what to believe. After all the timeline had changed, he had no way of knowing which of his memories were real or which were left over from a reality that now never happened.

'You tried to warn me,' Logan continued, 'tried to save me, but I wouldn't listen and it cost us Temperance. I should have been at home looking after her, not following Nathaniel around like a trained puppy. I failed her, just as I failed you,' he shook his head sadly. 'Why didn't you tell me?'

'Tell you what?' Theo asked carefully.

'You know what,' he whispered. 'You and Temperance both have magical abilities and so did our mother, and...' His gaze cut across to James who wisely chose not to interfere with this moment between the two brothers, '...your father.'

So, he knew about James, Theo thought.

'You may not have known about James when we were children, but you knew that you and Tempy were different. Why didn't you come to me?'

'I was protecting you,' Theo replied quietly, 'and us.' He blew out a deeply frustrated breath and raked both of his hands through his hair.

'I didn't know what to do. I made the best decision I could at the time, but I've always regretted it.'

'I would have protected you,' Logan said quietly.

'Would you?'

'Of course I would have,' he replied, 'you're my brother and I love you. When I found out the truth about you, I came to a Crossroads in my life. I had to make a choice, between what I had been taught was right and wrong and what my own conscience was telling me. I chose you... I knew I had to get you as far away from Nathaniel as I could, that's why I treated you the way I did. I needed you out of Salem and back at the farm, where I knew you'd be safe.'

'But all the things you did, the accused...'

'You saw exactly what I needed you to see,

everyone did.'

'I don't understand,' Theo frowned.

'He saved them,' a new voice spoke up from the doorway.

James and Theo turned to see a tall blond haired man step into the room. For a moment Theo's stomach jolted; he looked almost identical to his best friend Jake back in Mercy.

'Justin,' James replied in confusion, 'what are you doing here?'

'I'm a part of Logan's story,' he walked into the room.

'Theo,' James introduced them, 'this is my friend Justin Gilbert.'

Theo nodded in acknowledgment. 'What do you mean he saved them?' he asked, latching on to what he'd said when he walked in.

'When Logan had his epiphany he came to me. He wanted to find a way to stop the killing, to stop Nathaniel,' Justin picked up the story. 'He was going to publicly denounce Nathaniel. Being the closest one to him, he was privy to many of his secrets. However, being a part of Nathaniel's inner circle made him far too valuable. We needed to see how far Nathaniel's reach stretched, so Logan agreed to stay close to Nathaniel and work with us. We managed to save so many, thanks to Logan's information. That's what this place is, 'The Salted Bone', it's a safe place for the accused to hide until we could smuggle them out of Salem.'

'You were the one who told Justin that Nathaniel was holding me at his house?' James turned to Logan.

He nodded slowly. 'I'm sorry it took us so long to get you out, we needed to know that Justin had the backing of the Governor in case Nathaniel refused to hand you over.'

'You saved my life,' he replied quietly.

Logan shrugged, 'don't waste your gratitude on

me, I don't deserve it. Whatever lives I had a hand in saving in no way makes up for those I failed...for those poor souls who were hung on Gallows Hill.'

'Logan,' Justin sighed.

'It's true Justin,' Logan insisted, 'you know it is.'

'So you both have been playing Nathaniel?' Theo frowned trying to understand. 'You made him believe he could trust you and you used that information to save those he'd had accused or arrested?'

'It's so much more complex than that,' Logan told him, looking to Justin.

Justin met his gaze and an unspoken agreement seemed to pass between them. Finally, he nodded as if giving his permission for Logan to continue.

'Theo,' Logan spoke softly, 'we know what Nathaniel is. We know that he is a demon.'

'What?' Theo gasped.

'Once we understood what we were dealing with, we realized this went far beyond merely denouncing him and having him arrested. We knew it wouldn't do any good. Have you read Mother's journal yet?'

Theo shook his head. 'James has, but I didn't get the chance.'

'Mother saw a great many things, she was an incredibly gifted seer. She knew about Nathaniel and his search for a book she called Infernum.'

'The Hell book,' Theo nodded.

'You know about that?'

'That's why we're here, to stop Nathaniel from getting his hands on it.'

'That is part of our goal too and it goes way beyond just the two of us.' Logan pulled back his sleeve revealing a mark seared into the flesh of the inside of his wrist.

Justin too pulled back his sleeve to reveal the same mark. It was a small cross with a loop at the top which looked as if it had been burned into their skin with a branding iron. Theo's gaze narrowed as he studied the mark. He recognized it, he'd seen it before in one of the history books on ancient civilizations that Olivia had shown him back when he'd first arrived in Mercy. It was Egyptian, an Ankh, the universal symbol for truth.

'That is the symbol for truth,' he looked up at his brother.

'Yes' he smiled, pleased that Theo knew what it was. 'That is what we are.'

'I don't understand,' he shook his head.

'We are 'In quibus sit veritas' which translates from the Latin, as Men of Truth,' he told him. 'We are a secret order which started with Justin and I, then Thomas Murphy joined us and then Benjamin Linden. Joseph Green, who will replace Samuel Parris as Minister, is also one of us. Our order is growing slowly, but soon we hope to place a few more of us in positions of power.'

'To what end?' James frowned.

'To protect the innocents and those of magical descent from persecution,' Justin told him. 'Most of the order are descended from magical families who fled the persecution of Europe and the Old World. They thought that this would be their new world, a place they would be safe, but instead they were met with greater fear and ignorance than they'd left behind in England and Ireland. All they have ever wanted was a safe place to call home and we are going to make sure that they have it.'

'If we can get a few of our order into the highest ranks we can make sure that the trials never happen again. But more than that, we will protect them from creatures like Nathaniel. This isn't just about protecting our kin from persecution, it's about protecting all the innocents, even those of non-magical descent. They won't know and they won't thank us, but it's the right thing to do,' Justin told them.

'We're here to stop Nathaniel,' Logan stepped closer to Theo, 'and we're going to start by getting your woman back.'

'How?' Theo asked.

'There's another way in and out of the house, a secret entrance that he had designed when he commissioned the house to be built. I will take you in that way, but we must wait until dark; we cannot be seen.'

'We can't wait until nightfall,' Theo paced to the window anxiously. 'What if she doesn't have that long?'

'Trust me brother,' Logan said stopping beside him and placing his hand on his shoulder, 'I wouldn't leave anyone in that house a moment longer than necessary, but it's not just Nathaniel who is a danger to her.'

'What do you mean?'

'Nathaniel is still highly placed with the governor and the other officials. If your Olivia really can do the things Mother described in her journal, we cannot risk her being exposed to the selectmen. The trials may be over, but witchcraft is still a crime. If she is revealed as a witch she will still hang for it. Once we get her out of the house and away from Nathaniel, we must get her out of Salem as quickly as possible. We stand the best chance of success under the cover of night.'

Theo's jaw clenched tightly. He could see the logic in what Logan was saying, but it still made him sick to think of Olivia trapped in that house with Nathaniel.

'Tonight is the dark of the moon,' Logan told him. 'It lasts three days and there is a ritual Nathaniel performs. He doesn't know that I know this. He will be distracted for about an hour, that is our window of opportunity to get her out without risking a confrontation with him.'

'How do you know about the dark of the moon?' Theo frowned.

'We are the Men of Truth, we seek all forms of truth because knowledge is power. When we founded the order Justin and I began to learn everything we could about magic, demons and witchcraft. We sought out and read every forbidden book we could get our hands on, right under the noses of the selectmen. We know a great deal about Nathaniel, but we still don't yet know how to kill him. Therefore we must avoid a confrontation if we can.'

Theo nodded, turning back to the window and letting out a deep frustrated breath. The sun was starting to dip lower on the horizon, but it was still a goodly way off sunset and every minute felt like an eternity as his gaze locked on Nathaniel's house.

'Hold on Olivia,' he murmured, 'I'm coming for you…'

19.

Nathaniel looked up at the sudden knock at the door. Scowling in annoyance he glanced down at Olivia whose head had dropped forward limply as she gasped for air.

'I do apologize for the interruption,' he told her pleasantly. 'I'll be right back.'

He stepped out of the study, heading toward the door. Opening it slowly his gaze dropped to the hunched, hooded figure standing on his doorstep. His beady black eyes narrowed suspiciously at the stranger, his nostrils flaring with the ripe stench of decaying flesh.

'Yes?' he queried.

The figure looked up, the hood of his cloak falling back slightly to reveal his rotting mismatched face and the deeply embedded stitches in his mouth.

'What the…?'

He stared at the goblin of a figure who looked back up at him silently. Looking deeper he saw past the gruesome mask of death, past the milky half blinded eyes to the face beneath and what he saw caused his eyes to widen in surprise. He looked up suddenly, glancing into the street to make sure no one else had witnessed the stranger at his door. The sun was already setting giving everything a dim bruised cast, but it was still light enough for witnesses.

'Get inside before you are seen,' he hissed, stepping aside so the hunched figure could shuffle past him.

He paused in the hallway, turning to face his unexpected guest.

'You are me,' it was more a statement than a question. He grabbed the figure's face in his cold bony fingers, examining the stitches at his mouth.

'Magic,' he mused, 'but not unbreakable. Come with me and I will remove the stitches, then we can talk.'

The other Nathanial nodded, shuffling along behind him with an uneven gait until he was shown into the study. Once there his damaged eyes fell upon the broken and bloodied figure, hunched over and tied to a hard wooden chair with witch rope. If he'd had teeth he would have bared them. A strange muted growl vibrated deep in his throat as he regarded her with venom filled eyes.

'I see you two have already met,' Nathaniel said, his mouth curving in amusement as he bent down to retrieve a knife.

It was a seemingly innocuous implement. Small with a non-descript handle, but along the blade itself symbols and sigils were deeply etched.

'Hold still, this might sting a little' Nathaniel murmured as he once again grasped the ruined face of the other demon.

Gripping his jaw tightly, he tilted his face up and ran the knife edge along the seam of his lips, cutting the stitches and splitting his mouth open like a raw wound, releasing a pungent smell that even Nathaniel grimaced at.

'You stink of rotting human' he snorted in disgust. 'What have you done? How in all the Hells did you end up stitched up into this pile of decaying pig flesh?'

His visitor coughed a couple of times, savoring once again the freedom of movement in his jaw.

'It doesn't matter how,' he answered, his voice a disturbing wet growl. 'All that matters is that we can help each other.'

'Is that what you think?' Nathaniel raised a brow condescendingly. 'If you were stupid enough to get yourself trapped inside a mortal body, I think I can live without your help.'

'I'm you, you moron,' he growled, 'so unless you want to end up like this you'd better start listening, because trust me, being trapped in here is even worse than you can imagine. You think it looks bad on the outside, you should be stuck in here breathing in this filthy stench.'

'Very well,' he conceded after a moment, his eyes narrowing dangerously, 'I'm listening. What exactly is it you think you can do for me?'

'I can hand you the Wests,' he said simply.

'Why should I believe you?' he asked suspiciously.

'Was I ever this stupid?' he shook his head muttering to himself. 'Because you have one of them sitting right in front of you, you idiot.'

Nathaniel spun around to stare at Olivia, who had raised her chin defiantly as she witnessed their conversation.

'Hello Nathaniel,' she smiled at the misshapen man. 'Still looking pretty then.'

He growled angrily and took an involuntary step toward her, his teeth bared.

'You really want to kill her don't you?' the Salem Nathaniel smiled slowly.

'I can't...' he ground from between clenched teeth.

'And why exactly is that?'

'Because it was her mother who trapped me in this body. She sealed it with blood magic, both hers and Olivia's blood. I can't harm her.'

'No?' Nathaniel raised an eyebrow questioningly. Letting the knife he'd used on the stitches dangle teasingly from his fingers, he circled the chair Olivia was tied to until he stood behind her, facing the deformed version of himself. 'But I can harm her, can't I?'

He drew the knife across her collarbone leaving a trail of blood in its wake. Olivia bit back a hiss of pain. That was no ordinary knife. It held power, a lot of it, which burned even as it sliced.

'Would you like me to kill her for you?' Nathaniel purred as he skimmed the blade lightly across the skin of her exposed throat, gauging his counterpart's reaction and seeing the undisguised arousal in his gaze. 'Would you like to watch?'

'Yes,' he whispered.

'Well then,' Nathaniel straightened, 'let's talk terms.'

'We're both after the same thing. We want Infernum and we want to raise Seth from Hades' domain.'

Nathaniel nodded in agreement.

'In order to do that you need to get your hands on the West girls or their mother. They are the only ones who currently know its location.'

Nathaniel looked down at Olivia.

'She doesn't know where it is,' he told him. 'She doesn't matter, neither does her mother.'

'So what about the girls and their mother?'

'There are three of them, Abigail West and her twin daughters Hester and Bridget West, but before I tell you their location I want something from you.'

'And what's that?'

'I want you to free me from this body.'

Nathaniel stared thoughtfully at him, 'I can't do that. If it was created with blood magic, only blood can break it.'

He looked down at Olivia.

'It can't be her,' he mused, 'as she was part of the original spell. Nor her mother, but perhaps someone else of the West bloodline. You said there were three of them?'

He nodded slowly.

'We need at least Abigail West or the oldest of the daughters alive until we can ascertain which one of the them knows the location of the Hell book. But the spare, the younger sister? Her blood will break the prison.'

'Very well, but the other half of my price is that I get to watch you kill Olivia and I want you to do it slowly.'

Nathaniel smiled slowly, 'then we have a deal?'

'We have a deal,' he nodded. 'They are in a cabin in the woods just North of Salem. Olivia's mother is with them. I will take you to them once you deal with this witch.'

His hungry gaze fell on Olivia once again.

'Very well,' Nathaniel replied, 'how would you like it? Choked, watching the life slowly leave her eyes? Or would you like to watched her bleed?'

'Make her bleed' he whispered eagerly. 'Pull out her insides and make her watch.'

'As you wish,' he set the point of the knife against her sternum and pressed.

A bright trickle of blood seeped through her linen shift, her heart began to pound in her breast and a strange buzzing filled her ears. The candles in the room suddenly flared up, filling the space with a bright flash of light. A violent wind came out of nowhere and ripped through the room churning up papers and books, yet did not extinguish the candles which continued to sputter and flare. The heavy leather bound Grimoire, which had lain dormant on the desk, suddenly flipped itself open and the pages began to fan frantically as if caught on an unseen reel.

'What the hell?' Nathaniel released the pressure of the blade against Olivia's skin and stepped around the chair so that he was facing her. 'How are you doing this?'

But Olivia wasn't listening, he was now the equivalent of a pesky fly buzzing in her ear. The moment the book opened the whispering began again, this time so loud, so consuming, it was a roar in her mind, building higher and higher until it was screaming in her head. She threw her head back, her mouth opening in a silent scream as her eyes blazed a deep lavender. Suddenly the rope at her throat and wrists burst into dark purple flames.

'NO!' Nathaniel roared. There was no way she could overcome the witch rope, it was supposed to bind any witch's power.

'WHAT ARE YOU?' he thundered angrily.

Olivia still wasn't listening to him, she could feel the overwhelming power of the purple flames licking along her skin, filling her soul. When she'd conjured Hell fire it had felt vast and ancient, carrying with it a deep sense of responsibility. Her silver Spirit fire was cool and ageless and encompassed within it the sense of an infinite number of souls. Her Earth fire was gold and red and brought with it life and warmth, but this…this fire was incredible and she instantly knew beyond a shadow of a doubt what it was, as if the knowledge had been deep inside her all along.

It was Witch fire.

She reached out for it and let it consume her, bringing with it a deep sense of joy and belonging. It was as if all her sisters were crying out in one voice. Thousands and thousands of generations of witches who'd come before her calling to her soul, lending her their strength and resolve. It was like a hive mind, generations of memories and shared thought passed down to her. This was her greatest weapon.

She let the fire loose. It burst from her body exploding outward, knocking the other more damaged version of Nathaniel to the ground. Candles tumbled over and slowly the red and gold flames caught and began to spread, devouring the papers and books in their path with a roar.

Her blazing violet gaze locked on Nathaniel's as he stood opposite her, his fists clenched and his black eyes burning with fury.

Her mouth curved into a smile as she let her power loose. He screamed, locked in place, unable to move as his body was engulfed in purple flame. A circle of violent fire ignited around his feet keeping him trapped and immobile. Her gaze was locked on his, but she was unable to rise from the chair because of her injuries and he was unable to leave the circle of fire. Trapped in a Mexican standoff she didn't notice the other Nathaniel climb to his feet, nor did she hear him growl in anger before stumbling from the room and fleeing the fire. They were surrounded as the red and gold flames spread throughout the house, consuming everything in its path.

'I guess I'll see you in Hell Nathaniel,' Olivia smiled.

'You first,' he growled.

'FIRE!' Justin leapt to his feet and stared out of the window.

Bright red flames exploded out of the windows of Nathaniel's house and were already licking up the timber frame engulfing the roof. The shouts of panic filled the street below as everyone scrambled to gather buckets of water to stop the blaze from spreading to the adjacent buildings.

Theo leapt to his feet and was already down the stairs and running out onto the street before James and Logan could catch up with him.

'OLIVIA!' he screamed as the two men grabbed him roughly and wrestled him back from the snapping flames.

'Theo NO!' James shouted, 'the building is already too far gone.'

As he struggled against them James caught his foot and his injured leg threw him off balance. He stumbled to the ground losing his grip on his son's arm. Seeing an opportunity Theo swung around, his fist crashing into his brother's jaw forcing him to release his grip. He ran for the house kicking down the door and, covering his mouth with his sleeve, plunged into the dark smoky depths of the burning building.

He pressed forward through the wall of heat which made his skin feel impossibly tight. His eyes teared up as a beam crashed down beside him. Forcing himself deeper into the building he called for her again, his voice muffled by his sleeve as he tried to keep the smoke fumes from his mouth.

'Theodore!' A voice had him looking up, trying to see through the smoke before his eyes locked on a familiar looking slave woman.

'Tituba?' he coughed.

'This way,' she tugged at him urgently, strangely unaffected by the heat or smoke.

Tituba ran through the flames before stopping in the doorway, her gaze surveying the destruction. Flames rolled up the walls and across the ceiling and trapped in the center Olivia was still in the chair and Nathaniel was imprisoned in a circle of violet fire. Her eyes fell on the Grimoire still lying open on the burning desk and she rushed forward to grab it before it was consumed. A glint of metal caught her eye on the ground. She grabbed it quickly, wrapping her fingers around it, feeling the blade pulse with magic.

She turned as Theo burst into the room. His eyes immediately fell on Olivia and he rushed forward to scoop her into his arms. As he lifted her from the chair Logan came crashing through the doorway behind him, covering his mouth with his sleeve.

'Theo! Quickly the house is collapsing.'

'Tituba!' he called out to her.

'Get Olivia out of here,' she shoved the book and the knife into Logan's hands.

'What about you?' Theo yelled above the roar of the fire.

'I will deal with Nathaniel,' she eyes locked on the

demon who glared at her behind the wall of purple flame.

'Tituba!'

'GO!' she commanded.

'Theo we have to move now!' Logan coughed.

He threw one last look at Tituba and rushed from the room, following his brother. Once out in the hall they backed up as the ceiling crashed in blocking the door.

'Come on,' Logan yelled, 'I know another way out.'

Turning blindly Theo followed his brother into the smoke and flames.

Tituba turned and watched Nathaniel, completely unfazed by the smoke, heat or flames. She didn't even flinch as more of the building collapsed around them.

'They don't even know who you are, do they?' Nathaniel sneered. 'They have no idea that you're not even human.'

'They'll know soon enough,' she replied calmly. Although her voice still held the musical island accent it was no longer the poor speech patterns of a common slave, but instead was articulate and well spoken.

'I wasn't sure until just now,' his eyes narrowed, 'but I know who you are now.'

She watched him dispassionately as another part of the house groaned, followed by a crash of splintering wood.

'You could have escaped at any point before I shackled you,' he glared at her accusingly. 'You had the power not only to walk out, but to make those around you suffer, and yet you didn't. You allowed yourself to be subjected to slavery and abuse. You allowed them to beat you, condemn you and imprison you, and still you did not use your powers to defend yourself.'

'You want to know why?'

'Tell me,' he growled. 'You were never Tituba were you?'

She shook her head. 'The real Tituba died of fever back in Barbados months before Samuel Parris even sailed for the Colonies. He didn't even notice the difference; to him slaves are no better than animals. In his eyes every black woman looks the same.'

'So why? Why this elaborate ruse?'

'I would have thought that was obvious even to a stupid demon like you,' she scowled. 'I was waiting for her.'

'What's so special about Olivia West?'

'I wouldn't want to ruin the surprise for you so soon,' she smiled.

'You don't really think you can protect her do you?' he sneered.

'She has more allies than even she realizes,' she replied. 'We have waited a long, long time for her. Do you really think we would allow any harm to come to her.'

'I don't care what you think,' he growled, smashing his fist against the wall of flames holding him and ignoring the searing pain of his smoking flesh. 'This fire won't hold me indefinitely and as soon as I get free the first thing I will do is kill the West girls, take possession of the book and then… I'm coming for her.'

'And I will make sure she's ready,' she threatened menacingly.

'You don't have time,' he hissed. 'This fire will burn out within hours and I will be free.'

'Oh you think so?' her brow twitched as she raised her hands, 'we'll just see about that shall we?'

Her eyes burned deep ocean blue and her skin glowed with a mesmerizing luminance. The scent of briny salt water filled the air and the distant sound of waves echoed around her. The floor at his feet cracked and splintered, splitting open like a skin. The ground churned as she thrust deep, deep underground with her power, cracking open soil and rock until she reached a deep natural well of water.

Prizing the ground open even further the water surged upwards, a violent swell that ripped up through the layers of sediment until it reached the ground level. It erupted into the room with a steamy hiss as it made contact with the red and gold flames of the house fire. The purple flames however weren't doused by it. Instead the water swirled in a huge wave, curling around the flame encased demon until it coalesced into a writhing churning mass, a sphere comprised entirely of water, completely impenetrable and airtight. Inside the prison of water, the violet flames of Olivia's Witch fire continued to burn. He screamed and beat his fists against the fire, but it was no good.

She smiled coolly as the writhing sphere plunged deeply back into the earth taking the burning demon with it. The ground folded over and closed once again, sealing him in a watery prison.

'Enjoy the next fifty years,' she murmured.

Suddenly the beams above her cracked and gave way. With a thundering crash the house collapsed in on itself, but by the time the beams and burning timber hit the ground the strange dark skinned woman was already gone. The only evidence of her presence was the smell of salt water in the air and the lone call of a dark strange looking bird with a huge wingspan, who swooped high above in the sky, surveying the carnage below with a dispassionate eye.

Theo and Logan burst out into the blessedly cool air. With a loud crack the house behind them crashed in on itself as they stumbled away from the cloud of burning ash and smoke that was thrown up into the air.

'Come on,' Logan coughed, 'we have to get her out of the street.'

The exit had brought them out on the other side of the house. The only way around was to skirt past the next house along and down a long thin alleyway. Theo cradled Olivia closer and Logan tucked the Grimoire under his coat. They hurried away from the burning pile of timbers and by the time they exited the alleyway back onto the main street it was in chaos. James rushed toward them pulling off his cloak and throwing it over Olivia's body.

'Quickly,' James told them, 'the fire has brought out the governor himself who only lives two streets over. Get her inside before anyone starts asking questions.'

People were running down the street screaming, and buckets of water were being passed along hand to hand. There was no use trying to save Nathaniel's house anymore and they were now concentrating their efforts on dousing the buildings either side to stop the fire from spreading. Huddling Olivia closer to try and hide her from prying eyes, they pressed through the mass of panicked bodies and acrid smoke filled air, and dived down the alley toward The Salted Bone.

James limped ahead and banged on the door. As it swung open they ducked inside and headed straight up the stairs to the room they'd been encamped in earlier.

'Get me some clean water and some linen strips to bind her wounds,' Theo instructed as he laid her out carefully on the bed. 'Olivia?' he smoothed the hair from her soot smeared swollen face.

'Theo?' she croaked, opening her eyes and trying to sit up.

'Don't move, not yet,' he pressed her gently into the bed. 'We need to take a look at your injuries.'

'Nathaniel?'

'Tituba is dealing with him,' he told her softly. 'You are safe for the moment.'

'No,' she shook her head struggling to rise.

'Olivia,' he pressed her back once again.

'Sweet Jaysus,' a strong Irish accent gasped from the doorway.

Theo turned to see Thomas Murphy looking down at Olivia, while crossing himself. Theo steeled himself as he turned back to her, forcing down the fresh wave of guilt that he had let Logan talk him into waiting. He was horrified at the extent of her wounds.

Her right eye was completely swollen shut, her lips bitten ragged and split. Her jaw was severely bruised and so swollen it made her face look lopsided. There was a long thin wound along her collar bone, which was still bleeding, and a rapidly darkening bruise was spreading across her shoulder and down her arm towards her left hand which was mangled beyond repair. In fact, it didn't even look like a hand any longer, just a mangled lump of flesh and protruding splintered bones.

A patch of dark blood stained her shift at the top of her rib cage and her right leg had small cruel looking puncture marks leading down her shin. He wished that had been the worst of it, but she still had three vicious looking pins protruding from her shoulder, her thigh and her forearm. He reached out to touch them tentatively and she sucked in a painful breath.

'Olivia, we need to get these out,' he told her gently as she closed her eyes and nodded.

'No wait!' James stopped him as he reached for them again. 'I'm very familiar with these,' he grimaced rubbing his lame leg unconsciously. 'They screw down into bone and flesh, if you just pull them out they will cause more damage.'

'Jesus Christ,' Theo shut his eyes and clenched his fists. 'I am going to find Nathaniel and when I do I'm going to fucking destroy him.'

A small smile tugged at the corner of Olivia's swollen mouth. It always sounded strange when Theo swore, as he did it so rarely, but when he did he sounded just like Jake. A sudden wave of homesickness washed over her and she ruthlessly gritted her teeth.

'Just get them out,' she ground out.

'You have to twist them back out slowly,' James told Theo, 'and it's going to hurt like hell.'

'Do it,' she nodded.

James wrapped his arms around her carefully, holding her tight.

'We've got you Livy love,' James told her and as the endearment fell unconsciously from his lips he sounded so much like his son.

Setting his jaw determinedly, Theo reached for the first screw and that's when the screaming began. It killed him, absolutely destroyed him, to cause her such prolonged and systematic pain, but there was no other way to get the sadistic pins from her body. It seemed to take forever and as the last one was pulled from her thigh, she slumped back against the bed breathing heavily, her whole body shaking violently. Theo reached for the bowl of water and gently cleaned her wounds and bound each of them tightly with strips of linen. He was just binding the last one when Justin rushed into the room carrying a handful of men's clothing and a cloak.

'We need to move quickly,' he told them, handing the clothes to Theo. 'The wind changed direction, the fire jumped to the next street and they can't keep ahead of the flames. If they don't pull down some of the houses as a fire break we could lose half the town.'

Theo stood quickly as James helped Olivia into a sitting position. Between the two of them they managed to help her dress in the breeches and linen shirt, being careful of her heavily bandaged hand and her various injuries. Olivia moved to sit on the edge of the bed, cradling her broken hand close to her body and holding onto her elbow trying to relieve the relentless shooting pain in her shoulder. Her whole body burned with the pain of even the smallest movement and in that moment she would have given anything to just slump down in exhaustion and sleep.

'Is the fire heading this way?' Theo asked, gently easing the woolen stockings up her damaged leg and slipping her feet into the smallest pair of leather shoes Justin could find.

'Not yet,' Justin shook his head, 'but it's only a matter of time.'

'Which direction is the fire burning in?' Olivia croaked, as Theo wrapped a warm cloak around her trembling body.

'East towards the harbor.'

'We need to head North' she told them.

Justin shook his head, 'it's too dangerous. If the wind changes again the fire will blow straight across our path.'

'Olivia,' James told her softly, 'we're going to take you back to my house. You'll be safe there.'

'No,' she shook her head, 'we can't go back. We have to go North.'

'What? Why?' Theo asked.

'Because that's where my mother is and she's already with Hester and Bridget. The other Nathaniel was at the house before and he now knows how to break the body my mother forced him into. If we don't get to him in time, he's going to kill one of the girls and free himself.'

'Shit,' Theo swore.

'But there's more than that, Zachary is here.'

'Zachary?' Theo's gaze snapped back to hers.

'Who's Zachary?' Logan asked stepping closer, still holding the book and the knife Tituba had thrust into his hands.

'He's another demon,' Theo told him, 'Nathaniel's second in command.'

'Where is he?' Logan asked. 'Was he in the house when the fire started?'

Olivia shook her head. 'No,' she looked up at Theo, 'Nathaniel sent him to kill you.'

'He's welcome to try,' Theo's tone was flat and dangerous.

'No,' she insisted worriedly, 'not just you, the other you as well. The younger version of you.'

'What?' James gasped.

'Someone needs to go to the Beckett farm and protect the other version of you until Sam shows up and drags your ass to Mercy,' Olivia told him, 'and it can't be you or me because he can't know about us.'

'I'll do it,' James stood abruptly.

'I'll go too,' Justin agreed.

'Good,' Olivia let out a deep breath of pain as she shifted her body. 'Now someone get me a horse please, we need to get to Hester before the other Nathaniel does.'

'Olivia, you don't know how to ride a horse,' Theo frowned.

'Fine, you get me on a horse then, but either way we need to go now.'

'Olivia, you are in no fit state to take on Nathaniel or your mother. You need to rest.'

She grasped his hand with her one good hand and tugged him down to her level so she could touch his face.

'Theo,' she whispered softly, 'this is what we came here for. We can't stop now.'

'Nathaniel nearly killed you,' he replied angrily, 'and you want me to take you out into the woods broken and defenseless, and let him have another shot at you?'

'Not defenseless,' she corrected him. 'My hand may be useless and I can't walk unaided, but I can still use magic. I still have enough strength for that. I know my body may be a bit worse for wear right now and I'm not going to lie to you Theo, I'm in a hell of a lot of pain. All I want to do is lie down and sleep until the pain stops, but we have a responsibility. This is the choice we made, stop Nathaniel, stop my mother, no matter the cost.'

'Even if the cost is your life?'

'Even then,' she whispered, touching his face lovingly. 'I found you once in the Otherworld, don't think I can't do it again,' she smiled painfully, wincing as her lip split again. 'We're forever Theo, in this life or the next and everywhere in between.'

'Forever?' he traced the undamaged side of her

jaw with his thumb.

'Forever,' she promised. 'We'll always find each other Theo, no matter what happens. But I'm really not planning on dying, you know you did promise to marry me.'

'I did, didn't I?' he smiled slowly.

'Yes you did, and I want a dress and a ring,' she replied, 'so let's get this done and go home.'

'Alright then,' he sighed.

'Alright?' Logan repeated incredulously, 'are you mad? She's in no condition to go up against Nathaniel.'

'You don't know her very well Logan,' Theo scratched his chin thoughtfully. 'You can try telling her 'no' if you like, but I wouldn't recommend it. It didn't work out too well for the God of the Underworld.'

'What?' Logan's face paled.

'Logan?' Olivia glanced at Theo. 'Is this your brother?'

'Let's save the introductions for later,' Theo told her, 'we can talk on the ride out of Salem, but right now we need to get ahead of the fire before the wind shifts its course again.'

'Very well,' Logan replied grudgingly, 'but I'm going with you.'

Theo nodded.

'Logan?' Olivia reached out toward him suddenly, 'where did you get that knife?'

'This?' he handed it to her, 'the slave woman gave it to me.'

'Where is Tituba?'

She looked at Theo who met her eyes sympathetically. 'I'm sorry Olivia, we tried to get her to come with us, but she stayed behind to deal with Nathaniel. She never made it out of the house before it collapsed.'

Olivia shut her eyes briefly against a wave of grief for the woman who'd shown her such kindness.

'Here take this,' she handed the knife to James. 'It's powerful, it should work against Zachary.'

James accepted it with a nod, tucking it carefully inside his clothes.

'You'd better take this back now,' Theo told Olivia as he lifted the compass from his neck and removed it.

'Thank you,' she murmured as he slid the chain over her head and tucked it into her shirt.

'The horses are ready,' Thomas appeared at the door, 'they're around back. You should get going.'

Theo bent down and carefully picked Olivia up, cradling her against his body. They all hurried back down the steps and out the back door, into the smoke filled street. James and Justin were the first to mount up, their horses dancing expectantly beneath them, as they watched Logan take Olivia, while Theo slid up into his saddle. He passed her up to his brother carefully and Theo settled her onto the horse in front of him, wrapping his arms around her protectively as Logan mounted his own horse.

'We'll head North,' Theo told James. 'If all goes well we'll meet you at the farm.'

'Be careful,' James nodded as both he and Justin turned their mounts in the opposite direction and headed out.

'I guess that just leaves us then,' Theo turned to his brother. 'You know the town better than I do, now get us the hell out of Salem.'

20.

Isabel placed another couple of sticks in the fireplace and stoked the fire absently as Abigail cleaned away the dishes from the table.

'Hester,' Abigail called softly, 'come wash the dishes.'

'But it's Bridey's turn,' she complained.

''Tis not,' Bridget frowned.

'It is too,' Hester replied not even bothering to look up from where she lay, comfortably splayed on her stomach in front of the fire watching the dancing flames.

'Actually,' Isabel smiled up at Abigail, 'I think it is Bridget's turn.'

Hester looked across to Isabel as she leaned back in Abigail's favorite rocking chair. Their gazes met for a moment and Isabel winked.

'But it's not fair,' Bridget grumbled.

'Come on,' Abigail smiled, 'I'll help you.'

Isabel watched as Bridget and her mother disappeared from the room taking a bucket with them to fill with water. Once they were alone, her gaze again fell to the small dark haired girl lying on the ground, who was watching her warily.

'What?' she asked softly after a moment.

'I see you, you know.'

'Do you?' Isabel replied in amusement, 'and what exactly do you see Hester?'

'I see you, I see your daughter, I see blood of my blood.'

'And do you know what that means?' Isabel replied slowly. Despite the incredible power she felt emanating from Hester, she was still just a child and she knew she had to tread cautiously.

'You come from me, from my family.'

'Yes that's right,' she smiled. 'I am a West too,' she whispered, 'but we probably shouldn't tell the others just yet.'

'Why?' Hester frowned.

'Because there are people looking for me and I don't want to put your mother and sister in danger.'

'But I know.'

'Yes,' Isabel nodded, 'but you are very special Hester. I think you know that, don't you?'

'I'm not like Mama and Bridey,' she replied quietly. 'I see things, things they wouldn't understand.'

'Like what?' Isabel leaned in closer 'What do you see Hester?'

'A crossroad…' she whispered, her whiskey colored eyes darkening, 'and an old woman…'

Isabel's eyes widened in surprise.

'I know what you gave up,' Hester continued. 'You think you won't miss it, but you're wrong. Its absence will change you. It already has, you just don't know it yet.'

'You're wrong,' Isabel replied warily.

Hester sighed and climbed to her feet so she was directly in Isabel's eye line.

'You're chasing something that will never be yours,' she told her softly, 'and it will cost you the most important thing in your life.'

'Really?' Isabel scoffed, 'and what is that?'

'Family,' Hester replied easily. 'Family is all that matters.'

Throwing one last look at Isabel, she turned toward the door as her mother and sister re-entered the cabin, laughing and carrying a bucketful of water between them. She wandered over to her family throwing them a warm smile.

'Can I help?' she offered.

'Bridget can wash, you can dry,' she handed her a cloth, 'and I'll put the dishes away.'

Isabel watched the three of them with a troubled expression. It was clear they were an unassailable unit, bound together not just by magic and legacy, but by love.

She'd had that once, although it seemed like a lifetime ago now. She wasn't the same woman anymore. That woman was long gone; she'd made her choice and she wouldn't allow herself to question it now. Especially not because some child had touched a nerve she didn't even realize was still tender.

She was so close she could taste it. She had more power than she'd ever dreamed and soon she would have the book too. It was her legacy, her birthright and no one was going to get in her way. Not a demon, not her daughter, not a child who knew far too much for her own good and certainly not her own conscience.

A slow familiar presence suddenly made the hairs on the back of her neck stand up. Her spine stiffened warily as she cast a glance to the window. It was already dark outside and she couldn't see beyond the light in the room. Hester looked up from the plate she was drying and also looked around curiously, as if she too sensed something.

'I'm just going to fetch some more firewood,' Isabel told them smoothing down her dress. 'It's going to be cold tonight.'

'Do you need some help?' Abigail offered.

'No, it's fine,' Isabel wrapped a thick woolen shawl around her shoulders. 'I'll be right back.'

She slipped from the room, closing the front door

behind her and hearing the latch click into place. Pulling her shawl tighter against the bite in the air, she stepped down from the porch and ignoring the pile of loose sticks stacked neatly against the side of the house, she disappeared into the trees.

The canopy of trees above her head was patchy, like an old man, partially bald. Several bare branches twisted and reached upward like spindly arms and the discarded leaves littered the ground around her, tumbling restlessly on the wind as if they could sense her unease. The moon split the dark sky like a great silver disc and tiny pinpricks of light shone around it in a halo of starlight, but she paid it no mind. She hurried deeper into the concealment of the trees, as far from the tiny ramshackle cabin as she could.

She could almost feel him breathing down her neck, feel the way her skin cringed at his repellent proximity. Her mouth set in a hard, unforgiving line and her eyes flattened angrily. She came to a small clearing far enough from the cabin Isabel hoped, for Hester not to sense his presence. She stood, silently watching as he ambled from the underbrush and stopped in front of her, lifting his head into the pale moonlight.

Isabel's eyes flashed furiously. The light was dim and he still wore a heavily hooded cloak which was pulled far over his head to conceal most of his face, but she could still tell that the magical stitches she'd used to seal his mouth shut were no longer in place.

'What have you done?' she demanded. 'How did you remove the stitches?'

He looked up at her. Although his milky eyes were now so lost to decay, they were unable to convey any emotion, she could've sworn she saw them dance in amusement.

'Did you forget who you were dealing with Isabel?' he answered dangerously. 'You may have double-crossed me back at the Crossroad and you may temporarily have more power than you have ever had in your life, but you are still only a second rate witch. Whereas I was here in the very beginning, and I will be here long after you and this world of yours are nothing but dust and memories.'

'Be very careful Nathaniel,' her eyes narrowed. 'I may be only a second rate witch, but I hold all the cards right now and you would do well to remember that…'

She held up her hands and he felt the tightness in his mouth once again, as the stitches began to form.

'Don't you want to hear about Olivia?' he replied quickly, before his mouth was sealed shut once more.

Isabel closed her fist and the pressure in his mouth dissipated.

'What about my daughter?' she asked warily.

'She's on her way here…'

'What?' Isabel scowled angrily, 'I told you to keep her away from here.'

Nathaniel shrugged, a strange gesture with his misshapen shape. He had no intention of telling Isabel about his old house in Salem, nor what the other version of him had done to her daughter. After all, Isabel could be quite unpredictable when it came to Olivia, and she didn't need to know for the moment. She would find out soon enough when Olivia and Theodore caught up with them.

He knew she was with Theodore now. After he'd fled her Witch fire he'd hidden close by, watching and waiting. He'd expected the other Nathaniel to emerge from the burning wreckage, but he hadn't. Instead Theodore and his brother Logan had emerged with the injured girl. He'd followed them to a building across the street into which they'd disappeared, only to emerge a short time later. It was obvious they'd dressed and tended Olivia and then the three of them had saddled up and headed out.

He knew they were heading in this direction and that they couldn't be far behind. The only reason he'd beaten them was because he knew exactly where he was going and he had flogged his horse almost to death to get it to a constant flat out run. It had finally collapsed in the underbrush not far from the clearing to die. Humans were so tender hearted with their mounts. He could guarantee that the others wouldn't make such a sacrifice with their beasts, therefore giving him the window he needed.

He just had to make sure he pushed the right buttons with Isabel. He needed her to lure the West girls out into the open. Once she did, and Olivia and the Beckett boys showed up, he would find a way to subtly lead them to Isabel. While they were busy distracting her, he could grab one of the sisters. At this point he didn't care which, all he wanted was to get out of the disgusting body he was festering in. Once he was able to break free he would once again be in his true form, and then Isabel would see if she truly had the talent to take on a demon.

'Nathaniel?' Isabel hissed breaking him from his thoughts, 'I told you to keep her away.'

'She's not alone.'

'Let me guess?' she replied, 'she has Theodore Beckett with her?'

'And his brother Logan.'

'His brother?' her eyes narrowed thoughtfully. 'Wasn't he one of your playthings?'

'He served as a Witchfinder during the trials.'

'And Abigail would know that,' Isabel murmured to herself.

'Enough,' he brushed aside her thoughts, 'have they told you where the book is?'

'Of course not you imbecile,' she snapped angrily, 'I need more time. The book is the one secret they've had passed down to them through generations. They're not ready to trust me yet, not with that. Besides, the youngest Hester…'

'Yes?' Nathaniel prompted.

'I'm not sure yet,' she mused, 'she knows things…'

'What things?' he asked carefully. 'Does she know

the location of the book?'

Isabel's gaze snapped up and her mouth suddenly tightened.

'You need to leave Nathaniel,' she told him bluntly. 'I can't be sure she won't sense your presence, she's more powerful than the other two. Get away from here and stall Olivia and the others for as long as you can. I need more time with them.'

'You should get them to move,' he suggested.

'Tell them the Witchfinders are coming for them?' Isabel considered. 'Abigail would know who the Becketts are. She told me she kept up with what was happening in Salem in case they came for her and the girls. If I tell her they're coming for them and get her to leave with me...'

'It would go a long way to making her trust you,' Nathaniel coaxed.

'Maybe,' her eyes locked on him warily. 'You just stop the others and stay out of my way.'

'As you wish,' his ruined mouth curved into a wry smile.

Nathaniel melted into the darkness as Isabel turned and hurried back towards the cabin.

'Theo!' Olivia gasped, 'Stop!'

He reined the horse in as she struggled to climb down.

'Olivia wait!' he tried to hold onto her, but she slid from the saddle, painfully crashing to the ground. He swung down from the horse as she crawled a few feet away and started heaving.

'Is she alright?' Logan reined in and swung down himself, catching hold of the reins of Theo's horse.

Theo threw a worried glance at his brother, but it was lost in the darkness of the dimly moonlit sky.

'Olivia?' he pulled her hair away from her face and soothed her.

She heaved again. There was nothing for her to

expel from her stomach, but every involuntary movement wrenched her damaged body and sent an agonizing pain shooting through her shoulder.

'Livy,' he breathed in worry, 'you are not well enough to face your mother and Nathaniel.'

'That's why I brought you two along with me,' she laughed weakly. 'You're my henchmen.'

'Livy I'm serious.'

'So am I Theo,' she looked up.

Unable to focus on his face in the darkness, she snapped the fingers of her good hand and three of her dragonflies burst into flame. Slightly larger than usual and comprised entirely of red and gold flames, they bathed the three of them with warmth and light.

'Sweet Mother Mary,' Logan gasped, his eyes widening in shock.

Olivia glanced across at Logan's expression and smiled thinly. She wasn't surprised at his reaction, after all this was probably the first time he'd experienced true magic first hand.

'They won't hurt you,' Theo spoke to his brother but kept his eyes firmly locked on Olivia. 'Livy…'

'Don't,' she shook her head. 'We've come too far now, we have to finish this.'

His eyes betrayed his turmoil, torn between what he knew they needed to do and wanting to protect her.

'I want to go home Theo,' her eyes filled with tears. 'I'm tired and I'm in so much pain, but the only way we are going to get home is to deal with my mother and Nathaniel. If we don't stop them and make sure Hester is safe, we might not have a home to go back to. We don't have a choice, we have to go on.'

'You don't have the strength for this,' he took her face gently in his hands.

'My body is failing,' she admitted, 'but I still have my magic. Get me close enough and I will deal with my mother. I'm the only one who can,' she dragged her gaze away from Theo and looked up at his brother who was hovering close by in concern. 'Logan…'

He tore his gaze from the blazing dragonflies and looked down at the broken woman sitting in the mud.

'Your job is to get the girls away from Nathaniel no matter what,' she told him seriously. 'No matter what happens,' she repeated firmly as his gaze was drawn back to the dragonflies, 'you have to get them and their mother somewhere safe. Can you promise me that?'

Logan studied her carefully before finally dropping to his knees next to her and taking her good hand in his.

'I promise,' he nodded, 'I will protect them with my life.'

'It still leaves the problem of Nathaniel,' Theo frowned.

'Well you are right about one thing,' Olivia replied.

'What?'

'I don't have the strength to go up against Nathaniel and win. I'm gambling that my mother doesn't want me dead. The best I can hope for at the moment is to distract her long enough for Logan to get Hester and the others away from her and Nathaniel, especially Nathaniel. After all mom won't risk any harm to Hester because she's also directly of her bloodline. If anything happens to that little girl, not only will I never be born, she won't either. But Nathaniel doesn't feel any such restriction. He needs the blood of a West and he's going to do whatever he can to see that he gets it.'

'I won't let that happen,' Theo told her.

'I know,' she sighed painfully. 'I don't want to, but I need you to take on Nathaniel, to keep him away from me while I deal with mom, but also to keep him away from Logan and the girls.'

'Trust me, it will be my pleasure to deal with Nathaniel,' he said darkly as his eyes flicked over her wounds. 'He and I have a debt to settle.'

'Theo, I don't want you to put yourself in

unnecessary danger. Don't let your anger at what he has done blind you.'

'I'll be fine,' he replied tightly.

'No you won't, not at the moment, but I have something to give you. Something I think will help.'

'What do you mean?'

'When you rescued me from Nathaniel's house, do you remember seeing the purple fire?'

Theo nodded.

'I know what it is now,' she told him softly. 'It's Witch fire.'

'Witch fire?'

'Yes,' she answered, 'and it will hurt him. Back at the house I caused him real pain and while he was in his true form. Now it may not kill him, but it will, at the very least, slow him down.'

'You want to give me the fire?' he realized slowly, 'like you did back in Mercy when you gave me the Spirit fire.'

She nodded slowly.

'Only…' she hesitated, 'I know it will cause you pain. I can give you the fire and it will become part of your blade, just like the Hell fire and the Spirit fire did, but it will hurt like hell.'

'Do it,' he told her firmly.

'Are you sure?'

'Livy,' he brushed his lips gently against hers trying not to disturb her split lip, 'I know you don't want to hurt me, but I need a weapon I can use against him. I need to be able to protect you.'

'What is happening?' Logan asked in confusion, 'what do you mean you are going to give him fire?'

'It's a bit hard to explain,' Theo told him. 'I need you to trust me and not interfere, no matter what you see, alright?'

Logan frowned, but wisely chose not to argue. He knew they just didn't have the time.

'Are you ready?' Olivia asked.

He pulled back his sleeve revealing the winding veins of blue, black and silver, which wound and coiled up his arm, and nodded.

Taking a deep breath, she held up her undamaged hand. Once again she reached for her magic and felt the violet colored fire deep within her, felt the voices of all her sisters, of all the witches who had come before her. She felt the rush and adrenalin surge through her body and run along her arm. Her fingers curved like talons and her hand erupted in vivid lavender colored fire. When her eyes opened and fixed on Theo her eyes blazed the same deep amethyst.

'Take my hand.'

Unable to resist her softly spoken command, he reached out and locked his fingers with hers. There was a sharp jolt and a searing pain. The breath caught in his throat as his back arched in agony, and he could barely breathe as the fire raged unchecked through his veins. A high pitched buzzing filled his ears and bright vivid flames of deep purple mixed with the palest lilac blinded him. His body felt like it was burning, being consumed from within as he experienced the vast inescapable ancient power, and with it came the sense of thousands upon thousands of voices. Not just any voices, witches…only they weren't anything like he'd expected. Nothing like he'd been raised to believe. He'd always known Olivia was different, but a part of him had believed that she was the exception rather than the rule. But experiencing that one moment, hearing all those women's voices crying out as one, feeling every moment, every heartbeat, every experience of every life, he finally understood.

Thin vines of violent purple snaked up his arm alongside the blue and black coils left seared into his flesh from Olivia's Hell fire. Looping around the silver vines, the violet colored swirls intertwined with the other lines and embedded itself deep into his skin, permanently etching itself into his arm.

Slowly the fire began to ebb, the high pitched buzzing subsided until he could hear the frantic drumming of his own heartbeat hammering in his ears. His breath was rapid and ragged as he tried to calm his racing heart. He gingerly flexed his fingers and then his arm. The flesh was sore and swollen, branded by fire and magic.

Nodding to Olivia, who watched him in concern, he flexed his fingers once again and reached for his blade, for the magic that belonged to him. He felt the blue, black, silver and now purple coils slide down his arm like liquid, pooling in his palm and coalescing to form a blade. Theo turned the knife over in his hand and studied it. Before it had been the length and shape of a large hunting knife, the hilt a highly polished onyx decorated with a thin vein of silver interwoven with tiny little silver leaves. The blade itself had been a strange metallic blue black inscribed in a strange language he had not been able to read and when he turned the blade and it caught the light, some of the lettering would glow a dim phosphorescent blue and some a pale spectral silver. Now there was additional lettering, blazing violet, and along the hilt the silver vine of tiny leaves now had delicate purple flames.

Helping Olivia to her feet, Logan held her upright as Theo swung back into the saddle and helped Olivia up in front of him. Logan remounted also, watching as Olivia reached out with her hand. One of the dragonflies landed on her palm, while the other two danced around her head.

'Find them,' she whispered to them. 'Find Hester and her sister.'

The dragonflies shivered and darted off into the trees.

Theo gripped the hilt and felt the weapon pulse with power. He glanced across to his brother whose eyes were now wide with disbelief and his mouth curved into a cool smile.

'Let's go hunt a demon…'

'Abigail! Abigail!' Isabel rushed into the cabin.

She looked up from where she sat, brushing Bridget's long dark hair.

'What is it?'

'We have to leave now!'

'What?' she stood abruptly causing her favorite rocking chain to clank heavily against the floor. 'Why?'

'They're coming,' Isabel breathed heavily, trying to catch her breath as if she'd been running.

'Who are?' Abigail asked in confusion.

'Witchfinders,' Isabel's eyes widened in fear. 'I felt them, they are close by.'

'Witchfinders here?' Abigail grabbed her girls, unconsciously squeezing them close to her, 'but why? I don't understand.'

'This is all my fault,' Isabel dashed forward her eyes filling with tears. 'I should never have stayed here with you, it was just that you were so kind and I'd been alone for so long. I did this, I brought this upon you. I should've known Theodore and Logan would not have stopped looking for me.'

'The Beckett brothers?' Abigail's eyes widened in fear. 'The Beckett brothers are who you are running from.'

'You know who they are?' Isabel frowned in confusion.

'I know of their reputations,' Abigail swallowed hard. 'I've heard what they did in Salem town.'

'Then you know we have no choice,' Isabel grabbed her arms desperately. 'We can't let them find us or the girls. We have to run…Now!'

Abigail nodded.

'Bridget bank the fire,' Abigail turned and began grabbing things, laying them out on a blanket. 'Grab what you can Hester, but only what we can carry.'

'Mama?' she whispered as Isabel turned to grab whatever food she could from the cupboard. 'What about the book? You said we couldn't allow it to fall into anyone else's hands. Are we going to go and get it? Will they find where it's hidden?'

Abigail glanced at Isabel, checking that she was too busy to take in what they were saying.

'Hester,' she whispered, 'it's too dangerous to go to it now. We can't risk anyone finding it. You and Bridget both know where it is. If anything happens to me you must protect it, that is our most sacred duty. Do you understand?'

She nodded solemnly.

'Get your cloak then, we don't have much time.' She turned to retrieve her own cloak, missing the small smile that curved the corner of Isabel's mouth.

'Mama?' Bridget pulled her cloak on as Abigail knotted the corners of the blanket, creating a small bundle of clothes to take with them.

'Yes my love?'

'Will we ever come back?' she asked in a small fearful voice.

'I don't know,' she shook her head, 'I just don't know, but right now we have to get some place safe. There are some very dangerous men coming this way, we must hide from them.'

'But Mama,' Hester frowned, reappearing wrapped in her winter cloak. 'The men that are coming, they're not what you think they are.'

'What do you mean?'

'I don't think they're coming to hurt us,' she struggled to explain herself. 'There is something dark out there, but I don't think it's them.'

'Do you sense danger?' Abigail asked urgently.

Hester nodded.

'Then we can't take the risk,' she stroked her face. 'We have to run.'

'But…'

'Your mother's right,' Isabel told her.

Hester turned, but chose not to say anything else. Grabbing what they could carry, the four of them slipped out of the door and disappeared into the woods.

21.

Isabel's eyes narrowed as she peered further into the darkness. Fortunately, the trees were sparser in this area of the woods and although it wasn't well lit, the moonlight filtered through the bare trees illuminating the path ahead of them. For the most part the four of them walked in silence, albeit a tense, wary one. The two young girls had followed along with barely a complaint, but Abigail's eyes darted about nervously as she clutched the bundle of clothes she carried. Hester had been the most worrying. She'd not said a word, yet her gaze had not left Isabel since they'd departed from their cabin. It felt as if she was studying her, trying to come to a decision of some sort. Her tiny face was somber and her eyes filled with sadness.

'It doesn't have to be this way you know,' she spoke quietly, appearing beside Isabel.

Isabel glanced behind her to make sure the others were not listening.

'What doesn't?' she questioned.

'You think there's no way back,' she clarified, 'but you're wrong. There is always forgiveness.'

Isabel's jaw tightened.

'Not for some.'

She suddenly felt a small hand slip into hers and

squeeze gently. She stopped abruptly, staring down into the small serious face.

'Just promise me you'll try to remember one thing.'

'What's that?'

'It's never too late to do the right thing.'

'What is it?' Abigail caught up to them. 'Why did you stop?'

'It's nothing,' Isabel murmured turning her gaze away from Hester as she released her hand. 'Where's Bridget?' she looked behind Abigail with a small frown. 'I thought she was walking with you?'

Abigail's eyes widened in horror as she dropped the bundle she was holding and spun around.

'She was just here,' she breathed in a rush. 'BRIDGET?' she called out into the darkness.

'Wait!' Isabel caught Abigail's arm.

'Let me go,' she jerked her arm free and ran.

Isabel swore under her breath and turned to Hester. 'No matter what happens you stay close to me, do you understand?'

'It won't make a difference,' she shook her head, 'they're already here.'

'Damn it,' Isabel growled and grabbed Hester's hand as they chased after Abigail.

Abigail ran back through the woods calling out to her daughter. Her panic and the desperate need to find her child clawed viciously inside her chest and reached up, wrapping itself around her throat until she felt like she was choking. She suddenly skidded to a halt in the damp leaves, her heart pounding in her ears and her mouth going dry.

Bridget stood in the path, eyes wide with fear and tear tracks staining her dirty face. A grotesque deformed hand clamped over her mouth and a cloaked figure hunched over her small trembling form, it's milky white eyes glowing maliciously in the dark.

'Let her go,' Abigail's eyes went flat with anger.

His rotting hand slid from her mouth and encircled her tiny throat feeling her pulse flutter frantically like the wings of a trapped bird.

'No,' he replied as his hood slid a little further back, revealing the damaged decaying mess that should have been a mouth. It split into a monstrous smile filled with brown loose peg-like teeth. 'She has something I need.'

He pressed his patchwork face to her cheek and inhaled deeply.

'The blood of a West,' he crooned, 'untainted and mine for the taking.'

'If you so much as spill one drop I will destroy you,' she threatened.

Nathaniel barked out a laugh, a disgusting mucus filled sound, which was more likely to inspire a cringe of revulsion rather than one of fear.

'Pathetic bitch,' he sneered. 'Just the same as the rest of your worthless bloodline, you think you're so superior,' he mocked. 'The chosen ones, given the Hell book to protect as a sacred duty.'

Abigail's eyes widened.

'The truth is you stole it… thieves you are,' he scoffed in disgust, 'nothing more. I will have the book from you, but first I need to shed this filthy infested body and your daughter's blood is going to help me do that.'

'Is that what you think Nathaniel?' Isabel's smooth amused voice cut across the distance between them.

Nathaniel's eyes moved across to the tall woman striding into the tiny clearing they were standing in, a small girl tucked protectively behind her skirts. His eyes narrowed in blind hatred, his lips peeling back into a snarl as his fingers convulsively gripped harder around Bridget's neck.

'Don't Isabel,' he warned. 'The second you raise your power against me I will snap her neck like a twig.'

'Go right ahead,' she replied coldly, 'it won't do

you any good. Alive or dead her blood won't set you free. That's what you think isn't it?' her mouth curved mockingly. 'That the blood of a West will break the spell I used on you? Who told you that, the other Nathaniel?'

His hate filled eyes remained locked on hers as he watched her in silence.

'Did you really think I didn't know you would go running straight to the other version of yourself, whining for help? Thanks to you I have what I want,' she reached behind her and gripped Hester's arm tightly. 'Go ahead, kill them both. It will make no difference,' she shrugged.

'NO!' Hester darted around her, but Isabel caught her and wrenched her back. 'I told you,' she whispered into the little girl's ear, 'I told you some things couldn't be forgiven and that some people don't ever change.'

'And I told you it is never too late to do the right thing,' she looked up into Isabel's eyes pleadingly. 'Follow this path and you will damn your soul.'

'It's already damned,' she replied flatly as she turned her gaze back on the demon.

'Well Nathaniel, what's it to be? Are you willing to take the risk? Her blood or Abigail's…either way it won't save you and the minute you're done with them, I will make you suffer for your disobedience.'

For a moment time seemed to freeze, even the trees themselves drew up and held their breath, watching the witch and the demon locked in a battle of wills.

'Then make me suffer,' he hissed savagely, as his fingers curled tighter and Bridget's mouth fell open. Her face started to change color as she clawed at his hands and frantically tried to suck air into her lungs.

'NO!' Abigail screamed. Throwing her hands out, the sudden and violent punch of her power knocked Nathaniel back a couple of paces.

His grip loosened just long enough for her to dive forward, ripping her daughter from his grasp and throwing her away from the demon.

'RUN!' she screeched wildly.

She turned to follow her daughter, but stopped abruptly. Her eyes widened in shock and a thin line of scarlet suddenly appeared horizontally across her throat. A gush of blood spilled down the front of her dress saturating her bodice like a grotesque waterfall. Her legs collapsed under her and her eyes rolled upward and the last thing she thought she saw was a dragonfly made of pure fire dancing above her.

'MAMA!' Bridget screamed.

Nathaniel growled, clutching a knife in his hand as the witch folded to the ground. Ignoring the child, he dropped to his knees and sank his teeth into the wound, feeling her weak pulse faltering and the blood slowly oozing from the deep slash.

After a few moments he still felt nothing. He tore his mouth away from his grisly feast, and knowing he didn't feel any different he let loose an animal howl of rage and frustration.

Isabel threw her head back and laughed.

'Moron! Her blood won't do you any good. It doesn't have enough power to counteract the spell.'

His eyes locked on Abigail's lifeless body, his eyes suddenly narrowing as he processed Isabel's words. He needed something incredibly powerful and there was only one thing more powerful than blood magic... A human soul.

His gaze turned back to Isabel and smirked.

A warm golden light suddenly appeared above him and they both looked up to see a trio of fiery dragonflies hovering over Abigail. They had run out of time. Turning back to Isabel he saw the exact moment she realized his intention. The cocky confidence suddenly drained from her expression and her eyes widened in alarm.

'NO!' She rushed toward him her hand outstretched with a startled scream on her lips, but it was too late. As she reached for him he plunged his hand into

Abigail's chest, filling the night air with the sickened crunch of rending flesh and broken ribs.

Before Isabel could reach him a burning sphere of sapphire blue and jet black flames streaked through the darkness. It crashed into her, throwing her clean across the small clearing and into the thick gnarled trunk of a nearby tree.

Two horses closed in on the scene, hooves thundering loudly against the ground. Theo threw himself from the saddle, crashing into Nathaniel, his burning blade already in his hand. It burst into purple flame and he plunged it into his chest. A high pitched scream tore from the demon's throat, a shockingly human sound filled with pain and surprise.

Olivia clutched the reins tightly with her good hand, desperately trying to keep control of the horse she no idea how to ride. Placing herself between Theo and the hunched figure of her mother who was still slumped at the roots of the vast tree, her horse danced expectantly in circles.

'LOGAN! GET THEM OUT OF HERE!' she yelled desperately.

Logan dug his heels into his horse's flanks. Nudging the beast toward Bridget he leaned down in his saddle and plucked the sobbing girl from the ground, hauling her into the saddle in front of him. He spun the horse around and headed for Hester who seemed to understand he was their only chance at survival. As she held up her arm he grasped her and swung her up behind him.

'GO!' Olivia screamed at him, sensing his hesitation.

Taking one last look at Olivia he took off through the woods at a dead run.

For a second Olivia allowed herself to breath in relief. Whatever happened from this point on, at least Logan had gotten the girls away from her mother and

Nathaniel. Now she could only pray he managed to hide them safely.

Tugging on the reins the way she'd seen Theo lead the horse, it turned under her instruction. Her gaze locked on Nathaniel and Theo who were wrestling across the muddy leaf strewn ground. Theo's knife sunk into the demon's body over and over again and each time it did it blazed hotter with Olivia's Witch fire and Nathaniel howled in agony.

His milky white eyes blazed in pain and fury as he managed to throw Theo off him. Nathaniel peeled his bloodied lips back in a feral snarl, his expression filled with a desperate kind of madness as he clawed his way across the sodden earth towards Abigail's corpse.

Olivia could do nothing but watch in horror, a kind of sick slow motion reel of images as he thrust his hand into the dead woman's chest. This time he wrenched out a writhing, living sphere of blazing white light. Theo rolled over and scrambled back toward Nathaniel reaching for him, but it was too late.

The demon threw his head back and crammed the pulsing ball of light into his mouth shoving it down his gullet. His throat lit up from within as the light descended, illuminating his chest cavity with a muted glow. Deep cracks began to appear in his skin, like the floor of an arid, dried out riverbed, revealing the pure white light beneath. His skin bubbled hideously and began to melt, sliding off him like a sick horror movie effect. He began to claw at his skin, tearing off chunks and peeling back huge strips of flesh. They watched in abject horror, knowing it was too late to stop him and unable to tear their gaze away. It was like witnessing a huge chrysalis breaking apart.

'What have you done!' Isabel suddenly screamed.

Olivia turned her head and saw her mother struggling to her feet, her eyes blazing angrily.

Unable to spare her mother any attention she turned back to Nathaniel, her eyes desperately searching the dark ground for Theo. She tried to urge her horse forward, but the shining light from his body was now so bright she had to raise her forearm to shield her eyes. The horse shied away, instinctively backing away from the sheer luminance.

'Theo!' she shouted blindly.

But it was no good. The air was filled with a trill whistle, like a kettle about to boil, as the light grew brighter and brighter. Suddenly the sound cut out and for just one second the night was filled with an ominous silence.

Then Nathaniel exploded.

A great roar and Nathaniel's prison of flesh burst like an overripe cyst. The shock wave of energy exploded outward with such violence it uprooted trees. Olivia suddenly found herself thrown from the horse. She lost sight of it, of everything, as she hit the ground with a sickening impact.

For a moment she couldn't even breathe from the pain and shock. Then everything roared back with sharp acuity. Pain ripped through her body and she was unable to hold in the scream of agony. Her broken body had already sustained far too much injury to absorb such an impact.

Her breath caught in her throat, shallow and labored. A high pitched buzzing filled her ears as she blinked a couple of times, her vision blurry. She could make out trees, some had toppled over fully, some were pitched at precarious angles, but all of them leaned outward in a circular pattern from where Nathaniel had been the epicenter of the explosion. A fine dusty mist hung above the ground filling the night with a strange snowy shroud. Olivia blinked again, trying to get her vision to swim back into focus. She could see a tall naked figure standing in the mist. Her vision sharpened and she could make out his jet black hair, his coldly handsome face and dark eyes. Their gazes locked for a moment and a small smirk grazed his perfect mouth then he was gone.

She blinked again, her mind so dulled by the pain and shock it was unable to process what she'd just seen. Her eyes tracked up to the sky, now more fully revealed through the voids where trees had stood only moments before.

A loud and ominous cracking sound rent the air above her. It seemed to her she should be alarmed or at least try to move, but she just couldn't, she wasn't capable of it. Her whole body lay motionless in a thick carpet of leaves, barely aware of the cold and damp seeping through her clothes. The loud cracking noise came again, this time accompanied by a shower of tumbling leaves which fluttered down settling on top of her prone body, and when a thick gnarled trunk filled her vision, crashing down toward her she could do nothing but close her eyes and wait for the darkness to take her. Resigned to her fate she did not even feel the soft warm arms that suddenly enveloped her, cradling her broken body gently.

'OLIVIA!' Theo screamed in warning, but it was too late.

More dust, dirt and leaves were thrown up into the misty air as the tree hit the ground with an almighty resounding crash. Coughing violently, he climbed over felled trees and debris, desperately trying to reach her. He ripped branches out of his way calling to her frantically, but there was no answer.

'OLIVIA!' he hauled a huge branch out of the way and stared at the tree trunk. It was split vertically as if it had hit some kind of invisible barrier, which had caused it to snap clean in two, falling either side.

He climbed up on top of one half of the tree and leaned down, peering into the gloom. His eyes widened in surprise and his expression hardened at the face that greeted him.

Isabel looked up at Theo as she cradled Olivia in her arms. Ignoring his murderous expression, she turned her attention back to her daughter. Smoothing back a lock of dark hair from Olivia's swollen and damaged face, she felt Theo drop down beside her.

'Did he do this to her?' she asked accusingly as she took in the bruising and swelling on her face, before picking up her damaged hand carefully.

'The other one did,' Theo replied grudgingly, 'the Nathaniel from this time.'

'She's dying,' Isabel whispered.

'No,' Theo's jaw tightened, 'that's not going to happen.'

'And how do you think to stop it?' Isabel asked, her eyes narrowing on his face in interest. 'Her body is damaged, her heart is failing. How do you propose to stop the laws of nature?'

'I will not lose her,' Theo looked down at Olivia's closed eyes, his voice a whisper and the expression on his face indescribable. 'I will summon Hades himself if I have to.'

'A God?' she replied, quietly studying his face. 'You would go up against a God, to save my daughter?'

'I have followed her deep into the belly of the Underworld… I have faced Titans and Judges…I have crossed centuries of time…waited a lifetime…all for her…' He looked up at Isabel, into the face that looked so much like the woman he loved that it made his heart clench painfully. 'I would do anything for her.'

'Yes,' she murmured thoughtfully, 'I believe you would…'

Theo held out his hands as his expression hardened. 'Give her to me.'

Isabel stared, first at his outstretched hands then his determined expression, before finally shaking her head.

'You can't help her… not this time,' she stroked Olivia's face softly, her voice barely louder than a whisper. 'Only I can.'

'What do you mean?' he asked suspiciously.

Isabel ignored him. She cradled her daughter's

cheek in one hand taking in her features. Despite the injures Nathaniel had inflicted on her, she could still see an echo of the child she had once been. For a moment the years and everything else fell away and she could almost see her little dark haired girl flushed from a nightmare, being soothing in her arms as she slipped back into a dreamless sleep.

While her mind swirled with memories and regrets Isabel reached down inside herself for her magic. Before she'd been so weak. She'd never had the same kind of power that had come so easily to the West women. Even as a child the most basic charms and spells wouldn't work for her. She'd been a disgrace to the West name, that's how she'd always felt. Defective, unwanted, unloved. She'd seen the disappointment in her mother's eyes time and time again, when she'd failed to master even the most basic elements of witchcraft.

Her Aunt Evie had been the same. They'd never said it but she knew. Aunt Evie had tried so hard to teach Isabel her beloved art of healing, a skill every witch had to varying degrees. All, except her. Well, that was no longer the case. Ever since the Crossroad, ever since the deal, she'd felt the enormous amount of power coursing through her body, as vital as oxygen, as addictive as heroin. But with the power had also come knowledge and with it a greater understanding of the worlds and her place in them. Hester was right, it had changed her. An unconscious frown marred her brow as she laid her hand gently on Olivia's chest, feeling her heartbeat falter, stuttering like the fragile wing beat of a caged bird. She let the light and heat of her magic seep into Olivia's body, healing as it went.

Theo watched intently as a pale lavender glow pulsed softly beneath Isabel's hand. Slowly, the bruising on Olivia's face began to fade and the swelling recede, until her face was once again its normal shape. The split in her lip knitted itself back together, leaving her lips soft and full with no scarring. He was unable to see what was happening to the rest of her body beneath the layers of heavy clothing, but her flushed skin was once again a beautiful creamy color instead of ashen grey, and her breathing had changed from shallow and labored to deep relaxed measured breaths. He could only imagine her body was being healed the same way her face was.

Isabel's eyes suddenly widened in surprise and then she frowned. She pulled in a deeper breath and seemed to be concentrating even harder on something. The light beneath her palm pulsed brighter and then suddenly dimmed. Isabel pulled back, breathing heavily, as Olivia's eyes fluttered open.

Her gaze landed first on Theo, her brow furrowing slightly when she realized it wasn't his lap she was laying in. Turning her head, her eyes widened in shock at the sight of her mother. Reacting instinctively, she sat bolt upright, even more confused when she realized all the agony in her body was gone.

The pain in her shoulder was no longer there, the same with her leg. She no longer felt the bone weary fatigue and sickness which seemed to have plagued her for weeks. She looked down at her hand and flexed it slowly. It didn't hurt anymore. Pulling off the layers of linen strips which had been holding her broken hand together, she looked down at the unmarred skin. Her bones were once again whole and perfect, there wasn't even any slight bruising and she even had all her fingernails back. Flexing her fingers once again just to be sure, she looked up at her mother and then across to Theo.

'What the hell is going on?'

'I'll tell you what's going on,' Isabel replied irritably as she climbed to her feet and brushed off her skirt. 'You two let Nathaniel loose and now we have a big… big problem on our hands.'

'We let Nathaniel loose?' Olivia's eyes widened incredulously as her voice climbed an octave in disbelief.

'That's a bit rich coming from the woman who broke him out of the devil's trap in the first place.'

Theo stood quietly, reaching down to help Olivia stand. Although her attention was fixed on her mother she kept her hand firmly in his.

'I had him under control for as long as he remained inside the human body,' she replied as she climbed over the wreckage of the tree and dropped down the other side.

'Well clearly you didn't,' Olivia and Theo followed her over the fractured tree.

'We really don't have time to play the blame game here Olivia,' Isabel sighed. 'As I said we've got a bigger problem.'

'Bigger than the fact you're a psychotic killer who let a demon loose?' she replied sarcastically.

'You must realize by now that Nathaniel is going to go after Hester and Bridget?' Isabel answered calmly, ignoring the insult.

'Which we'll deal with,' Olivia scowled. 'I'm getting used to cleaning up your mess.'

'It's really not as simple as that.'

'What do you mean?' Theo asked suspiciously.

'I mean Nathaniel has broken loose and is in his natural form.'

'Yeah we know,' Olivia rolled her eyes. 'Believe me I've been up close and personal with the other version of him.'

'Where is the other one?' Isabel suddenly asked.

'We don't know,' Theo shrugged. 'He disappeared after his house burned.'

'Well,' Isabel mused, 'let's not borrow more trouble than we need to. If he's disappeared let's just leave him to it. We've got more trouble than we can handle without going after him too. I'm sure he'll resurface sooner or later, like he did the first time around, and then Hester can snare him in the devil's trap as she's supposed to. For now, let's just concentrate on stopping this Nathaniel before he gets to Hester.'

'What's all this WE, business?' Olivia snapped. 'There is no WE; there's me and Theo and then there's you.'

'Don't be so childish Olivia,' Isabel hissed waspishly. 'You can't do this on your own. I know how powerful you are, I sensed it when I healed you, but I also know it's untapped and undisciplined. You may have the firepower, but you don't have the knowledge or skills to take Nathaniel down. Only I can.'

'I held my own against him back at his house. Even tortured and wounded I still managed to light him up with Witch fire and I know damn well that hurt him.'

'It may have done,' she replied testily, 'but that was the old Nathaniel. This one is something entirely different.'

'What do you mean, different?' Theo demanded. 'He should be the same; after he broke free of the mortal body he reverted to his natural form.'

'Yes,' Isabel sighed trying to find her patience, 'but this is the super turbo charged version of him.'

'Ohhh,' Olivia's eyes suddenly widened in understanding, 'he ingested a human soul.'

Isabel nodded.

'There is nothing more powerful in this world than a human soul. Right now he's amped up to the roof. It's going to take a hell of a lot more than Witch fire to take him down.'

'And you think you're the one to do it?' Olivia scoffed.

'I don't know,' Isabel answered honestly. 'I forced him into that body for a reason. I never expected to have to go up against him in his natural form, especially one that has been supercharged. The best I can hope for is to get him away from the children.'

'And you're just doing that out of the goodness of

your heart, right?' Olivia replied in disgust. 'You seriously expect us to just trust you, after everything you've done? You expect me to let you anywhere near Hester and Bridget, where you can find out the location of the Hell book? After all, that's all you care about isn't it? All of this…healing me, trying to gain my trust is just part of some larger manipulation to get your hands on Infernum.'

'You want to believe it's all about the book?' Isabel snapped.

'Isn't it?' Olivia shouted back.

Isabel drew back, her eyes livid and her jaw tensed.

'Fine,' she replied tightly, 'believe what you want, but right now nothing is more important than Hester's survival. If Nathaniel gets his hands on the girls he will wring the location of the book from them and once he has what he wants he will kill them both. Need I remind you that if Hester dies, both you and I will never be born.'

Olivia stood silently as she stared at her mother in fury.

'If you can't trust any other motive from me, then at least trust in my desire for my own self-preservation.'

'Olivia,' Theo muttered reluctantly, 'I don't want to admit it, but we need to protect Hester at all costs and we stand a better chance with her powers added to your own.'

'Well at least one of you is thinking straight,' Isabel murmured.

Olivia glared murderously at her mother, sick to her stomach and knowing that she was backed into a corner.

'Don't think for one second that healing me cancels out everything you've done,' Olivia told her coldly. 'This doesn't even come close to making us even.'

'No Olivia,' Isabel smiled slowly, 'what this makes us, is partners…'

22.

Olivia crouched down silently, fighting the urge to roll her eyes when her mother ducked down next to her.

'Can you see him?' Isabel whispered.

'No,' she snapped, 'it's dark.'

'I can see you're not going to make this easy, are you?' Isabel retorted.

'Why the hell should I make this easy on you?' she turned to her mother, her eyes blazing in anger. 'You killed innocent men to raise Nathaniel and then you let him kill Abigail, and those are just the ones I know about. How many people have you killed Mom? How many have had to die in your pursuit of this obsession?'

'You wouldn't understand Olivia,' she answered quietly.

'No you're right, I don't understand,' she turned back to watch out for Theo, 'and I don't want to. Do no harm…our most basic principle, the very core of who we are and the first thing you ever taught me or have you forgotten?'

'I've forgotten nothing.'

'But you conveniently ignore it when it suits your purpose.'

With Isabel not willing to respond they settled into

a tense silence. When they'd emerged from the woods they'd headed for the nearest farm. Knowing that Logan was going to head straight for the Beckett farm with the two West girls, they had to get there quickly.

With Nathaniel going after them, they knew that the only chance they had of making it in time was to steal some horses. Olivia knew her mother could ride, she remembered seeing photos of her astride her horse as a child and although Isabel had offered to accompany Theo, sneaking into the stables to saddle a couple of horses for them, he'd declined. He didn't trust her, that much was painfully obvious, but strangely he also seemed convinced she wouldn't harm her daughter.

Olivia seriously doubted that. She'd done nothing but hurt her since she was eight years old. It wasn't only the physical trauma, but the emotional pain that left scars and she'd had plenty of both, courtesy of her mother. In fact, her shoulder still bore the scar from the bullet wound she'd received from Isabel the night Nathaniel had been raised from the devil's trap.

'Was it worth it?' Olivia asked suddenly.

'What?'

'Whatever it cost you at the Crossroad,' she replied quietly. 'The price you paid for your power.'

'You know nothing of cost,' Isabel answered coldly.

'Maybe,' Olivia conceded, 'but I do know I would never have abandoned my child and my husband to chase a myth.'

'It's not a myth,' Isabel replied, 'it's my birthright.'

'Is that all that matters to you?' Olivia asked softly. 'A tale that has been passed down our family for generations? How do you know it's even real? The knowledge has passed from daughter to daughter, but what of the actual book. When was the last time one of our bloodline actually, physically, held it in their hands?'

Isabel watched Olivia carefully, her brow marred

by a tiny frown.

'Hester knows where the book is.'

'Does she?' Olivia replied, 'or has she just been told a bedtime story like the rest of us? If Abigail had it in her possession, do you really think she'd leave and not take it with her? She couldn't because she never had the book, none of them did. It's just a story, that's all it ever was.'

'It's not,' Isabel hissed. 'I wouldn't expect you to understand, you're not a believer, you have no faith.'

'I do have faith,' Olivia answered. 'I have faith in what I can see, I have faith in what I can touch, I have faith in the people I love.'

'A waste of time,' Isabel scoffed, 'they will only let you down.'

'Like you did?'

'You were too young to understand,' Isabel shook her head.

'I'm not anymore,' she replied, 'so explain it to me now.'

'Olivia,' she breathed, 'you can't possibly know what it was like for me to be born into this family. The weight of expectation…of our legacy. It's the first thing we're taught, our sacred duty to the book.'

'But you didn't want to protect it, you wanted to use its power. The one thing that was forbidden to us.'

'Not at first,' she shook her head, 'all I wanted was to be worthy. I thought it was such a great honor to be chosen to protect it. I was so full of foolish noble ideals such as honor, duty and loyalty.'

'So what changed?'

'Nothing changed, that was the problem. I wasn't good enough. The runt of the litter, born with barely any magical powers. Did you know mama tried to get pregnant again?'

'What?' Olivia frowned in confusion.

'Right up until my father died in Vietnam,' Isabel replied bitterly. 'She knew the moment I was born, the moment she held me that I was defective, a West born with barely any natural ability. Such a disappointment, I always knew it, always felt it. She couldn't love me; she did try for a while, but she was incapable. She was always so cold, so distant. She started trying for another child as soon as she was able to.'

'How do you know?'

'Because my father told me,' a small smile played at the corners of her mouth, the first real emotion Olivia had detected from her mother in years. 'He was home on leave and he told me he had a secret, that he and mama were trying to get me a brother or sister. Such a sweet man,' she shook her head, 'he didn't understand that it was impossible. No West had ever given birth to more than one child unless it was identical twins, and certainly never a boy. Mother knew and yet still she tried and tried, knowing that it was pointless. But I was such a crushing disappointment to her she kept trying. Even after my father died, she had affairs, hoping one would result in another child.'

'No,' Olivia shook her head, 'that's not true. Not Nana Alice, she wasn't like that. This woman you're describing, I don't know her.'

'No, you wouldn't,' Isabel murmured, 'because right from the beginning she was different with you. Do you remember that night back in Mercy, in the library, after I came back?'

'How could I forget?' Olivia replied coolly, 'you punched me and knocked me out so you could steal Hester's Grimoire.'

'Do you remember what I told you?'

'Oh you mean the fact that you didn't want me?' Olivia answered bitterly. 'Or my personal favorite, when you told me you contemplated smothering me as a baby because you didn't want me.'

'That wasn't true,' Isabel replied quietly. 'I wanted to want you, but she ruined that for me.'

'I don't understand,' she frowned.

'I loved your father,' Isabel breathed quietly, 'like I'd never loved anyone else and for the first time in my life I felt loved in return. Truly loved, in a way I hadn't since my own father had died. We didn't plan on me getting pregnant, it just happened. We were so young...but I wanted you, I wanted a child of my own to love the way I hadn't been. At first I wasn't going to tell mama. I wanted it to be just us, you, me and Charlie, but she knew. She knew the minute she saw me. Even if I'd wanted to have an abortion she wouldn't have let me, she'd have done anything to stop me. I had what she wanted, a child of powerful magical ability. Even in my womb I could feel the magic in you. The problem was, so could she. Once you were born she had the child she always wanted and I was pushed further and further out. She made sure you had a strong bond between you, I had served my purpose so I was no longer needed.'

'But you still killed her,' she accused.

'There was no other way,' Isabel's voice hardened. 'It could've been so different; she set this path in motion.'

'No!' Olivia hissed angrily, 'you will not put this on her. You chose to kill all those people, including her. You made that decision. No matter what has happened in your life there is no excuse, none, for taking an innocent life.'

'She was far from innocent,' she scoffed.

'So you say,' Olivia replied, 'but the others? Adam Miller? Remember him? You butchered him for his bones. He was a sweet guy and because of you he'll never get to see his child grow up. He didn't even know he was going to become a father because you robbed him of that. Or how about Lucas Campbell who was only nineteen, barely more than a child when you ripped out his eyes and his tongue? What about James Talbot who was one of dad's best friends, someone he loved? Did you think about that at all when you were busy removing his brain?'

'I have never taken a life that wasn't necessary,' Isabel replied. 'You wouldn't understand.'

'No I wouldn't and I never want to,' Olivia whispered painfully. 'No matter what you think your justification is, you broke our most sacred law when you chose to harm another, and then you abandoned me and Dad. You let him take the fall for you and you let me spend twenty years believing my mother was dead.'

'Olivia…' she began.

'No, I'm done,' she whispered. 'I'm just…done. I can't forgive you and I'll never trust you. After we've stopped Nathaniel you'd better run as far and as fast as you can, because if the book really does exist and you think you're going to get your hands on it, you can think again. I will stop you and then I am going to make sure you answer for the lives you have taken.'

Isabel leaned back studying Olivia carefully.

Suddenly she heard a noise and when she looked around Theo was heading back toward them, as quietly as he could, while leading two saddled horses.

'We should move quickly before they discover the horses are missing,' Theo told her as he came close enough. 'Do you ride Isabel?' he asked.

She nodded.

Theo handed the reins of the other horse to Olivia and cupped his hands so he could boost Isabel up into the saddle. When she was seated comfortably Theo grasped the reins, forcing her attention back on him.

'And just so that we are clear,' he warned her in a low voice so Olivia couldn't overhear, 'if you betray Olivia again, I will kill you.'

Isabel leaned back in her saddle, an amused smile curving the corner of her mouth.

'I do like you Theo,' she laughed.

Glowering at her, he turned and helped Olivia into the saddle before swinging up behind her. Wrapping his arms protectively around her, he shook the reins nudging the horse into a slow canter.

'Follow as closely as you can,' Theo called over his shoulder to Isabel. 'We're heading for my family's farm, and if we hurry we'll make it before dawn.'

Isabel nodded in agreement and as soon as they were far enough away from the farm they spurred their horses into a run.

Theo looked up from the flickering lamplight at the sound of the latch and shut his journal abruptly. After a few seconds he let out a relieved breath and relaxed the tension in his shoulders. It was just the wind tugging restlessly at the barn door. For the moment he remained as he preferred, alone. Dipping his hand into the deep pocket of his coat he pulled out his most prized possession, a stick of lead wrapped in string.

He'd traded his bible for it from a traveler. He closed his eyes momentarily, his fist tightening around the innocuous object. If his father had still been alive he would have whipped him for it, whether or not he was now a man. Shaking his head at the thought he settled himself on a low bale of hay, tucking the lamp more securely atop another bale so it wouldn't topple and catch light.

Slipping a leaf of paper free, he pressed the lead to the sheet and began to sketch in quick confident strokes. The face which took shape was one that had haunted his dreams for as long as he could remember. He did not know who she was, but he could draw every line and curve of her face with his eyes closed. Her hair was a deep dark pleasing brown, which fell in loose curls, spilling over her slim shoulders and down her back. Her eyes burned gold, the depths of which seemed to go on forever and her rose colored lips were soft and full, curved into a small half smile.

It was the first time he had put her likeness to paper. It felt strange to see her there staring back at him through layers of black and white, and he found himself wishing he was able to put color to the paper. Tracing his fingers along the edges of her face he could hear her voice in his mind as clear as a bell and as fragile as a whisper.

'Infernum exists Theo and we have to find it before they do or all the gateways will fall.'

He did not understand what her strange words meant, but he had heard them so many times he had them committed to memory. He felt as if he knew her, he felt her urgency, her desperation. He felt her love. If only he could find her. He sighed, it was impossible. Even if he did know where to start looking he would never escape Salem. He would never escape his family, his life had become his prison. Maybe he deserved it, maybe it was his punishment for the terrible things he had done. Shaking his head in resignation he tucked the picture into the pages of his journal.

His head snapped up as the door rattled louder this time and swung open. Theo stood abruptly as a familiar man entered, dragging two dirty ragged looking children with him.

'Logan?' Theo's expression darkened in confusion.

'Theo,' Logan breathed heavily, 'where is James? Is he here?'

'James? James Wilkins our neighbor? Why would he be here?' he replied his gaze falling to the two little girls standing either side of Logan, clutching his hands tightly.

'What are you doing here and who are these children?' he asked.

'We have to hide them Theo,' Logan told him urgently. 'James was supposed to be here with Justin.'

'Who is Justin?' Theo replied in confusion, 'Logan you're not making any sense. What is going on? Who are these girls?'

'They are important Theo, we have to protect them at all costs.'

'I don't understand.'

'Nathaniel is coming, we have to hide them. We can't allow him to find them.'

Theo's expression darkened. Nathaniel Boothe was not a man to be trusted, there was something about him that made Theo's blood run cold. He was always there in the background, quiet and self-effacing. A true man of God according to his father, but Theo knew that there was something much darker and dangerous about the man.

'Why would he want the children?' Theo asked.

'He doesn't want them, he wants something he thinks they have. He wants Infernum.'

Theo's head snapped up at the strange word that had echoed in his mind for as long as he could remember.

'You know about Infernum?' Theo asked urgently. 'Logan this is important, do you know what it is?'

'There isn't time to explain, we have to find James and…'

He was cut off abruptly, his eyes widening and his mouth falling open in silent shock as he looked down and saw a knife blade protruding from his chest, surrounded by a rapidly expanding circle of crimson that saturated the fabric of his clothes.

'Logan!' Theo rushed forward as his brother collapsed into his arms and sank to the hay strewn floor.

One of the girls screamed and was dragged to the side of the barn by her sister as they watched on in horror.

Theo looked up from his brother's limp body and found himself staring into the grinning face of Stephen, Nathaniel's avid supporter and his brother Logan's usual companion. The long knife he held in his hand still dripped with his brother's blood.

'Why?' Theo's fists tightened. 'He was your friend, why would you do this?'

'Nathaniel's orders,' he smiled. 'However,' he added, 'he's not the one I'm after.'

Theo stood slowly, his gaze flickering to the two

small girls huddled together in fear.

'Don't worry I'll get to them in time,' his black eyes narrowed, 'but for now Nathaniel wants you dead.'

'ME?' Theo frowned. 'Why?'

'You're in his way.'

Stephen lunged forward and Theo grabbed his wrist with one hand and his throat with the other, spinning him around and slamming him into a thick wooden post. As he did two men came rushing into the barn. He recognized one of them as James Wilkins.

'Get them out of here now!' he yelled as he fought to keep Stephen pinned.

'Don't go too far,' Stephen smiled as he called over his shoulder, 'I'm not finished with them yet.'

'You will have to get past me first,' Theo breathed heavily, as he pitted his strength against Stephen's.

Something was different, he was stronger. A lot stronger than he remembered. After all this was not the first time he'd gotten into a fight with the man. He'd never liked him. Stephen had always taken a little too much pleasure in the trials and the questioning of the accused for Theo's liking, not to mention the part he'd played in his wife Mary's death.

There was something about this Stephen. His face still held the same streak of cruelty, but now it was kept solidly in check by a ruthless control that hadn't been there before. There were also his eyes, they were the wrong color. He'd known Stephen since they were children and his eyes had never been black.

At the edge of his vision he saw another man, whom he assumed was the one called Justin his brother had spoken of. The man was ushering the two terrified girls out of the door followed by James Wilkins, who was dragging Logan's limp body from the barn.

Stephen shoved Theo back, breaking his grip and planting his fist in his face. Theo stumbled back blocking the doorway, his eyes wary, his only thought to keep

Stephen from the open door. He knew he had to give them as much of a head start as he could before Nathaniel Boothe arrived.

Laughing mockingly at his attempt to shield his half dead brother and the two small children from him, Stephen rushed at him with his blade held high. Theo moved to meet him, raising his arm to block the downward stroke. A searing pain speared up his arm as the knife passed clean through his forearm protruding from the other side. But before Stephen had a chance to pull the blade clear Theo twisted his arm with a determined cry.

As he had hoped the hilt snapped off leaving the blade embedded in his arm and denying his enemy a weapon. Balling his good hand into a fist he drove it into his stomach. The air whooshed from Stephen's lungs forcing him to buckle forward giving Theo the opportunity to bring his fist up under his chin. Stephen's head snapped back and he stumbled backward, trying to pull in a deep breath.

Theo grasped the detached blade tightly and pulled it through his arm, ignoring the stinging pain as it bit into the palm of his hand. The useless piece of metal clanged to the ground, as it fell from his wet bloodied hands.

Stephen glanced at Theo, it was blind madness meeting cold fury. Stephen's teeth peeled back in a snarl as he launched himself forward, tackling Theo's torso and slamming him against the wall. From that point on there was only hate and madness between the two of them. They grappled and rolled into the wall and across the floor, slamming each other into any hard surface they could find, landing a punch wherever they could. It was a dirty fight in which neither was willing to give any quarter.

They were barely aware when they slammed into the bale where the lamp sat. They certainly didn't notice when it teetered precariously on the edge, nor did they care when it toppled to the ground with a resounding crash.

Fire caught the straw littered floor immediately, like a great claw of flame devouring everything in its path. The fire let out a great roar and the beast grew. Flames licked up the wooden supports toward the beamed roof. A huge sheet of red, gold and orange broke and rippled like a gigantic wave.

Smoke choked the air as the two men continued to wrestle across the floor. Suddenly there was a loud cracking and Stephen looked up from where he had Theo pinned to the ground with his hands around his neck. The beam gave way and crashed to the ground as Stephen rolled clear. Theo coughed through the dust and ash that was thrown into the smoky air. His lower body was pinned to the ground and he struggled to pull himself free but it was no use.

'Well it seems my work here is done,' Stephen shouted above the roar of the fire. 'Your soul is going to burn in Hell my friend.'

'Then I'll see you there,' Theo ground between his teeth as he watched Stephen turn towards the doorway.

'You first Beckett,' Stephen smiled as the roof gave way, sealing the doorway.

Theo dropped his head back against the floor and roared in frustration. He tried once again to pull himself free, but it was no use. So this was how it was all going to end. He prayed to God the children got away. If he had done nothing else good with his life at least he hoped they would get to live theirs, away from Salem and free from Nathaniel.

He coughed again as the thick oily smoke invaded his lungs. It was like inhaling burning hot brands from the fire. He looked up as he heard another huge groan of timber and an alarming splintering sound. He drew in a painful breath and the whole world seemed to slow. He watched with the quiet dispassion of a man who had accepted his fate, as the roof broke apart and plunged directly down toward him. Unable to do anything else he closed his eyes and waited to die.

Suddenly he felt a strange pressure on his upper arms, as if someone had grabbed him. The next thing he knew everything around him lurched and he found himself upright and standing on a strange hard surface in the freezing night air.

He stumbled as he tried to regain his equilibrium. Leaning forward with his hands on his knees, he coughed up thick black spittle and dragged the crisp clean air into his lungs. Slowly, his breathing evened out and he regained his balance.

He stood warily and took in his surroundings. He didn't recognize where he was, he almost certainly was no longer on his family's land. The burning barn was nowhere in sight and the air smelled and tasted clear with the cold bite of autumn. He could hear the rustle of huge trees in the night breeze although he could not make them out in the darkness. The clouds moved across the sky, suddenly illuminating his path with silvery moonlight.

He stared as a figure was revealed by the pale light. The man standing in front of him was as tall as him and broad. His dark hair seemed to curl slightly at the ends, his skin was as pale as the moonlight and although Theo couldn't make out the color of his eyes, they watched him calmly and patiently as if waiting for him to adjust to his new surroundings.

'Who are you?' Theo croaked. His voice sounded foreign to his own ears, so he cleared his throat and tried again. 'Who are you?'

The man in front of him smiled warmly in amusement.

'A friend,' he replied.

'Where am I? How did I get here?'

'A better question would be - when are you?' the man replied casually.

'I don't understand,' Theo shook his head.

'Theodore Beckett,' he began.

'How do you know my name?' his eyes narrowed suspiciously.

'I know more than you can possibly imagine Theo,' he sighed. 'But now is not the time. I can only tell you that you are no longer in Salem and the year is no longer 1695.'

'I don't...' he shook his head, 'I don't understand.'

'Theo,' he said gently, 'you are in a town called Mercy and the year is 2015.'

'No, that's not possible,' He shook his head again. 'It's not possible. I died... I died in the fire...This is Hell. I'm in Hell.'

'You might feel that way once you've watched a couple of episodes of Jersey Shore,' he murmured under his breath.

'What?'

'Nothing,' he grinned. 'You're not in Hell my friend. I hate to throw you in at the deep end, so to speak, but I'm sure you'll adjust'

'What am I doing here? I don't understand, I don't understand any of this'.

'Back that way,' he indicated over his shoulder, 'through the woods you'll find a house by a lake and in it lives a woman you might just recognize.'

'Who?' Theo asked suspiciously, 'who is she?'

'Oh I wouldn't want to ruin the surprise,' he smiled, 'but whether she likes it or not, she needs you. She's now your responsibility.'

'I don't think so,' Theo's expression darkened. 'I am not a wet nurse, I don't intend to be responsible for anyone.'

'Not your choice,' he replied good naturedly. 'I know what you've done Theo and I know what you want'

'And what's that?' Theo hissed.

'Redemption,' he shrugged. 'Trust me, she's your ticket to peace and forgiveness, but first you need to protect her.'

'From what?' he frowned.

'You'll find out soon enough.'

'What if she doesn't want me to protect her?'

'You'll figure out the details Theo, I have the utmost confidence in you. Oh and by the way,' he leaned forward as an amused smile tugged at his lips, 'watch out for the car'

'What's a car?'

But he was talking to thin air, the man before him had disappeared. Hearing a strange noise behind him he turned and threw his hands up to protect his eyes from the sudden glare of two bright lights.

23.

Zachary smiled as he stepped out into the night air. He could feel the heat of the burning barn at his back, a curious experience. He could never quite get used to wearing human skin, it processed tactile sensations completely differently to his own form. Hopefully he wouldn't have to wear it for long and at least that was one of the Theodore Becketts crossed off his list. Now all he had to do was find the other one. But first...

His gaze tracked over to the two men who had crashed into the barn and disturbed him. One of them was on the ground, leaning over that fool Logan Beckett and the other was trying to shield two small human girls. His eyes narrowed curiously. He'd heard Logan mention Nathaniel's name and that he had a specific interest in the two girls. Perhaps he would intervene on his behalf.

He took a step toward them and stopped abruptly. He could feel the human hairs on the back of his neck begin to prickle and rise, like the air was charged with energy. He turned as he felt a presence and his eyes widened curiously.

'Nathaniel?'

Nathaniel stood before all of them, naked except for a pair of breeches he'd managed to find. He was seemingly unaffected by the cold night air and he looked different somehow. Zachary was used to seeing Nathaniel in his true form, but there was something about him that he couldn't quite pinpoint.

It wasn't the Nathaniel from this timeline, that was for sure. He seemed older, but that wasn't it. His shiny black hair fell to his shoulders and his skin was smooth, in fact it almost seemed to glow, radiating power. But when he looked across and their gazes locked Zachary found himself drawing in a sharp breath of sudden understanding. Nathaniel's usually beetle black eyes were now pure white.

'Nathaniel,' Zachary shook his head slowly, 'what have you done?'

Nathaniel's mouth curved into a slow and deliberate smile.

'Absorbing human souls is forbidden,' he breathed in alarm. 'That is a line even we don't cross. Did you learn nothing from that pathetic addict, Charun?'

'Nothing is forbidden,' Nathaniel replied indifferently. 'There is only power and those too afraid to seize it.'

'Not like this,' he hissed. 'Human souls are like a drug, the power they give is an addiction. Once you start down this path it can only end with you as a slave to your hunger for it.'

'I am not stupid,' Nathaniel replied coolly, 'and I am nothing like that pathetic creature Charun. I only needed one to break free of the body Isabel West forced me into.'

'One is all it takes,' Zachary warned.

'I am strong enough to resist it,' Nathaniel turned toward the girls as Justin pushed them behind him protectively. 'Once I have the book I will have all the power I require.'

'You are never going to get your hands on the book,' Justin growled.

'And who are you little human?' Nathaniel asked

in amusement.

Justin's mouth tightened as he took an involuntary step back, keeping tight hold of the girls.

Suddenly a streak of bright purple skimmed through the air, hitting Zachary in the chest. He shrieked loudly and was knocked back with such an intense amount of force it knocked him clean out of the human body he'd been using. Stephen's vacant husk folded to the ground with a huge smoking hole in the chest. Zachary himself was lying naked in the mud, terrible burns covered his chest and torso as he wheezed and fought to suck in a painful breath.

Olivia slid down off the horse, her flaming bow of Witch fire trained on Nathaniel, as she sent another bolt of violet colored flame through the air with a punch of power. Nathaniel smiled, raising his hand and brushing it aside as if it were as harmless as a paper airplane. She drew her bow again, but this time she felt her mother's hand on her forearm.

'I've got this Olivia,' her eyes were hard and fixed on Nathaniel. 'This time I'll clean up my own mess.'

'How sweet,' Nathaniel taunted, 'what a lovely little family reunion. Did you two kiss and make up?'

Olivia's eyes blazed with anger as her bow flared even brighter.

'OLIVIA!' her mother's voice snapped with authority, 'STAY OUT OF THIS!'

Gritting her teeth her fists tightened, but her fire banked slightly.

'LOGAN!' Theo leapt down from the horse, seeing his brother slumped lifelessly on the ground beside James.

'Go,' Olivia told him, 'we'll handle this.'

He hesitated, torn between his dying brother and protecting Olivia.

'Go!' she flicked her eyes toward him sensing his indecision.

Nathaniel watched in amusement.

'Well, well, well,' Nathaniel's glinting gaze swept across to Bridget and Hester, then to Olivia and Isabel. 'Three generations of Wests, I am being spoiled for choice today.'

'Smirk all you like Nathaniel,' Olivia followed him with her bow. 'You're not getting out of here alive and you're certainly not getting your hands on the book.'

'We'll just see about that Olivia,' he replied, holding his hand up as it burst into flame. 'You see, you're not the only one who likes to play with fire.'

She barely had time to shout out a warning, when he launched the fireball directly at her mother. Isabel didn't even flinch. One minute she was standing there, the next there was a sudden swirl of purple colored smoke, which absorbed the impact of the fireball, then just as suddenly she reappeared.

'Witch smoke?' Nathaniel's brow rose in surprise, 'you have learned some new tricks, haven't you?'

'You have no idea,' Isabel peeled her lips back and hissed.

She threw herself toward him in a running leap, but as her feet left the ground her body whirled and disappeared into a funnel of writhing violet smoke. Nathaniel drew himself up, his body melting into a churning mass of deep green colored Demon smoke. The two clashed mid-air in a swirling, writhing, violent maelstrom of mashed colors, flickering purple and green.

Olivia was thrown to the ground and her bow tattered and dissipated. She looked across to see Theo and James protecting Logan, and Justin shielding the two small girls. It was like being caught on the violent edge of a tornado. The wind whipped up and churned, the sky boiled with heavy storm laden clouds, punctuated with bursts of lightning generated by the static electricity of the churning funnels of smoke. The wind blew apart the remnants of the burning barn, sending a spray of lit embers across to the main farmhouse, which caught and began to burn.

Olivia looked across to the burning rubble that was once the barn. For just a second before the main supports had given way she'd felt a familiar presence inside the building and she knew beyond a shadow of a doubt that her Sam had gotten the other Theo out, just as he was meant to. Even now he was probably dropping him in the middle of the road back in Mercy, where she would find him.

Something inside her, that she hadn't even realized was wound so tight, relaxed and she breathed a sigh of relief. At least that part of the timeline was still intact. Theo had been pulled forward to Mercy and they would meet. Now she just had to make sure Hester survived.

The two gigantic funnels of colored smoke twisted and coiled madly like a gigantic corkscrew through the dark storm clouds, which lit up ominously. The ground shook and roiled beneath their feet. Olivia blinked suddenly as everything around her suddenly blurred then sharpened into focus.

Something was wrong, she could feel it. The nearby fences started to rattle and were suddenly pulled violently from the ground and launched across the farm in rapid succession, like a round of ammo. The ground heaved and rolled, and once again everything blurred and shifted then sharpened into focus.

Olivia glanced back toward the barn her mind working furiously. She gasped in surprise as the compass still tucked carefully inside her clothes, burned white hot and began to throb. She quickly pulled it out and flipped it open. The sundial was spinning madly and pulsing in her hand. Suddenly she understood what Sam had been trying to tell her all along, about fixed points in time. This was a fixed point in time, the barn burning, Theo being pulled into the future and the girls being saved.

She stood abruptly, staring up into the sky as the

brutal wind buffeted her body. Widening her stance, she braced herself against the violent down draught of air. This wasn't supposed to happen, the battle between her mother and Nathaniel was creating a build-up of power.

She could feel the crackle of electricity in the air, but this was a fixed point in time, it couldn't be changed without ripping a massive hole in the fabric of time. This timeline had already sustained too much damage, the blurring and shifting was time itself trying to expel them and reset itself. If she didn't stop them, her mother and Nathaniel were going to tear this place apart.

'I see you've finally figured it out,' a deep smooth voice spoke from someplace close behind her.

Olivia spun around, but there was no one there. Frowning in confusion she watched as time began to slow all around her. Tiny embers of fire danced and swirled languidly on the air. The sky above her moved so slowly, turning and spiraling with green and purple smoke. Even the roaring of the wind had muted. She turned slowly, taking everything in.

'The answer is right in front of you,' the voice came again.

Whoever it was, she didn't feel threatened by him but sensed an innate curiosity and wry amusement coming from him. She felt him step close and although, when she turned to look there was no one there, she could make out a figure in her peripheral vision. As long as she wasn't looking directly at him, she could make out a tall attractive figure wearing what looked to be a well-tailored dark suit. He seemed to be young, but his hair was almost pure white.

'Who are you?' she asked quietly.

'I am one of many,' came the soft reply, so close she could almost feel his breath brush against her ear.

'I don't understand,' she frowned.

'You will.'

She felt his head tilt as he looked up to the sky.

'Their war will tear a hole in time itself, a gaping bleeding wound that will never heal.'

'I have to stop them,' she breathed heavily. 'I have to find some way to reach them.'

'You have the answer right in front of you,' she saw a slim arm snake around her, grasping the compass and holding it to her, nestled on a masculine palm of ivory skin.

'The sundial?' she frowned.

'The Time'dhal,' he corrected. 'We created the Time'dhal as a gateway across time and worlds. It is limitless…as are you Olivia.'

'How do you know my name?' she asked in confusion. 'And what do you mean limitless?'

'Do you think it a coincidence that the Time'dhal came into Hades' possession? And that he then gave it to you? The demon Seth was a means to an end, the Time'dhal was never truly his.'

'Are you saying you wanted me to have it?' Olivia shook her head in denial, 'that you made sure Hades got his hands on it with the express purpose of him passing it to me?'

'That's exactly what I'm saying,' she could hear the acerbic humor in his voice.

'But why? Why me?'

'I would have thought that would be obvious by now Olivia,' he replied, 'or did it escape your notice how many Gods and Goddesses have taken a very specific interest in you. You're special, and you're the only one who hasn't figured that out yet. You know, for a very extraordinary woman, sometimes you can be a little slow.'

'Thanks,' she replied sarcastically as she glanced down at the slightly tarnished compass in her hand. 'So how exactly is this supposed to help?' She flipped it open. 'The compass takes you to another point geographically and the sundial takes you to another point in time.'

'You are thinking too linear, too three

dimensionally,' his arms encircled her intimately and his hands cupped hers as she held the Time'dhal in her joined palms. 'It is limitless; reach beyond what your eyes are showing you. We placed it into this form as a diversion, a commonplace item so easily discounted and overlooked, but like so many things, on the inside it is so much more. It only takes a truly exceptional person to unlock its secrets.'

As she stared at the curious little golden object laying so innocently in her palms everything else seemed to fade away. She could feel it pulsing against her skin like a tiny throbbing heart. Strangely it felt like her Earth fire. She could feel golden vines winding from the Time'dhal down into her skin, spreading down into her flesh like ancient roots. There was no pain just a deep sense of connection, the metal became liquid swirling in her palms, the same molten gold as her eyes.

It swirled and pulsed and grew. Opening up like the heart of an exotic flower it bloomed in her hands until she was holding a huge golden sphere, which looked like the innards of a clock. Hundreds of golden dials of varying sizes, some as tiny as a pea, some as large as a tennis ball, spun and rotated elegantly, suspended between tiny mechanisms that looked too beautiful, too intricate and delicate to be man-made.

The tiny mechanism suddenly parted and folded in half and then half again, revealing a golden hourglass containing infinitely pouring sand. She watched it for a moment, mesmerized, until the metal of the hourglass frame melted down to a molten liquid and circled her palms and the sands of time swirled to join it. Suddenly the whirling slowed and her breath caught in her throat, her eyes shimmered, reflecting back the spiraling galaxies and infinite universes sitting in the palms of her hands.

'Now do you see?' his voice whispered seductively in her ear, 'do you see the endless possibilities?'

She watched the birth of a universe as planets and

voids swirled out of nothingness, the beginning and end of time as an endless circle. She was so intently watching the pulsing sphere in her hands she didn't see the strands of gold surrounding everything around her, the threads of time binding everything together. Nor did she see those threads pull taut and begin to fray every time the violent funnel of Witch smoke and Demon smoke crashed into them.

'Olivia,' the voice crooned softly, 'you know what to do.'

Strangely enough she did. She concentrated on the sphere in her hands and the galaxies and stars disappeared. She pulled back in the molten metal and in her mind began to manipulate it. It coiled and twisted in her palms, slowly taking shape. A circular shape like a portal with an ornate golden frame appeared, but she was so focused on the beautiful shape in her hands she didn't see an enormous replica of it appear high up in the sky.

A small smile appeared on her lips when she finally looked up. The portal in the sky shimmered and pulsed, and suddenly the purple and green tornado of smoke was pulled inside, both of them howling and shrieking in fury.

Staring up in satisfaction into the now clear sky which was filled with the pale rays of dawn, she turned her attention back to the glowing sphere in her palms. Closing her hands together the golden light disappeared and when she opened her hands again the Time'dhal was once again sitting sedately in her palm, looking for all the world like a plain old tarnished compass.

'Very good Olivia,' she heard the amused voice fading behind her. 'There may be hope after all.'

She turned, but the enigmatic stranger was gone, she no longer even felt his presence. Her gaze fell on Theo, who was cradling his brother's body gently in his arms. She slowly approached, but even from this distance she could tell it was too late. Her heart broke when she saw the sheer grief weighing down on Theo. His head hung low and his shoulders slumped as he wrapped his arms tightly around his brother.

'Theo,' she whispered, placing her hand on his shoulder and dropping down next to him.

'He's gone Livy,' he whispered brokenly.

'I know,' she murmured, 'I know.'

He leaned his head against hers as a tear slid down his face. She ran her fingers through his hair and just sat with him, staring down at Logan's peaceful face.

'Theo,' Justin laid his hand comfortingly on his other shoulder, 'you need to move. The house is burning now.'

Theo raised his sorrow filled face long enough to see his childhood home engulfed in flames and with it all his memories both the good and the bad.

'It doesn't matter anymore,' he muttered. 'They're all gone now, there's no one left to care.'

'I know,' Justin replied sympathetically, 'but the smoke will bring others and as far as anyone will know, you died in that fire. We can't risk anyone seeing you.'

'Theo,' Olivia stroked his head gently, 'he's right. We've damaged the timeline enough.'

'It doesn't feel right just leaving him like this.'

'I will take good care of him,' Justin told him. 'You have my word.'

'Theo,' James leaned over Logan's body and grasped his forearm. 'Take the girls back to my house. Justin and I will take care of Logan, I promise.'

Theo looked up at his father and nodded slowly. Olivia's heart broke again as Theo wrapped his arms around his brother and held him tightly. Cupping the back of his head in his hand he pressed him into the crook of his neck, tears spilling silently from his closed eyes. He rocked him for a several long seconds before pressing a kiss to his forehead.

'Goodbye brother,' he whispered as his voice

cracked. 'Be at peace.'

He laid him gently on the ground and stood up. His gaze swept the grounds surrounding the house. The barn had collapsed into a smoldering pile of ash and the main house still burned. Nathaniel and Isabel were both gone and Stephen's discarded body lay crumpled on the ground.

'Where is Zachary?' Theo asked in a deadly voice.

'He's gone,' Olivia told him. 'He crawled away, while we were distracted.'

'We'll find him,' Justin told him, 'but judging from the hit he took from Olivia, I'd say he's crawled away to lick his wounds. We probably won't hear from him for a while. It will be safe to take the girls back to James' house.'

Theo nodded. Olivia turned to the two little girls standing to one side. Hester was calmly staring at Olivia, her arms cradling some sort of journal to her chest, while her sister stood behind her with her arms wrapped around her protectively.

'Hey,' she dropped down in front of them and smiled carefully. 'I guess you are both pretty scared and confused right now.'

'I know who you are,' Hester spoke up.

'You do?'

'You're her daughter, aren't you?' she replied.

'Yes I am,' Olivia sighed. There wasn't much point in lying to them now, not when she needed their cooperation.

Bridget gasped and pulled Hester further away from her.

'I'm not going to hurt you,' Olivia held up her hands slowly. 'I just want to get you someplace safe. Pretty soon there are going to be a lot of other people here and they are going to start asking questions.'

'She won't hurt us Bridey,' Hester pulled herself free from her sister's death like grip.

'You don't know that,' she replied stubbornly.

'Yes I do,' she answered confidently.

'What do you have there?' Olivia asked curiously, indicating the journal in Hester's hands.

'I found it in the barn,' she held it out for Olivia to take. 'It belonged to the other man, the one who looked like him.' She pointed to Theo.

Olivia recognized the book as soon as Hester dropped it into her hands. She flipped it open to reveal journal entries and sketch after sketch signed TB. It was Theo's journal. She'd found it hidden in a trunk in her house along with Hester's journals when she'd first arrived back in Mercy. With a small smile she closed the book and handed it back to Hester.

'Will you do something for me?' she asked softly.

Hester tilted her head questioningly.

'Will you look after this book?' she told her, 'it's very important. You need to keep it safe.'

She nodded slowly.

'Will you come with us?'

Hester looked at her for a moment before finally reaching out, tentatively taking Olivia's hand.

'Hess!' Bridget hissed.

'It's alright Bridey,' Hester looked up at Olivia and smiled shyly, 'she's mine.'

Olivia held out her other hand. Bridget stared at it as if it were a poisonous snake before ignoring it completely and walking past them and waiting. Sighing in resignation she turned and nodded to Theo. The four of them set out, back across the field toward the woods and headed for James' orchard.

It was well into morning by the time they arrived at the house, dirty, tired and hungry. They sat the girls at the table, while Theo found them something to eat and Olivia disappeared into the bedroom.

She stripped down quickly out of the borrowed men's clothing she wore, removing the blood stained rags wrapped around various parts of her body where her wounds had been. Washing quickly in freezing cold water she pulled on the dress and petticoats she'd left behind and stepped back out into the main room in time to find Theo pouring out cups of warm spiced apple cider.

She sat down at the table opposite the two dark haired girls and sipped slowly from the cup Theo passed her, feeling the delicious liquid warm her weary body. Theo sank down onto the bench next to her and she slipped her hand in his reassuringly. They sat in companionable silence for a while, but Theo didn't drink, instead he sat and stared blankly at the cup.

'You haven't asked us about the book,' Hester piped up suddenly.

'What?' Olivia tore her concerned gaze from Theo and focused on the little girl who was studying her curiously.

'Your mother wanted the book. She didn't say it, but I knew.'

'Hess!' Bridget kicked her under the table in warning.

'It's alright Bridey trust me, it's meant to be hers, not Isabel's.'

'I don't want the book,' Olivia sighed.

Hester nodded, her gaze serious as it locked on Olivia.

'That's why it's meant to be yours.'

'I really don't want it,' Olivia whispered.

'We don't get to choose our destiny, it chooses us,' Hester replied sadly. 'That's what Mama always said.'

'I'm so sorry about your mother,' Olivia shook her head. 'I was your age when I was told my mother was dead and although it wasn't true, I thought it was for a long time. I know how painful it is.'

'She would have wanted us to help you,' Hester replied. 'She was always helping people.'

'And look where that got her,' Bridget interrupted bitterly. 'She's dead.'

'Don't do that Bridget,' Theo told her sharply. 'Your mother was a good woman, she wanted to see the best in people. She trusted in them and that is a trait too few people have. What happened to her was not her fault. Yes, she trusted the wrong person. Isabel West has taken from all of us, but your mother loved you, she gave her life to save you. So if you hold onto anything, hold onto her love for you, not your bitter feelings, or it will end up changing you.'

'I want her back,' Bridget's lip trembled and her eyes filled with tears.

'I know,' he stood slowly as he walked around the table and knelt down to her level, beside her. 'I want my brother back too, but they're gone. All we can do is carry them with us for the rest of our lives and then a part of them will live too.'

Bridget threw her arms around him, buried her tiny face in his neck and sobbed. Theo wrapped his arms around her and picking her up he settled down on the bench next to Hester with Bridget in his lap and rocked her slowly, while she purged herself of her grief.

Olivia watched them both with sad eyes.

'Olivia?'

She turned her gaze back to Hester.

'Ask me about the book,' she insisted.

Olivia shook her head slowly.

'Ask me.'

Olivia blew out a resigned but reluctant breath.

'Is it even real?' she asked, 'or is it just a myth?'

'It's real,' Hester nodded.

'Where is it?' Olivia finally asked.

'I don't know.'

'Sorry?'

'It's hard to explain,' Hester frowned. 'It's in a different place for each of us.'

'I'm not sure I follow,' Olivia shook her head in confusion.

'All mother said was when you are ready to find it, the book will find you.'

'That's it?' Olivia replied incredulously. 'It will find me?'

She nodded.

'You're different than the rest of us,' Hester frowned. 'Your threads are different, so are his,' she nodded in Theo's direction as he continued to soothe Bridget gently.

'Threads? How are they different?'

Hester yawned tiredly.

'You both need some sleep,' Olivia looked over at Theo who nodded in silent agreement. Bridget had cried herself out and fallen asleep in Theo's arms.

'Come on,' Olivia held out her hand for Hester.

They stood and followed Theo into the bedroom, watching silently as he settled the sleeping child in the bed and removed her shoes. Hester turned to Olivia and hugged her tightly.

'I won't see you again Olivia,' she told her softly. 'You'll be gone when we wake, but thank you for saving us.'

She nodded, unable to find adequate words.

Hester kicked off her own shoes and climbed up into the bed next to her sister, wrapping her arm tightly around her comfortingly.

'We'll be alright,' she whispered sadly as she closed her eyes, although whether she was reassuring her sister or herself Olivia couldn't tell.

She pulled the covers up over the girls and kissed each one of them gently in turn, before turning and creeping from the room.

She stepped back into the main room and Theo pulled her into his arms, kissing her roughly. She sank into him, wrapping her arms around him and losing herself to his kiss. By the time he pulled back they were both breathing hard as he pressed his forehead to hers.

'Olivia,' he breathed painfully.

That one word seemed to convey everything he was feeling. All the love and loss and relief rolled into one messy sticky ball of emotion.

'I know,' she whispered, holding the hands that cupped her face tenderly. 'I know.'

And she did. Words weren't needed between them. She knew exactly what he was trying to say, even if he didn't.

'It's time to go home Theo,' she told him softly, 'we can't stay here any longer.'

'I know,' he whispered, 'but how?'

'I can get us home,' she told him confidently. 'We'll stay and say goodbye to James and then we have to leave.'

He nodded looking up as the latch lifted and the door swung open. Both James and Justin walked in wearily, stopping abruptly when they saw them both.

'Where are the children?' James asked.

'In bed sleeping,' Olivia reassured him.

He looked at Olivia and Theo quietly for a few moments. 'You're leaving, aren't you?'

'Yes,' Theo replied, 'we have to.'

'I wish we had more time,' he swallowed painfully.

'I do too,' Theo stepped closer, 'but I'm grateful for the time we had, and I'm grateful I found out the truth.'

'Are you?'

'Yes,' he nodded, 'and I'm glad I had the chance to know you, to know that my father was a good man.'

'Father?' Justin replied startled.

'Theo,' James tried to speak, but his voice caught in his throat.

Theo simply wrapped his arms around him and pulled him in, hugging him tightly.

'I'm proud to call you father,' he whispered.

'Son,' James wrapped his arms around him and

held him as if he never wanted to let go.

'Why don't we give them a moment,' Olivia suggested to Justin. 'You can help me.'

Nodding quietly, he followed her across the room. While James and Theo said their goodbyes Justin helped Olivia retrieve her backpack from beneath the floorboards. She also gathered up Hester's Grimoire and Emmaline's journal. When she was finally ready, she approached James and Theo.

'Olivia,' James wrapped his arms around her and hugged her tight, 'I love you. You've been a daughter to me.'

'I love you too,' she hugged him back, her eyes filling with tears. 'I'm going to miss you so much.'

'I'll miss you too,' he smiled sadly. 'I don't suppose you'd be able to come back and visit?'

She shook her head slowly.

'Once we leave I have to seal this timeline,' she replied. 'We can't risk any more damage than it has already sustained. Once I seal it we can't return, but then again neither can my mother or Nathaniel. Sooner or later the other Nathaniel will resurface, but hopefully by then Hester will be old enough and powerful enough to deal with him.'

'I will make sure they're safe,' Justin told her. 'They are both under our protection now. I give you my word they will be safe and cared for.'

'Thank you Justin.'

'What about you father?' Theo asked James. 'Will you be alright?'

'I'll be just fine,' he smiled. 'I know both you and your sister are out there and you are safe and happy. I can't ask for more than that.'

Theo nodded.

'Will you tell her? Temperance?' James asked. 'Will you tell her about me?'

'Of course I will,' Theo promised.

'Tell her I love her and I want her to be happy.'

'I will,' Theo answered painfully.

'I will be alright Theo,' James assured him. 'Justin has asked me to join the Veritas, to take Logan's place in the secret order of the Men of Truth. We will make sure he is never forgotten; his name and the sacrifice he made will live forever in the order's memory. We will guard against Nathaniel's return and protect Olivia's family.'

'We will also find Zachary,' Justin promised.

'I guess this is goodbye then,' Theo said quietly.

James nodded, he hugged them both one more time and then stepped back.

Theo picked up the backpack and hooked it over one shoulder. Picking up the books and holding them tightly, he reached for Olivia's hand. She looked up at him as she pulled the Time'dhal from the collar of her dress. Clutching it in her fist she breathed in, her eyes filling with tears as they locked on James.

She felt the Time'dhal pulse in her hand, the metal growing warm under her touch, her voice barely more than a whisper.

'Take us home…'

Part 3.
Present

24.

'You missed a spot.'

Roni put the paintbrush down and took a step back. Hand tucked on her hip and her head cocked to the side, her eyes narrowed as she studied her handiwork.

'No I didn't,' she frowned and turned to see Jake smirking.

'What color is this again?' Jake asked.

'It's oatmeal.'

'It's beige.'

'No,' Roni replied slowly, 'it's oatmeal.'

'How do you know Olivia will even like it? After all, it's her library.'

'Are you kidding? Did you see what was in here before?' her lips pursed thoughtfully. 'Besides its neutral, it's warm, its inviting, its…its…'

'It's beige,' Jake supplied helpfully.

She threw him a dry look.

'I thought you were supposed to be helping?' she asked pointedly.

'I am helping,' he wiggled the roller in his hand.

She chuckled, shaking her head as she turned back to the wall.

'So where is the bit I missed?' she waved her hand dismissively. 'Because I gotta tell you I'm just not seeing it.'

Jake dropped his roller back into the tray of paint

and stepped closer to the wall, the side of his body innocently grazing hers.

'It's just…about…here,' at the last minute he turned his head angling his face away from the wall and crashing his lips down on hers.

She dropped the paintbrush and wound her arms around his neck, turning slightly so their bodies aligned. It wasn't fair, nobody should be this good at kissing. Every time his lips met hers every single intelligent thought drained from her head, in fact she was sure her IQ even dropped a few points.

His hand snaked up and grasped the nape of her neck, squeezing then releasing gently until chills danced the length of her spine, before he tilted her head slightly allowing him better access to taste her. He bit down gently on her lower lip and she was helpless against the low moan which caught deep in her throat…totally worth the IQ points.

His hands skimmed down her spine, leaving her skin tingling in their wake. He lifted her easily and she wrapped her legs around his waist. He pressed her back against the wet, freshly painted wall leaving long strokes of color down the back of her hair and shirt. Her hands slid under the hem of his shirt, feeling ridges and hard muscle as her fingertips lightly scraped his smooth flesh.

'Ahem,' a throat cleared behind them.

They both froze.

Roni's eyes widened on Jake's face as they broke apart. They both slowly turned their heads to find Olivia and Theo staring at them in amusement.

'I totally called it,' she whispered to Theo, 'you owe me twenty bucks.'

'Something we should know about?' Theo's mouth twitched as he looked at Jake who still had Roni pinned to the wall with her legs wrapped around him.

They continued to stare speechlessly, eyes wide in shock as Olivia leaned slowly to the side, glancing around them.

'Is that a butt print on my wall?' her eyes narrowed.

Roni released her legs and slowly slid down the wall as Jake lowered her to the ground. His eyes ran over Olivia and Theo, dirty and disheveled and still wearing their 17th century clothes.

'Dude, you're wearing tights,' Jake's mouth curved.

'They're socks, asshole.' Theo's face broke into a wide smile as the two of them laughed and wrapped their arms around each other tightly.

'Boys,' Olivia shook her head, rolling her eyes in amusement as she turned to her friend.

'Hello Roni,' she smiled.

Roni let out a low cry and wrapped her arms around Olivia, swaying gently as she hugged her firmly.

'You're real,' she laughed as her eyes filled with tears. 'You're really here?'

'Yes we are,' Olivia replied quietly, swallowing past the knot of emotion burning at the back of her throat.

She was finally home.

'Move aside Roni,' Jake released Theo and moved over to Olivia.

'Jake,' she grinned.

'Olive,' he wrapped his arms around her and squeezed her gently. 'Missed you,' he whispered, burying his face in her neck.

'Missed you too,' she sighed, relaxing into his arms.

She looked up as she heard a sudden desperate scrabble of claws on wood. Breaking away from him she hunkered down on the floor as a ball of golden colored fur came barreling into the room.

'BEAU!' Olivia gasped happily as he dived at her.

He was a lot bigger than when she last saw him and although he was still a small dog he had a lot of weight and enthusiasm behind him as he leapt on her, knocking her to the ground on her ass. She laughed in delight as he rolled and trod all over her, licking every inch of her he could reach, his large soft paws padding over her belly and thighs and his tail whipping around as he rubbed his face all over her.

'I missed you too baby,' she smiled as her eyes filled with tears.

Theo leaned down and Beau suddenly abandoned her and jumped all over him, lavishing him with affection.

'You looked after him for us?' she looked up at Roni.

'Yeah,' she glanced over at Jake and smiled, 'we both did. We also made sure he got his next lot of shots as well.'

'Thanks.'

'Yeah well, he wasn't too thankful,' she grimaced. 'He demonstrated his opinion by peeing all over my bed.'

'Oh no,' Olivia chuckled, 'last time it was the back seat of my car.'

'I had to buy a mattress,' she laughed and shook her head.

'How long have we been gone?' Olivia asked.

Roni threw a look at Jake who stared back.

'How long?' Olivia stood slowly as Beau continued to climb all over Theo.

'Olive,' Jake told her gently, 'you've been gone nearly six months.'

'Six months, really? Shit…' Olivia breathed slowly, her forehead creasing, 'I've still got that library book.'

'How long did you think you'd been gone?' Roni asked curiously.

'I have no idea,' Olivia shrugged. 'Time passed differently for us in the Otherworld and the Underworld. We kinda lost track, although time went back to passing normally when we were in Salem.'

'Salem?' Jake frowned. 'You were in Salem and

you couldn't call to let us know you were only an hour away?'

'Um not Salem now,' Olivia replied, 'Salem 1695.'

'1695?' he repeated slowly.

'Why do you think we're dressed like this?'

'Oh my God 17th Century Salem? Are you serious?' Roni's eyes widened and her historian's heart began to beat wildly. 'That must have been insane.'

'You have no idea,' she muttered. 'Trust me, it's not as much fun as it sounds.'

'Hold on,' Jake frowned suddenly, 'the Underworld?'

'I guess we've got a lot to catch up on,' Olivia replied quietly. 'What did you tell everyone? I mean, about where Theo and I were?'

'Well apart from those of us who knew the truth, we told everyone else you were on a research trip and Theo went with you.'

Olivia nodded and looked across to Roni who'd pulled out her phone and was scrolling through her contacts.

'What are you doing?' Jake asked.

'Letting everyone else know you're back, we've all been so worried.'

Theo's eyes locked on Olivia's and she knew what he was asking.

'Have you got Tammy Burnett's number?'

Roni said nothing, but her eyes were filled with understanding as she scrolled through to the right number and passed the phone to him.

He waited as it rang, his heart beating wildly in his chest.

'Hello Roni,' the smooth female voice answered, 'what can I do for you?'

Theo's voice caught in his throat as he heard the one voice he thought he never would again. It was older, more smooth and polished, but it was still her.

'Roni?' the voice came again, 'is everything okay?'
'Tempy?' Theo whispered.
The line went silent for a few moments.
'Theo?'
'Yes,' he smiled.
'Where are you?'
'At Olivia's house.'
'Is she with you?' Temperance asked.
'Yes,' he replied again.
'I'll be right there.' The line suddenly went dead and he handed the phone back to Roni.
'I guess she's on her way over.'
'I guess so,' he replied quietly.
Olivia sank down onto her old couch, which was covered with a dust sheet. Beau immediately jumped up into her lap, padding her down a couple of times before curling up with a contented sigh. Olivia smiled and stroked his soft coat lovingly.
'So why are you painting my library oatmeal?'
'See,' Roni smirked at Jake as she mouthed the word 'oatmeal' to him. She perched comfortably on the arm of the couch and looked down at Olivia. 'The library was in a pretty big mess when you disappeared.'
Olivia thought back to the last time she'd been in her favorite room. It was the night they'd gone to the old abandoned hotel high up on the cliff overlooking the lake, in order to look for Charon, the Ferryman of the Underworld. God, it seemed like a lifetime since that night. But Roni was right, the library had been an absolute mess, as that had been not long after her mother had broken into the house and trashed the room while looking for Hester's Grimoire.
'When you disappeared,' Roni continued, 'I borrowed a lot of your books trying to find a way to locate you and bring you back.'
'I thought there were a lot missing,' she glanced around the almost empty room.

'Well a lot of them are stacked up neatly in Theo's studio with his paintings. We didn't want them to get damaged while we were decorating. Anyway, if you remember we briefly talked after your mom trashed the room, about you redecorating and sorting through all the mess in here. I figured I'd get started while you were gone as a surprise,' she replied rather sheepishly. 'It gave me something to do other than worry. I'm sorry, I hope you don't mind.'

'Mind?' Olivia chuckled, 'no I don't mind. Knowing me I would have gotten distracted and the room would have stayed that way for years, with piles of books stacked everywhere. At least it's one job off my list.'

Roni breathed a sigh of relief.

'I'm so glad,' she smiled, 'but I have to ask you…what do you think of the color?'

'I like it,' Olivia decided, staring at the walls. 'It's neutral, but warm and inviting.'

Roni turned and smirked at Jake again.

'Plus it goes really well with the dark wood of the shelving.'

'That's what I thought,' Roni nodded.

'So how are things going at the museum?'

'Really well,' she beamed. 'The renovations were finished a few months ago and the new exhibits have been a big hit.'

'And?' Olivia prompted.

'And?' Roni repeated in confusion.

'Did they give you the job permanently?'

'Oh,' Roni blushed, 'well yes…yes they did. They decided I was adequately suited for the job so my probationary period is over and I am now the permanent curator'.

'Adequately suited?' Jake laughed, 'they couldn't offer her the job quick enough. She's done incredible things at the museum, in fact, she had the new wing dedicated to Renata. The Renata Gershon Memorial wing now houses an exhibition on Mercy during both World Wars, and a whole section on the Holocaust and the Jewish community who chose to make their home in Mercy. Then there's her new intern program that students are climbing all over each other to apply for, plus her young curator program.'

'Young curator program?' Olivia asked in interest.

'We give children from the local schools a chance to experience what it is to be a curator. They have a chance to learn how to preserve and display items of historical significance, as well as some insight on what it's like to run a museum. We also have a night at the museum once a month, where the children get to have a sleepover actually on the premises. We have specific night time exhibits and they get to have a midnight feast.'

'That sounds amazing,' Olivia laughed in delight. 'I want a sleepover in the museum.'

'Well you might just get your wish, we're always looking for volunteers to help out. Mrs Bailey has been an absolute Godsend when it comes to managing thirty over-excited kids.'

'That's because they're scared of her,' Jake coughed.

'Mrs Bailey?' Olivia's eyes widened in surprise.

Roni nodded. 'Don't listen to him,' she threw a look at Jake. 'She's been great, in fact, I think working with the kids has softened some of her sharp edges. After Mr Bailey passed away she couldn't bring herself to return to the store, so Tommy's been managing it for her and she started volunteering at the Museum.'

'Tommy? What Louisa's Tommy?'

'Yeah,' Jake explained, 'he's been honorably discharged from the army now. Louisa's happy to have him home permanently and its given them a chance to work out some of their problems. They're doing okay at the moment.'

'That's good then,' Olivia agreed.

'In fact now you're home, once you've settled back in, I have a project I'd love your help with,' Roni told her.

'Oh?' Olivia looked at her curiously.

'It's going to be an exhibit of the role of women in Puritan society. As you've written a book on the subject I thought you might like to help me and maybe even give a guest lecture?'

'I'd love to,' Olivia smiled, turning toward the open window as she heard a car pull up outside.

A few moments later the front door opened and she heard footsteps.

Olivia moved off the couch, disturbing Beau who gave a disgruntled sniff and jumped down just as Tammy Burnett walked through the doorway.

She stopped dead, her eyes locked on Theo and for a moment neither of them spoke.

'Tempy,' he finally whispered.

Her eyes filled with tears as she rushed across the room and threw herself into his arms. Olivia's own eyes filled with sentimental tears as she watched them hug each other tightly.

After a while she pulled back slightly and with her arm still wrapped around her brother she reached out and pulled Olivia in and hugged them both.

'Temperance,' Olivia smiled.

'Oh,' she pulled back smiling, tears of happiness shimmering on her long dark lashes, 'it's been a very long time since anyone has called me that.'

'You'll always be Tempy to me,' Theo tugged her hair playfully as he did when she was a child.

'I've waited so long for this day,' she wiped away a tear with her fingertips.

'Why don't we give you three some privacy,' Jake grasped Roni's hand and pulled her from the room, closing the door behind them with a quiet click.

'I want to know everything,' she told them,

'everything that happened from when Sam pulled me out of the house to the moment you arrived back in Mercy.'

'I have so much to tell you Tempy,' Theo pulled her over to the couch and sat with her while Olivia pulled up the chair from her desk. 'But first tell us what happened to you, when Sam pulled you out.'

'Well,' Tammy replied, glancing back and forth between Olivia and Theo, 'as you know Sam had been really sick, first from his extended exposure to the Underworld then from being infected with Demon fire.'

'You know about that?' Olivia asked curiously.

'Sam told me,' she nodded, continuing with her story. 'By the time he got to me he was better, but still very weak. When he jumped us through time he intended to bring me here to your present, but he didn't have the strength, nor the experience, as it was only the first time he'd made the jump through time. We fell short and ended up in 1983.'

'1983?' Olivia repeated in confusion, 'that's not right. If you landed up in '83 and stayed there that would put you in your forties. I read your bio when I first returned to Mercy and that says you're just over fifty.'

'I'll get to that part of the story in a moment,' she smiled. 'As I said we ended up in Mercy, Christmas 1983. I was really sick, I had pneumonia with a secondary bronchial infection. They managed to treat me, but I was out of it for weeks. When I finally woke up Sam was there, but the jump through time had made him really weak. He said he had to go home, he couldn't bring me forward until he'd healed himself. He left me here in Mercy and told me he would be back for me, but not to tell anyone my real identity. Then he disappeared. I don't need to tell you how shaken up I was. I didn't speak for months, but as I had no apparent family and they didn't know who I was, I ended up in the system and fortunately I was fostered by the Burnetts. They called me Tammy.'

'Were they good to you?' Theo asked in concern.

'Yes they were,' she squeezed his hand reassuringly. 'Susan and Ed were lovely people, they loved me so much. I had a good life with them. After a while Sam showed up looking older and healthy. He'd come to jump me forward to find you, but he could see how attached I'd become to Susan and Ed. So he gave me a choice.'

'You chose to stay and be their daughter?' Olivia realized.

'Yes I did,' she smiled, 'we were a family. I knew it meant I would have to wait longer to see you both, but I didn't want to leave them. They'd come to love me as much as I loved them, it would have hurt them terribly to lose me. I told Sam I wanted to stay, so he arranged false papers for me, a social security number and a fake birth certificate. He made me a few years older than I actually was and changed my name from Temperance Beckett to Tammy Jones just in case Nathaniel ever came looking for me. Eventually Susan and Ed officially adopted me and I became Tammy Burnett.'

'Were you happy?' Theo asked quietly.

'I was,' she nodded, 'I was cared for. Once I got used to this new place they put me in school and I excelled. I went to college, got a good job and ended up as Mayor. Sam always stopped by to check in on me and over the years we've become very close.'

'Sam kept an eye on you?'

'Of course he did,' she smiled at him. 'What did you think he was going to do? Drop me three hundred years into the future and then abandon me? I was a child, he always made sure I was okay.'

'It seems I owe the man more than I can ever repay,' Theo murmured. 'First for bringing me to Olivia and then for taking care of you when I couldn't.'

'So tell me what happened after I left,' she looked first to Theo then to Olivia.

'We jumped forward ten years to 1695,' Olivia

replied softly.

'How?'

Theo looked across to Olivia, who nodded silently in agreement and so he began to talk. He told her everything, from Olivia being kidnapped from James' house, to the fire in Salem. He explained about Hester and Bridget, Logan, Justin and the Veritas, with Olivia filling in the blanks on The Time'dhal, telling Theo at the same time as they had not yet had a chance to discuss what had happened at the Beckett farm after Logan had died.

'Poor Logan,' Tammy replied sadly. 'I mean obviously I knew he was dead, after all it's been three hundred years, but seeing you and hearing about what happened, it all feels like it happened yesterday.'

'For us it did,' Theo replied quietly.

'He found his peace Theo,' she squeezed his hand again.

'I hope so,' he sighed before turning to Olivia. 'This man you saw?' he asked, 'the one who told you about the Time'dhal, you don't have any idea who he was?'

'No,' she shook her head, 'I didn't even see him clearly.'

'But he told you how to use it, how to open the portal?'

She shook her head again, frowning. 'That's just it, he didn't. I already knew, the knowledge was already there inside me. I didn't just open it, I created the portal.'

'Where did you send them?' Tammy asked curiously, 'your mother and Nathaniel?'

'Antarctica,' Olivia replied, with a deadpan look.

'Antarctica?' Tammy laughed, 'are you serious?'

'Yes,' she confirmed. 'I couldn't risk leaving them both in the past so I had to bring them back to the present day and I didn't want to dump them down in the middle of a populated area. Neither of them care much about collateral damage so I dropped them down on a gigantic ice shelf and let them fight it out. Sooner or later one or possibly both of them will likely show up here, but for now...' she shrugged, 'it was the best I could do at short notice. I do feel sorry for the penguins though.'

Tammy laughed, 'God Olivia, you truly are priceless.'

'There is something else I have to tell you Tempy,' Theo told her. 'It's about James Wilkins.'

He glanced across at Olivia who gave him a small smile of encouragement.

'What is it?' Tammy asked.

'He was our father.'

'What?' she replied in confusion.

'Logan was Matthias Beckett's son, he was our half-brother, but you and I are both James Wilkins' children. He and mother were in love,' he shook his head in frustration. 'It's a really long story.'

She sat quietly for a moment just staring at her brother, not knowing what to say.

'She left us her journal,' Theo told her.

'Who? Mother?' Tammy asked.

Theo nodded.

'It will explain things far better than I ever could. Once I'm done with it I will give it to you to read, but I also have this for you.'

She watched as he reached into the pocket of his long dark coat and pulled out a letter sealed with red wax and pressed into the wax was the shape of an apple.

'He wrote this for you,' Theo handed it to her. 'I don't know what's in it, but he wanted me to tell you that he loved you very much and all he ever wanted was for you to be happy.'

Tammy's eyes filled with tears as she clutched the letter.

'I wish I'd known,' she shook her head sadly, 'he was such a dear sweet man. He was always so good to me.'

'I know,' Theo replied quietly.

There was a knock at the door of the library and

as the three of them looked up the door swung open and Roni stepped back in.

'Sorry to disturb you.'

'It's fine Roni,' Theo smiled, 'where's Jake?'

'He ran out to the store. No one has been staying here for the past six months, so there's no food or milk or even basics. He said after six months you're going to want coffee and a lot of it.'

'He's not wrong,' Theo smiled.

'I hope you don't mind, but I called the others. I wanted to let them know you guys were alright and that you're back in Mercy, but you know Louisa, wild horses couldn't hold her back. They're all heading over here and she said she'll bring takeout.'

'Yes,' Olivia fist pumped the air, 'real food. Call her back and tell her it'd better be Chinese or I won't speak to her for another six months.'

'Okay,' Roni laughed.

'Right then,' Olivia stood up absently smoothing down her skirt and petticoats. 'I'm sorry Temperance, but you have no idea how long I've been dreaming about a hot shower and a toothbrush. Are you staying?'

She nodded smiling.

'Good, and by the way, what would you prefer me to call you?'

'Best stick with Tammy,' she replied. 'I'm used to it now and it's how everyone knows me. Besides if Nathaniel is heading back this way, I don't want to advertise the fact that I'm Theo's sister.'

'Probably a good idea,' Olivia nodded. 'Okay, well make yourself comfortable. I'm going to get washed and changed,' she grinned, 'because it looks like we're about to have a welcome home party.'

25.

Olivia looked up as her mouth filled with warm water. Swishing it around and spitting it out she let the water wash over her face, drenching her hair as it ran down her body. Sighing in pleasure she tried to squeeze the last of the toothpaste out of the almost empty tube and onto her brush. Scrubbing her teeth again she briefly contemplated squeezing the toothpaste directly into her mouth and bypassing the toothbrush altogether. She'd cleaned her teeth a total of six times so far and they still didn't feel clean enough. They probably were, but she couldn't seem to help herself. No matter what she did she didn't feel clean enough.

Rinsing out her mouth once again she discarded the now empty tube of toothpaste. Squeezing soap onto her toothbrush she used it to scrub the deeply embedded dirt from her nails and made a mental note to add a new toothbrush to her shopping list. Finally satisfied they were clean, she shampooed her hair again, feeling that delightful tingling on her scalp from the vigorous amount of scrubbing. Never again would she underestimate the pleasure of washing, nor would she take for granted the simple act of being able to shave her legs. Pressing her hands against the tiled wall she stuck her head back under the spray and sighed again.

'Olivia?' Theo called through the steam in amusement.

'Uh huh,' she replied absently.

'Are you planning on getting out of the shower sometime today?'

'No,' came her very definite reply.

'You've been in here nearly an hour and a half.'

'And I plan on being in here for at least another two.'

'Louisa's here…with food.'

Olivia stuck her head out of the shower, dripping water on the floor.

'Did you say food?'

'Yes,' he chuckled. 'She also said if you don't get downstairs in the next ten minutes, she's coming up here, whether you're naked or not.'

Olivia laughed as her eyes swept over Theo appreciatively. His dark hair was wet and brushed back from his face and hanging past his collar, so long now it almost brushed the tops of his shoulders. He was freshly washed and shaved and back in his trademark jeans and black Tee shirt. Her mouth curved into a slow smile.

'You know, you could get undressed and get in here with me.'

'You didn't want company,' he smiled, 'you were very specific about that. That's why I had to use the guest bathroom.'

'I've changed my mind,' her gaze trailed slowly down his body.

'Food Olivia,' he laughed, as her stomach growled loudly.

'Fine,' she shut the water off and stepped out to stand in front of him, unapologetically naked.

His eyes darkened and the laughter died on his lips. This time it was his gaze that slowly slid down her body, like the droplets of water still clinging to her wet skin. He skimmed over the graceful curves and dips, the arch of her collar bone, her full breasts, the curve of her hips.

How long had it been since he'd just looked at her, taken his time appreciating her body, appreciating her? Since they'd found each other again in the Otherworld and after that when they'd been in Salem, all they'd had were stolen moments that they'd been able to snatch together. He reached out, tracing his fingers slowly down the line of her throat, down between her breasts to her stomach then drifting lower.

'Theo,' she breathed stepping into him.

His arms wrapped around her, pulling her in close as his mouth closed over hers. Stretching up on her tiptoes she raked her fingers through his damp hair, tugging gently as her tongue danced with his in long indulgent strokes. His hands skimmed down her spine pulling her in closer, his heart pounding with need for her, this woman in his arms who was everything. When the insistent need for air finally drove them apart she pressed her face into the line of his throat and inhaled deeply.

God he smelled good, she thought randomly. After the rather questionable hygiene of the 17th century she now understood why he had always been so obsessed with the scent of her. She could spend all day breathing in the deliciously clean smell of his skin.

His mouth closed over hers again and she was lost, all other thoughts drained from her mind. Her hands fisted desperately in his shirt dragging it up and over his head, pressing them skin to skin.

'Livy,' he breathed against her mouth.

Her fingers scraped down his stomach to the waistband of his jeans. Popping open the buttons one by one and hooking her fingers in she slid them past his hips, taking his boxers with them. His hands slid over her soft skin, cupping the backs of her thighs and lifting her easily.

She could feel him pressing intently between her thighs, hot and hard and ready for her. God she was desperate for him. She could feel it burning through her veins like wildfire, this intense need to feel him inside her, as close as they could possibly get.

'Theo please,' she gasped against his mouth as he slid into her with agonizing slowness.

She closed her eyes and her head fell back against the cold tiles, savoring the delicious friction of each slow and deliberate movement. Everything else faded away and in that one moment of time nothing else existed. It was just the two of them in their own little pocket of reality.

'I love you,' she breathed against his ear.

His grip tightened on her and his movements intensified, all languidness gone. He tilted her hips changing the angle, each thrust deep and intense, robbing her of breath. Her toes began to curl and her eyes rolled back in her head. She could do nothing to stop the groan of pleasure humming deep in her throat. He could sense the change in her body, feel the tension begin to climb as she dug her fingers into the corded muscles of his shoulders.

'Let go Livy,' he whispered against her throat, 'let me watch you come apart for me.'

Her thighs tightened around his hips and he pulled back just far enough to watch her face. Feeling her inner muscles tighten he watched in satisfaction as her eyes locked on his and blurred with intense pleasure. Watching her shatter, he could do nothing as his own body tightened and followed her.

Neither of them moved. They remained where he had her pinned to the cold wall, bodies trembling and breaths coming in deep heavy gasps. There was nothing they needed to say, they just absorbed the simple pleasure of being home together, and for the first time in months they began to relax.

Olivia jolted at the sudden pounding on the other side of the door.

'Don't think I don't know what you two are doing

in there,' Louisa's irritated voice snapped. 'Theo I sent you in there to get her out, not distract her.'

Olivia pressed her face into Theo's neck and laughed tiredly.

'Give me a moment,' she called out as she unwrapped her legs from Theo's waist.

'Fine,' she huffed, 'but you'd better hurry up or I'm going to break down the God damn door.'

This time Theo laughed.

'She's probably serious you know,' Olivia told him as she slid her legs to the floor and shivered.

'I don't doubt it for a moment,' he smiled as he pulled her bathrobe from the back of the door and wrapped her up gently.

She pulled a towel out and wrapped up her hair, watching him as he cleaned up and refastened his jeans, scooping his wrinkled Tee shirt from the floor and pulling it back on.

'Ready to face the wrath of hurricane Louisa?' she grinned.

Theo rolled his eyes. 'I'm feeling really sorry for Tommy right now,' he murmured.

'Don't be,' the voice called from the other side of the door. 'He loves me just the way I am.'

'Seriously, how did she hear that?' Theo asked incredulously.

Olivia smiled and opened the door. She'd barely stepped into the bedroom when there was a sudden blur of color and the impression of blonde hair and she found herself bundled up in a tight embrace. They stood for a moment, neither woman moving, absorbing the bone deep love and friendship that had bound them together since childhood.

'Missed you,' Louisa whispered.

'Missed you too,' Olivia smiled, but as she did something occurred to her. Louisa's body shape didn't feel right. She pulled back and looked down, her eyes widening in surprise at her friend's hugely swollen belly.

'You're pregnant,' Olivia gasped on a delighted laugh.

'Yeah,' she pulled back from her best friend, wiping the tears from under her eyes. 'Tommy went and knocked me up.'

Olivia wrapped her arms around her and gave her a squeeze before pulling back and stroking her belly.

'How far along are you?'

'About six and a half months. Turns out I was pregnant before you left, but I didn't realize it.'

'Oh my God, I'm going to be an auntie?'

'Yes you are,' Louisa nodded smiling, 'now hurry up and get dressed. I'm starving and Tommy has learned the hard way never to get between a pregnant woman and her food.'

'Yes ma'am,' Olivia teased.

'Come on Theo,' Louisa dragged him from the room with her. 'I don't trust you not to distract her again.'

He threw Olivia a sweet smile and followed the very bossy pregnant woman from the room.

Smiling to herself Olivia crossed to her dresser and pulled out a pair of panties and a matching bra. It felt so good to be wearing proper underwear again. She twirled happily and then yanked on a comfortable pair of yoga pants and a tank top. Finally, she picked up her favorite old sweater from the chair in the corner of her room, where she'd left it the last time she was home. Stopping suddenly, she took a long look at her bedroom. She may have changed in the last six months, as apparently had everyone else she mused, thinking of Roni and Jake's relationship and Louisa's pregnancy, but it was comforting to know some things hadn't changed. Her room was exactly as she'd left it. Her eyes suddenly filled with tears.

She was finally home.

'Hey, those are my egg rolls,' Jake complained.

'Not when Louisa gets her hands on them they won't be,' Tommy grinned.

Shaking his head in disgust Jake unpacked more cartons of food and spread them across the coffee table.

'Here,' Roni handed him a beer, 'let Louisa have the egg rolls if she wants them. After all you wouldn't want to deny your future niece or nephew would you?' she asked innocently.

'Welcome to my world,' Tommy took a swig of his own beer. 'You wait until it's your turn.'

Jake rolled his eyes, wisely choosing not to comment.

'Tell me you brought coffee?' Theo walked into the room, closely followed by Louisa.

'Yeah we brought coffee,' Tommy replied holding up a beer, 'but that's for breakfast.'

Theo took the bottle from him with a smile.

'So,' Tommy grinned looking over at Theo, 'I hear you were wearing tights?'

'They weren't tights,' he sighed loudly.

'No, they were woolen stockings, which everyone wore back in the seventeenth century,' Roni supplied helpfully.

'Stockings?' Tommy choked on his swig of beer. 'Dude, that's even worse. Now I just keep picturing the Rocky Horror Picture Show.'

'The what?'

'Trust me sweetheart you don't want to know,' Olivia walked into the room.

'Hey, there she is,' Tommy jumped up and gave her a hug.

'Hey daddy,' she smiled up at him and he blushed in pleasure.

'God, you're so cute,' Olivia laughed.

'Where's the egg rolls?' Louisa panicked, rummaging through the bags.

'Jake…' Roni warned.

'Uh, fine,' he hissed, handing them over from where he'd been hiding them.

Tammy chuckled, looking up from where she sat next to her brother, slowly sipping from a glass of wine as she watched the interaction between them all.

There came another knock at the door. Leaving Louisa and Jake to their arguing Olivia slipped out of the room. She swung the front door open and smiled at Mac, who stood on the other side grinning.

'Well I'll be damned, it is true,' he laughed, wrapping his arms around her.

'Hey Mac,' she squeezed him back, 'come on in.'

She stepped aside as he walked past, shutting the door behind him. Smiling softly, she turned back toward the library, with him following beside her. She would almost have missed what happened next if she hadn't been looking directly at Tammy when they both entered the room. She looked up from where she was smiling beside Theo and as soon as her gaze landed on Mac her expression cooled and her mouth tightened, before she deliberately turned away.

'Is there something I should know about?' she asked quietly, turning back to watch Mac's expression carefully.

'No,' he sighed.

So that was a big fat definite yes, Olivia thought to herself. Still she wasn't going to try and prize it out of either of them tonight as she was starving and extremely tired. The events of the last few days were beginning to catch up with her, not to mention the fact that she hadn't slept in over thirty-six hours. At this rate she'd probably be falling asleep in her noodles.

'Are you hungry Mac?' she asked.

'No I'm alright,' he shook his head. I grabbed something down at the station but...' he scanned the cartons and bags, 'if you have egg rolls...'

Louisa glared at him dangerously.

'Probably best not,' Olivia told him sympathetically.

'Ah,' he nodded diplomatically.

'Here Mac,' Jake tossed him a beer, 'you're off duty now.'

'Yes I am,' he blew out a deep breath as he popped the top and took a deep gulp.

'Well it looks like we have just about everyone.' Olivia took a seat on the floor sitting comfortably between Theo's legs, as Mac pulled up a chair covered in a dust sheet and sat down. 'Did you call my dad, Roni?'

Roni looked up from the carton of rice she was digging into and threw a look at Jake, who looked at Louisa, who then looked to Tommy, as Mac shifted uncomfortably in his seat.

'What's going on?' Olivia asked suspiciously. 'Why are you all looking at each other like that? Where's my dad?'

'We don't know,' Mac told her gently. 'He fell off the grid not long after you two both disappeared. No one has spoken to him in months.'

'What about Davis or Danae?' she frowned in confusion.

'Davis is the same. I don't know if he's with your dad or not but no one has seen or spoken to him in months either.'

'And Danae?'

'Back in Mercy,' Roni told her. 'She left both of her brothers and came back to Mercy when the Soul Collector was on the loose and after it was over she stayed. She's back at work with Mac and Jake.'

'She's on duty tonight,' Mac told her. 'She said she'd stop by and see you tomorrow sometime, but I don't think she knows where her brothers are. They don't seem to be speaking to her either.'

'I bet she's not taking that too well,' Theo answered.

'No,' Roni muttered, 'the last couple of months have been rough on her.'

Olivia nodded, taking the carton of noodles Theo handed her.

'I gotta say,' Jake began as he bit into a pork ball, 'we're all dying to know what happened to you guys. So start at the beginning and don't leave anything out.'

Olivia looked up at Theo and smiled, digging her chopsticks into her noodles and taking a huge mouthful. Knowing that she would rather eat than talk, Theo sipped his beer and went back to the beginning, telling them about the Crossroads then the collapse of part of the Otherworld into the Void. He went back over Hades and the Underworld, recounting everything he'd told his sister earlier. They all listened intently, every now and then asking questions, while Olivia filled in gaps or expanded on something Theo was describing. Finally, he caught up to them arriving back in the library, omitting with a smile in Jake and Roni's direction the position they'd caught them in.

'Wow,' Mac scratched his chin, 'so your mother and Nathaniel…'

'Pretty pissed,' Olivia nodded, discarding her carton and picking up another. 'At each other and in general.'

'So what happens now?'

'I don't know,' she shook her head, sighing as she chewed a piece of pork thoughtfully. 'They're both extremely dangerous, way more than before. My mother is packing some serious juju, her powers are incredibly advanced and as for Nathaniel, well now we have a demon on the loose in his natural form, who is just as powerful as my mother.

Fortunately for us, at the moment they're so pissed with each other they're ignoring us, which gives us a little breathing room. But make no mistake, sooner or later one of two things are going to happen. Either one of them destroys the other or they kiss and make up. Either way, at that point they're going to head in our direction and when that happens we're in serious trouble.'

'Damn,' Jake frowned.

'Yeah,' Olivia nodded, dropping the empty carton and picking up another.

'So they're still after the book?'

'Looks like,' Olivia bit into a chunk of chicken. 'Although they're pretty focused on each other right now, the book is still their goal.'

'And you don't know where it is?'

'No I don't,' Olivia shook her head staring at her kung pao chicken thoughtfully. 'I need a drink.'

'Do you want a glass of wine?' Roni offered.

'No thanks,' she murmured. 'What I really want is a milkshake.'

'A milkshake?' she asked dubiously, 'with Chinese takeout?'

'Yeah, did you guys bring milk?'

'Yes,' Louisa nodded, 'and bread.'

'I just want the milk. I'm sure I have a tub of Nesquik somewhere in the pantry.'

'Well if you're sure that's what you want,' Roni got up. 'I'll go check.'

'Thanks,' she beamed up at her.

Roni slipped out of the room, returning five minutes later with a tall glass.

'You only had chocolate flavor, I hope that's okay?'

'Perfect,' Olivia smiled, taking a long sip and licking the milk mustache from her top lip, before picking up the carton and starting to eat once again.

'That's gross Olivia,' Tommy shuddered, 'and I've seen some of the things Louisa's been eating.'

'Okay whatever,' Jake shook his head. 'Focus on the problem people, not on Olive's poor taste in beverages. So we have time to figure it out then?'

'Yeah, but I don't know how long,' she shook her head frowning, 'or what the hell to do? I mean how do we stop an incredibly powerful witch and a pissed off demon?'

She sighed in frustration and Theo leaned down and squeezed her neck gently. She looked around the room taking in the morose expressions and made a decision.

'You know what we need?' she asked no one in particular, 'we need something happy, something normal. I mean, if our lives are about to turn to shit we should at least have a party first.'

'Something happy and normal?' Tommy repeated. 'You got any ideas?'

'As a matter of fact I do,' Olivia looked up at Theo. 'I don't want to wait,' she told him quietly.

'Neither do I,' he smiled back at her.

'What's going on?' Jake asked curiously.

'Oh,' Louisa's eyes filled with tears as she caught on. Tommy looked over at her in concern.

'Don't worry about me,' she waved her hands, blinking rapidly. 'Hormones.'

'Don't I know it,' Tommy muttered under his breath.

'What was that?' Louisa asked.

'Nothing sweetheart,' he smiled innocently.

'So what's going on?' Jake repeated.

'Olivia and I are getting married,' Theo explained.

'No way!' Jake's face broke into a wide smile, 'really?'

'Yeah, weddings are happy, right?' Olivia grinned. 'We don't want to wait, so I say we have ourselves a wedding.'

'Hell yeah,' Tommy raised his bottle and the room erupted in smiles and congratulations.

'So when do you want to get married? Louisa asked.

'As soon as possible,' Olivia replied. 'We want to get married here, down by the lake and then just have a party afterwards,' she turned to Theo, 'unless you want a church?'

'I'm happy with whatever you want,' he smiled.

'Wise choice man,' Tommy slapped him on the shoulder. 'Best thing to do is let the women have their way and then just show up on the day and say I do.'

'That's pretty much what I plan to do,' he absently toyed with the label on his beer bottle. 'I don't care how we get there, I just want to marry her.'

'Awww.'

Theo looked up to see both Roni and Louisa smiling at him.

'Anyway, Jake,' Theo frowned and turned back to his friend, 'I was hoping you'd stand up with me.'

'You mean be your best man?' he froze with his beer halfway to his mouth.

'Yeah, if that's what you call it,' he mumbled.

'Of course man,' he blinked, clearing his throat.

'Good,' Theo nodded.

'Good,' Jake repeated.

There was a choked little sound and they looked across to see Louisa and Roni tearing up while they watched them. Olivia smiled at Theo as she scooped up her food.

'How much of that have you eaten?' Jake frowned at Olivia. 'You're putting Louisa to shame.'

'I'm hungry,' Olivia shrugged. 'Do you have any idea what it's like in seventeenth century Salem? The food sucks.'

'I can imagine,' Roni replied sagely.

'So the wedding then?' Louisa changed the subject.

'Yeah,' Olivia replied, 'you two are going to be my bridesmaids, right?'

Louisa's eyes filled with tears again.

'Okaay,' Olivia replied slowly, 'waterproof mascara for you on the day.'

'I'm fine, I'm good,' she wiped her eyes, 'and I'd love to.'

'Me too,' Roni nodded.

Olivia turned to Tammy who sat watching her and Theo with an unreadable expression on her face.

'Tammy?' Olivia looked over at Theo.

'We wondered if you would perform the ceremony for us?' Theo asked.

'Really?' she replied, 'you'd like me to be part of the wedding?'

'Of course we do,' Olivia answered as if the answer should be obvious. 'You're family.'

'Yes,' she smiled widely. 'I'd love to.'

'Well then,' Louisa clapped her hands together in a brisk business like manner, 'looks like we've got ourselves a wedding to plan.'

The discussions went on well into the night and Olivia was grateful to her friends. It was what she needed, a little bit of normality. A chance to celebrate what she and Theo felt for each other. Her life had been a circus from the moment she'd landed back in Mercy, filled with murder, magic and impossible expectations. Everyone seemed to feel she had some kind of weird destiny thing going on. And with Gods, and Goddesses and strange white haired strangers poking their noses into her business, the truth was, the pressure was starting to get to her.

Nathaniel was coming for her and this time it was personal. Not only that, she had unfinished business with her mother, who she didn't want to see. She didn't want to admit there was any truth to what she had told her about her grandmother and their relationship, but the fact was, the more she looked back at her memories the more she could see things from her mother's point of view.

She didn't want to feel anything for her mother, especially not sympathy. She was a killer and a dangerous one at that. She was manipulating her, she knew she was, but there was still that small part of her, the eight-year-old child in her, that missed her mom. The mother she had known, the mother she had remembered, but most of all the mother she had loved.

It was all getting too complicated, too hard. All she wanted was a life with Theo, and her friends. A life that didn't include Hell Books and demons and legacies. Unfortunately, she knew she probably wasn't going to get her own way, not this time. Her mother and Nathaniel were coming for her and she didn't have a clue how to stop them. All she knew was that she needed a break and this wedding was their breather, a moment out of time where they got to be normal.

As the evening wore on her eyes grew heavier, her mind became fuzzier and as the low voices of her friends began to lull her into sleep her head began to droop against Theo's knee.

'Okay, party's over,' Theo spoke up. 'Olivia and I need some sleep, so I'm kicking you all out.'

There was a murmured consent and a great deal of shuffling around followed by hugs and goodbyes.

'Why don't you go up to bed,' Theo said to Olivia quietly. 'I'll lock up and be up in a while.'

She nodded as she stifled a yawn.

'Okay, but there's something I need to do first,' she told him softly.

He watched as she crossed the room and picked up the phone. Nodding in understanding he left the room, closing the door behind him to give her some privacy.

She sat down on the couch and dialed the number she had memorized. After a few rings a familiar voice answered.

'I'm not available right now, leave a message.'

Olivia drew in a long shaky breath as she listened to the beeps.

'Hello dad,' she whispered, 'I'm home...'

26.

Olivia rolled over and burrowed deeper in the pillows, face first. As she slipped back down into the dream she'd been roused from, she felt a furry nuzzling and a soft snort. A wet nose pushed against her ear, followed by a long wet flat tongue.

'Ugh, Beau cut it out.' She reached out and shoved his face away gently.

Realizing he'd achieved his goal and woken her he padded up the bed on soft paws and proceeded to flop onto his back and roll over her head. Unable to stop herself she giggled, and shoved him away again. Tail thumping happily along the bed he continued to nuzzle and roll all over her.

'Alright, alright,' she laughed, 'I'm getting up.'

Swinging her legs over the side of the bed she yawned and glanced at the clock. It was late again. She'd been sleeping on and off for the best part of the four days since they'd returned to Mercy. Theo had been up at the crack of dawn again. His body had naturally reset itself to farmers' hours when they'd been in Salem and it was a habit he'd been unable to shake. After that first night of being back in the house, Theo seemed to have caught up on his sleep with no problem whatsoever. She on the other hand was still permanently tired. Of course her body had been through a lot more trauma than his. After jumping them through time, conjuring Witch fire, purging Sam of Demon fire, being tortured by Nathaniel and then healed by her mother, she wasn't at all surprised her body couldn't seem to regain its natural balance.

Pulling in a deep breath as she yawned again, she climbed out of bed and slipped her arms into her robe. Absently tying the belt, she wandered over to the window. The sun was shining, its warm peaceful rays bouncing off the lake, glittering like rhinestones. She opened the window to let the warm breeze in, which carried with it the hazy scent of long summer days and warm nights.

Down on the grass leading to the water a white arch was currently being erected and chairs were stacked everywhere, strewn with big loops of tulle. Further along a temporary square floor was being laid, the framework above it was strung with thousands of tiny twinkling fairy lights, and it was surrounded by circular tables.

Smiling to herself she absently reached down to pet Beau as he rubbed against her legs as if he were a cat.

'Crazy dog,' she muttered lovingly. 'I missed you too.'

Her eyes were drawn back to the bustling activity down by the lake. Even from this distance she could see her very pregnant best friend marching along and giving orders. The woman was nothing if not frighteningly efficient.

She was getting married tomorrow.

She couldn't believe it. Given the childhood she'd had, she'd never given any thought to marriage and family, had never wanted to, seeing how it destroyed her parents. But with Theo it was different, everything was going to be different. She was not going to make the same mistakes as the women in her family who had come before her. This was a completely fresh slate, she was not going to continue to perpetuate the mistakes of her ancestors. There was one very important decision she had come to late last night and it was time to tell Theo.

She wandered silently from the room followed happily by Beau. The dog seemed content to permanently trail along behind her, as if he was worried she was going to disappear again at any moment. Padding down the stairs on bare feet she stuck her head into the kitchen, but he wasn't there. Ever since they'd been back he'd been more or less permanently attached to the coffee machine, he was lucky he hadn't overdosed on caffeine yet. Shaking her head in amusement she quickly made herself a cup of tea and headed out of the kitchen. If he wasn't in there or outside helping, which she didn't think he was because she hadn't seen him, then there was only one other place he could be.

Bingo.

She stood in the doorway to his studio, idly leaning against the door frame and sipping her tea as he painted onto the canvas with broad confident strokes. His stance was relaxed and his focus intent. Not wanting to disturb him she stood and watched while finishing her drink.

Her gaze wandered across the room and there lying open on the table was his mother's journal. He'd obviously been reading it. Curiosity about Emmaline Beckett was gnawing at her like a sore tooth, but she wasn't going to pry. This was something intensely personal for Theo, a way for him to connect with the mother he missed so much, and she didn't want to intrude. She wasn't going to ask, she'd just wait for him to come to her if he wanted to. She just hoped he would tell her about it when he was ready.

Finally Theo stopped and put down his brush, picking up a rag and wiping the oil paint from his fingers.

'Hey,' she spoke softly.

He looked up and smiled at her.

'Hey.'

'I'd have thought you'd be outside helping,' she

stepped further into the room.

'I was, but Louisa is terrifying,' he shook his head. 'I don't know what I did, but she yelled at me and then burst into tears.'

'You don't have much experience with pregnant women do you?' Olivia chuckled.

'None,' he frowned. 'Are they all like this?'

'No,' she smiled, 'the craziness varies.'

'I just thought I'd be better off keeping out of her way and letting her do whatever she wanted.'

'Probably a good idea,' Olivia replied, placing her empty cup down and perching comfortably on the edge of the table. 'Still, I know I said I didn't want to wait to get married, but I can't believe she's managed to pull together a wedding in less than a week. The woman missed her calling in life, she should have been an event planner instead of a doctor.'

'She'd terrify all her clients,' he laughed lightly, 'they'd be too afraid of her. Besides she loves being a doctor.'

'I'm surprised she managed to get time off from the hospital,' Olivia frowned.

'You remember Dr Achari?'

'Sachiv?' she nodded.

'Well he made her take some time off. He was worried about her blood pressure, plus she kept making the residents cry.'

'How do you know?' Olivia asked curiously.

'Tommy.'

'I swear,' she smiled in amusement, 'sometimes you two gossip like little girls.'

'We don't,' he frowned, 'we converse in a very manly fashion.'

'Yeah, yeah,' she shook her head her eyes glittering with mirth. 'Speaking of the wedding,' she became serious again, 'there is something I think we should discuss.'

'Oh?'

'My name,' she told him. 'You know it's a tradition in my family for all the women to keep the West name instead of taking their husband's?'

'I do know that Olivia,' he walked over to her and wrapped his arms around her. 'I knew that when I asked you to marry me and its fine. I don't want you to take my name.'

'Why?' she frowned.

'I don't know,' he sighed. 'I suppose ever since I found out that Matthias wasn't really my father, that I wasn't a Beckett, it just doesn't feel like my name anymore.'

'You want to take the name Wilkins? After James?'

He shook his head slowly.

'I'm not really a Wilkins either because they were never married…. I don't know,' he blew out a frustrated breath. 'I feel like I'm caught in between them, just like my mother was.'

'Theo,' she took his face in her hands gently, 'it doesn't matter who was married to whom, or who your biological father was. What matters is who you are. You're Theodore Beckett and the name Beckett isn't all bad. I know what kind of man Matthias was, but you're forgetting Logan was a Beckett too. Keeping the name is a way to honor your brother, to show that not all the Becketts were heartless bastards. For all his mistakes, in the end Logan was a good man.'

'Yes he was,' Theo murmured.

'Keep the name,' she smiled, 'and make it yours…and mine.'

'What?' he looked at her sharply.

'I don't want to be like the other women in my family,' she told him. 'I want to belong to you, I want to take your name.'

'But your name will die out with you.'

'Then I'll keep both,' she smiled. 'I'll be Mrs Olivia Beckett-West.'

'Beckett-West eh?' he pulled her closer, smiling.

'Yes, what do you think?'

'I love it,' he brushed her lips gently with his own. 'It suits you perfectly.'

'Just as your name suits you,' she traced his jaw absently with her fingertips. 'Let's make a deal, here and now, we're drawing a line on the past. Let's not drag all our families' baggage with us. Our marriage, our life together is a fresh start and from here on in we decide who we're going to be.'

'I think I can agree to that,' he smiled, kissing her thoroughly.

She finally pulled back and smiled.

'What are you painting? Can I see?'

He took her hand and pulled her over to the canvas and as she stopped she drew in a sharp breath and her eyes filled with tears.

'Do you think it's okay?' he frowned hesitantly. 'Do you like it?'

'I love it,' she whispered. 'I think it's perfect.'

A tear spilled down her cheek as she stared into the familiar eyes of James Wilkins. Theo had recreated him perfectly on the canvas, from nothing more than memory, even managing to catch the curve of his mouth when he smiled in amusement, but that was not what had Olivia's heart clenching. He'd painted James with his arms wrapped around Emmaline, who was staring out of the painting happily. They looked so intimate, so in love and so happy.

'It's beautiful Theo,' she wiped away a tear, 'it's them as they should have been, if they'd been given the chance.'

'I know he's gone,' Theo replied painfully. 'I know for us it's only been a week since we last saw him but…'

'In reality it's been nearly three hundred years,' Olivia replied in understanding.

He nodded slowly.

'Do you think they found each other?' he asked

her. 'I mean in the Otherworld, like we did?'

'Yes,' she turned to him and squeezed his hand, 'I do.'

'I hope so,' he turned back to the painting and studied it.

He'd painted them both in regular clothes so that anyone looking at them wouldn't think that they'd been born and had lived in the seventeenth century.

'You know what?' Olivia mused, 'we should have them at the wedding.'

'What?'

'We'll set up a stand in the front row and put the portrait there. That way it'll be like they're kind of there,' she looked over to him. 'What do you think?'

He swallowed slowly and nodded, not quite trusting his voice.

Suddenly there was a pounding at the front door. Dropping a kiss on her lips, he let go of her and headed out to answer the door, with Olivia trailing along behind him, smoothing down her bed hair.

The door swung open to reveal a stocky man with a clipboard and a box at his feet.

'Delivery for Olivia West?'

'Yes,' she stepped forward smiling widely. 'I'm so excited about this. I've been waiting for days.'

'What have you been up to?' Theo's brow rose curiously.

'You'll see,' she replied.

'Sign here please,' he handed her the forms which she scrawled her name across. 'Where would you like the others?'

'Others?' Theo peered around the man to his partner, who seemed to be unloading at least twenty more boxes like the one at his feet.

'We'll take this one,' Olivia told him. 'Just go on through to the back and stack them in the kitchen.'

He handed her a large thick envelope and nodded,

picking up the heavy box at his feet and handing it to Theo.

'No problem,' he replied trotting back down the steps to help unload the boxes.

'Come on,' she told him excitedly as she headed back into the studio.

'What's all this?' he asked.

'A surprise for you,' she watched him set the box on the table.

'For me?'

She nodded enthusiastically. Picking a craft knife out of one of the pots on the table she slit the tape and opened it up. Theo peered inside. There seemed to be about twelve bottles of an amber colored liquid. She lifted one out and handed it to him. He turned it over in his hand to read the label and his heart gave a hard knock.

Wilkins Orchards, Apple and Peach Cider, the bottle read.

'How?' he whispered.

She smiled and opened the thick envelope the delivery guy had given her and pulled out a huge color brochure, handing it to him.

'Tammy told me the other day that she'd looked up the orchard a few years back, out of curiosity. It's still there. Wilkins Orchards is not the biggest, but it's one of the oldest and most respected cider mills on the East coast. It's still operating today, and producing all of James' original recipe for ciders and applejack. It's very famous. People come from all over to visit the orchard and the mill which is open to the public for tours, as are their cider cellars and…' she pointed to the front of the brochure which showed a picture of James' barn.

It was the same barn! It had survived three hundred years, but strangely enough the only thing different about it was that a tree seemed to be growing out of the roof.

'What's that?'

'That,' she smiled, 'is what the locals affectionately refer to as the tree of Temperance. You have to love the delicious irony when you consider that the word Temperance, apart from being your sister's name, means sobriety or abstinence of alcohol. The story goes that God made the tree grow right there in the middle of the barn, cracking through the floorboards and up through the roof, as a reminder to the God-fearing puritans to drink responsibly.'

Theo started laughing. He laughed so hard he doubled over, his eyes watered and he had to clutch his sides.

'What?' Olivia asked in amusement.

'It wasn't an act of God,' he wheezed in a gasping breath smiling. 'It was witchcraft.'

'What?' she chuckled.

'James was demonstrating to Temperance what he could do with his gift. He made an apple seed sprout in his hand. He put it down on one of the barrels intending to plant it out in the orchard, but it must've slipped down between the floorboards and taken root.'

'Oh that's perfect,' Olivia laughed happily. 'You know it's a major tourist attraction? I thought after the wedding we could take a drive out to Danvers and go visit the place, if you'd like.'

'Danvers?'

'They renamed Salem village Danvers after the trials. They were trying to distance themselves from the bloodshed, but they still retained all their magical heritage. In fact, I think there are still some of the original buildings left.'

Theo settled down, staring down at the bottle in his hand.

'I can't believe you did this for me.'

She shrugged, 'it wasn't completely altruistic. I have to admit I became very fond of James' apple and peach cider while we were with him. Although Jackson is taking care of the drinks, I thought it might be nice to have it at the wedding for the guests.'

'Yes it would,' Theo smiled. 'I wonder what happened to him after we left.'

'James?' Olivia replied, 'well after we left he continued on at the Orchard. After a few years his nephew William came to live with him. He was the oldest child of James' sister. His father passed away and his mother remarried and had another two children. He didn't get along with his stepfather and so he went to live with James. It appears they got along very well, he seemed to love the orchard as much as James did. Coming from the city, because he'd been born in Boston, he fell in love with the Orchard the moment he saw it. He and James expanded it and improved it over the years, building it into a profitable business, unrivaled for miles around.

When William married a local girl, they expanded James' house to include them both and their three children. James passed away an old and happy man surrounded by his family. He left the orchard and the cider mill to William and his wife and it eventually passed down their line, but they kept the Wilkins brand and all its traditions.'

'How do you know all this?' he asked.

'Roni,' Olivia shrugged simply. 'The woman is unparalleled when it comes to research. When I first started looking at the Orchard and putting in an order for the cider, she dug up everything she could on James and his family tree. Don't say anything but I think she's putting it all together for you as a wedding present.'

'She really is a sweetheart,' Theo smiled, shaking his head.

'Yes she is,' she agreed, pulling out another bottle. 'What do you say we crack these open and see if they taste like the real thing?'

'I say yes,' he grinned.

They both snapped the tops off, toasting the

picture of James before taking a deep swig.

'God that's good,' Olivia blew out a breath.

'Amazing,' Theo stared down at the bottle, 'it tastes just the same, only better.'

'To James,' she raised her bottle.

'To my father,' Theo tapped his bottle to hers with a soft clink before taking another sip. 'Have you heard anything from your dad yet?' he asked.

'No,' she shook her head with a sigh. 'I left a message on the emergency contact number he gave me but nothing…you know my dad, he'll turn up when he feels like it.'

Theo nodded sympathetically. He wrapped his arm around her shoulders and pulled her in close to his body. They both stood in comfortable silence, sipping their cider and staring at the portrait of Theo's parents.

Charles rolled over, the sheet draping across his naked body as he stared up into the darkness. His arm crooked over his head and his hand tucked under the back of his hair, his face creased into a troubled frown. The sweat clung to his body in the oppressive heat and wet humidity. Every breath was like breathing underwater. He glanced towards the open window, for all the good it did. The air was still, but filled with the sounds of the night; the cacophony of bush crickets and grasshoppers, interspersed every now and then by the loud croak of a bull frog. The air hung heavily with the scent of vegetation and algae covered waters, which lapped against the supports beneath the window.

The constant chatter of Katydids perched in the nearby Cypress trees was shattered by the loud lonely cry of the night heron circling the bayou, high above them. The bed dipped as he felt the warm soft body next to him shift and a long slender arm, with skin the color of honey, wrapped around his waist. Unable to sleep, he slid slowly out from underneath the arm of his companion and sat on the edge of the bed, picking up his phone and turning it on. Still no signal, not a surprise. Out in the swamp it was patchy at best.

Davis had been by the day before with a message, as he'd been keeping an eye on Charles' voicemail.

Olivia was back.

'You know, you gon' have to speak with her sooner or later Cher,' Cora rolled over and propped her head on her hand.

'I know,' he muttered.

'Are you gon' tell her the truth?'

Charles frowned, and stood. Brushing the sheets aside irritably he strolled naked across the cabin and grabbed his pants, yanking them on roughly, leaving the top button undone.

He paced the floor in agitation until he finally stopped in front of the window, looking out into the murky water surrounding them.

'She's not ready to hear the truth,' he finally replied quietly.

'She's not ready?' Cora's brow rose questioningly, 'or you're not ready?'

'Does it matter?' he scowled.

'One is your choice,' she climbed out of the bed wrapping her nude body in the white sheet, 'the other is not. You have no right to make that decision for her, not now, especially not now.'

He turned and looked at her sharply.

'Can you not feel it?' she whispered as she stepped closer to him. 'Something has changed. It vibrates in the very air we breathe. I can taste it on every breath.'

'What has changed?'

'That I cannot say Cher,' she stroked his arm, trailing her long nails down his tanned skin, 'but she is the very center of it.'

'No,' he shook his head in denial.

'You know it is true,' she stroked him gently. 'You

have always known it.'

'I didn't want this for her,' he shook his head slowly.

'She is in great danger,' Cora told him, 'and she doesn't know it. She thinks the worse she has to worry about is her mother and the demon, but that is no longer true. They will come…all of them.'

'Who?'

'The fallen, the unwanted, the damned, every dark creature that hides in the shadows will be drawn to Mercy, to her, like a moth to a flame. The book is awake now and they all hear its call and they know she is the only one who can find it. They are coming for her and there is no stopping them.'

'What should I do?' he looked down at her with dark, grief filled eyes.

'Go home Charles,' her eyes burned into his. 'It is time.'

27.

Olivia sat perched on the edge of her bathtub nibbling her fingernails nervously. She knew she shouldn't, somewhere in the back of her mind she could hear Louisa's voice telling her not to ruin her French manicure before the ceremony.

Her hair was soft and shiny, curling at the ends and caught at the temples with delicate pearl and crystal combs, which swept it back from her face. Her make-up was done and tiny little pearl studs sat at her earlobes in place of her usual small hoops. Her dress hung in her bedroom. She'd decided, after much internal debate, to wear her grandmother's dress. It was simply stunning. The 1950's style slashed neckline and long sleeves were a delicate cream colored lace, the dress nipped in tightly at the waist and flared into a full skirt of tulle, partly overlaid with more lace and falling to mid-calf. A tiny row of satin covered buttons ran the length of her spine, matching her satin covered stilettos.

She'd found it in the attic and Roni, bless her heart, knew someone who restored vintage clothing. They'd been able to repair the minor tears in the fabric and have it cleaned and adjusted, with just a day to spare. She'd felt amazing when she'd tried it on and she couldn't wait to see Theo's face when she walked down the aisle but…

Her heart banged anxiously in her chest and she nibbled even more ferociously at her nail. She knew it was perfectly normal for all brides to be nervous on their wedding day, the trouble was she wasn't nervous about being married to Theo…her eyes fell on the small white test sitting on the edge of the sink. Her eyes flicked back to her phone, where she'd set the timer and watched it count down the last 60 seconds.

She'd finally found her phone and charged it. She'd been surprised it still worked, she'd had it with her the night they went to the lake. It had not only survived a dunking in the icy water, but also a trip to the Otherworld, a trip to the Underworld, being thrown back in time…twice, and being hidden under a floorboard in a 17th century farmhouse for a decade and still, when she charged it, it had lit up and switched on just like 'the little engine that could'. She'd leave it a hell of a product review but really what was she going to write?

'Excellent model, long battery life, quality sound, good features, affordable…oh and will survive a plunge into an icy lake and a trip to the Underworld…'

Yeah, probably best just be grateful the damn thing still worked. Unfortunately for her, her problems had started the moment she switched it on. She had a dozen updates, hundreds of messages and several reminders on her calendar, one of which being a reminder to go get her contraceptive shot.

Shit…

Yes, she'd counted back and given the amount of time she'd spent in both the Otherworld and the Underworld, where time didn't pass the same as the real world, then adding in the time she'd spent in Salem, she should've had a period by now, shouldn't she? Then things really began to click into place. The tiredness and the sickness; so it turns out the sheep was off the hook, as it probably wasn't the mutton that had made her sick. She glanced across at her phone again.

18...17...16...

What the hell was she doing? There was very little chance she was actually pregnant, she was just being paranoid. Really, it was probably just all the stress that had thrown her body out of whack. How often had she and Theo even made love since they left Mercy?

Shit...

Okay, well probably best not to panic. So they'd made love a few times, okay so several in fact. It was funny because she didn't think that they'd managed to spend all that much time together, but when she actually counted...

She held her breath as her phone started beeping. Turning it off she picked up the test and looked down.

Two blue lines...

What the hell did that even mean? She grabbed the instructions and read down quickly before looking back at the test. Definitely two blue lines.

Shit...

She swallowed nervously and looked down again at the test in her trembling hand. Louisa was now, officially, not going to be the only hormonal basket case in town.

She was pregnant.

She let that sink in for a moment. She was pregnant with Theo's baby, she was going to be a Mom. The corners of her mouth began to twitch and she let out an unexpected laugh as she covered her mouth with her hand. She stood up and let her hands drop to her belly where her child grew. Their child she smiled, as she felt an intense wave of love for the child they had created. Her eyes filled with unexpected tears and she had to blink them back rapidly, knowing Louisa would kill her if she ruined her make-up.

Blowing out a quick calming breath she unhooked her robe from the back of the door and slid it on over her underwear, tying the belt as she walked out of the bathroom. She padded down the stairs amidst the bustle and chaos. People were everywhere carrying drinks, food, centerpieces and all sorts of things. She headed for Theo's studio knowing he wouldn't like the crowds and hoping to find him there alone.

She wasn't disappointed. He sat in the ratty old chair by the window, in his shirt and pants. The collar was open at the throat and his sleeves rolled up to his elbows. His bow tie hung over the back of the chair with his tux jacket. He had a sketch book open in his lap, while he scribbled away with a stubby half chewed pencil.

'Hey,' she walked in quietly.

'Hey,' his face broke into a wide smile as he held up the sketchbook. 'Louisa wouldn't let me paint.'

Olivia laughed.

'You know you shouldn't be down here,' he put the book down and rose from the chair, wandering over to her. 'I got a two-hour lecture on how it's bad luck for the groom to see the bride before the wedding.'

'But you saw me at breakfast,' she smiled.

'That's what I said, but she gave me that look.'

'Oh I know the look.'

'I decided at that point to shut up.'

'Very wise,' she snickered, 'Louisa can be terrifying and efficient all at the same time. In fact, if I ever decide to invade a small country I'm having her as my general.'

'You know if she finds you down here she'll murder us both.'

Olivia smiled, fidgeting nervously.

'What's wrong Livy love?' he frowned.

'I have something to tell you,' she breathed, 'before we get married.'

'Okay.'

'I...it's something good, something happy. Well I think it is, but I don't know what you'll think because it wasn't expected and we've never discussed it.'

'Livy,' he smiled slowly, interrupting her nervous babbling, 'why don't you just tell me what it is?'

'I'm pregnant,' she replied.

'What?' he whispered as his eyes widened.

'I'm pregnant,' she twisted her hands uneasily. 'I know we haven't discussed having children, I mean I don't know if you even want kids, but I...'

She was silenced when his mouth crushed down on hers and his arms wrapped around her tightly.

She pulled back after a moment and looked into his dark eyes.

'So, does that mean you're okay with this?' she asked hesitantly.

'Livy,' he smiled as he pressed his forehead to hers, 'we're going to have a child?'

She nodded, 'you're going to be a father.'

He sank down to his knees wrapping his arms around her waist and pressing his face into her belly.

'Our baby,' he murmured, kissing her stomach lovingly.

Her eyes filled with tears again as she ran her hands through his dark locks of hair.

'Ahem.'

They both turned their heads and looked across to the doorway to find Louisa, Roni and Tommy standing there.

'You're pregnant?' Roni smiled.

Olivia nodded.

'Alright,' Tommy grinned. 'Dude, high five!'

Louisa shot him a look.

'Obviously not a high five moment,' he corrected himself.

'Hey what's going on?' Jake walked past, carrying what looked to be a box of Wilkins Orchards cider. 'Why is Theo on his knees? I thought he'd already done that part.'

'He's not proposing,' Roni smiled.

'He knocked Olivia up,' Tommy told him.

'Jeez another one?' he looked at Roni in alarm.

'Don't worry, it's not catching,' Roni smiled in amusement.

'You say that now,' Louisa murmured.

'What?' Jake's gaze snapped to his sister.

'Nothing,' she replied brightly. 'Well I think congratulations are in order.'

They all filtered into the room exchanging hugs, while Theo stood with a beaming smile on his face.

'I'm so happy for you,' Louisa whispered as she hugged Olivia tightly.

'I know,' Olivia smiled happily, 'we can terrorize them all together with our scary hormones.'

'It'll be so much fun,' Louisa laughed, 'and you know what?'

'What?'

'I'm so happy our kids will grow up together.'

'Me too,' Olivia nodded.

'Do you know how far gone you are?' Louisa asked.

'No,' she shook her head. 'I've only just done the test, but I don't know how long it's been since my last period.'

'Not to worry,' she replied easily, 'after the wedding I'll get you booked in with my OB and we'll get her to give you an ultrasound, to see how far along you are.'

'God,' Olivia blew out a breath as her eyes teared up again. 'I'm a mess.'

'You'll get used to it,' Louisa smiled. 'I cried for an hour yesterday, at a toothpaste commercial.'

'She's not kidding either,' Tommy replied, 'an hour and forty-two minutes to be exact.'

'Come on,' Louisa rolled her eyes at her husband and took Olivia's hand. 'Roni you too, let's go get dressed.'

'Yeah you go,' Jake grinned, 'we're going to get Theo a drink and celebrate,' he slapped him on the back.

'Don't get him drunk,' Olivia called out as she was

towed from the room.

'Does she think I'm a moron?' Jake frowned, 'now where's that bottle of Johnnie Walker Blue.'

Olivia twirled in front of the mirror, the full skirt spinning out in a mass of tulle and lace.

'You look beautiful Olivia,' Roni dabbed her eyes with a tissue.

'So do you,' she smiled taking in Roni's pale blue chiffon dress.

She looked over to Louisa who was also dressed in pale blue.

'Louisa...'

'Don't say it,' she frowned, 'I look like a whale.'

'No you don't,' Olivia smiled.

'What are you doing with that monstrosity around your neck?'

She looked at the compass which was laying on top of her lace bodice.

'I can't really take it off,' she murmured, picking it up. 'It's kind of a big deal, I can't just go leaving it lying around.'

'But it ruins the whole look,' Louisa complained.

'She's right you know,' Roni agreed.

'Maybe I can do something about it,' she mused thoughtfully, turning it over in her hands.

She could feel it pulse and throb against her skin. It had been like that ever since she'd unlocked it and created the portal. It was almost as if it was specifically attuned to her now. The metal felt warm beneath her touch. She held it out in her palm and watched as it began to melt. The hot liquid swirled in her palm much as it had the day she had stood outside the Beckett farmhouse, only this time it was a lot smaller, more muted. She built a picture in her mind and allowed the flowing metal to take shape. When it finally solidified in her palm she looked down.

No longer a clunky, slightly tarnished compass, it was now a delicate golden locket with intricate filigree and swirling designs on its face, which resembled star charts. She pressed the tiny little button at its side and watched it flip open. Inside where there would normally have been a lock of hair or a photograph, there were tiny little cogs and dials which whirred and ticked like a little mechanical clock.

'There,' she closed the face with a little click and let the small oval locket rest against her breastbone. 'Is that better?'

Louisa and Roni both stared at her.

'Okay,' she replied slowly, giving them a moment, after all they hadn't even witnessed a fraction of what she was actually capable of.

There was a sudden knock at the door and Louisa went to answer it. She exchanged a few muffled words with what sounded like Tommy and then turned back to Olivia.

'Um,' she chewed her lip nervously, 'I have a little confession to make.'

'Alright,' Olivia replied warily.

'I may have invited someone to the wedding,' she grimaced slightly. 'Please don't be mad at me, but she's important to you and no matter how mad you are at her, I think you'll regret it if you don't have her here.'

'Okay?' she repeated in confusion.

Louisa opened the door and an older woman stepped through, immaculate in a peach colored dress and matching jacket. Her hair was perfectly styled and small tasteful diamonds sat at her earlobes, she also wore a matching bracelet.

'Mags?' Olivia whispered.

'Hello Olivia,' she smiled nervously.

'Why don't we give you both a moment?' Louisa motioned for Roni to join her and they both stepped out into the hallway and clicked the door softly shut behind them.

It felt like a lifetime ago since she'd seen the woman who had been a mother to her. The last time they'd seen each other was during the murders, when she'd learned the truth.

Margaret Hale had been a lot of things to her, friend, confidant, mentor, literary agent and most of all family. When she'd had no one, when she'd moved from town to town unable to settle, unable to reconcile her past, it had been Mags who'd been there for her, who'd filled all the hollow parts of her life. It was only when she'd returned to Mercy that she'd learned who Mags really was. She'd always believed they'd met by chance but that couldn't have been further from the truth.

Mags had been intimately involved with her great aunt Evie, they'd been in love for years and when Evie couldn't look after Olivia herself she'd sent Mags to do it for her. Only Mags had never told her the truth. When she found out she'd felt betrayed, fooled, lied to. At the time she'd been under so much stress after being accused of murder, she'd lashed out and said some pretty awful things to the one woman who'd always stuck by her.

They stared at each other in silence for a moment, neither knowing what to say until Mags finally spoke.

'I hope you don't mind me coming?' Mags asked her quietly. 'If you don't want me here I'll leave.'

'No,' Olivia shook her head, 'I'm glad you're here Mags. In fact I owe you an apology.'

'No Olivia,' she began.

'I do,' she cut off her denial with a wave of her hand. 'I'm sorry, I should never have said all those horrible things to you. I was upset, but that's no excuse. You've always been there for me, been such a big part of my life and I've missed you.'

'I've missed you too,' she replied softly, 'but I also owe you an apology. I never should have lied to you for so long. I knew it was the wrong thing to do, but Evie was so adamant and she was so bull headed when she had her heart set on something. But I should have stood up to her.'

'No, its fine,' Olivia shook her head. 'Aunt Evie and I have settled our differences now.'

'You've seen her?' Mags' eyes filled with tears.

'When we have more time I will tell you the whole story. It's very long and very complicated, but she asked me to tell you something,' Olivia stepped closer.

'What?'

'She loves you,' Olivia told her softly, 'and she's waiting for you.'

A tear spilled over followed by another as Mags dragged in a deep breath.

'Her death must have been so hard for you, not being able to tell me the truth, not being able to grieve her openly.'

'She was my whole world for more than forty years,' she breathed heavily, 'my only family.'

'Not your only family,' Olivia whispered. 'You still have me.'

'Do I?'

Olivia nodded and wrapped her arms around the older woman. Mags pulled her in tight and held her, the girl she had watched grow into a woman.

'Besides,' Olivia sniffed pulling back, 'I'm going to need someone to step in and play Grandma.'

'You're pregnant?' she whispered, smiling as her eyes shone with tears.

Olivia nodded.

There was a sudden knock at the door and Louisa stuck her head around.

'I'm sorry to interrupt, but it's time.'

'Well okay,' she blew out a breath. 'How do I look?'

'You look beautiful,' Mags smiled.

'Why don't I take you down and find a seat for you?' Roni asked Mags as she stepped into the room.

Mags nodded, throwing Olivia one last smile before following Roni out the door.

'Ready?' Louisa asked, handing her a small bouquet of pastel colored roses.

'Yes I am,' she smiled, 'let's go have us a wedding.'

Louisa hooked her arm through Olivia's and the two best friends walked from the room arm in arm. As she descended the stairs she caught sight of a familiar face and a mop of white hair. By the time she hit the last step she bypassed Davis and her gaze landed on another even more familiar figure, strikingly groomed and wearing an impeccably cut suit.

'Dad,' Olivia smiled as she crossed the distance and wrapped her arms around him.

'Jelly bean,' he crushed her to him and lifted her up so her toes were barely grazing the ground, sighing as he swayed her slightly.

'Where have you been?' she frowned, pulling back as he set her back on her feet. 'I've left you messages.'

'Sorry sweetheart,' he apologized. 'I didn't have a signal.'

'For six days straight?'

'Yes.'

'Where the hell were you? The jungle?'

'That's not far off actually,' he replied candidly.

'Dad, where have you been?' her eyes narrowed suspiciously.

'I'll fill you in later,' he brushed the question off, 'just let me look at you.' He held her hand and stepped back to get a better look. 'You're stunning.'

'Dad,' she flushed in embarrassed pleasure.

'Well,' he shrugged, 'you didn't think I was going to let anyone else walk you down the aisle did you?'

'Um dad?' she frowned, 'not that I wouldn't love you to give me away, but I have half the town out in my back yard and you're still technically a wanted criminal. Not to mention the fact that I think Mac still wants to shoot you.'

Charles smiled slowly.

'Trust me,' he held his hands up to his face then ran them over his hair and down past his ears. As his hands passed over his skin his features changed, until the man standing before her bore a small resemblance to her father, but no one would be able to pick him out of a line up.

'A glamour?' she raised a slender brow.

'This way no one will recognize me and I still get to walk you down the aisle.'

'Sure,' she replied sardonically, 'and no one's going to question the fact that I'm walking down the aisle with a complete stranger?'

'There's still enough of a resemblance for me to pass as family,' he chuckled. 'Just tell them I'm a distant uncle or something.'

'Fine,' she rolled her eyes smiling, 'you can walk me down the aisle.'

'Good, then that's settled,' he grasped her arm and wrapped it over his, patting her hand gently.

Louisa stepped closer and settled Olivia's skirt.

'Hello Mr Connell,' she smiled.

'Hello Louisa,' he smiled back, his eyes sweeping over her protruding belly in amusement. 'You're looking radiant.'

'I look like a balloon and I still have two and a half months to go,' she replied testily, 'and you can stop smirking Grandpa, the radiance is catching.'

His eyes widened as he looked sharply at Olivia.

'You're pregnant?'

'Surprise!' she shrugged as she gave him a small smile.

'That's...great,' he replied, 'that's really great.'

'Jeez don't strain yourself there Mr Connell,' Louisa murmured.

For a moment Olivia could have sworn she saw a

worried look pass over his face before it was replaced by a smile.

'Are you happy?' he asked Olivia.

'Yes I am,' she replied.

'Then I am too,' he nodded. 'So I'm really going to be a Grandpa then?'

'Yes you are,' she grinned, 'unless you want to be Pops?'

'Pops?' he smiled standing taller, 'I like that.'

She laughed softly.

'You ready?' he asked.

'Yes I am.'

'Then let's go get that boy to make an honest woman of you,' he led her towards the door.

'Right,' her silvery laughter echoed throughout the room, 'that'll happen.'

The ceremony was beautiful. She walked down the aisle strewn with petals, to join Theo who stood with Jake at his side. His eyes widened when he saw her, then settled into a frown when he saw the stranger standing next to her. Smiling she nodded toward Davis who was taking a seat at the back. Figuring out who it was next to her she saw Theo visibly relax.

By the time she reached the alter she saw Temperance standing on the small raised dais, dressed in a gorgeous deep blue dress, which hugged her body and swirled around her knees in a fluid shimmering material, that looked as soft as a cloud. Roni and Louisa moved to stand the other side of her and the sun smiled down on them, highlighting the lake which lapped and glittered behind them.

Later she wouldn't remember any of the words, only the way Theo looked at her. She wouldn't remember the guests, only the kaleidoscope of butterflies that suddenly appeared, dancing around their heads as they made their promises to each other. And as he slid the ring onto her finger she would forever remember the smooth metal against her skin and his soft lips against her own, as Temperance pronounced them man and wife to thunderous applause.

The bright sunny afternoon gave way to the soft balmy evening. The canopy of lights twinkled like starlight above the dance floor as she made the rounds to speak with all their guests, her husband firmly planted at her side. The music played softly on the night air as they took the floor for their first dance as husband and wife. Every eye turned and watched them both, mesmerized as they twirled and swayed to the music, lost in each other.

They stayed on the floor through another two dances, content to just hold onto each other. Olivia's eyes roamed the gathering. Louisa was sitting with her shoes discarded next to her chair and her swollen feet propped up in her husband's lap, as Tommy was laughing at something Sachiv had said.

Her eyes scanned the floor again and she found Jackson happily bouncing a seven-month old Miller in his lap, watching Shelley, his friend and part time bar manager talking to a man Olivia didn't recognize, but judging by the way he leaned in and kissed her and the way Jackson's expression darkened, she assumed it was Shelley's fiancé.

Mrs Bailey was sitting grilling her father extensively over a cup of fruit punch, probably trying to ascertain who he was exactly. Bless her heart, once a busybody always a busybody. Roni and Tammy were sitting chatting with Harriet and John Gilbert, Jake and Louisa's parents, and as she'd discovered earlier in the evening Harriet knew Tammy extremely well, as she had been the nurse on duty the night Sam had turned up in 1983 with her dying of pneumonia.

Her young and beautiful aunt Danae was on the dance floor pointedly ignoring her brother Davis, who was frowning as he watched her dancing and laughing with Mac.

Suddenly her gaze fell on a heart-stoppingly familiar person. He was leaning casually against the makeshift bar, his dimples deepening as he smiled and raised his glass to her.

'Theo,' she murmured nodding in his direction, 'look.'

Theo's eyes fell on Sam and he turned back to Olivia.

'Give me a moment?'

'Sure,' she smiled as he dropped a kiss on her upturned lips.

Letting her go, he crossed the dance floor and stopped next to Sam, accepting the drink he offered. This was the Sam he remembered, the older Sam who'd pulled him from the burning barn, not the younger one who'd almost died after being poisoned by Demon fire.

'Sam,' he took a sip of his champagne.

'Theo,' he smiled, 'congratulations.'

'Thank you,' he nodded, 'and thank you,' he added pointedly.

'For?'

'My sister.'

'Ahh…well,' he replied, 'she and I have grown extremely fond of each other.'

'What you did for her,' he shook his head. 'You didn't just save her, you took care of her when I couldn't.'

'Would you believe me if I told you it was my pleasure?'

Theo stared at him.

'Your sister has an exceptional mind and an extremely wicked sense of humor. She has been one of the highlights in my life,' he sipped his own drink. 'You should try to take some time and get to know the woman she has become.'

'I intend to,' he nodded, as his eyes fell on Olivia and he smiled.

She was holding Miller, bouncing him in her arms

as she chatted with Jackson. She threw her head back and laughed as Miller reached out with pudgy little fists and grabbed her face, leaning in and banging a sloppy kiss to her mouth. Theo felt his face melting into a smile as he watched her with Jackson's son. Soon that would be their baby she was holding and kissing.

'She looks happy,' Sam looked in Olivia's direction.

'She is,' he turned back to Sam. 'I can't seem to thank you enough times. If you hadn't brought me here I wouldn't have all this. I owe you more than I can ever repay. I wish there was something I could do for you.'

'Oh trust me,' Sam sighed heavily as he stared into his empty glass, 'be careful what you wish for Theo.'

'What's that supposed to mean?' he frowned.

'You're going to get the chance to repay the favor and sooner than you think.'

'What?'

'Just treasure moments like this Theo,' he told him quietly, 'it'll keep you going through the hard times ahead.'

'What do you mean?' he turned to Sam, but found himself talking to thin air.

Olivia smiled as she juggled the wriggling baby in her arms.

'Oomph, he's a strong one isn't he?' she laughed as Jackson reached out and took him back into his arms.

'Aye that he is,' he tossed the baby up and then caught him as Miller squealed in delight. 'A champion wrestler I'll bet.'

She stroked his silky blonde hair sweetly.

'I'd have thought he'd have red hair like his mother,' she murmured, while wondering what her own child was going to look like.

'Aye he did for a while, but it lightened to a blonde,' he grinned. 'A heart breaker this one is already, the ladies love him.'

'I'll bet,' she laughed.

'Excuse me?' A cool authoritative voice spoke, drawing their attention.

Olivia turned, her eyes widening in surprise as her gaze fell on the inky blue black hair, pale skin and the impeccably attired tux of the man standing before her. His eyes glittered as he held out a hand adorned with an elegant signet ring embedded with a deep blue stone.

'May I steal the bride away for a moment,' he asked.

'Of course,' Jackson smiled stepping back.

Olivia allowed herself to be lead back out onto the dance floor and twirled around, before settling into his arms.

'Hello Hades,' Olivia greeted him casually, eying his perfectly tailored tux. 'Nice outfit.'

'Is this not customary attire for a mortal bonding ceremony?' he frowned.

'For the bridal party yes, not usually for the guests unless it's a black tie event,' she chuckled. 'We're not quite that formal.'

'Oh,' Hades replied blandly, 'Aeacus will be displeased.'

'Aeacus?' Olivia repeated thinking back to the most ill-tempered of all three of the Judges of the Underworld. 'Why would he be bothered?'

She followed his eye line and gasped in surprise. Across the room sitting at a table arguing with Mrs Bailey was Aeacus. Minos, one of the other Judges sat next to him uncomfortably adjusting his collar and tugging at the bow tie he had obviously never worn before in his entire existence. Her gaze tracked over further and she saw Rhadamanthus the third and final Judge, who seemed quite comfortable sitting back in one of the tulle draped chairs as he lifted a glass of champagne in her direction, smiling at her before taking a sip.

'Hades?' she asked quietly, 'why are the Judges of

the Underworld at my wedding?'

'They all wanted to come and visit you,' he shrugged, 'and I didn't have the heart to say no. After all they haven't been topside in several thousand years.'

'Um what do you mean... all?' she frowned.

Her gaze swept the dance floor and the surrounding tables and she surprised herself by laughing out loud. Eris was sitting next to Jackson, wearing a violent red dress that matched her lips, a dynamic contrast to her pale blonde hair. She sipped from her cup slowly and every time she smiled at Jackson he looked slightly dazed.

Eris looked up at Olivia and toasted her with her cup.

'NO APPLES!' she mouthed firmly at Eris, who simply shrugged and turned her attention back to Jackson.

Hecate sat in a corner by herself wearing a slinky black dress and sipping dark red wine from an elegant glass, her expression polite, but tinged with sadness.

'Is Hecate okay?' Olivia asked in concern.

'She still feels the loss of the Crossroads deeply,' he sighed. 'I fear it is a pain she will always carry now.'

'What is she drinking?' Olivia frowned.

'Dionysus sends his best wishes and his best wine,' Hades told her. 'He's over there by the mechanical musician.'

She turned to look at the tall, good looking man propped up against the vintage jukebox Louisa had hired for them.

'Ah, who's that next to him?'

'That? Oh that's just Hephaestus, you'd get on well with him actually. He likes fire too.'

'Likes fire?' her eyes widened, 'Hades he's the God of fire.'

'Yes' Hades nodded, 'I do believe he is.'

Shaking her head, she glanced across at three small identical women who were scavenging for food at the buffet table.

'Hades' Olivia sighed, 'please tell me you didn't bring the furies to my wedding?'

'What?' he shrugged innocently. 'They'll be on their best behavior you have my word.'

'Hades,' she replied dryly, 'they're eating the centerpieces.'

'Better that than the guests,' he pointed out.

'What?'

But Hades wasn't listening. His attention was fixed over her shoulder on the shore of the lake. Olivia turned to look and saw a dark haired woman dressed in a long green gown. Her long dark hair was loose instead of in her customary braid and a coronet of holly sat on her head. Beside her stood a tall pure white stag with silver antlers. Olivia watched curiously as Hades inclined his head respectfully. Diana returned the gesture and with a small smile for Olivia both she and the God Herne disappeared.

'Hades,' Olivia spoke softly, as they continued to sway to the music, 'why did you crash my wedding?'

'You know Olivia I am inordinately fond of you.'

'Thanks,' she replied dryly.

'The truth is Olivia,' he sighed, 'I came to warn you.'

'Is that concern I hear Hades?' she smiled in amusement.

'Olivia,' he frowned, 'I am concerned for you. Your mother and Nathaniel now believe that you have the location of the book.'

'I don't.'

'But they think you do,' he answered, 'they believe Hester told you and they are not the only ones. You are a target now Olivia. Isabel and Nathaniel are not the only ones coming for you or the book.'

'I know,' she sighed.

'You know?' he replied slowly.

'I've known for some time,' she whispered.

'It seems I never give you enough credit Olivia,'

he mused as he gazed down at her. 'Are you ready for them?'

'No,' she shook her head, 'but I guess I'll have to be.'

Her gaze swept over to Theo, who was laughing with Tommy.

'He doesn't know yet,' Olivia told him quietly. 'I didn't want to worry him.'

'You need to tell him Olivia,' Hades told her seriously. 'He will not be happy that his woman or his child are in danger. He deserves to know the truth.'

'I know,' she nodded and with a deep sigh she laid her head on Hades' chest.

His eyes widened momentarily in surprise before he relaxed and laid his head affectionately against hers, while they swayed to the music.

'Hey Theo,' Jake wandered over to him, 'who's that guy dancing with Olivia?'

Theo's eyes drifted over to his wife on the dance floor.

'Hades,' he shrugged.

'What?' Jake scoffed.

'Yeah,' he replied.

'THE Hades?' his eyes widened in shock.

'Why does everyone keep saying that?' Theo murmured. 'Yes, THE Hades.'

'Seriously? The God of the Underworld?'

'Didn't I just say so?'

'What does he want?' he asked worriedly.

'I don't know,' Theo replied easily.

'Shouldn't you go and find out?'

'They'll let me know if they want me,' he shrugged.

Jake stared at him with huge eyes.

'Come on,' Theo laughed, slinging his arm around Jake's neck. 'Let's go get you a drink. Don't worry, the shock will wear off after a while.'

The moon rose bright and full of light, shining high above. Deep in the dappled shade of the woods dozens of pairs of curious eyes watched the celebration from afar. All of them looked eerily similar, with pale white blonde hair and dressed in dark expertly tailored suits.

'You are sure she is the one Rhys?' one of them asked.

'Yes,' he replied. 'She was able to use the Time'dhal without instruction or help.'

'It responded to her?'

Rhys nodded, 'she is the one.'

'Then it has begun.'

'It has,' he answered carefully, 'the book is awake now. It's calling out and there are many that will heed that call.'

'It cannot fall into the wrong hands,' the first man spoke quietly.

'It is beyond us now,' Rhys replied. 'We are witnesses only.'

'I cannot believe the fate of everything rests in the hands of a human.'

'She is an exceptional human.'

'Maybe,' he mused, 'we'll just see.'

'See?'

'See if she is up to the task.'

And slowly one by one each of them disappeared into the darkness.

Keep Reading…

The Guardians Series 1
Book 5

Infernum

Infernum, the Hell book. There have been whispers of it down through the centuries. The most powerful book to have ever existed, so powerful wars have been fought over it, families torn apart and betrayed for it, souls have been lost to it and countless rivers of blood have been spilled for it. It is said whoever possesses it will have limitless power. The humans want it, so do the demons and every supernatural creature in between.

When Olivia finally returns to her hometown of Mercy with her husband Theo the relief is short lived. Her mother and the demon Nathaniel have also returned and they are under the disturbing impression she knows where the Hell book is, and they're not the only ones.

With supernatural creatures pouring into Mercy at an alarming rate, in a desperate attempt to gain possession of the lost book they head straight for Olivia. With Theo and her friends trying desperately to protect her, she knows she has run out of time.

Infernum is awake now, she can hear it whispering to her. It wants to be found and when an old friend she thought was long dead arrives in town Olivia realizes, in order to stop her mother and Nathaniel before they can use her to get their hands on the book, she must summon the most ancient and dangerous fire of all, demon fire.

If she doesn't they will fail, hell will be unleashed on earth and Mercy will be the gateway. But with everything hanging in the balance can she really risk her life and the life of her unborn child, or this time is the price just too damn high?

1.

Olivia climbed out of her car and smiled. God, she'd missed Dolly. She looked down at her trusty little banged up old Camaro and she could've sworn it was smiling at her. Okay, well maybe not, but after spending an uncomfortable amount of time on the back of a horse or in a rickety wooden cart, she was sure as hell glad to be back in her car again. She watched from the sidewalk as Theo unfolded himself from the driver's side and walked around to join her.

'I still don't like your car,' he frowned.

'Shush, she'll hear you,' Olivia replied.

Theo had never got on well with her cramped car. Not only was he a tall guy, but he'd been spoiled by learning to drive in Jake's brand spanking new, shiny black truck. He'd only driven into town instead of Olivia, as she'd insisted he needed the practice. After all, it had been a while since he'd been behind the wheel of a car.

'Maybe we should get something new.'

'We'll probably have to when the baby comes' Olivia sighed, looking forlornly at her beloved Dolly. 'I'm not getting rid of her though. We'll have to build a garage or something to store her in.'

'Whatever you want love,' he leaned down and kissed her lips softly.

'You're just trying to soften me up because you want a shiny new truck like Jake's,' her eyes narrowed suspiciously.

'No,' he grinned taking her hand, their matching wedding bands glinting in the bright sunlight as he slipped his sunglasses on, 'but they are very reliable and roomy.'

'Roomy?' her brow rose questioningly. 'Since when do you use the word roomy?'

He shrugged, smiling as they began to walk down the street.

'You've already been looking at trucks with Jake haven't you?' she shook her head. 'I'm going to kill him.'

'No you're not,' Theo laughed and wrapped his arm around her shoulders, 'you love him too much. Besides he does have a point. We need something more practical than Dolly. If you don't want a truck, we'll look at something else.'

'Hmm,' Olivia huffed, slightly mollified.

'What time's your appointment?' he asked.

'Four thirty,' she replied as his face lit up.

'Yes, we've got time to go to the coffee shop first,' she rolled her eyes in amusement. 'Honestly I don't know how you managed without coffee while we were away.'

'I had a lot of headaches,' he admitted.

'I'll bet.'

'Morning Olivia, Theo!' Shelley called from across the road. 'Hell of a wedding!'

'Thanks,' she called back as they waved and continued on down the street.

'So we're seeing a...'

'OB/GYN,' Olivia filled in for him.

'And he...she?'

'She.'

'She,' Theo continued, 'can tell us how many weeks pregnant you are?'

'Yes,' Olivia nodded, 'seeing as I haven't got a clue.'

'Because you don't know when your last period was?' he frowned.

'Yes, but also you have to remember when we were in the Otherworld time ran differently, which has confused everything.'

'I see,' Theo nodded thoughtfully.

'Morning Theo! Olivia!' Fiona yelled at them from outside the grocery store. 'Brilliant wedding!'

'Thanks Fiona!' Olivia waved.

'Stop by for a spot of tea when you have a moment!'

'Will do,' she nodded as they carried on down the street.

'It really is incredible though,' Theo said excitedly, 'that we will actually be able to see our baby inside your womb and hear its heartbeat.'

Ever since he'd found out she was pregnant he'd been pouring over books on pregnancy and childbirth, trying to learn every detail of what was going to happen to both Olivia and their child.

'I know,' Olivia smiled, 'but just so you know, when the time comes you're going to be there in the delivery room with me.'

'You want me in the room when our baby is born?' he asked in surprise.

'Duh,' she replied flippantly. 'Look, I know the guys from your time just stand around outside listening to the women scream, but not in the 21st century buddy. You are going to be in that room with me, experiencing every second of pain, even if I have to get you in a neck lock or break every bone in your hand...and that's meant with all the love in the world.'

'Livy,' he stopped abruptly, and took her in his arms. 'There is nothing I want more than to be with you, watching our child being born.'

'You might not be saying that afterwards,' she smiled. 'You know, when you're traumatized for life.'

'Not going to happen,' he smiled as they started walking again.

'Hey Olivia, Theo!' Harriet, Jake's mother waved to them from inside the shop window they were passing by. 'Fantastic wedding!' she mouthed through the glass and gave them two very enthusiastic thumbs up.

'Thanks,' Olivia smiled and waved as they wandered past.

'You know, I'm starting to get the impression our wedding is going down in the history books as the most uncivilized wedding ever,' Olivia sighed.

'Well it certainly did get a bit wild,' Theo replied.

'A bit wild?' Olivia repeated. 'A bit wild? Theo, Fiona streaked naked across the shore of the lake.'

'Yeah,' Theo laughed out loud in remembrance.

'Tommy and Jake were having a medieval joust using traffic cones as lances.'

'I know,' he smiled, 'I think that was my favorite part.'

'I don't even know where they got the damn traffic cones from in the first place, and they were using two of the other guests as horses.'

Theo chuckled and scratched his jaw thoughtfully.

'Well they did all drink Dionysus' wine. It was bound to get a little rowdy.'

'A little rowdy?' she repeated slowly. 'Mrs Bailey dirty dancing with the God Hephaestus isn't something I can ever unsee.'

'Yeah,' Theo snickered, 'I can't believe Louisa got that on camera.'

'You know, now I understand why the Ancient Greeks' parties were considered debauched and wild. I'll bet they were all on Dionysus' wine.'

'Probably,' he replied. 'I think at this point we should just be grateful it didn't degenerate into an orgy.'

'You know I was expecting a few people to maybe get a little tipsy, but I certainly didn't expect Hades to show up with a bunch of drunk, dead Greeks.'

'Can immortals really be considered dead?' Theo wondered.

'I think you're missing the point,' she laughed, unable to help herself.

'What does it matter? They all enjoyed themselves and I had the best time ever,' he pulled her in close and kissed her. 'And now I have the most beautiful wife in the world and we're about to have a baby. Things just can't get any better.'

'Espresso?'

'I stand corrected,' he grinned as they passed by the pub.

Olivia suddenly stopped and glanced across the street, her eyes narrowing.

'What is it?' Theo asked.

'Nothing,' she murmured after a minute, 'I just thought I recognized someone is all.'

'Who?'

For a second she could have sworn she'd seen a woman who looked just like Tituba.

'No one,' she shook her head and smiled. 'Come on, let's get that coffee or we're going to be late for our appointment.'

Taking her hand, they set off once again toward the coffee shop.

Jackson looked up from the bar as the door opened and a beautiful woman with skin the color of cocoa walked in. There was something about her, an air of confidence that made her own the room. Her long, wild, curly corkscrew hair fell down her back like a wild waterfall and she wore an expensive deep blue pantsuit with really thick yet elegant heels. Her eyes immediately locked on Jackson as she headed his way and slid onto a stool at the bar.

'Afternoon darlin',' he smiled at her.

Her ocean blue eyes glittered and for just a strange brief moment Jackson could've sworn he heard the waves crashing on the shore and smelled the briny tang of salt water.

'Good Afternoon Mr?'

'Jackson,' he offered his hand.

'Mr Jackson,' she replied.

'Just Jackson' he smiled, his gaze dropping to her throat where the strangest necklace lay. It was a small blue sphere suspended from a leather thong and for a moment it looked like a tiny spike of lightning was trapped in its crystalline depths.

'Cally Atlass,' she offered in return.

'Stopping or passing through?' Jackson asked.

'I'm staying for a while, I'm here to see a very old friend…' she smiled slowly. 'She and I have unfinished business.'

Also Available

The Guardians Series 1
Microbook

Boothe's Hollow

It's summer in the sleepy little town of Mercy Massachusetts. For eight-year-old Olivia West and her two best friends Louisa and Jake Gilbert it should mean ice cream sundaes at Miz Willow's scoop'n'shake, playing pirates down by the caves, endless hikes through the woods and skinny dipping at the lake on the shores of her grandmother's old rambling stick style house.

But as the long summer days drag on Olivia has no idea that the town has been rocked to its very foundations by a string of vicious and violent murders. All she knows is that her parents are fighting again. Sent to stay with her grandmother and great aunt for the summer, at the house by the lake, she finds new and ingenious ways to get into trouble.

It's all harmless fun until suddenly something in the woods begins to stir. She can feel it. Whatever it is, it's very old and its calling to her. It wants her to come and play...

This mini prequel book is available in E-book format FREE! When you sign up to my mailing list at:
www.wendysaundersauthor.com

Author Bio.

Wendy Saunders lives in Hampshire, England with her husband and three children. She spent twelve years caring for her grandmother but when her grandmother passed away she decided the time was right to pursue her own dream of writing. Mercy is her debut novel and the first of a five book series.

Also in this series
Book 2 The Ferryman
Book 3 Crossroads
Book 4 Witchfinder
Book 5 Infernum

Come find me!
On my official website
www.wendysaundersauthor.com
Don't forget to subscribe to my mailing list via my website to receive a free copy of my e-book Boothe's Hollow, a companion/prequel short story to Mercy.

On Facebook
www.facebook.com/wendysaundersauthor

On Twitter
www.twitter.com/wsaundersauthor

On Instagram
www.instagram.com/wendysaundersauthor

If you would like to rate this book and leave a review at Amazon or Goodreads.com I would be very grateful. Thank You.

Printed in Great Britain
by Amazon